RECOIL

RECOIL

By BRIAN GARFIELD

WILLIAM MORROW AND COMPANY, INC.
NEW YORK   1977

Printed in the United States of America.

1   2   3   4   5   6   7   8   9   10

Library of Congress Cataloging in Publication Data

Garfield, Brian Wynne (date)
    Recoil.

        I. Title.
PZ4.G2315Rc   [PS3557.A715]   813'.5'4   76-45211
ISBN 0-688-03158-7

BOOK DESIGN   CARL WEISS

FOR

BRYAN AND

NANETTE FORBES

Revenge, at first though sweet,
Bitter ere long back on itself recoils.

—JOHN MILTON, *Paradise Lost*

PART ONE

THE HUNTED

CHAPTER ONE

New York State: 18–19 July

1

THE DOOR CLOSED BEHIND HER WITH A SHUDDERING STEEL crash. The corrections officer at the desk looked up once, dropped his eyes to the stack of forms and did not look at her again. "Name?"

"You know my name."

"We get a lot of visitors."

She said, "Anna Pastor. Mrs. Frank Pastor."

He filled in a space at the top of a form, writing with a ball-point. "You're here to see . . . ?"

"My husband." She took one step forward and placed the visitor's pass on the desk. She kept her hand on it.

It took forty minutes; then she sat in a hard chair at the long table. It ran wall to wall: The mesh partition filled the space from tabletop to ceiling. She had learned how to ignore the flyspecked green walls and the men who stood just inside the doors with their pot bellies cinched up by black pistol belts.

Frank came in and faced her through the mesh in his drab uniform. She smiled at him. He drew out the chair and sat down.

"They all send regards."

"How are the girls?"

"Sandy has a cold. I'm keeping her in bed today. Ezio told me he heard a rumor about your parole."

When he smiled it made her think of the early days. He was still thin but he'd gone bald on top and that had aged him. She said, "We'll have to get you a hairpiece."

"What rumor?"

"Two months at most. Maybe six weeks."

"Well now." He smiled again; he began to relax.

"It's only a rumor, Frank."

"Sure."

She said the rest with a nod: The parole board had been reached, the petition would be affirmed; the fix was in.

"Eight years," he said.

"Don't think about it, Frank."

"Nothing else to think about. Nothing else to do except think about it." He looked around from guard to guard; his voice dropped. "There was a piece in the *Post* last week. Page five."

"I saw it. I gave it to Ezio."

"You ask Ezio for me, ask him to find those four gentlemen."

"We'll see if we can't give them to you at the front gate. As a coming-out present. Gift-wrapped."

It inspired his quiet laughter.

THREATENED WITNESSES LEAD NEW LIVES

Federal Marshals Provide Protection

WASHINGTON, July 18—More than 1,000 American families are living false lives under assumed names given them by the U.S. government. Their new identities are all that protect them from violent retribution.

Last week's congressional budget hearings brought to light the formal existence of a federal witness relocation program, a key element in the Justice Department's effort to grapple with organized crime.

When witnesses are threatened by organized crime figures

against whom they intend to testify, the government offers to protect these witnesses by giving them new identities, new locations, new jobs, and sometimes even new citizenship if the case is judged so dangerous that it seems advisable to relocate the witness abroad.

The protective service is granted to witnesses both before and after they give testimony: In many cases it is a lifetime service. (Witnesses need protection not only from those against whom they have testified, but also from other criminals who may fear being squealed on by the same witnesses.)

Head of the program is F. Scott Corcoran, associate director of the U.S. Marshal's Service. Interviewed in his office in Falls Church, Va., Mr. Corcoran expressed surprise at what he called "all this sudden interest by the press."

Mr. Corcoran said, "We're not a clandestine organization. We've been on the books of the Justice Department seven years now. We don't hide our budget appropriations under phony headings or classified listings. We're out in the open. The only secret here is the identities of the people we service."

Last week's congressional budget hearings included debate over an $11-million annual appropriation request for the Witness Security Program, a joint operation of the Justice Department's Criminal Division, the U.S. Marshal's Service and the FBI.

"We're surprised but pleased by this sudden attention," Mr. Corcoran said. "I think the publicity definitely helps. A big part of our job is assuring potential witnesses against organized crime that they can avail themselves of our protective services."

Witnesses' names are changed legally, in closed federal court sessions, so that no unlawful acts are committed by administrators of the program. "We're not perpetrating frauds on anyone except the Mob," Mr. Corcoran insisted.

But he conceded that some known criminals, granted immunity from prosecution in return for their testimony, have been relocated under new names without the knowledge of local law enforcement agencies. "We couldn't very well broadcast the witness' new name to every police department in the country," Mr. Corcoran pointed out.

Asked about the program's degree of success, Mr. Corcoran replied promptly, "Our batting average is 998. We've had two witnesses attacked out of more than a thousand we've relocated. There's no binding evidence that either of the two victims was discovered by the Mob—the murders haven't been solved, but they may have been coincidences."

Mr. Corcoran added, "I'd like to point out that there have been certain instances of witnesses refusing our protection. In a large number of cases those people have gone home and been shot to death or blown up when they started their cars. We're providing the only successful defense against that kind of retribution. The program has been very successful in encouraging witnesses to step forward. It's putting a big dent in the operations of organized crime in this country. This program is the main reason why you're seeing a lot more prosecutions of organized crime leaders today."

But he admitted it could be a severe jolt for a witness to start life over again under a new name. "He's got to leave all his friends behind. Sometimes he's got to take a step down, professionally or financially. Sometimes he's got to face his children, confess his wrongdoing to them so they'll understand why they've got to live the rest of their lives under new names. But it's been a great advantage to some of these people. Some of them have done very well for themselves. We've got two witnesses we relocated several years ago who've become millionaires under their new identities."

The program has grown rapidly over the past few years. "Sometimes we process two new families in a single week," Mr. Corcoran said. "People are getting the word—there *is* a way out of their dilemma, and we're here to help them."

2

She put the soup pot on the front burner, heard the doorbell and glanced at the monitor screen above the refrigerator. It was Ezio's face, a pattern of gray dots; he stared gravely into the camera.

She pressed the door-release button and saw him walk out of the picture; then she heard the front door.

"I'm in the kitchen."

His wide body filled the doorway. "How's Frank?"

"I haven't seen him smile like that in years. He even laughed."

"Yeah." The cigar had gone out. Ezio snapped his gold lighter. He didn't look at her; he rarely did. She was still the outsider: He did not let her forget she was the second Mrs. Pastor.

She put the lid on the pot. "Sandy's got a cold, I'm making her some lentil soup. Want some?"

"No. I'm on my way to a meeting. Just checking in."

"He saw the article in the *Post*. He wants the four of them found." She searched his face. "Any progress?"

He was looking at the monitor screen; his answer was reluctant. "You could say so. We're getting close to their files."

"How close?"

"We'll know Thursday, one way or the other."

"Better find them, Ezio."

"I know. Say hello to the girls for me." He put his hat on and left.

She took the lid off. It was bubbling. She opened the cabinet and took down a soup bowl. On the monitor screen she saw Ezio walk away toward the elevator.

The youth had crow's-wing hair and a pointed face. He called himself C. K. Gillespie but Ezio called him Charlie because he didn't like the arrogance of people who used initials in place of a name. He thought of Charlie as a flyweight kid, although Charlie was ten years older than he looked, had a busy law practice in Washington and had done satisfactory work for the Pastor organization.

Charlie came into the office at ten minutes to four. Ezio was reading the *Wall Street Journal*. "You're twenty minutes late."

"We were in the holding pattern. This place swept for bugs?"

"Once a week. And the jammer's always running. You ought to apologize a little for being late."

"I never apologize for something that isn't my fault."

"It's just good manners, you know."

Charlie sat down. He was slim in the sharkskin suit. It looked vaguely Sy Devore, Ezio thought—something West Coast about it. He couldn't wear clothes like that; from the age of six he'd been built like a beer truck. He had decided he looked best in winter tweed and summer seersucker, and those were all he ever wore.

"And you ought to wait for somebody to ask you to sit down before you sit. It's presumptuous."

"Ezio, I like you a lot but I don't need courtesy lessons from you. I match my manners to the company I'm in."

"Don't patronize me, Charlie, I'm not one of your Texas hillbilly clients."

"No." Charlie smiled a little and that made Ezio wonder how the kid actually did picture him. As a gorilla with an education, probably. Charlie still had a lot of things to learn and one of them was about jumping to oversimplified conclusions.

Ezio said, "Mr. Pastor's anxious for news from Washington."

"I met Mrs. Janowicz this morning."

"And?"

"The security's pretty tight there."

"We already knew that, Charlie."

"I'd prefer you didn't call me that."

"When you're in this chair you can call yourself anything you want. Right now I'm in this chair and you're in that one, Charlie. Now tell me about that secretary—what's her name again?

"Janowicz. Mary Janowicz."

"Polack?"

"Irish. She's married to a Polack."

"Polish-American, Charlie. An important attorney like you shouldn't stoop to ethnic slurs. Only thugs and bigots use words like that."

Charlie smiled again: He didn't rise to it. But Ezio liked to bait him because someday he was going to find out whether the kid had balls.

"She's got a girl friend she loves once or twice a week. She wouldn't want it broadcast. The people she works for are stuffy about that kind of thing."

Ezio made a face. "So am I, as a matter of fact."

"We've got three hundred feet of infrared film. She's a little fat but you could possibly get six bucks a ticket in a Times Square porn house. She got the idea all right. Then also of course we offered her money to cooperate. Enough money to make her start thinking about the possibilities."

"How did you get onto her?"

"We put an investigative staff on everybody working out

of Corcoran's headquarters. She turned out to be the apple. All it takes is time and patience."

"They've got their own security checks. If you could turn her up why haven't they tumbled to it too?"

"It only started a few months ago. She's been married three years. The honeymoon wore off and she got seduced by this lesbian after a bridge game. That's how we cottoned onto it— Mrs. Janowicz always stayed behind for an hour or so after the other women left."

"So why hasn't the federal security found out?"

"They probably will, next time they run a spot check on the people out of that office. That's why we've got to get it done fast."

"What's the hang-up?"

"Access. She doesn't work in the file section. She's the secretary to the GS-8 who runs the assignment section."

"What does that mean?"

"He prepares the new identities. New job, name, location, all the details. He's got to get the birth certificate, driver's license, credit cards, all the ID documents. All that stuff has to be legitimate, so it takes time. They've got this one official who does it full time. His name's Fordham, if it matters. Janowicz is his secretary."

"How the hell can they provide a new legitimate birth certificate for a man who's full grown?"

"The same way you get one for a phony passport or license. Graveyard registrations. They take, say, a forty-year-old guy that they need papers for. They go back forty years in a newspaper file somewhere, they find a death notice for an infant. Then they check back to the birth notice for that same infant. They go to the hall of records and they buy a notorized official copy of the birth certificate. That's how they pick the new names for the witnesses—the name originally belonged to some baby that died young. So it's a real birth certificate."

"Charlie, you were going to tell me about the delay."

"Fordham deals only with the new people that come in. Looking after the ones who've already been relocated, that's another department. Bureaucracy, you know, everybody's a specialist. Witnesses they've already relocated go into a

19

standby status after the marshals pull their surveillance off them. It's an active file because they do regular spotchecks to make sure the people are still secure. But it's a different department."

"Then what good does this woman do us?"

"She's got access but it's spotty. When they finish work on a new identity for some family they give the file to Janowicz. She takes it to the filing section and puts it in the appropriate file drawer. The drawers are organized by cross-reference. Both under the new phony name and under the old real name. That's because sometimes they have to call these people back to testify and they need to be able to find them themselves. So all we need is a peek in those files. We're looking for John Doe, say, so we just look up John Doe, and it says, 'See William Smith, four-six-two Chingadera Avenue, Podunk, Nebraska.' Janowicz goes into those files once or twice a week to enter a new file. She's given a temporary one-time clearance each time. It'd be easier for us if they had it in a computer, but they don't." Charlie cleared his throat, crossed his legs and resumed:

"When she does it she's in plain sight of the security guard. She can find a name and address for us all right. But she'd attract suspicion if she opened more than one drawer per trip, and sometimes weeks go by between trips to any particular drawer—maybe even months. They've had this operation seven years now and there are only eleven hundred individuals and families in those files. Figure it out—even if they're doing more business now, entering another new case every few days, there's still a couple of dozen file drawers in there and the odds of hitting the right one are kind of puny. We give her a name, we might get the answer overnight and then again we might have to wait a month or six weeks before she gets into that drawer."

Ezio watched Charlie screw a long cigarette into a silver holder. He didn't prompt Charlie. When the cigarette was burning Charlie spoke again:

"We've got to wait for her to get a new file that fits alphabetically into the same drawer that's got one of the four files we want. Am I boring you?"

"When I get bored I'll yawn."

"For instance we want her to find the file on Walter Benson, right? But she's got to wait for them to get a new file on somebody whose name starts with *B*. You follow?"

Charlie's smile hardened like a trap abruptly sprung. "I've got Benson for you. She came through with it last night. He's calling himself William Smithers, he's working as an assistant manager in Maddox's Department Store in Norman, Oklahoma, and he lives at one-eighteen Bickham Place in Norman."

Ezio wrote it down. He made a point of showing no emotion. "All right. Now go back and get the other three."

CHAPTER TWO

Los Angeles: 29 July–1 August

1

FRED MATHIESON LOCKED THE OFFICE SAFE AND WENT OUT through the reception office. He heard movement across the room—Phil Adler, leaning through the doorway of his office. "Didn't realize you were still here, Fred."

"Heading home."

"Got a minute?"

"Jan will roast me if I'm late."

"Only take two minutes. Time me." Adler, red-faced and forty pounds overweight, backed out of sight.

By the time Mathieson strolled into the office Adler had sat down behind the desk, as if to assume command.

"Good thing you caught that sequel-and-remake clause in the Blackman contracts." The air whistling through his nose commanded Mathieson's perverse attention.

"That's what I get my ten percent for."

"The lawyers missed it. You caught it. I always told you you should've been a lawyer."

"That's right, I should have been a lawyer. Your two minutes are ticking, Phil. We've got dinner guests."

"I just wanted to ask you one question."

"Ask."

"Well it's kind of hard. I've been rehearsing how to do this but there just isn't a simple way."

Mathieson tried not to look uneasy.

Adler said, "To put it bluntly, what would you say if I offered to buy you out?"

"That's out of left field." It was; but he was relieved.

"I know. I've been thinking about it but I didn't know how to put it to you without it sounding like an insult. God knows it's not an insult. You've been a terrific partner. The absolute best."

"Then why do you want to buy me out?"

Adler leaned back. He was trying to look relaxed but his hands gripped the chair arms and he might have been waiting for the dentist's drill. "Five years ago you and I figured we could multiply our clout by joining forces. We did a pretty fine job of . . ."

"Spare me the history, Phil, your two minutes are up."

"I have an ego problem, I guess. I'd rather be Adler Enterprises than Mathieson and Adler. I'm getting more into the production end of the business—I've got an associate producer credit on the Colburn movie, did you know that? And I just feel I'd prefer to have a free hand."

If it had been anyone else he would have laughed. But Adler had no sense of humor, no picture of himself other than the surface image he'd buffed and polished; laughter would hurt him, so Mathieson didn't laugh. What he said was, "What would happen to the clients?"

"Your clients, you mean. Nothing would happen to mine."

"My clients, then. Do you keep them, is that the idea? Or do I take them away with me and set up my own independent agency again?"

"That's however you'd prefer to do it, Fred. I certainly don't want to steal your clients away from you. But if you'd like to sell your end of it completely, I'd be willing to pay a substantial hunk for your string of clients. Provided each of them was willing to be represented by me instead of you, of course."

"What's a substantial hunk?"

"You pick a figure and we'll dicker."

Mathieson said, "You wouldn't have maybe sent out a feeler or two in the direction of my principal clients?"

"I might have. But I made it clear it was hypothetical."

"I see. Something like, 'If Fred should retire, or die, or anything, how would you boys feel about being represented by good old Phil Adler?' Something like that, Phil?"

"Don't get mad at me, damn it. Don't try to put a sinister cast on it. I'm not doing anything underhanded."

"I'm a little slow today but I still don't understand why you want to dissolve the partnership. We're making damn good money. We're having fun—at least I am. What's wrong with it?"

"I want to be on my own. I don't want to have to consult anybody about decisions. Call it power hunger, call it vanity. I can't explain it, really. I just want my own business again. Look, Fred, you're late, you'd better get on home to Jan and your guests. But just think about it, all right? Will you do that?"

"Yes, I'll think about it." He left the office uncertain whether to be angry or only sad.

2

The traffic on Sunset Boulevard had thinned out and he made good time up over the top of the canyon and down the turns to his house on Beverly Glen. He recognized the Gilfillans' Chrysler wagon parked in the oval driveway: They lived only five hundred yards away but they had become true Californians. He navigated the Porsche into the garage beside Jan's convertible and went inside.

Roger and Amy Gilfillan were down in the Pit looking at television news. They rattled their highball glasses at him. Jan came out of the kitchen, cross with him but she put on her company smile. It changed the patterns of her freckles. They kissed with dry lips.

"It's late, you're sore and I'm contrite."

"All right." She glanced at the clock. "You may as well go and pacify our lonely guests. I'll have it on the table in fifteen minutes."

He went down into the room. An aspiring television star had built the house in the era of the Conversation Pit and this one looked like an indoor Olympic pool that had been emptied for the winter. It dwarfed even Roger Gilfillan, who had made a career out of being big enough to stand up to Duke Wayne in Republic prairie operas before he'd won a Supporting Actor Oscar as a genial drunken Texas millionaire in a soapy MGM titillation. Forty-six and still bemused, he seldom made anything but mindless action movies but he stood well up in the box-office top ten.

Amy was tiny and blonde and cherubic. "You look like you just got trampled in a thousand-cow stampede. Come and set and let Roger mix your drink."

Mathieson settled into black leather cushions. Roger was uncoiling his grasshopper legs. "Bourbon?"

"God no. See if you can find Bloody Mary mix in there."

"Rough lunch?" Roger pawed through the bar refrigerator.

"You could say that. Like a combat mission."

Roger had a high whinnying laugh. "We ought to take Amy and Jan on patrol some time, let them find out how their warriors earn combat pay. Who was it?"

"McQueen's people. Business manager and two lawyers." Mathieson stretched his legs out and bent his head back until something cracked in his neck.

Roger said, "Everybody trying to get you drunk enough to come down to their price. Who's the writer?"

"Bill Block."

Roger clawed at ice cubes and Mathieson grinned at him: Block had written Roger's Oscar part. Roger said, "Could I do it?"

"You and McQueen could do it together if somebody wanted to come up with enough to pay for both of you. It's a two-star script. But you'd have to talk to McQueen's people."

"They bought the script?"

"They bought it. It's a bank caper story, set in Oregon. Outdoor pursuit. The bank robber and the state trooper. Nice characters."

"Block always gives his actors something to do—which makes the bastard unique in this business." Roger stirred with

25

his index finger. "I'll call them in the morning before they've had time to hire Barbra Streisand for the part instead of me. Here y'go."

Mathieson took the drink out of Roger's gnarled hand. "How's Billy doing?"

"Back on his feet. Busted ankle never slowed no Gilfillan down. He'll make the track team in September—that's all he cares about. Kid ever grows up and gets married, his wife'll be a decathlon widow." Roger sat down. Amy sprawled sideways on the cushions, cheek propped on her palm; Roger tickled her foot and she kicked him absentmindedly. She was looking at the TV screen—the anchorman talking, behind him a black-and-white still photo of Sam Stedman looking grave. The sound was off; Roger said, "Turn that up, honey, let's hear about it."

She reached for the control but the screen went to a commercial. Roger said, "Shit."

Amy sat up. "Probably a hoax anyway. Old Sam, he'd do *anything* to get on the front page." She pronounced it *innything* without affectation.

Mathieson tasted the drink. "I don't think Stedman's that kind of a phony."

"That pious el creepo?" Amy lifted an eyebrow.

Roger said, "Sugar baby, look at it this way. Twenty years Sam Stedman's stayed on top of the box office because he's the only one of us who won't play the bad guy. Number-one public image, your God-fearing Bible-belt hero. Can you see him risk the image by settin' up a phony stunt to have his boy kidnapped?"

Mathieson shook his head. "I talked to his agent yesterday. The man's going through genuine anguish. It's no publicity stunt."

After the commercial the weatherman came on. Amy switched the set off. "What about that announcement he made there last night? About hiring Diego Vasquez to find the boy?"

Roger said, "I could've done all right without Sam's pious preamble but I kind of admired the rest of it. Man, he's right, you can't just lay down and let these fuckin' terrorists walk on you."

26

"He's taking too much of a risk," Mathieson said. "I wouldn't have done it if it were our kid. I might have hired an investigator like Vasquez but I certainly wouldn't have called a press conference to tell the world what I was doing."

Roger said, "If you think about it, it makes sense. He's threatening to spend every last penny he's got to find those bastards. He's siccin' Vasquez on them in public to emphasize the message—if they don't turn Sam Junior loose unharmed, they ain't no way on earth for them to get away alive. That's the message, clear enough."

Mathieson said, "Is Diego Vasquez all that terrifying? What makes him more of a threat than the FBI and the police?"

"The FBI and the police need courtroom evidence and they ain't too likely just to shoot the bastards on sight."

"And Vasquez will?"

"He's done it before," Roger said. "You remember that case two years ago, that Denver millionaire that hired Vasquez to find out who pushed poison heroin on his daughter after she died from shooting up pure uncut?"

"I think so . . ."

Amy said, "You couldn't hardly forget it. Diego Vasquez seems to make damn sure he's on the front page every time he wipes somebody out."

Roger went to the refrigerator. "I got time for another one, don't I? No, he got all the way to the top that time. Not just the street pusher but the one the cops don't never reach—the one that was financing it. Some real estate honcho up there."

Amy made a baby-faced smile. "Just like in the movies. Self-defense. Vasquez left that old boy in Denver dead on the living-room carpet with three forty-five Colt bullets inside of him."

"They dug a couple of thirty-eight slugs out of the ceiling plaster," Roger said. "And there was this thirty-eight automatic in the dead fella's hand. Fired twice. Everybody knows Vasquez just planted it that way after he killed that old boy. See, they never could have convicted the fella in court. That's the way Vasquez earns those five-figure fees."

Mathieson said, "Whatever happened to the days when there was a difference between the good guys and the bad guys? That's what tastes sour to me—how could a religious man like Sam Stedman hire a cold-blooded killer?"

"Didn't you ever see none of them Westerns where the sanctimonious town dads hire the gunslinger to clean up the town for them? Same fuckin' thing, ain't it?"

"Oh, hell, Roger."

"You're an old-fashioned moralist, Fred."

Jan emerged from the dining room. "It's on the table. Move it or lose it."

3

The Gilfillans left at midnight and there was the customary flurry of clearing up because Jan couldn't stand to face messes in the morning and the cleaning lady wasn't due again until Monday. Mathieson cleared the table while Jan loaded the dishwasher and then it was half past twelve and they slouched into the Pit for their nightcaps.

"Cointreau?"

"Yes, fine."

He poured himself a Remy Martin and carried the drinks to the couch. "I'm already a little squiffed. Ought to go on the wagon." He stood sipping the cognac. "You know I really should sign up with a health club. The old pot's growing. I need to get rid of fifteen pounds of this flab and get some decent exercise."

"You don't look so bad for an old-timer." She gave him a distracted glance.

"Well you get past forty, you need to start looking after yourself. I see myself five years from now gone to pot and gone to seed. I get nightmares about turning into a slob like Phil Adler."

"You won't. You'll always be long and lean. You're like Roger—lanky bones."

He slapped his paunch dubiously. Then he said, "He wants to buy me out."

"*Roger* does?"

"Phil Adler."

She carried her drink around the room, shifting little things, testing for dust with a fingertip. Mathieson sat down.

"He sprang it on me this afternoon. He wants to dissolve the partnership."

"Whatever for?"

"I think he's restless. He's been bitten by the big-shot bug. A lot of agents have become producers. Phil always hates to be left out."

She sat down across the room, the drink in both hands. "Are you going to sell out to him?"

"He only sprang it on me tonight. That's why I was late. I haven't had time to think about it."

"What was your first reaction?"

"You can't always go by that."

"Sometimes you can."

"We did that once. You remember what happened."

Her fingers crept under the neckline of her dress to pluck at something awry. "In the long run it worked out. You enjoy what you're doing now—more than you did when you were practicing law."

"We don't talk about that, remember?"

She uttered a short bark of unamused laughter. "I suppose Frank Pastor has microphones all over this house."

"It's better to stay in the habit of never talking about it."

"Doesn't it make you feel foolish? Melodramatic?"

"I like it here. I don't want us to take stupid risks."

His eyes followed the lines of her body as she stood up and walked aimlessly around the room. She was tennis-slim and her fine long hair was sunbleached. She seemed unaware that she was in a chronic state of irritation. "Ronny's coming home Friday. I hope you haven't forgotten."

"I haven't but I've got a lunch on with a client from Seattle. It's the only day he's here—I tried to change it but I couldn't. Can you meet the plane?"

"We both ought to be there."

"I'll see how early I can get away."

"It lands at half past two."

"I'll try."

"Please do." She took his glass and carried both empties out to the kitchen. When she reappeared she looked drowsy— the drinks were catching up. "Well take me to bed, then."

It took him by surprise but he walked her to the bedroom with his hand on the small of her back; he felt through the thin fabric the warmth of her skin. They undressed in silence, peeled back the covers neatly and got into bed. He reached up for the light switch; they made love in darkness and she did not kiss him.

4

By the time he reached the airport Jan had already collected Ronny. Mathieson saw them coming along the concourse to- gether, the boy maintaining a stiff distance from his mother: Ronny was eleven and painfully determined that no one mis- take him for a momma's boy. He seemed to have grown at least another two inches since June.

Ronny held out his hand gravely and Mathieson shook it. "How you doin', son?"

"Fine, Dad. How're you?" Very grown up.

They walked toward the baggage-claim turntable. "You look damn near bowlegged, boy. Didn't they ever get you off a horse in the past ten weeks?"

"Oh sure. We had all kinds of activities. Man, you wouldn't believe it, that's a *bad* place."

Jan said, "When 'bad' comes to mean the spectacularly good, I wonder what that tells us about ourselves?"

"Oh, Mom, sheesh."

The boy stood straight up and flashed his white California smile and Mathieson was proud of him. Ronny rattled on about his adventures while they waited for, and collected, his duffel bag. They walked out into the thick heat of the parking lot. The boy got in the narrow bench that passed for a back seat in the Porsche and Mathieson gave him a critical look. "You're growing too long to scrunch up back there."

Ronny was alarmed. "You wouldn't sell it!"

"No. But I might have to hang a U-Haul trailer on behind for those mile-long legs of yours." Mathieson flipped the bucket seat up for Jan; but she was looking back toward the terminal and she'd gone bolt still.

He peered back that way. A man was standing on the curb by a taxi, looking at them. Then the man stooped to enter the taxi.

Jan said, "Isn't that . . . ?"

"Bradleigh."

"But I thought . . ."

"If he wants to see us he knows where to find us."

Ronny leaned forward. "Who's that?"

"Just an old acquaintance." But sensations of alarm rubbed against Mathieson. He fitted the key into the ignition. Jan's eyes had gone wide. He gave her hand a quick squeeze.

5

When they walked into the house the phone was ringing. He put down Ronny's duffel bag and went to the receiver.

"Hello, Fred?"

"Yes." He recognized the voice. Jan was in the doorway watching him and he contrived an indifferent shrug to reassure her.

"You were right, that was me at the airport. I'm glad you didn't try to approach me. I'm in a phone booth right now— I've got to talk to you."

"Go ahead, talk."

"Not on the phone. You remember where we had that drink together the first time we came to Los Angeles?"

"Wasn't that at the——"

"Not on the phone. But you remember the place. Is it still there?"

"Far as I know." Mathieson watched Ronny lug the duffel bag toward the back of the house. Jan was locking the front door. It was something she almost never did in the daytime.

"Meet me there in half an hour."

"Look, it's an awkward time. My son just got home from summer camp and we . . ."

"It's important, Fred. Important, shit, it's vital. Make sure you're alone before you show up there. You get me?"

"I—Should I bring Jan and the boy along?"

"Does he know?"

"No."

"Then don't bring him. I won't have time to explain things to him. You'll have to do that yourself, later on."

"Why? There's no reason why he ever has to . . ."

"There is now."

Mathieson gripped the phone hard. "Why?"

"Have you got neighbor friends Jan and Ronny could go visit for a few hours?"

"The Gilfillans. They've got a kid Ronny's age . . ."

"Send your wife and the boy over there."

"But they just came home and . . ."

"I don't want them home alone right now. You get me? Hang up and get a move on."

Click.

She was still by the door; now she came toward him, anxiety on her face.

"Glenn Bradleigh. He wants me to meet him."

"What is it?"

"He wouldn't explain on the phone. Those guys are all paranoids."

"Something must have happened."

He said, "Maybe it's a routine drill of some kind."

"You don't need to tell me reassuring lies, you know."

"I don't see what else it could be. But he wants me to send you both over to Roger and Amy's until I get back."

"He'll be so disappointed—he's bursting with things to tell you about camp."

"He can tell me when I come back. I won't be long."

Ronny came through from the back of the house with a clumsily gift-wrapped package. "For both of you."

Mathieson began to rip at the Scotch tape. Jan had the boy's face between her hands: "Oh Ronny, how sweet." Ronny shied away and regained his composure at a wary distance. He eagerly watched the opening of the package.

They were belts, Indian style, beaded with multicolored patterns.

32

"I made them in shopcraft."

"My God," Mathieson said, "that's fantastic!" He wrapped the belt around his middle and laughed. "It's a foot too long. Trying to tell your fat old dad something?"

"We can cut it down. See, I wasn't sure so I figured I'd better make it too big, so I didn't punch holes for the buckle yet either . . ."

Jan's was a perfect fit and she wore it over her skirt and beamed at her son.

"We'd better go," Mathieson said.

"Go? Hey, we just got home and I was going to . . ."

Jan said quickly, "Your father has an appointment, Ronny, and I know Billy Gilfillan's dying to hear about your summer. Why don't you and I go over to Roger and Amy's until Dad comes home?"

"We'll have a celebration dinner tonight, how's that sound?"

They'd said the right thing: The boy had adventures to mesmerize Billy Gilfillan; the prospect was enough to make him forget his disappointment.

Mathieson watched them stride down the curving pitch of the street, Ronny breaking into a run and racing on ahead. Mathieson locked up and got into the Porsche. He answered Jan's wave.

Downhill into Sherman Oaks and Culver City he had his eye on the rearview mirrors constantly; he saw no sign he was being followed but he put it up onto the freeway and went through a series of maneuvers designed to disclose pursuit. Eight years ago Bradleigh had taught him things he'd never expected to have to put to use but this was the sort of thing you didn't forget once you'd learned it. He went down an off-ramp and around under the cloverleaf and got right back up on the freeway. He went past Universal City, got off at Vine and got back on, northbound. He left the freeway in Burbank and drove completely around the same block twice. No car followed him. When he was positive about it he went up Hollywood Way and parked the Porsche on the concrete lot behind Berk's Bar.

His hands were sweating when he went inside.

It had no windows. The light was poor and each booth had a squat candle burning inside a red glass cup.

Mathieson searched the shadows but did not find Bradleigh. He slid into a corner booth at the rear and the barmaid took his order for a Bloody Mary. Mathieson wiped his palms on a napkin.

Bradleigh appeared and stood just inside the door acclimating his eyes to the darkness. When he began to search the room he found Mathieson. He came over, put his palms on the table and slid in across from Mathieson. "You didn't pick up any company, I hope."

"No. What's this all . . . ?"

The barmaid's approach silenced them. She set the Bloody Mary on the table and took out her order pad. "Yes, sir?"

"Just a ginger ale," Bradleigh said.

Mathieson studied him. Bradleigh had put on ten pounds or so but it only made his ruddy face squarer. His brown hair was still in a 1950ish brush crew cut and he was still wearing a conservative suit with a white shirt and plain brown tie; it might have been a uniform. His gray eyes picked up a little reflected candlelight and seemed frosty, as if he'd been affronted by something.

The barmaid went away and Bradleigh took an envelope from his pocket. "You'd better take a look."

It wasn't sealed. Mathieson reached inside—a folded newspaper clipping. STORE MANAGER SHOT BY SNIPER. He glanced down the paragraphs. One William Smithers had been gardening in his yard in Norman, Oklahoma, when a rifle bullet had struck him in the back. Apparently it had been fired from a passing car. Smithers had been taken to a hospital and was on the critical list: The bullet had broken a rib and done some internal damage.

He handed it back to Bradleigh. "So?"

"This was a last-minute squib in this morning's Oklahoma City paper. The later editions probably ran photographs of him. Smithers is Walter Benson."

It hit him like a fist. "Oh boy. Oh boy."

"It could be a coincidence."

"You don't think it was, though."

"If I did I wouldn't be here."

"Is he going to pull through?"

"Nobody knows. We've transferred him to another hospital under wraps. We're guarding the place like the mint."

Mathieson tried to compose himself. "What does it mean?"

"Obviously we think the mob found him."

"I thought Frank Pastor was still in prison."

"He is, but he's up for parole in a matter of days. And his organization's not in prison. Ezio Martin's still running things."

"And if they found Benson they may find the rest of us."

"Fred, they may already have found you."

He reached for the Bloody Mary. It had too much Tabasco and pepper in it; his throat burned afterward.

Bradleigh said, "I sent people out this morning to cover Draper and John Fusco. Maybe Benson was a fluke, maybe they haven't got a line on the rest of you but we can't take the chance. Not until we know more. I came here myself because if they do have information on all four of you then you'd be the prime target. You were the one who put Pastor away—the others were corroboration but we could have done it without any of them. You were the key witness."

"That's a comforting reminder."

"I know."

"How did they find Benson?"

"God knows. We're investigating everything. Including ourselves."

"Yourselves?"

"It's always been our nightmare. The chance of a leak in our office. We don't think it happened. We don't see how it could. But we've got to check it out. Until we prove there was no leak we've got to assume all four of you may have been blown."

"Terrific. That's terrific."

"Look, the way it probably happened, some guy happens to be passing through Norman, Oklahoma. He just happens to spot Benson in the street. Maybe just some uninvolved guy who gets back to New York and goes out to dinner and says, 'Say, you'll never guess who I saw on the street out in of-all-the-Godforsaken-places Norman, Oklahoma. It was old Walter Benson, you remember how he disappeared right after that sensational Pastor trial where he testified?' And somebody over at the next table with big ears passes the word back to somebody in Ezio Martin's crowd and they figure there's probably nothing to it but it can't hurt to send somebody out to Oklahoma just to check it out."

The barmaid brought Bradleigh his ginger ale. He tasted it.

When the girl was gone Mathieson said, "It's been eight years. Nearly nine. Why should Pastor's mob give a damn any more? Benson wasn't doing them any harm in Oklahoma."

"You still don't know those people, do you?"

"Nor want to."

"They shot Benson for reasons that make perfect sense to them."

Mathieson said, "What reasons? What reason justifies trying to murder somebody who's doing you no harm?"

"For one thing it's an object lesson. They want the world to know they'll catch up with their enemies no matter how far they run or how long they hide. It's a deterrent."

Mathieson scowled at him. Bradleigh went right on:

"Then there's the matter of revenge. Those people are very primitive that way. Revenge is a religion with them. They carry it along from generation to generation. Vendetta. It amounts to their law."

"What a grisly waste."

"They're weaned on it." Bradleigh lit a filter tip.

"You're saying we'll never be safe."

"Who's safe? You could get hit by a truck. The chances are they stumbled on Benson by a fluke. The chances are you're in no danger at all."

Mathieson said, "You fly out here on the first plane and you alarm the hell out of my wife and me. And we're in no danger at all. I see."

"Look, Fred, it's my job. I'm not trying to be an alarmist. I'm just preparing for a contingency. A remote possibility."

Mathieson burned his throat on another swallow. At the

bar a fat TV character actor whom Mathieson knew by sight but couldn't name returned from the jukebox to a glass of something that looked like a potted plant. The jukebox bleated heartbrokenly.

Mathieson tried to compose his ragged emotions. "What do you think we should do?"

"Disappear. Take your family on vacation for a while. Don't leave a forwarding address. We'll send agents along for protection. And I'd like to set up surveillance on your house—see if anybody snoops around."

"What if they do? You can't arrest them for snooping around."

"But we'll know, won't we. If nobody snoops around then we can assume your cover's intact. If they do show up we'll be warned. We might have to do another identity switch."

"No."

"Fred . . ."

"I couldn't put Jan through it again." The marriage was barely intact as it was. "And Ronny. I'd have to tell him what we were doing and why."

"He's old enough to understand it."

"He'd have to keep the secret for the rest of his life—or at least for the rest of mine. He's too young for a responsibility like that."

"You may not have a choice."

"There's always a choice," he said with empty stubbornness.

"Like for instance?"

"Shouldn't we wait and see what happens?"

"I want you to be prepared, Fred. It's my job to protect you but I also kind of like you, you know. Most of the people we service are losers. Opportunists like Benson. Most of them are in the mob themselves. We nail them for something, then we offer them immunity if they'll finger the higher-ups. Once in a while a guy like Benson accepts our offer and we go to work for him. But we don't get too many good honest citizens who choose to testify because they see it as a moral duty. You were a breath of fresh air from the moment I met you. I don't want anything to happen to you. We'll send some good men to look after you. They'll be there if you need them, you know, but they won't get in your way. Where'd you like to go?"

Mathieson drummed his fingers on the table. "Hell. We've never been to Hawaii."

"Sounds perfect, if you can swing the tab."

"We've got high-priced clients nowadays. In fact we're doing so well my partner wants to buy me out."

"Does he. Well I hope it doesn't come to that but you may have to accept his offer."

"The hell. I just decided not to. This morning."

"Did you tell your partner?"

"Not yet."

"Then don't. Tell him you want to get away for a couple of weeks to think it over."

"It's rough to get away right now, Glenn. I'm right in the middle of contract negotiations . . ."

"Nothing's as urgent as survival."

"Maybe. But I think you may be ——"

The bartender yelled across the room: "Hey, everybody listen here!"

He was turning up the volume of the radio behind the bar. It was a news announcer's voice:

". . . promises to hold a news conference at nine tomorrow morning, Los Angeles time, at which time he expects to have been reunited with his son, Sam Stedman Junior. The star's sixteen-year-old son, who was kidnapped last Saturday, is being taken by helicopter from his place of rescue in Baja California to a hospital in Hermosillo, Mexico. Mr. Stedman stressed that his son appears to be unharmed, according to his reports from private investigator Diego Vasquez, who rescued the youth this afternoon. But he said his son had been drugged with sedatives by the kidnappers to prevent his escaping. The flight to Hermosillo hospital is purely precautionary, Mr. Stedman said, and his son will be flown home to Los Angeles tonight in a private chartered plane which Mr. Stedman, a licensed pilot, will fly himself. On his way to Los Angeles airport, Mr. Stedman spoke briefly with this reporter."

There was no mistaking the deep heartland twang of Sam Stedman's voice. "Through the grace of God and the mercy of Jesus Christ my son has been set free. I'm clasping my hands in a prayer of profound thanks to Almighty God."

"Mr. Stedman, is it true that your son was rescued by an armed assault on the kidnappers' camp by Mr. Vasquez?"

"Yes, sir, it was Diego Vasquez's show, pure and simple. My son and I owe a great deal to that fine man—more than we can ever repay. I pray to God to bestow His blessing on Mr. Vasquez and his fine family."

"We've heard reports that three or four of the kidnappers may have been shot during the rescue operation. Can you confirm that, sir?"

"No, I can't. I think we'd just better wait and find out the truth from the people who are actually down there. You have to excuse me now. Bless you."

The bartender turned the radio down and beamed at everyone in the room. "Well now how about that, folks?"

The fat actor lurched to the door. He looked around owlishly. "Hallelujah," he muttered, and went.

Conversations picked up again. The waitress plugged the jukebox back in. Bradleigh seemed annoyed: "Vasquez. I'm sick of hearing Vasquez, Vasquez, Vasquez. You'd think he was Emiliano Zapata. Fucking gunslinger. He's found a way to commit legal murder and the press loves the son of a bitch. In a sane society he'd be locked up in a rubber room."

Bradleigh lit another cigarette and inhaled ferociously. "They say he gets the job done. Well the bastard that tried to murder Benson in Oklahoma—he almost got the job done too. Where's the difference? Come on, let's get out of here." He signaled for the check.

Mathieson said, "Where can I reach you?"

"Right behind you. I'll tag along in my car and hang around until we've got you packed and on the plane."

7

Going up toward the top of the canyon drive he heard sirens somewhere nearby. There were always sirens in the valley; the sound carried up the gorges.

He saw the blue Plymouth in the rearview mirror, Bradleigh's left hand propping up the frame of the open window.

By habit he had the car radio tuned to KGEB, the all-news station; a fraction of his attention absorbed the Stedman-Vasquez story and the hour's catalog of disasters while he stopped and waited for a Datsun to back out of a driveway. He was starting to move again when his ear picked up the name Mathieson; he shot his hand to the radio knob to turn it up.

". . . explosion evidently was caused by a powerful bomb that was thrown from a passing car. The bomb was hurled into the house through a front window, shattering the glass and exploding violently inside the living room. Jim Schott reported from the scene of the explosion a few minutes ago that police and rescue workers still are not certain whether the Mathieson residence was occupied at the time of the blast. Firemen and police are sifting the wreckage . . ."

He was jammed up behind the lackadaisical Datsun with traffic flicking past in the opposite lane; he held the horn down and hooted the Datsun right off the road and went up to the crest ramming the gearshift around, swinging the Porsche fast through the bends, squealing. In the mirror Bradleigh's Plymouth was lodged behind the Datsun, dwindling.

At the top he squirted recklessly across the stop-sign intersection; down the turns on the north slope he rode the brake, teetering around the sharp curves, hunched forward over the wheel.

He heard the grind of a siren starting up. One last bend and then he swerved through it, nearly banging nose to windshield as he tried to see ahead.

Maddeningly his view was blocked by a great red fire truck that was beginning to pull away. He slewed toward the curb behind it.

A cop ran forward, gesturing at him angrily. The lawn was aswarm with men in uniform. Three patrol cruisers were drawn up at haphazard angles, askew on the road. He saw the Gilfillans and Jan, standing in a rigid little knot like mannequins: Jan was pale, she had both fists clenched at her sides, she wasn't looking at the man in the business suit who was talking to her with a notebook in his hand.

"Get back in that car and move along out of here, buddy."

He was searching for Ronny; he still had his hand on the car door and he felt the Porsche begin to roll—he hadn't pulled the brake. He dived back into the seat, stabbing for the pedal. That was when something made a loud sharp *crack* over his shoulder.

He hadn't heard that sound in twenty-three years but his instincts knew it: the crack of a high-velocity bullet passing near—a tiny sonic boom.

He threw himself flat across the seats and heard the distant cough of the rifle, delayed by range. He jackknifed his legs inside the car and the brass of fear coated his tongue with sudden bitterness. The next shot clanged against metal and sighed away whistling: again the distant bark of the rifle.

The Porsche was rolling slowly. The third bullet starred the windshield and then his ears thudded with the shockingly close-by boom of a handgun shot. Another explosion, and he realized it was the cop shooting back.

The car whacked the curb. It threw him against the dash and wedged him down toward the floor; his knee cracked the shift knob and sharp pain shot up his leg. The curb chocked the wheel and the car didn't move again; he heard the cop empty his revolver methodically. Other guns opened up and the racket was intense, like a battlefield. Someone kept yelling—he couldn't make out the words. Heedlessly he lifted himself off the floor and searched the lawn. The plainclothesman must have knocked Jan down; the man was down on one knee, hiding her behind his own bulk, sighting his revolver up across the street at the high canyon slope beyond. Roger had his arm across Amy's shoulders and was running her toward cover, the hedge on the property line. Then he saw Ronny and Billy, both of them diving into the ruins of the house.

Bradleigh's blue Plymouth came lurching downhill. The cop just outside the Porsche was belly-flat with his revolver extended in both hands toward the slope.

He heard the distant cough and sputter of a kicked-over motorcycle engine and he spun his eyes toward the far slope. The cycle roared and abruptly appeared in flitting bursts, ramming through the trees on the ridge line above the houses.

It drew police gunfire from the lawn but the motorcyclist dropped off the skyline, disappearing beyond the crest.

Bradleigh was running forward, bellowing: *"Get that mother!"* A cruiser plunged away, siren unwinding from a growl. Cops swarmed past Mathieson and slammed into their cars.

Mathieson backed out of the Porsche, dimly aware that his body was doing the necessary things: pulling the hand brake, ducking to clear the opening with his head, turning to face Bradleigh. "Jesus Christ, Glenn——"

"Are you all right?"

"Yes. I'm not hit. But they——"

Bradleigh's relief took the form of a surge of anger: "Get back in there and get the fuck away from here."

"That's *my* house."

"The hell. It's the insurance company's now. You damn fool."

He stared at the ruins. Half the house was gone: just debris. The back walls were intact and part of the roof sagged inward; the rest was junk.

Roger had his arms around Ronny's shoulders. Mathieson couldn't see Jan in the wheeling crowd. Bradleigh thrust him into the car. "Shove over, damn you." Then Bradleigh was at the wheel, finding the gears, making a tight U-turn, squalling away.

"My kid—my wife . . ." He twisted around, watching Jan step forward on the lawn with one hand lifted.

Bradleigh batted him across the back of the head. "Get down. Quit making a target out of yourself."

"What?" But he slid down in the seat, knees against the dash.

"You fell for it like a rube buying the Brooklyn Bridge. Why do you think they posted the sniper up there? The bastard was there to pick you off when you showed up to rubberneck the wreckage. You dumb bastard. God knows why you're alive."

CHAPTER THREE

Los Angeles: 1 August

1

ROGER'S STATION WAGON SLID TO A STOP ON THE GRAVEL AND Jan came out into Mathieson's arms; Ronny dived out of the car. There was a confusion of embraces: He couldn't stop touching them, he had to keep reassuring himself that they were alive.

They were inside the Gilfillans' house but he didn't remember getting there. Bradleigh was on the phone. Two ambulance doctors were filling syringes. Ronny sat subdued on the couch with his hands in his lap, holding Jan's hand. Billy and Roger stood around like funeral mourners, uncertain what to do with their hands. Cops flowed in and out of the house endlessly. A plainclothes sergeant with a notebook and pencil was talking to Roger.

Mathieson refused sedation and the white-uniformed doctor moved away. Mathieson sat on Roger's cowhide ottoman right back in the corner of the room with his shoulders wedged against the intersecting walls. Words flew past and he tried to catch them.

The nurse with Amy glanced at him. He felt her stare and dragged his eyes around. The nurse was young and pretty and had one of those meaningless professional smiles that

43

clicked on whenever anyone looked at her. She was pretending to listen to Amy's drugged babblings: Amy was flat on the divan, struggling to communicate something.

A cop lifted back an end of the drape to look outside. Mathieson saw past his arm through the window. He had no reckoning of time: It was after dark but the Gilfillans' lawn glared with a blaze of television lights. He saw a TV-remote panel truck and a reporter on the lawn talking into a camera.

The cop dropped the drape back in place and turned toward Mathieson. "Anything I can get you, sir?"

"No."

Bradleigh cupped the phone in his palm and spoke to the cop: "Get him a drink. Straight booze and an ice cube."

"Yes, sir." The cop moved briskly. Mathieson watched everything; it all swayed around him and never seemed to touch him—he felt weightless.

Uniformed cops shifted in the room like organisms under a microscope.

There was a drink in his hand and someone was forcing his arm up toward his mouth. "Come on, drink it." Bradleigh.

He took a swallow. He couldn't taste it. "Glenn—what's the matter with me?"

"Shock. Go on, drink up. You want a coat or a blanket or anything?"

"No."

"Chug-a-lug. Come on, attaboy."

The nurse put a blanket over Amy Gilfillan. Mathieson had never seen Amy so pale—like a death mask. She was muttering, scowling with a little-girl frown of concentration.

Bradleigh was back on the phone. "The hell with that. I want both of them tucked away out of circulation, right now this minute. Arrest them if you have to; I don't care what they want. Pass it on, all right? . . . Right. Switch me over to the DAC, will you? . . . Dan, me again. Did you ask the police to cover L.A. International? All right, let's try to cover the rest of the area airports too—everything from Burbank and Santa Barbara to San Diego. And get teams out to the New York airports. . . . What? . . . Hell, because we know who set this up and they're from New York. . . . Maybe not but we've got to cover it. . . . No. No positive make on it. Couple people saw a dark sedan going like hell—one makes it green, the other blue. You know how those are. No make on the motorcycle but what the hell, how many people can tell one motorcycle from another? . . . No, the car was probably boosted an hour before the hit anyway. We'll find it abandoned five miles from here. They must have switched cars four times on the way in and out, these guys aren't tyros. See if you can run a make on Vietnam combat veterans in the New York mobs. They used plastique, they must have learned how somewhere . . . Frank Pastor *what?* Jesus H. Christ, doesn't that just figure. . . . All right, you've got the number here."

The alcohol was getting to Mathieson. Jan was sitting on the edge of the ottoman holding his hands. "Darling?"

She looked up at Bradleigh. "He's coming out of it."

"I'm freezing to death. Look at me—goose bumps."

"Get him a blanket." Bradleigh sent the cop away. "You with us now, Fred?"

"I think so. Funny, it's like Inchŏn. Artillery flashes—it's lit up here and there but I can't make the picture stand still. Give me another shot of that stuff."

The cop brought a blanket and Bradleigh swapped the empty glass for it. "Refill."

His teeth were chattering. He clutched the blanket around him like a Sioux. "Been a long time since I got shot at. But I wouldn't have thought I'd have gone all to pieces like this."

"You want a cigarette?" Bradleigh shook out his pack.

"I quit six years ago."

"That was six years ago."

"I'd only burn holes in this blanket."

The cop gave him the refilled glass and he drank it straight down. It burned. Bourbon, he realized.

Bradleigh took the empty glass. "That's probably enough. You don't want to get schnockered."

"All right, I'm mostly here. Tell me what the hell happened."

Jan looked up at Bradleigh and caught his nod. She said, "We were all here in Roger and Amy's house. We heard the blast. Then a lot of sirens, and somebody phoned Roger and told him our house had exploded. We all went up there."

Bradleigh said, "A few people heard the car going away fast but only a couple of people saw it. There haven't been any descriptions we could use. One of your neighbors had phoned the police and they got up there fast, if it matters. The way we've reconstructed it, the car came down from the top of the canyon, at least two men in it—a driver and the guy who threw the bomb. Are you all right?"

"I'm just peachy. For God's sake."

"Look, at least nobody got hurt."

"Go on, then."

"I don't know what else to tell you. Frank Pastor was awarded parole today. He'll be out in a day or two. How does that grab you, Goddamnit?"

Jan burst into abrupt laughter. Mathieson reached out and she sagged against him, burying her face against his chest, the laughter going into sobs.

"You're alive," Bradleigh said in his stern monotone.

"Are we supposed to be grateful about that?"

"You will be when you've had time to think about it."

"What about right now? How are we supposed to feel right now?"

"They don't make rules about it."

"I just want this to be a bad dream."

2

By midnight Amy Gilfillan was in bed, drugged to sleep, and the house had emptied out but there were still cops outside standing guard. The TV trucks and lights were gone. Ronny dozed on the couch; most of the lights were off; Roger had taken Billy back to put him to bed; Jan sat half drunk on the ottoman.

Mathieson went to the bar. Anger made his hands shake

and Bradleigh shouldered him aside. "I'll do it. What are you having?"

"Might as well stick with bourbon. Rocks."

He waited without patience and finally took the glass from Bradleigh; he turned. "What now?"

"We'll have to get you out of here. They'll try again." Bradleigh closed the refrigerator door. He was drinking orange juice. "It was my job to prevent this."

"Don't get maudlin, Glenn. You're not responsible. You didn't sling any bombs."

The phone rang and Bradleigh took it; Mathieson couldn't hear what he said but afterward Bradleigh came across the room and stood beside him. "Looks like they've slipped the net. If we were going to collar them locally we'd have had them by now. Either we'll get a tip from a CI or we'll have to go at it from another angle."

"CI?"

"Sorry. Confidential informant. We've made some progress toward finding the leak in the office—narrowed it down to three or four people. As soon as we pin it on one of them we'll go to work. We'll find out who bought the information, I promise you."

"We know who bought it."

"Not to get a prosecution we don't. We've got to have evidence."

"When does Pastor go out in the street?"

"Tomorrow morning."

Silence dragged along for a while. Jan had fallen asleep sitting up, one shoulder tipped against the wall, the hair falling across her eyes. Mathieson looked down at Ronny's sleeping face.

Some time later he said, "I feel like a goldfish here. Suppose they throw a bomb into this house? We ought to clear out."

"We may as well." Bradleigh looked embarrassed; he was a poor dissembler.

"What's the matter, Glenn?"

"Guess I've been playing dirty pool with you. Chalk it up

to an excess of zeal. We should have moved you out of here six hours ago."

"Hell, I know that. You've kept us here because you wanted them to make another try."

"Believe me this place is covered inside out and upside down. They'd never get near you." He put his glass down. "But you're right, we'd better move out. Let's start waking them up."

CHAPTER FOUR

Long Island: 2–3 August

1

FRANK'S DAUGHTERS CARRIED THEIR STRIDENT RIVALRY ONTO the screened porch and Anna Pastor slumped with the fatigue of dealing with them. She retreated from the parlor, out onto the flagstones.

Beyond the statuary the lawn was neatly cut, two acres of grass sloping down to the beach. She could see Frank on the dock with Ezio: In silhouette against the silver water of the Sound they looked like cutouts of Mutt and Jeff. Ezio used his body expressively whenever he spoke; his arms rode up and down incessantly, his head rocked back and forth, he pivoted and stamped and took up defiant poses. Frank stood motionless, perhaps asking and answering, but there was no sign of it at this distance. Frank had outgrown the mannerisms of the streets long ago and prison had put a kind of rigidity into him.

This morning when he'd come outside the walls he'd stood on the curb with his head thrown back and his eyes half closed, presenting his face to the sun as if to draw strength from it. It had been ten minutes before he'd got into the car and then he'd just sat beside her holding her hand, letting Ezio's rapid-fire talk roll off him.

They'd driven straight out to the Island and he'd gone upstairs with her and without a word made love to her without even bothering to draw the curtains; then he'd put on his whites and told her he needed to be alone because he hadn't been alone in eight years and he'd taken the outboard onto the Sound.

He'd been gone until an hour ago; at midafternoon he'd tied the boat up to the dock and Ezio had gone down there to meet him and they were still talking.

In the meantime there'd been twenty phone calls and for a time the place had crawled with men but Ezio had sent nearly all of them away, some on errands and some simply away. Only two were left, somewhere around the place— George Ramiro down at his post in the gatehouse and C. K. Gillespie who had been on the phone in the dining room when she'd gone past a moment ago.

Every summer for eight years she'd brought the girls out here; every summer it had got harder as they'd got older. She had never lived out here with Frank: They had been married the year before he went to prison and they'd taken a honeymoon in Italy that summer and spent the rest of it in the Brooklyn house while Frank's lawyers tried to delay the sentencing.

The two men came up across the garden. Frank took her in his arms. He held her close and tight, not moving; she slid her fingers up his spine and rubbed the back of his neck. She felt a shudder run through him. "Jesus Maria," he whispered, "sometimes I thought it'd never be." Then he turned past her and patted her rump. In the house a phone was ringing; Ezio hurried inside. Gillespie had come outside and was politely looking away, down toward the water. Frank moved to the marble table and pressed the buzzer under its lip; after a moment Gregory Cestone appeared at the French doors in black trousers and white shirt and black bow tie. "Yes, Mr. Pastor?"

"Let's have some drinks out here."

"Right away, sir." Cestone neither nodded nor smiled. He had been in some kind of fire years ago; there were legends about it and none of them coincided; whatever the incident, Cestone's face had been burned. Plastic surgeons had reassembled it but the facial muscles were gone and it was an immobile mask. It had taken her years to get used to it.

Cestone turned back inside and Ezio brushed past him, coming out. Frank caught Ezio's eye and Ezio shook his head. "There's nothing. They've all gone to ground."

"That's not good enough, Ezio."

"We'll get them, Frank. It'll take a little time."

"This time it's taken eight years. How long do you figure on the next one?"

"It won't be any eight years, I can promise you that."

"Can you?" Frank never raised his voice but she edged away from him; when he spoke in that tone she felt uneasily as if she were in a cage with something untamed. Yet she had never seen him lift his hand to anyone. It was what had attracted her to him in the beginning; the sensation of raw savagery absolutely controlled by the power of his will.

Cestone pushed the wheeled drink cart outside through the doors. Gillespie came from the parapet and they gathered around the cart while Cestone made the drinks. She thought how handsome Frank looked in his nautical whites and cap.

But then he took the cap off and rubbed his pale scalp. "Those four gentlemen made me into a bald-headed old man, Ezio. They took eight of my best years. That's something a man can't ever get back."

"I know that, Frank."

"No. You don't. You've never been inside. Eight years with those stinking black animals. If I hadn't been who I am, I'd have got raped in there twice a day. Two thousand black junkie fags locked inside those walls. That's what I lived with those eight years."

"You look damn good, though."

"I kept fit. I made a point of it. You go too soft in there, it doesn't matter who you are or who your friends are. You have to keep command. Nobody respects a flabby leader."

"Well you've never been flabby, Frank, that's for sure."

Gillespie said, "Personally I never trust a fat man."

It made Ezio look at him angrily. Ezio wasn't fat—he was thick but it was all solid—but she hadn't missed the insinuation in Gillespie's remark and she was surprised he had the nerve to utter it.

It hadn't escaped Frank but he decided to ignore it; he had other things on his mind. He gestured toward his wife with his drink; she smiled; Frank took a healthy swallow and turned toward Ezio. "What's in motion?"

"Hell, Frank, we're looking for them. What else can I tell you until we start hearing back? The word only went out a few hours ago. We've got photographs going out to every city and town where we've got contacts. Some of the cops here and there, the organizations, you know how it goes. It's the biggest manhunt we've ever started. We'll find them."

"Particularly Merle. Edward Merle."

"Particularly him, Frank."

"I want all four of them. But the other three are just window dressing compared to him."

"We know that."

Frank turned his head. He was eyeing C. K. Gillespie. The younger man met his glance. She saw the flicker of a smile at the corner of Gillespie's thin mouth.

Frank said, "What about you? What are you doing about it?"

"Well I have an idea, Mr. Pastor."

"You do? Let's hear it."

"Sir, I wouldn't want you to take this the wrong way. Right now it's just kind of a wild idea I'm trying out. I'd just as soon not go into the whole thing before I find out whether it pans out."

Ezio said, "Mr. Pastor doesn't like smartass young lawyers, Charlie."

Gillespie spread his neat small hands openly. "Look at it this way, Ezio. If the idea works we'll all benefit from it. But if it's a dud, then I just raise Mr. Pastor's false hopes and I make a fool out of myself by bragging about it at this point. All I can say is I'm working on something and I think it's got a pretty good chance of producing results."

"You coy little——"

"Let it go," Frank said. "C.K. may have a point. In the meantime you get on the phone to Los Angeles and build some fires under those people."

2

They walked together along the shore; she held Frank's hand. With the toes of her canvas shoes she kicked at seashells. Out on the Sound little sailboats wheeled like butterflies. Frank said, "You've done a job with the kids. I mean a fabulous job, Anna."

"Forty lashes a day keeps them in line."

"I'm serious about this. I married you—let's face it, I married you because you had good brains and good looks and a body that just won't quit. I wasn't looking for a mother for my kids; I wasn't even thinking that straight in those days. Nobody around me wanted this marriage. They all hated it. They put you through hell, I guess. And then those four gentlemen sending me away for eight years. But you're still here and you're the one that got me out of there, you more than anybody else——"

"Now that was Ezio, Frank; he's the one who reached the board."

"Just between us and the seashells, little Anna, I get a feeling Ezio wouldn't have minded having a free hand to go on running the organization by himself for a while longer. You were the one who kept sticking the prod to him. What I'm saying, you turned out to be a lot more wife than I figured I was bargaining for and I'm not forgetting it."

But then it went both ways and he knew that. All she'd had before she'd met him was her wits and her looks. She was a coal-dust brat from a rancid miner's shack thirty miles from Hazleton, Pennsylvania. She'd won a high-school beauty contest and quit school to go to New York and be a high-priced model, and she'd ended up getting two TV commercials because the director liked sleeping with young brunettes, and that was the extent of her life—that and a fifth-floor walk-up in the East Village that she shared with another girl and a hundred cockroaches and the occasional influx of freaked-out junkies with Beatle haircuts; and the promise of maybe eight or ten good years as a hooker before her looks got battered away and she disappeared from the world.

She didn't remind him; he became annoyed whenever she brought up her past. What she said was, "I love you, Frank."

3

For an hour she and Nora played badminton against Sandy: Sandy was the athlete and won more games than she lost to the two of them. They were going inside to clean up when Gillespie drove down the driveway from the road. Anna saw George Ramiro go back into the gatehouse after closing the big gates. There was electric wire along the top of the wall all the way around the three landward sides of the six-acre estate.

The girls raced inside; Anna waited at the door while Gillespie parked the rented Cadillac and came up the slate walk with his briefcase, his sharkskin suit and his gentle friendly smile. "Been getting your exercise, I see."

"The girls keep me hopping."

"They're a great pair of kids," he said. "I've got some good news for Frank."

"In that case let's not keep him waiting." She led him through the parlor and knocked on the door of the office. When she heard Frank's voice she opened it and stepped back and Gillespie went past her into the office.

Ezio and Frank were at the table leaning over a litter of blueprints. Gillespie stopped two paces inside the room. "That idea paid off."

Over the back of Gillespie's shoulder she watched Frank's face. One eyebrow went up inquisitively. Ezio glanced at her disapprovingly but she stayed where she was.

Gillespie said, "I think it'll lead us to Edward Merle."

Ezio said, "Shouldn't this be private, Frank?"

"Anna has a right to hear this. Come on in."

She stepped into the room and pushed the door shut behind her.

Gillespie was opening his briefcase on the arm of a chair. The room had been built for a nineteenth-century millionaire; it was all deep rich woodwork—glass-enclosed bookcases, wainscoting, Dutch doors onto the garden, an Italian Renaissance chandelier. It was huge for a study; Frank was not a large man but he dominated it, and very few men had that quality.

Gillespie drew a single sheet of paper from the briefcase. "Name, vital statistics, fingerprints. Photograph in here as well."

"On Edward Merle?"

"No, sir," Gillespie said. "They'll probably be changing his name again, giving him a new identity, relocating him, all that. It would take quite a while to get that information. I think this is faster."

Ezio said, "Then spill it."

"The government knows the four witnesses are targets. They've put all four of them under wraps."

Ezio's voice became sharp. "We know that, Charlie."

Gillespie smiled. "Sure. The government assigns caseworkers to look after these witnesses, shepherd them along, get them resettled. You know how it is. Now I managed to get this information from our contact in the Witness Security office because I asked for it. She wouldn't have volunteered it—I don't imagine it would have occurred to her."

Ezio spoke through his teeth: "You don't imagine *what* would have occurred to her, Charlie?"

Gillespie put the sheet of paper on the desk and put the photograph on top of it. "The name and picture of the agent who's assigned to take care of Merle. His name's Glenn Bradleigh. We find Bradleigh, we've found Merle. And I don't think Bradleigh is trying to hide. Why should he? He ought to be easy enough for your people to find. Start them looking in the Los Angeles area." Gillespie picked up the photograph and looked at the face. "You find this man, he'll lead you to Edward Merle."

She looked at Frank. He was walking forward, a hard shine on his eyes. He took the photograph gently out of Gillespie's hand. "I like a man who uses his head."

"Yes, sir. I'm glad it worked out. I wasn't sure she'd be able to get us the name but she came through."

"You're all right, C.K." Frank turned to Ezio and put the photograph in his hand. "Find him."

CHAPTER FIVE

California–Arizona: 3–6 August

1

EXPLAINING IT TO RONNY WAS THE WORST PART. RONNY SAT on the motel bed watching both of them. Mathieson said, "I know it sounds kind of comic book. But it happens all the time. Glenn Bradleigh has more than a thousand families just like us on his roster."

Ronny only watched him; it unnerved him. Jan was hugging herself and Mathieson went to the air-conditioner under the window. "You could hang meat in here." He switched it off. Jan gave him a brief distracted smile.

The boy's puzzled eyes searched him: Ronny wanted to understand but it was a lot to absorb. "What was this thing you testified to?"

"Bribery. Frank Pastor was involved in a real estate lawsuit. It wasn't a criminal trial, it was a civil suit, but if he lost it he might be liable for fraud charges. And there was a lot of money involved in the case—hundreds of thousands of dollars.

"He wanted to buy the judge, to make sure he'd win the case."

"Which side were you on? Whose lawyer were you?"

"Nobody's. I wasn't involved in the case."

57

"You just said you used to be a lawyer, though."

"I was trying another case in another courtroom in the same building. I went into the men's room to wash some of the subway dirt off my hands and I happened to walk in just when Frank Pastor was slipping an envelope to the judge in the back of the men's room. They didn't realize I'd seen the envelope change hands."

"How come?"

"They were around behind the row of stalls. I happened to see it in one of the mirrors over the washstands. It was an accident—a total coincidence. Things happen like that all the time but they're always hard to believe when you try to explain them later."

"They believed you, though, didn't they? They must have, if Pastor went to jail."

"It was my evidence that triggered the investigation, but they had a lot more to go on than just what I happened to see in the men's room."

"How come you knew who this guy Pastor was?"

"Everybody in New York knew him by sight in those days. You used to see him all the time on the television news, his picture in the magazines, all that kind of thing. He was a spokesman for some sort of antidefamation league and he was always in the public eye."

"But if everybody knows these guys are gangsters, how come they're not all in jail?"

He glanced at Jan. "Sometimes it's very hard to get proof against them. They're very clever people."

"Doesn't sound to me like this Pastor was so clever. He went to jail, right?"

Mathieson nodded. "I washed my hands and left the men's room. I suppose they'd seen me by the time I left, or at least heard me, but neither one of them came out of the back of the room. I went right to the phone and called the District Attorney's office. I had several friends there. I told them about the envelope I'd seen change hands in the men's room. It could only have been one thing—a bribe. People don't pass over harmless legitimate messages in secret like that. The District Attorney got a warrant from a criminal-court judge right away and they searched this judge's chambers about two hours after I'd phoned. They found the envelope in the desk because he was in court all morning and hadn't had time to get it away from his office."

"What was in it, anyway? Money?"

"Seventy-five hundred dollars in cash. The envelope had both Pastor's and the judge's fingerprints on it."

"Dumb," Ronny said.

"Well they didn't expect anybody to find it, did they."

"I still think it must've been pretty stupid for Pastor to do that in person. He could've had anybody deliver the money for him. Some flunky."

"Normally he would have. But the judge insisted that Pastor pay him off in person. If anything went wrong—and something did—the judge wanted to be able to take Pastor down with him. He didn't want Pastor double-crossing him afterward. You understand, Ronny?"

"I think so. So they got caught. Did this judge fess up?"

"He might have, but as soon as he was released on bail he was killed. Shot to death on his own doorstep."

Ronny drew air through his teeth. "Cripes."

Jan said, "It's not a TV movie we're talking about, Ronny. These are real people. It's real blood and real pain . . ."

Ronny scowled at Mathieson. "They killed this judge to keep him from talking, right?"

"Yes. That's why sometimes it's so hard to get evidence against them—they make people afraid to testify."

"But they didn't scare you, did they."

"They scared me."

Jan said, "Your father stood up and testified to the truth in open court. A lot of people told him he was crazy."

At the time, he was thinking, it seemed the right thing to do.

Ronny said, "How come they didn't arrest Pastor for killing the judge, then?"

"Nobody could prove he'd ordered it done."

They talked on. It was hard to explain to the boy; he'd grown up on adventure shows that always wrapped the villains up neatly in the fourth quarter-hour.

There was a discreet knock at the door—three raps, an interval, three more. Mathieson admitted Glenn Bradleigh. There were two men with him, lugging suitcases. They set the cases down and left without a word. Mathieson said, "It's still cold in here. You can leave the door open."

Bradleigh crossed to the door. "No, we don't want to talk to the world." He shut it and locked it.

"Talk about what?"

Bradleigh tossed a large bulky manila envelope on the bed. "Morning, Jan. Ronny. You folks are looking a lot healthier today. Had breakfast?"

"Mr. Caruso brought it on a tray for us."

"Caruso's a treasure." Bradleigh was snapping the latches of the suitcases. "We rescued as much of your clothes as we could from the house. One of the boys ran it through one of the dry cleaners yesterday. Had a lot of plaster dust but I think you'll find most of them pretty clean now."

Jan got up and rummaged through the suitcases. She beamed at Bradleigh. "We didn't expect to see any of these again. Thanks so much . . ."

Bradleigh looked away. "Don't thank me. Don't ever thank me again for anything, all right?"

"Glenn, it wasn't your fault."

Bradleigh wouldn't look at any of them. "We dug quite a bit of other stuff out of the house. Odds and ends, you'll want to sort through it—we've taken it to the FBI office downtown, you can claim the stuff later. Amazing the kind of things we found intact. A balsa-wood model airplane, believe it or not."

She smiled; a sidewise glance at Ronny. "He put that away in the closet last November. He'd probably forgotten he ever had it."

"I did not."

Mathieson was looking at the manila envelope on the bed. "Who are we?"

"Mr. and Mrs. Jason W. Greene." Bradleigh emptied the envelope's contents onto the rumpled bed: documents of various shades and sizes. "Best we could do on short notice— we'd been putting these together for another family but they can wait. I'm afraid it'll make you both out to be older than you are but it's the closest we could do. The birth certificate on the boy is a flat-out forgery but we're slipping a copy of it into the Binghamton hall of records if anybody ever checks back that far."

"Binghamton?"

"Right. Because you spent some summers there, didn't you?"

"Long time ago. With my uncle and aunt."

"Then you knew the town a little, at least. We couldn't give you a background you knew nothing about at all. Jason W. Greene. Margaret Johnson Greene. Don't forget it."

"What do I do for a living?"

"Your wife used to be a librarian. You were an investment counselor. All right?"

"That'd be hard to put over on anybody who knows anything about stocks and bonds."

"You won't ever have to practice the profession. It's just part of the background, like last time. You came out here with a phony background as an insurance executive, remember? Letters of reference, testimonials, the works. It's all in that pile of papers. Read through it, familiarize yourselves with all of it. Memorize what you have to."

"What's our program?"

"Like last time. Whatever suits you—whatever you folks think you can handle. We'll grease wheels to help you get started. After that it's up to you. If you start a business and it goes bust that's your own problem. We'll help with the relocation costs but we can't bankroll you beyond a few hundred a month for seed money. It'd be against policy and anyway we haven't got the funds."

Mathieson pawed through the documents on the bed. "Massachusetts driver's license. I don't know the first thing about Massachusetts."

"Don't have to. You apply for a new license, you turn in the Mass license. It's just to get bona fides on your applications. You did all this before, Fred."

"It's been eight years. I'd forgotten a lot of this."

"It'll come back to you." Bradleigh lit a cigarette. "Think

61

about it, let me know what you both decide. And incidentally I think you both cught to change your appearance. Jan, try a short haircut. Fred, I'd do a crew cut for a while and get one of those compounds that cover gray. You might think about growing a moustache."

2

They brought him a typewriter and he sent brief letters to each of his clients. After lunch Caruso, a man whose face Mathieson always had trouble remembering, drove him several miles to a shopping center in Santa Monica. Mathieson changed ten dollars into coins in a bank; he made his calls from an outdoor phone booth while Caruso sat in the car keeping watch.

His first call was to Phil Adler. "Do you still want to buy me out?"

"Well naturally I'll do whatever you want, Fred, but I'm sure right now you don't want to have to be thinking about——"

"Is the offer open or not?"

"Well, you know, of course it is."

"Draw up the papers. I'll take whatever you think's fair. A man named Bradleigh will conclude the deal with you, he's got my power of attorney, he'll be in touch with you in a few days to clean out my office and take care of the details."

He finally got off the line and made the rest of his calls— the lawyers, the bank, his good-bye calls. Most of them had seen the news on TV or in the papers; he tried to keep his answers short and fend off their sympathies.

Finally he called the Gilfillans. Amy answered the phone. "Wait, I'll get the string bean and put him on the extension."

In a minute they were both on the wire. Roger said, "How're they hangin', partner?"

"We've got to clear out, I'm afraid."

"I know. No forwarding addresses, I reckon."

Amy said, "Billy's going to miss Ronny."

"It's worse on the kids than anybody else."

"Like some kind of fuckin' divorce," Roger said. "Listen,

there's some clown hanging around up at your place. About your size and he's wearing that red and yellow sport shirt of yours."

"Must be one of the government people," Mathieson said.

"I told him it was a dumb thing to do, making himself a target like that. Man said, 'That's my job, sir.' Just like one of them brave heroes in the movies. Stupid fuckin' idiot."

Amy said, "Fred, you and Jan and that boy take real good care of yourselves, hear?" Her voice broke; he heard the click when she hung up her extension.

Roger said, "I hope all your trails keep downslope with the wind at your back, old-timer."

"Maybe one of these days we'll come back."

"Yeah."

"At least I'll see you in the movies."

"You do that."

"Christ this is a pain in the ass."

"Just look after that good family you got, Fred."

"So long, Roger." When he hung up he couldn't stop the tears.

3

Bradleigh woke him up, banging on the motel room door. Mathieson crawled out of bed, glanced at Ronny on the cot and went to the door. When the three-and-three knock repeated itself he opened up.

"Come next door a minute." Bradleigh talked in a whisper.

He locked the door and carried the key with him, padding along the galleried porch in his pajamas. It was still dark.

When he entered the room Caruso gave him a tired nod. The bed was made; nobody had slept in there. Bradleigh closed the door and handed Mathieson a styrofoam cup of coffee.

He stumbled to the chair with it. "Thanks. I need it."

"A little hung?"

"You could say that." He'd thrown the empty vodka bottle in the wastebasket; it was the last thing he remembered.

"I had a call from Washington. They've found the leak. I

thought you wouldn't mind being rousted early for that bit
of news."

"Uh-huh. Time's it, anyway?"

"Quarter to five."

"Jesus Christ don't you guys ever sleep?"

"When we have time to. It's one of the secretaries in our
office. They were blackmailing her—never mind for what.
Ever heard the name C. K. Gillespie—a lawyer in Washington?"

"No. Gillespie? No. You mean he was blackmailing her
and he was stupid enough to tell her his *name?*"

"No. She was smart enough to follow him after one of their
meetings. She took down his license number."

"He's a lawyer? Then it's a dead end. He'll plead confidential privilege."

"He doesn't know we're onto him. We're keeping the woman
on ice. We're going to bug Gillespie every way from Sunday.
Phones, office, apartment, car, even his clothes. After a while
he'll realize she's disappeared—then we're hoping he'll panic
and start calling people."

"This wiretapping and bugging. Is it legal?"

"Warrants from the Circuit Court, sure. We want them
airtight, we're not going to fuck around with illegal taps."

"She's the one who fingered me to this Gillespie?"

"And Benson and John Fusco and Draper. All four of
you. We've got the other three under cover, we're relocating
them all. Incidentally it looks like Benson's going to make
it all right. But don't worry about C. K. Gillespie, he's a drop
in the bucket." The smell of Bradleigh's cigarette was slightly
nauseating. "We may have a chance at the whole megillah
this time, Fred. All we need is a few breaks. If we can get
enough on Gillespie we can make a deal with him and maybe
bring the whole structure toppling down."

"Immunity from prosecution and a new identity if he'll
blow the whistle on Pastor and Ezio Martin and the rest of
them. That's the 'deal'?"

"Sure."

"So Gillespie set us up, and he ends up going scot-free."

"Come on, Fred, be sensible. He'll lose his law practice,

that's for openers. I told you, forget him. He doesn't matter; he's the smallest potato in the sack." Bradleigh picked up an ashtray; he kept his feet, holding the ashtray left-handed like a guest at a cocktail party. "Given any thought to where you want to go? Discussed it with Jan and Ronny any?"

"Ronny's all for doing a Swiss Family Robinson somewhere in the South Pacific."

"That what you want?"

"No. I'd go nuts if I didn't have people around me who talked the same language."

"So?"

"We've talked. I realize you want the decision fast but we're talking about the rest of our lives, Glenn. I'll let you know as soon as I can—we're not crazy about motel rooms either." He threw the empty styrofoam cup at the wastebasket, missed, ignored it and leaned back in the chair. "Got any aspirin?"

Caruso went toward the bathroom.

Bradleigh said gently, "Scared, aren't you."

"Sure I am. They found us—they can do it again. I don't really care how they did it, Glenn. I don't care if you've plugged this leak. They can find another one. That's what gives me nightmares."

"No more leaks."

"Suppose my kid had gone home to get his baseball bat or any damn thing. Suppose he'd been in the house when they threw the bomb."

"It's no good supposing. He didn't. Nobody was home. They tried Benson and they tried you and they came up losers on both. Mobsters aren't supermen, you know. They get power by keeping people afraid, but take away the guns and they'll never last a day in the real world."

"They may not be mental giants but they frighten the hell out of me." Mathieson took the aspirin with the glass of water Caruso gave him. He rubbed his eyes; they'd be bloodshot all day.

Bradleigh said with unusual heat, "It's a crazy mythology we've created about the mob. The cold professionals, the never-miss hit men. All they know is triggers and bombs. More often than not they can't even handle the simplest job without screwing it up. Look at you. Look at Benson. Benson's off the critical list, incidentally. About the worst they did to him was inconvenience him."

"Inconvenience." Mathieson clenched his eyes against the ache. "I'm sorry—I don't feel grateful. I don't even feel relieved. I'll feel grateful when there's nobody out there with guns and bombs looking for my wife and my son."

"I know how you feel."

Bradleigh's detachment enraged him. He sat with his eyes closed. He was remembering different people, different times. A cheerful young lawyer and his sparkling young wife and their bubbling three-year-old son. Friendships that were built on laughter and simple enjoyments. They had taken warm pleasure in one another: That had been the center of their world—warmth. He remembered the cramped apartment on Thirteenth Street and the laughter that always filled it—and then a man in a men's room had handed a white envelope to another man and it had all taken on weight and begun to sink beneath the surface.

He bestirred himself. "Phil Adler's drawing up dissolution agreements. You'll have to use that power of attorney for me, wrap things up with him."

"Sure."

"Sell the cars, handle the insurance people about the house, you know." *Scrape up the leavings of the life of Fredric Mathieson, 1967–1976—born by fiat and died of fear, aged eight and one half years.*

Bradleigh said, "We'll make it as though you never existed at all."

4

They had the pool to themselves: noon in a motel. A few cars were parked in the diagonal slots—the day sleepers who didn't have air-conditioned cars and drove by night. The pool was in the center of the two-story court, out of sight of the street; outside, Bradleigh's four operatives were positioned to enfilade the entrances. Caruso was the only visible official presence; he wore a loud Hawaiian shirt with the tails out over his slacks and Mathieson knew there was a revolver under his waistband.

"How about a drink?"

She shook her head. "It's not even one o'clock."

"What the hell, we're on vacation."

She was watching the boy swim across the pool. "I wouldn't call it that. For God's sake stop patronizing me, I'm not made out of bone china." Finally she looked straight at him. "I'm not going to pieces. You can stop treating me as if I were."

"OK. I'm sorry."

"And quit apologizing all the time."

"I'm sor——" And then they both laughed. But it was uneasy laughter.

Mathieson hitched his aluminum chair six inches closer to Jan's. "Been thinking about where we go?"

She pulled the sunglasses down off her forehead and adjusted them on the bridge of her nose. Now he could no longer see her eyes; but her face kept turning toward the pool. "My mind's still blank. I wish I could think." Her face dipped. "It's so damned unfair."

"We've got to make up our minds, you know. We can't stay here. Glenn's itching to get us out of here."

"I know—I know."

Ronny climbed the ladder, perched at the top of the slide, made sure he had an audience and chuted into the water. He went in straight, feet first, holding his nose. When he surfaced at the ladder he said, "I wish they had a diving board."

"Do your surface dives," Mathieson told him.

"Yeah but it's not the same thing." But the boy went off the ladder step, curving neatly through the blue water.

5

Bradleigh went out first. Mathieson heard his soft talk: "All right?"

"All clear."

Bradleigh waved them out. Mathieson went ahead of Jan and Ronny. "Feels a little foolish."

"Let's just play it by the rules," Bradleigh told him. They

walked through the archway to the back parking lot. Phosphor lamps on high arched stalks of aluminum threw pools of white light around the tarmac. The three cars were drawn up side by side. Caruso was feeding luggage into an open car trunk.

Bradleigh opened doors for them and stood to one side. "You understand the drill?"

"Seems melodramatic to me," Mathieson said.

"I know. Think of it as a game you're playing."

Ronny said, "Funny kind of game if you ask me."

"It won't last long," Bradleigh said. "A couple of days you'll be up in those Arizona mountains learning how to be an Indian scout." He gripped Jan's hand. "You take care of each other now."

"Glenn, you told us not to thank you but——"

"That's right." But Bradleigh smiled a little; Mathieson took his firm brief handshake. "Look after them, Jason. I'll check in with you in a few days."

Jason W. Greene. "Take care, Glenn."

Then they were in the back seat of the Plymouth and Caruso was sliding in behind the wheel. The doors chunked shut, starters meshed, headlights stabbed across the lot. The car on Mathieson's right pulled away and Caruso drove after it. Mathieson looked around: The third car rolled into place behind them.

They went up along the freeways with the two outrider cars bracketing them front and rear. Caruso kept a steady hundred feet behind the point car. Three in the morning: There was no traffic. Caruso's small talk dried up quickly. In the back seat Ronny fell asleep between them. Mathieson tried to sleep. He thought of the Gilfillans, the rubble that had been his own house, Phil Adler's complacent fat smile. He felt buffeted by events and resentful of his own passivity; but an innocent civilian on the battlefield couldn't make the war stop. You could only run for cover and hate yourself for it.

At El Centro the convoy stopped for gas and breakfast: Caruso made a phone call; after a while they were on the road again.

Ronny became restive; Jan gave him her place by the window but everything was shut tight, the air-conditioner feebly holding back the desert heat. The land was painfully bright, mirages in the road ahead, blinding slivers darting at them from the chrome of passing cars.

They crossed the Colorado River into Arizona and the temperature kept climbing. Twice the convoy left the Interstate and went two-laning along straight country roads, into the cotton and citrus towns, all dusty pickups and slow-moving tractors and endless irrigation hoses. The outrider cars ahead and behind were never out of sight. There was no pursuit but Caruso was obeying instructions.

The detouring and doubling-back ate up hours. At noon they were at a drab oasis somewhere near Buckeye and he tried to revive himself by splashing cold water in his face in the flyspecked lavatory. The overcooked hamburger kept coming back at him through the afternoon.

The procession took a roundabout route through the Phoenix suburbs; as the traffic thickened the outriders moved in closer like mother quail. One of the marshals spelled Caruso at the wheel of the Plymouth; Caruso slept with his head lolling while Mathieson and Jan kept Ronny occupied with Twenty Questions and Botticelli; after a while the boy grew tired of word games and took to counting telephone poles.

East past the Superstition Range, Florence Junction, up the grades through the smelters of Superior, the mines of Miami and Globe, the dark red earth of the Apache reservation. They switchbacked down the limestone cliffs of the Salt River Canyon, crossed the bridge and stopped at the filling station for gas and Nehis.

Going up the north cliff one of the cars overheated and they waited in the scenic overlook until it could cool down enough to empty a Thermos of water into the radiator. Caruso sat on the stone retaining wall and stiffened whenever a tourist car pulled into the parking strip. Ronny ran from point to point, plugged Mathieson's money into the coin-telescope, read the embossed metal legends about Indian battles and Spanish explorations.

Mathieson took Jan's hand and they stretched their legs. It was bright and dry but the altitude was enough to take the heat out of the air and there was a mountain breeze.

Above the canyon Caruso took them off the highway and they wound through the back roads of the reservation through Whiteriver and up the twisting bends of the Mogollon Rim into piney woods, with a trout lake on the left, and for the first time Jan gave Mathieson her slow smile. "Almost there."

They reached Showlow at suppertime. Caruso said, "End of the line, everybody out," and they trooped into a roadside steak house made of lodgepole logs. A heavyset Apache sat in a chair on the porch and tipped his head back to peer at them under the brim of his curled cowboy hat; he did not smile.

Mathieson pulled out a chair for Jan and then settled at the table. "All right. Tomorrow we start house hunting."

CHAPTER SIX

New York: 7 August

1

GEORGE RAMIRO HAD BLUE JOWLS AND A BELLY ON HIM; HE was comfortable in his fat.

Ramiro was smoking a Cuban cigar when he came into Ezio's office. His suit must have cost the better part of a thousand dollars but he made it look baggy. One jacket pocket bulged where he'd wadded his necktie into it; his shirt collar was open to the second button with coiled-wire hair bursting through the vee; his pot had puckered pleats into the shirt where it sagged out of his waistband.

"Mr. Pastor sent me over."

"Got a job for you, George." Ezio reached for the file. He opened it and glanced through it mechanically as if to remind himself of its contents, though he had committed it to memory. He pushed the file across the desk, picked a leaf of tobacco off his tongue and sat down.

Ezio said, "How's Alicia?"

"Fine, fine." Ramiro was married to Ezio's half sister. She was not a likable woman; the question and the answer were ritual; no further discussion was required.

"Justice Department agent," Ramiro said. He turned a page and held up the photograph, squinting at it.

"We've got a line on him," Ezio told him. "I want you to go out to Los Angeles and take charge personally."

"Take charge of what?"

"This guy Bradleigh, he's the one who's keeping Edward Merle under wraps."

"OK, I got you."

"The reason we're sending you, George, you were in the courtroom the whole time he was testifying, you know the guy's face. We can't have mistakes on this."

"Sure, Ezio. I don't mind. Getting too fat and lazy anyhow—I can use a little work."

"You make contact out there with a guy named Fritz Deffeldorf."

"Who?"

"Free-lance contractor. He's been on this a while. Don't step on him unless you have to, but he understands you'll be taking charge."

"He the guy that blew it the last time?"

"He's one of them."

"That's nice."

"He knows the setup, he's on top of things out there. I can't run in a whole new crew on this, George, we need people who know the Los Angeles area. Deffeldorf's the one who got us this line on Glenn Bradleigh. You work with him, all right?"

"Just so he knows who's running it."

"He knows." Ezio got the airline ticket out and pushed it across the desk. "You still carry that Magnum, don't you?"

"Sure."

"The license is no good for a plane. Leave it home. Deffeldorf will give you another piece when you get out there."

"When do I go?"

"Here's the ticket. Flight leaves La Guardia at one. You've just about got time to throw things in a suitcase and get out there."

"Miss my lunch." Ramiro gathered the file and reached for the airline ticket. He opened it and smiled wryly. "Glad to see it's round trip."

Ezio laughed quietly and watched him walk out of the office.

CHAPTER SEVEN

Showlow, Arizona: 9–10 August

1

JASON W. GREENE, HE THOUGHT. REMEMBER IT. BORN APRIL 1930 in Binghamton, New York. Antioch class of '52. Investment counselor, retired, had a minor heart attack, came out West for my health, writing a book, as he told the realtor who had come out to settle the lease.

He watched the realtor's Buick roll away—down the ruts of the driveway and a left turn into the road, past Caruso's car and quickly out of sight in the pines. Caruso waved to Mathieson from the front seat of the car. Mathieson saw him turn a page in his paperback.

In the kitchen Jan inspected the cabinets. She had a dinner plate in her hand, upside down. "South Korea. But they're not bad, are they."

"Sure you can hack this place?"

"For the rest of the summer at least."

"It's better than a motel. God knows. If we don't mind the winter we can look for a place of our own next spring."

"And otherwise?"

"Well, ma'am, I reckon we'll just drift on till we find a place that sizes up right."

Her smile was distracted. She turned a slow circle, looking at things. "All the mod cons." Her voice was a little dry. The refrigerator must have been twenty years old; the furniture was sturdy but battered—Salvation Army style. The uncovered log walls were self-consciously rustic and the high fireplace that separated kitchen from living room lent it a hunting-lodge flavor.

Ronny came in the back door. "That's a freaky old plow in the barn."

"It's a disk cultivator."

Jan said, "You've got grease on the knees of those Levi's and you just put them on an hour ago."

"Nag nag." Ronny made a face and dodged Mathieson's good-natured swat. He went outside again. The screen door slapped shut; Mathieson heard him running across the dry pine needles.

"I don't think we need to worry about his adjusting. He'd be more traumatized by a trip to Disneyland."

She said, "Were you worried about him?"

"I wasn't sure how he'd take all this."

"He's got all the bounce in the world. We'll rent him a horse for the rest of the summer—he'll be in seventh heaven." It was why they'd taken the rental—the three acres of woods behind it, the barn and the corral.

It was eight miles from town. The road served weekend and summer cabins—A-frames and mobile homes. It was the part of Arizona the world didn't know about: the piney-woods high country. Nothing elegant about the neighborhood but he didn't know how long their money was going to last; and it accorded with Bradleigh's dictum—*You can't just change the name. You've got to create a whole new profile.*

After lunch he took Ronny out to the rent-a-car to drive into town. Caruso's partner got out of the stakeout car at the foot of the driveway. The partner was a slight man with a round dark face and eyes that always seemed amused. Mathieson had had difficulty figuring out his name until he'd seen it written on a luggage tag: Michael Cuernavan. The accent came on the second syllable. "Welsh," Cuernavan explained.

Cuernavan rode into Showlow with them. They explored the village and did their shopping. At half past three they all had McDonald's milk shakes and then went car shopping. "If we've got to feed a horse we'd better look at pickup trucks."

At the third used-car lot they found a four-year-old El Camino. It was dented and the truck-bed had wisps of straw stuck in the corners but it seemed to run smoothly. Mathieson kicked the tires and slammed the doors. Ronny tested the radio. Cuernavan announced, "I'm the best amateur Chevy mechanic this side of the Bonneville Salt Flats," and prowled around under the hood while the used-car dealer watched with a great show of nothing-to-hide confidence, beaming at all of them, singling out Ronny as the most impressionable and zeroing in on him with amiable ebullience: "You'll have yourself a ball tootling around in this here machine. What's your name, son?"

"Ronny. Ronny Math—Ronny Greene."

Red-faced, the boy wheeled away on the pretext of ducking to look under the back of the pickup. Mathieson caught Cuernavan's sharp glance. Cuernavan spoke quickly: "Probably need a valve job in another ten, fifteen thousand." He went around to shut off the engine. "But she's reasonably sound."

They transferred the day's purchases into the bed of the truck and turned in the rental car. Mathieson drove the El Camino slowly, getting the feel of it. Ronny sat between the men poking at controls on the dash—air-conditioner, radio, cigar lighter. Finally he said in a low voice, "I'm sorry, Dad. It won't happen again."

"I know. Don't worry about it too much. I still think of myself as Fred Mathieson. It'll be a long time before it comes easy."

But it had unnerved him more than he liked to show. The burden on the boy would be heavy.

Cuernavan said gently, "Best way to handle it, just take your time every time somebody asks you a question. Any question at all. Wait a couple seconds before you answer. Give yourself time to make sure before you talk."

"Yes, sir," Ronny said.

When they returned to Cochise Road a Mountain Bell truck was pulling out of the driveway; they had to wait for it to emerge. Caruso was still parked at the side of the road. The truck drove away into the pines and Cuernavan let himself out of the pickup.

Caruso said, "I checked him out. Genuine telephone company. Your phone's connected. How you getting along, Mr. Greene?"

"Pretty good, thanks."

"We'll see you in the morning, then. Relief shift takes over in a little while; we'll be going off."

"How long do you have to keep watch on us?"

"Until Glenn Bradleigh pulls us off."

"It must be boring as hell."

"We get paid for it." Caruso had a kind smile. He displayed his paperback. "I catch up on my trash reading. Anyhow this is a picnic, running surveillance out in quiet countryside like this. Anybody comes along, we hear them coming from half a mile away. It's not like a city stakeout where you've got to watch everything that moves."

Cuernavan said, "Check the oil every hundred miles or so until you find out how much she's using."

"Will do. Thanks for the help."

"Thanks for the company," Cuernavan replied. He slid into the car beside Caruso.

Mathieson drove it into the driveway. Ronny said, "They're good guys."

"Aeah." He parked by the kitchen door and they unloaded into the house. Jan had the place dusted and swept to her satisfaction; it was time to line the shelves.

Mathieson picked up the receiver and listened to the buzz. Then he put it down; there was nobody he could call.

The air was crisp and thin. After supper he built a fire and they sat around it until it was time to turn in. They slept under doubled blankets. Somewhere in the run of the night he awoke briefly and thought how cold it was, and thought about the two men in the night-shift car at the foot of the driveway: They must be half frozen.

They had an early breakfast. Immediately afterward Ronny disappeared to explore the woods. Jan's admonishment followed him: "Don't go beyond earshot."

76

"Fat chance of him obeying that one," Mathieson said.

"I know. But there's no way Frank Pastor's people could find us here."

He hadn't told her about Ronny's slip of the tongue; he didn't tell her now. He set up the typewriter on a table near the fireplace; he stacked the paper beside it but did not sit down to write anything. That would come later. It needed some thinking first.

The phone. It startled him; the adrenaline made his hand shake when he picked it up.

"Hi, Jason. It's Glenn. How're you making it?"

"We're fine. Where are you?"

"Sky Harbor Airport, Phoenix. I'll be up there this evening, see how you're getting along."

"We're settling in. Your men are handling things beautifully."

"Caruso's a Goddamn gem," Bradleigh said. "See you around eight, OK?"

"Scotch and water, light on the water. Right?"

"Right."

At lunch Ronny described his discoveries—the overgrown wreckage of a 1949 DeSoto, the rotted remains of a tree house evidently built by an earlier generation of children. The lady two houses down said she had a son Ronny's age, he'd be home from camp on Sunday.

Jan stood to clear the table. Ronny said, "When are we going to go look at horses?"

"How about tomorrow morning."

"Hey, yeah. Then I better get the stable cleaned out." And the boy was off and running.

Mathieson broke the seal on the vodka. "Bloody Mary?"

"It's awfully early."

"I'm still jumpy."

"You go ahead then. I don't want anything." She was cool, distant.

He mixed the drink and sat at the kitchen table watching her rearrange things in the cabinet. She kept taking things down and putting them back. Then abruptly she took the drink out of his hand and swallowed half of it.

"I changed my mind." She gave the glass back to him. "I'm sorry. I'm feeling snappish."

"Yeah."

He drained it and went to the sink to wash the glass. Through the window he could see the open maw of the barn. Ronny was wielding a rusty rake, dragging piles of ancient straw.

"Fred?"

He turned. "Jason."

"I'm sorry. It doesn't fit you."

"Couldn't be helped. Those were the papers they happened to have. Short notice . . ."

"It's just not fair." She slammed a frying pan back onto its shelf. "I wasn't made for this rustic nonsense. I miss Roger and Amy—I miss everything."

He took her in the circle of his arms. "Go ahead."

She was still: rigid. She turned away from him and went to the fireplace. She kept her arms folded; he saw her shoulders lift defensively.

It was no good trying to go to her. He knew how she felt: She wanted to start smashing things. He said, "Right offhand I can't think of any platitudes that would help."

"I want my house back." She turned and stared at him. "I want my family's name back. Our friends. Our Goddamned life. I want our son to live like a normal human being again. Adjusting, hell—when would he ever be eager to go off by himself and muck out a falling-down barn? If he weren't desperately upset he'd be running all over the neighborhood making new friends. Look at him—he's crying inside, Fred, he's just barely holding himself together."

After a long time she said, "We're not going to last like this."

He took a long ragged breath. "What do you want me to do?"

"I wish I knew."

2

They waited for Bradleigh. The night shift came on but Caruso and Cuernavan stayed, taking coffee with them in the house.

Cuernavan and Ronny played gin rummy with a great deal of mock ferocity: They had struck up a friendship. Cuernavan seemed to sense that the boy needed it. Caruso sipped his coffee and remained inobtrusive. Jan had cut drapes from a bolt of streaked brown fabric and was running the sewing machine as if it were a Formula One racing car. She kept looking sharply over her shoulder as if to make sure Ronny was still there.

Mathieson drank the Bloody Mary too fast and tried to remember whether it was his fourth or fifth since lunch.

The downing sun threw a red blaze through the window. Caruso left his seat and went to the screen door to stand watch. "This is fine coffee."

Jan said, "Shouldn't he have been here by now?"

"I don't know," Caruso said. "I wouldn't worry about Glenn Bradleigh."

"Have you known him long?"

"Worked for him six years now. He's one of the best."

Mathieson was thinking: This is no good. We're just kidding ourselves. We've both got to find something sensible to do with our lives or we'll go insane up here.

"Gin."

"Hell, Ronny, you must have cheated. I've got at least seventy points here. Let's see, forty, forty-nine, fifty-seven . . ."

"Seventy-three." Ronny had always had a quick accurate head for figures. If he didn't devote the rest of his life to horses he'd probably turn mathematician or engineer or computer scientist. It was something he'd inherited from Mathieson: a quick deft competence with the exactitudes of numerical and mechanical things. He'd always been handy with tools and he could handle anything electrical. He enjoyed rewiring toasters and doing handyman carpentry: He'd built all their kitchen cabinets himself in Sherman Oaks.

Maybe I'll become a cabinet maker. Give me something to do with my hands at least.

It wouldn't work and he knew it but he explored the fantasy dutifully. He had been devoted to professions that involved human complexities; to sustain his spirit he had to deal with people, not with pieces of wood.

Twilight, then dusk. Jan left the sewing machine and moved behind Caruso toward the window. "He really should have been here by now."

"Might have got held up at the Phoenix office," Caruso said. "I'm sure he'll be——"

The phone. Mathieson shot to his feet, unnerved. "I'll get it." He strode past the gin players at the kitchen table and snatched the receiver up, breaking off the second ring in its middle. "Yes?"

"Glenn Bradleigh. Is Caruso there?"

"Yes. Are you——"

"Put him on. Fast."

Goddamnit I am so sick and tired of being pushed around. . . . But he waved Caruso over and stood back. "Caruso."

He watched Caruso's eyes widen and then narrow. "You sure? . . . Christ, that's going to be a pill for them to swallow. . . . Well how much time have we got, then? . . . I see, yeah. But we'd be stupid to take the chance, the town's just too damn small. . . . How the hell did they pull it off? . . . Christ, they must have put a lot of manpower on it then. Where do I report to you? . . . All right, I'll call in. We'd better do it from pay phones on both ends, so just leave a time and phone number at the office for me. I'll check in with them between six and eight tomorrow night. . . . Yeah, I'll need it. Thanks."

When Caruso hung up his face took on a studied blankness before he turned. Mathieson took a step forward. "What now?"

Jan came through past the fireplace and searched Caruso's face. "What is it? What's happened?"

"You're not going to like it. I'm sorry." Caruso's grimace was half angry, half apologetic. "This is our fault. Glenn made a mistake but it's something we all should have thought of. It looks like the Pastor organization got a make on Glenn. Either they picked him up in Phoenix or they've been tailing him all the way from Los Angeles. Either way, they shadowed his car up here from Phoenix. Apparently they're using at least two cars; they were leapfrogging him and that's why he didn't tumble to it earlier."

Jan reached out, braced her hand against the fireplace to steady herself and looked quickly from Mathieson to Caruso. "You mean they've found us again."

"No, ma'am. Not yet."

Cuernavan said, "Where's Glenn?"

"Next town up the road, calling from a gas station. He's going to keep driving as far as Gallup tonight."

"Where'd he disclose them?"

Caruso made a face. "Not until he turned into Cochise Road. The one that had jumped ahead of him on the highway hung a U-turn—that's what tipped him. He pulled over and waited, and both cars went right by him. He didn't recognize anybody but he's pretty sure. Both carrying California plates. Glenn ran them a little wild-goose hunt and got back on the highway. Tried to make it look as if he'd only pulled off onto Cochise Road to shake the tails. He's going to try to distract them as far as Gallup. But we can't take the chance they'll buy it. They'll come back to this town and they'll start asking questions about families who just moved in. It won't take them much time to find out about the Jason Greenes."

Cuernavan turned to Mathieson and spread his hands, palms up. Ronny was shuffling the deck. He set it down on the table and squared it neatly, with care, eyes fixed on it. "You mean we're going away again?"

Caruso rammed his hands in his pockets. "That's about the size of it."

Mathieson had trouble controlling his voice. It shook. "How long do we have?"

Caruso shook his head. "No telling. Long enough to pack, I guess. Jesus I'm sorry."

Jan turned away and walked back into the living room. She moved like a mechanical wind-up toy.

Mathieson's fists were clenched so tight they began to hurt. He opened his hands and studied them. *Dear God I can't take any more of this. I just can't do it.*

CHAPTER EIGHT

Arizona–California: 12–15 August

1

BRADLEIGH WAS WAITING FOR HIM IN THE PARKING LOT OF the Tucson airport—taking short quick puffs of his filter tip. The open ashtray under the dashboard was filled with butts.

Mathieson got out of Caruso's car and slid into Bradleigh's. The air conditioning blew the smoke around Bradleigh's face in fragile wreaths. Mathieson pulled the door shut. "You keep it idling in this heat with the air-conditioner on, you'll overheat the engine."

"Yeah, well it's rented."

Caruso was parking fifty feet away. Mathieson removed his sunglasses briefly to study Bradleigh's face but then he put them back on.

Bradleigh was waiting for him to say something. Waiting for his forgiveness. Mathieson didn't give it to him. "You get the papers for us?"

"In the folder." Bradleigh tipped his head back and Mathieson found the folder in the back seat. He unwound the string closing and opened the brown flap.

"Paul and Alice Baxter," Bradleigh said.

"Alice? She won't stand for it. It took her four years to get used to Jan."

"Jan for Janice. You could try calling her Al."

Mathieson shuffled through the documents. "Nothing in here for Ronny."

"We're still preparing them. He doesn't need paper ID right away—how often does a kid need ID? But we're doing a birth-certificate search. We want to find one for a kid named Ronald. We can doctor the last name. Whatever town it turns out to come from, you can always say you were just passing through there when he was born."

Mathieson stared at Bradleigh. "Do you think we'll have time to get used to the name this time?"

"Look, Fred—Paul—I know how you feel, and I wish there was——"

"Some way to make it all up to us? I understand, Glenn. I understand it's not your fault." He tapped his temple. "I understand it up here. But down in the gut it's something else. Have you ever felt real honest-to-God flat-out rage? Have you any idea how much it can corrupt your thinking . . . ?"

"You want to take a poke at me? Would that help?"

"Oh for Christ's sake."

Bradleigh stubbed the cigarette out. "You're not in a mood for much talk right now. All right, the tedious details, let's get them over with. I assume you've talked it over with the family. Otherwise you wouldn't have insisted on a meeting today. Where do you want to go?"

"We've got a place in mind."

Bradleigh shook out a cigarette and offered the pack. Mathieson ignored it. Bradleigh's smile came slowly. "And?"

"That's all. We've picked a place. It's on a need-to-know basis, Glenn. You don't need to know."

Bradleigh put the cigarette in the corner of his mouth. He braced both hands against the top of the steering wheel, straightening his arms, pressing himself back in the seat and staring straight ahead out the windshield. "You want off the hook?"

"Yes."

"I know how you feel. But it's not wise."

"I see. But it was wise to move to Showlow with a retinue a half-blind man could have spotted. It was wise to get tracked there within forty-eight hours."

"That was my stupid fault."

"Yeah, it was." He was in no mood to give Bradleigh an inch.

"All right. I asked for that. But there are still good reasons why you need——"

"It's my responsibility to look after the safety of my family, Glenn. It may be your job but it's my life. All I'm doing now, I'm taking the authority that goes with the responsibility."

"You're a novice. An amateur. Out there alone you three wouldn't last any time at all."

"We'll have help."

Bradleigh's face swiveled. "Whose help?"

"Need-to-know."

"The fact remains we're the experts at this. All right, we've blundered but don't forget we caught this blunder in time. An amateur might not have caught it until it was too late."

"I'm not going to sit here all day and argue the point. You know my position."

"Your position's counter to our policy. I'm committed to render every possible protective service."

"You'll be doing that best if you turn us loose."

"Not according to our regulations."

"Screw regulations, Glenn."

On the dashboard the temperature idiot-light began to flicker red. The engine idled roughly, skipping a beat now and then, shaking the car.

Finally Bradleigh said, "I'm not just a good German, you know. I don't just follow every order I get whether I like it or not. But this time I agree with policy. A fair number have turned state's evidence and then refused our protection. Tough guys. They figured they could hold out on their own. Mostly they get killed. I'm not bragging, Fred. That's just the way it is."

"I'm not being a tough guy. I'm not going to stand in one place and dare them to come get me. We're going to ground and they won't find us. But a secret's only a secret as long as nobody else knows it, and this time we don't want anybody at all to know where we are. Not Caruso, not you, not the President of the United States."

"You've always been a stubborn son of a bitch."

"Stubbornness got me into this in the first place. If I hadn't dug in my heels against the well-meaning advice of the whole world I wouldn't have got into this fix. All right. I haven't changed. Stubbornness got me in, it'll get me out."

"Don't count on it."

"It's all I've got to count on."

Bradleigh stirred in the seat. The red warning light flickered brighter. "I made a stupid mistake. I figured they were looking for you, not for me. It should have occurred to me they'd try to follow me to you. All right, it's a mistake I'll never make again. I lost them in Gallup and they haven't picked me up again. That's not conjecture. It's fact. You believe it?"

"Of course."

"I guess you do. If you didn't you wouldn't be sitting here with me." He crushed the butt out. Mathieson wondered what was going on in his mind: Usually Bradleigh was transparent; now he was struggling with something inside.

Bradleigh said in a different voice, "You know my office number. Call collect. Whenever you want to. If you want money we'll arrange a postal drop of some kind. Just let me know." He sounded hoarse and hollow: It was a confession of failure and his accession was a form of penance.

Mathieson had counted on it. It gave him no pleasure; neither did it sadden him. The coldness was something he needed to sustain close inside him for however long it might take to learn to live with the wild rage that these past days had thrown into his life.

Bradleigh leaned across him to open the glove compartment in the dashboard. A box of .38 cartridges rolled out onto the open hinged door. Bradleigh closed his hand around it and then slammed the compartment shut. He pulled his revolver out from inside his shirt and put it with the ammunition on top of the document case in Mathieson's lap. "You know how to use it, don't you?"

"Yes. But I don't want it."

"You'd better take it, Fred."

"I'm not a killer. That's one of the differences between me

and them. I doubt I'd shoot even Frank Pastor—even if I had the chance."

"Your life could depend on it." Bradleigh's voice hardened. "Jan's life. Ronny's life."

He saw that it was something that would make a great difference to Bradleigh. "All right," he conceded.

"I hope you'll never need it. Just keep a little oil on it." Bradleigh put the gun and ammunition into the envelope with the documents.

"How do you explain losing your gun?"

"I don't. It's personal property. I've got two more at home just like it. It's registered to me, of course. But if you have to use it you know damn well I'll support you all the way."

"All the way to my funeral, I expect. If I ever have to use a gun it'll mean they've got too close to us."

"Just keep it close at hand. Promise me you'll do that, Fred."

Mathieson made no answer; he wasn't going to make promises he didn't intend keeping and he wasn't going to spend the rest of his life with a gun in his pocket.

Bradleigh's shoulders drooped a little. "All right. You'll suit yourself, I guess."

Mathieson said, "I'd appreciate it if you wouldn't try to trace us. I'd appreciate it even more if you'd wipe these new names and ID's off our records but I don't suppose you can do that."

"No. I can't."

"All right. We'll settle for what we can get."

"I'll have to tell them you got away from us. I'll pull Caruso and Cuernavan away tonight at ten o'clock for a short conference. You'll have about ten minutes to be out and gone."

"Tell it any way you want. As long as they don't come looking for us."

"I'll do what I can. It's the least I owe you. Fred——"

"I know. Good luck yourself."

"Send me a postcard. Or give me a ring. Anything—just let me know you're all right. Will you do that?"

"Yes," he said, not sure whether he would do it. He opened the door. "You're about to boil over, Glenn." He picked up the heavy envelope and walked across the lot toward Caruso's car. He didn't look back.

2

When they drove away from the motel he saw no sign of pursuit but he doubled through the dark back streets anyhow, zigzagging through silent residential areas, avoiding the main arteries and keeping half his attention on the mirrors.

Jan and Ronny were silent with the washed-out enervation of something near hopelessness. He'd made the decisions himself. Jan had neither argued nor offered suggestions.

He avoided the freeway and drove south from Tucson along the highway to Nogales. It was fifty miles to the Mexican border; they were there in less than an hour. The station wagon needed only a few gallons but he made a point of filling the tank at a station within a few blocks of the border gate and he engaged the station's owner in conversation because he wanted the man to remember them.

At the border he applied for three temporary visitor visas in the Baxter family name. The visas weren't necessary for entry to the border town itself but they were required if you went more than a few miles deeper into the country. He was laying a false trail; it would buy them a little time.

They drove into the Mexican side of Nogales and ate dinner at the Cavern Restaurant; he'd been there once years before and remembered the turtle soup and it was still as good as it had been but he hardly noticed.

It was midnight when they put it back on the road. He'd studied the map and it looked like a rugged but passable highway; it proved to be a barely graded dirt track filled with chuckholes from the last rains and it took the rest of the night at snail's pace to cross eastward along the south side of the border, across the Sonora provincial boundary and through the dry hills to the village of Agua Prieta. At eight in the morning they crossed back into the United States. The Mexican guards merely waved them through; the American customs men tossed their luggage cursorily but showed no other interest and only glanced at the Mexican visitors' permits; he was sure they hadn't taken down the names and wouldn't remember faces for more than a day.

The next step was to get rid of the car because Caruso knew it, the year and color and plate number.

Sleeplessness laid a grit on his eyeballs but Jan was too groggy to drive and he made do on three cups of strong roadhouse coffee and a big breakfast of steak and eggs. It kept him going along the highway north from Douglas to Benson. He kept checking the mirror and found nothing alarming there. The station wagon's air-conditioner was inadequate against the Arizona desert and they sat three abreast because the cooling didn't reach into the back. He filled the tank and checked the oil in Benson; they had lunch in a café and went eastward. The Interstate brought them into Willcox in midafternoon and he drove down the exit ramp into the town.

He dropped Jan and the boy with all the luggage at the Trailways depot and checked the wall-posted schedules: There was a four o'clock express to Tucson, Phoenix, El Centro, Riverside and Los Angeles. It gave him forty-five minutes. He drove along one of the main streets until he found a shopping center; he parked the car in a slot near the edge of the big parking lot, left the keys in the ignition and walked to a telephone booth. He looked up the number of the local taxicab company, "Fast Service Radio Dispatched," and arrived back at the depot with fifteen minutes to spare.

They bought the tickets and waited for the bus; it was on time and they found seats without difficulty. He was speculating on how long it might be before someone spotted the keys in the ignition of the station wagon he'd left behind. Probably it would be stolen within twenty-four hours.

The Tucson stop was a dinner stop; they were on the road again at nine, out of Phoenix by midnight and barreling westward along the same route they'd taken last week coming the other direction with Caruso's three-car convoy. The starlit desert was nearly invisible through the tinted windows; the air conditioning was too cold in the half-empty bus and condensation gathered along the chrome strips of the overhead luggage racks. Mathieson slowly blinked his raw eyes and felt the anger eat at him like an ulcer.

It was nearly three o'clock when the bus stopped in El Centro. He made several calls from a booth and finally found a motel that was still open for business and had vacancies. He booked a double room with a cot and they took a taxi from the depot. At half past three they carried their bags into the room. Mathieson said, "We'll buy a car tomorrow. Let's try to get some rest—we'll talk tomorrow."

3

The Gilfillans were at the cabin waiting for them and he watched to see if the reunion would revive Jan. She was nodding and talking and smiling in response to things addressed to her but it might be automatic.

Finally the luggage was carried inside, Ronny and Billy were dispatched to the creek with Roger's fishing tackle, four chairs were set out on the porch, drinks were distributed.

He hoped that telling their story to Roger and Amy would restore reality to the nightmare experiences they had endured.

He let Jan tell it; he watched Roger's and Amy's reactions. As she spoke Jan became more animated, angrier; twice she laughed but it was laughter twisted inward. She drank too much too quickly and slurred. She'd had a headache all day; it became blinding and she went inside, moving like an old woman, Amy taking her along with an arm across her shoulders like a practical nurse.

It left him alone with Roger on the porch. Roger stood up. "Bourbon and branch again?"

"All right."

"Girl needs rest."

"Yes."

"I reckon you do too."

"I'll put the car away." Mathieson walked down to the old Ford they'd bought in El Centro and drove it around the house under the carport. When he emerged he found Roger on the steps holding both drinks.

Amy stood in the doorway. "She's out for the night, I expect. But the rest of us got to eat. I better repair to the cuisine department. You boys take a hike or something."

The men walked down along the edge of the pines. "We're right proud you decided to come to us, old horse."

There was nothing to say to that, nothing that wouldn't sound saccharine.

"Y'all welcome to stay on up here as long as you want. You know that."

"We don't want to weigh you down, Roger."

"Ain't no weight. But winters up here get pretty hard and kind of lonesome. You got to drive fourteen mile to the country store on the main highway. Sometimes it'll take you the whole day to do it."

Roger gestured with his drink toward the heavy interior of the forest. "Ain't likely to ever run out of firewood but this shack wasn't never built for winter living. You likely find yourselves spending two-three hours every day just cutting up dead trees to feed the fireplace. If y'all decide to stay on why I reckon I could bring in a Kohler plant."

"Roger, we're not going to move in permanently."

"Winters you need to keep the cover on the well when you ain't using it and keep a big rock on the end of a rope to bust the ice down there."

"We may only be here a few days."

"And then what? Where else you got to go?"

"I only came here to give us a chance to get our wind back."

"Where do you go afterward? Why not stay right here?"

Mathieson only shook his head, mute. They stopped along the edge of a mountain track that passed for a road. Roger said, "Jeep trail. The fire rangers use it. I brought in a grader last year, smoothed it out down to the county road. See, the reason we didn't spend anything on work up here, we don't own it. It's National Forest land. We got temporary possession—tag end of a forty-nine-year lease. When the thing expires the land reverts to the government. They'll demolish the cabin. They want to go back to virgin forest, all these old lumber and mining leases. Matter of fact that's why I figured we ought to meet up here. My name's not on any public record."

Roger hunkered down with his back against a pine. He

balanced the drink carelessly on his knee. "Old horse, you want to talk?"

"I don't know, Roger."

"You never did wear your feelings on your sleeve but this thing's got you clamped up tighter than a schoolmarm's cunt. You keep it all bottled up it'll start to rot inside you."

The stillness and the whiskey began to relax him. He watched the late sun rays flicker through the high trees. Needles and cones made a crisp resin fragrance.

Finally he said, "When you think about hiding out it looks like retirement. Pension, sixty-five years old and a gold watch. Spending the rest of your life trying to think of ways to kill time until you crumble away of old age. That's the vision I keep having and I can't stand the sight of it."

Roger tipped his head back against the tree and watched him. Mathieson said, "You know I grew up in New York. We had, you know, La Guardia and the Yankees and the Giants and the Brooklyn Dodgers. We were about a half a block from the Second Avenue El. My father was a druggist, we lived in the top two floors of a converted brownstone. It wasn't an elegant neighborhood then. It is now. But it was just middle class at the time. A lot of grit and that God-awful noise from the El trains. It was just New York, hell, nobody thought of it as a pesthole in those days."

"Uh-huh."

"We grew up on stickball and comic books and movie matinees, you know. Gangsters—to me a gangster was the same thing as the crooked banker in the Western movie, the guy that twists his moustache and forecloses on the girl's ranch. Bad guys—all right. But as far as I was concerned they were pure comic-book fictions. Something Hollywood dreamed up for the B-movie formula. To give Alan Ladd and Pat O'Brien somebody to fight it out with."

"I was raised on Jesse James, myself."

"The whole idea of willful evil was a comic-book fantasy. I guess I didn't grow up for the longest time. I mean, even combat in the army was like a movie. The reality was a bunch of ordinary people digging holes and eating out of mess kits and swapping dull stories to pass the time. It was like getting through your junior year. Waiting for mail, waiting for new orders. Thinking about girls. Lying a lot. Hell, there was an enemy army out there, there was a lot of noise and confusion but that was all part of the unreality. Am I making any sense?"

"Reckon you are, some."

"Frank Pastor, that whole world. Inside my head it's still a B movie. I keep thinking all I need to do is tell the writer to do a script rewrite."

Mathieson leaned forward and coiled his arms around his knees. "I want a crack at rewriting this script."

"Now I ain't sure I see what you're talking about there."

"Frank Pastor's had all the initiatives. He acts, I react. He shoots, I duck. He's the star, the writer and the director—the hell with it, Roger, I'm sick of being an extra in Frank Pastor's grade-B programmer."

"Well you had those cards dealt to you, old horse."

"If you're the mouse in the shooting gallery, sooner or later you're bound to get an urge to pick up one of the rifles and start shooting back."

Roger rolled his glass between his palms. "You mean that literally? I mean, picking up a gun and going after the son of a bitch?"

"That's not my line. I wouldn't stand a chance."

"Then that kind of thinking, it's only going to misery you. Torturing yourself ain't going to help."

"I'm not doing that."

"Amy must just about have supper on the table. Let's us go eat. Look here—you got a plan of some kind kicking around back there inside your head?"

"It's beginning to."

"You know there's one man you ought to go and see. You know who that is."

"Yes." Mathieson knew.

PART TWO

TURNABOUT

CHAPTER NINE

Los Angeles: 22 August

1

THE RECEPTIONIST HAD ABUNDANT DARK RED HAIR AND frosty eye makeup; she had the look of a cocktail hostess in a pricey lounge. "Yes, sir?"

"My name's Edward Merle. I phoned yesterday."

"Yes, sir. Your appointment was for ten-thirty."

"I know, I'm early. I took a chance . . ."

"Please have a seat? I'll see if he's free."

The reception office was old-fashioned like the lobby of a rail-depot hotel.

The red-haired woman put her headphone down and pulled a cord. "Would you come this way, Mr. Merle?" She gave him a quick smile.

He followed her down a short paneled corridor. She showed him through a door into the corner office.

Diego Vasquez came to his feet.

Shirt-sleeved, tie at half-mast, long sidewise shock of glossy black hair. Vasquez had the incongruous face of an intellectual gone to seed.

The redhead vanished silently. Vasquez sized up his visitor with sad dark eyes. "Mr. Merle."

The handshake was perfunctory as if Vasquez disliked the

touch of flesh. He was thin and not very tall; he looked fragile. How old was he? Fifty?

Vasquez circled his desk and got into the high-backed leather swivel chair, seating himself as if he were a pilot settling at the controls. "How may I be of service?" Courtly, low-voiced—as contrivedly old-fashioned as his surroundings. But the redhead was a giveaway: This was Hollywood country and Image was rarely truthful.

On the wall in a glassed frame was the headline from the *Times*. FOUR EX-CONVICTS REVEALED DEAD IN VASQUEZ RESCUE OF ACTOR'S KIDNAPPED SON.

Vasquez pinned him with a speculative scrutiny. He prompted: "Sir?"

"It's rather a confidential matter." A lame beginning; he wished he hadn't said it.

"They usually are." A quick smile that vanished abruptly.

"I want to contract for your services."

"So I gathered." Patient, polite; but the eyes became harder. *Spit it out. Get on with it.*

But it was the point of no return. Beyond this moment he would be committed.

"My family and I are being—harassed. By gangsters. Members of organized crime."

"Indeed."

"I testified against one of them. Some years ago."

"You're seeking protection? There are federal agencies that——"

"I'm not seeking protection, Mr. Vasquez."

"I see." The brown eyes narrowed. "Wear your hair longer, and take off that recently grown moustache, and yes. The photograph in the *Examiner*. It's Mathieson, isn't it? Fredric Mathieson?"

It jolted him. "Are you always that quick?"

"I read the newspapers, Mr. Mathieson. It's not every day that a house is blown up in Los Angeles. Why did you come here under a false name?"

"Edward Merle is my real name."

"Have you got any identification?"

"I've got papers in the name of Paul Baxter."

"Yet a third name. It must be rather confusing for you."

"Until a few days ago I was Jason W. Greene." He managed a sliver of a smile.

"I once knew a writer who used nine pen names. Sometimes he forgot his real name."

"My name is Edward Merle. That's my real name, it's the name the mobsters know me under."

"Then Mathieson is an alias, but you used it for rather a long time, didn't you."

"Until a few weeks ago, yes. More than eight years."

"I see. Let's see if I can reconstruct this. Your house is bombed by contract killers, presumably. Now it turns out the intended victim has been living under an assumed name and reveals that he testified against a criminal some years ago. You're not a Valachi type—you don't have the earmarks of a gangster gone rogue. You're not a defector from the syndicate, so I must assume you were an innocent witness to some criminal act. Correct?"

"Yes."

"The whimsies of fate allowed you and your family to survive; but you've lost your house and you've had to go into hiding again. You've had to give up your job and your name for the second time. And apparently the law can't do a thing to prevent this situation. So you've come to Vasquez. Is that a fair summation?"

"Close enough, yes."

Vasquez searched his face. "What you've got in mind takes more than resolve, Mr. Merle."

"I've got more than resolve."

"What have you got?"

"Time. A great deal of hate." He reached into his pocket. "And money." He laid the check on the desk.

Vasquez picked up a pencil and used its eraser to pull the check across the desk to him. He glanced at it. "Twenty thousand dollars. Rather impressive." He left the check where it was and tapped the pencil against his teeth. "Hate can wear off."

Mathieson said nothing to that.

"You're what, an agent for screenwriters?"

"I was, yes."

"And what was your profession before? When you were Edward Merle."

"I was a lawyer in New York."

"Criminal practice?"

"The firm I worked for had mainly business clients."

"But you did practice criminal law to some extent at least?"

"Now and then. Trivial matters. Sometimes a client would be arrested for assault in a bar, that kind of thing. Once or twice a year we'd take on a felony case for the Legal Aid Society."

"You had a fairly good practice?"

"I was a junior staff member. Not a very brilliant lawyer, I guess. But yes, I kept busy."

"Making, say, fifteen or sixteen thousand a year?"

"In that area. Why?"

"I'm trying to hold up a mirror for you. You witnessed some sort of offense perpetrated by an organized crime figure, I take it, and you stepped forward to testify to what you'd seen. Was your life threatened at that time?"

"Yes."

"Anonymous calls or letters?"

"Yes."

"Did you seek police protection?"

"Yes."

"And this led to your being provided by the Justice Department with a new identity. You moved three thousand miles and went into a new profession. Putting it another way, you decided your testimony was important enough to justify sacrificing your law practice and profession, your home, even your name."

Vasquez leaned back and crossed his legs. "Look in the mirror then, Mr. Merle. A man who distinguishes between right and wrong. A man who believes in the difference between good and evil. A man who believes in justice and law so deeply that he's willing to make extraordinary sacrifices for the sake of moral principle. Is that a fair picture?"

"Distorted. I never aspired to sainthood."

"Right now you're angry. Anger saps the reason. For a while it can neutralize inhibitions. It can even cancel out a man's deepest sense of moral rectitude—for a while. An angry man can make terrible mistakes. But anger wears off. If yours wears off after you've achieved your vengeance, how will you live with yourself?"

"I'll manage."

"Sarcasm would appear to be out of place just now. And if your anger wears off before you've exacted your revenge, what then? Suppose you find you've started something that can't be recalled?"

"I won't quit."

"Naturally you feel that way now. But you may begin to question yourself in time. You're a grown man whose life has conditioned you to accept certain values. You'll never escape that conditioning—not for very long."

Vasquez twirled the pencil in his fingers. "You'll question things. It may lead to one of two results. Either you'll become uncertain and your uncertainty will cause hesitation, or you'll be so corroded and corrupted by your own acts of vengeance that you'll have destroyed yourself along with your enemies. If the latter, the entire exercise is pointless. If the former then clearly a man who hesitates is more likely to be killed than to kill. I mean that both literally and figuratively. We are talking about killing, aren't we?"

"No."

For the first time he saw Vasquez taken aback. "No?"

"I'm not a killer. That's their style, not mine."

"Then what did you come to me for?"

"I want training. I want you to teach me how to get them off my back. How to neutralize them so that they never threaten me again."

"I don't quite understand."

"It's not a job I could hire anybody to do for me. I want you to teach me how to do it myself. Without murdering them." He felt the unconvincing tautness in his own smile. "The cliché happens to fit. Killing would be too good for them."

2

Vasquez did not smile. "Tall order, Mr. Merle."

"I know."

"Expensive, I should think."

"Naturally."

"Time-consuming. Do you have any experience of violence?"

"Infantry, in Korea. I was at Inchŏn."

"Combat officer?"

"Just a trooper. Private first class."

"Hardly a decision-making position." Vasquez looked to one side. "I've never attempted anything remotely like what you're proposing. This isn't a training academy. And you don't want them killed. Just what is it that you do want done with them?"

"If I knew the whole answer to that I wouldn't have had to come to you."

"I see. Then you don't really have a plan of action."

"No."

"As I said before, it takes more than resolve." Now the brown eyes came back to him. "How old are you?"

"Forty-four."

"After twenty years' office work. Do you smoke?"

"No."

"Drink?"

"Yes."

"To excess?"

"Sometimes."

"How often is sometimes?"

"Too often," he conceded. "But I'll go on the wagon."

"How's your heart? General physical condition?"

"Good."

"When was your last physical?"

"About eighteen months ago."

"Better have a thorough checkup." Vasquez pulled a yellow legal pad out of a shallow drawer and wrote something at the top of the page, underlining it with a flourish. Then he hesitated. "What do you prefer to be called? Mathieson or Merle?"

"I've got used to Mathieson but it was Merle who testified against them. It's Merle they're trying to kill and it's Merle who's going to stop them."

Vasquez wrote with his pencil—a swift crabbed hand. He looked up. "Who's the man you testified against?"

"Frank Pastor."

Vasquez's entire face changed when he smiled. He looked boyish. He wrote quickly on the pad. "Just Pastor alone? He's the one you want?"

"I want Pastor and Ezio Martin and a Washington lawyer named C. K. Gillespie. There may be others. Certainly I want to know who threw the bomb into my house."

"Enormous job."

"Of course."

"It's a huge organization," Vasquez said. "You must have seen the news two or three weeks ago—apparently they bought an entire parole board. Pastor walked out of prison, I suppose you knew that."

"Yes."

"Do you know anything about these men? Where they live, where their offices are, the patterns of their movements?"

"Not really. The New York area of course. I'm sure they're insulated by guard dogs and bodyguards and electronic gadgets and God knows what else."

"Those devices aren't as formidable as you may think. A man can always be reached. You need only to study the movements until you find patterns. They don't spend their entire time locked up behind walls and electric fences. They're active men. They manage a vast industry. They're always on the move. You can reach them. The hard part is to know exactly what to do when you've made contact." He laid the pencil down. "Normally I wouldn't touch this with a rake."

"But?"

Vasquez flipped to a fresh page in the pad and applied his pencil. "I'm going to draw up a contract. I'd advise you give it careful consideration before you sign it."

"Let's discuss it first."

"Discuss what?"

"The terms. Our separate obligations."

"Nothing to discuss. Either you put yourself in my hands or you don't. We'll hold that check of yours in abeyance but I'd like a small retainer from you. I'm licensed to practice law in California and a retainer entitles us to the protections of the privileged-communications statutes. You're employing me as an attorney and an investigator."

"Why so cut and dried?"

"It's the way I work. I'm arbitrary." Vasquez smiled again, off center. "Take it or leave it."

CHAPTER TEN

Long Island–Manhattan: 24–25 August

1

ANNA MADE A WORD ON THE SCRABBLE BOARD AND WATCHED him enter the score. "You look beautiful with hair."

"I was about to take it off."

"Please don't."

"All this humidity, you sweat. The thing gets hot."

"You'll get used to it. You look like a movie star."

He brooded at his rack of tiles. "I've got a seven-letter word here and no place to put it on that stinking board."

A gust came off the Sound and shook the windows; she heard the rain on the flagstones outside. It ran down the panes in rivulets.

She said, "Time."

"The hell. I'm going to sit here until I find a place to put it. It's a lousy board." He propped his chin in his hands and scowled. "One thing you learn inside. Patience."

"You can't take all night. It's not fair."

"Nothing's fair."

"What's the matter, Frank? You came home tonight like something with a lit fuse."

"All right, OK, I'm sorry. Look, I'm calm, everything's fine. What did you want to talk about?"

"First tell me what's the matter. Maybe you'll feel better."

He took his elbows off the table and leaned back in the chair. The fingers of his right hand slid back and rested against the rim of the table. His index finger tapped two or three times. "What do you think about C.K.?"

"I think he's got a lot of charm and he's in a hurry."

"Maybe too much of a hurry?"

"I don't know. You were ambitious too, I imagine, when you were his age."

"He's not a kid. He's older than he looks. He ever make a pass at you?"

"He wouldn't have the nerve."

"He's pretty—brash."

"No, Frank."

"But he butters you up a lot. I've seen him turn on the charm."

"He's only making points with the boss's wife, Frank. Are you jealous?"

"Sure I am."

"Not of C. K. Gillespie."

"Well I guess I'm jealous of anything in pants that looks at you twice. You mind?"

"No, I don't mind. I like that. You haven't been sitting here working up a rage about me and C.K., have you? Because it's absolutely——"

"No. It was something else. Forget I said that."

"It's Ezio. He's been putting things in your ear."

"He might have dropped a remark."

"Ezio hates C.K. He'd say anything to put a wedge between you and C.K."

"I know that. What I don't know is why. The kid ever do anything to him?"

"Not that I know of. But C.K.'s ambitious. He's young, he's very button-down, he doesn't want to spend his life as someone else's mouthpiece in Washington."

"That's what Ezio said. Ezio thinks he wants to carve himself out a piece of the organization."

"He probably does. Maybe he deserves it."

"You taking his side now?"

"I'm taking your side. I think C.K.'s useful to you. He's done good work. He uses his imagination—he's bright."

"He takes chances."

"So do you."

"I don't know. He bugs me."

"He bugs everybody—that's the way he is. But if you don't trust him that's something else, of course."

"You think I should trust him?"

"I don't know. But if you're suspicious of him I think it's just because of Ezio."

"Ezio's one of my closest friends. Christ, he's a cousin of mine."

"And how much do you trust him?"

"Well he got in the habit of running the company while I was inside. He didn't want to give that up, OK, he wouldn't be human otherwise. Ezio's a very old-fashioned guy. He was born in Palermo. He's an important man in the organization, with me or without me—I don't kid myself about that. You can see how he'd get nervous when he sees a sharp young dude trying to muscle in. Now you and Ezio, you never liked each other at all. I need to keep that in mind too, you know."

"I've never tried to get between you and Ezio."

"Damn right you haven't."

"Frank, what's bothering you?"

"I guess it's that Janowicz woman. You know, the secretary in that office. The one C.K.'s been getting this information from."

"What about her?"

"She's disappeared. He had a meeting set up with her yesterday she didn't come. He checked around. She's gone."

"On vacation?"

"No. Just gone. Her husband's gone too. They closed up the house four days ago. Now maybe that means the feds got onto her. If they did they'd have her under cover somewhere and they'd be squeezing her like a lemon. And they'd pack up the husband and put him in a hotel someplace just to keep him out of our reach. Now the thing is, C.K. says she can't finger him. He says he always wore dark glasses, never met her on his own turf, never gave her his real name. He says there's no way

105

they could trace him through her. Question is, can I trust him to know what he's talking about?"

"She's been missing four days. They haven't arrested C.K., have they?"

"Of course not."

"Does he think he's being watched?"

"No. He said he was looking for that but there's nobody shadowing him."

"Then he's telling the truth, isn't he? If they knew who he was, they'd have come after him by now."

"Would they? Sometimes those people try stunts. But either way it doesn't change the other thing. The other thing is, they squeeze that woman and they find out what she peddled, and it won't matter who she says she peddled it to—they'll know it was bought for me. So we start getting federals on the backs of our necks and I really don't need that kind of horse shit right now."

"We can live with that. We've lived with it before."

"Maybe. Hell, Benson got shot, Merle's house got blown up—they had to know that was us. But they'll never prove any connection and they know it." His hand dropped off the edge of the table. He scowled at the Scrabble board. "Eight years I had no privacy at all—that's enough shit for anybody."

"You could retire. We could move to Switzerland."

"Sure." The shade of a smile crossed his face. "You know it makes a difference having you to talk to. A lot of guys— you see Ezio discussing anything with that dame? She hasn't got two brain cells to rub together. You're something else, you know, I can talk with you. You've got it up here. I got a good bargain."

2

In the bedroom she watched him peel off the toupee. She laughed at him.

He was feigning ferocity: He stabbed a finger toward her. "I knew I was going to get ridiculed in my own bedroom, I wouldn't have let you con me into buying this thing."

She only laughed again. Frank slammed into the bathroom

and she heard the buzz of the shaver. She began to undress; she looked at herself in the mirror.

When he came out of the bathroom she was sitting on the bed setting the alarm: He had a morning conference in the city.

He stopped in his tracks and she looked up in alarm. He was staring at her.

"My God, Frank, what's the matter?"

"Sometimes I look at you, I just get choked up." The startled look in his eyes gave way to silent laughter. "You're the damnedest beautiful thing I ever saw."

It was slow and he was gentle this time; she said, "That was delicious."

He didn't reply and for a while she thought he was asleep. Then he said, "You wanted to talk to me. You said you had something you wanted to talk about. So talk."

"Turn on the light, then."

"I don't need lights to hear you talk."

"I want to see your face."

"The hell for?" But he switched it on. He was up on one elbow and his face was somewhere between puzzlement and impatience. "What's this you want to see my face? You going to lay something tough on me?"

"Sure. I'm leaving you for another man."

When he began to react she burst into laughter. "I'm running away with Ezio."

He lay back and made a face. "Come off it. Sometimes you pull too many jokes."

She brought her laughter under control. "I can't help it. The look on your face."

"The whole thing, getting me to turn on the light and everything—just for a lousy joke?"

"The thing I wanted to talk to you about. What if we started a family of our own?"

He hiked himself up on his elbow. "You want to get pregnant?"

"I want to make a son for you."

She couldn't make out his expression. "Christ sake I'm almost fifty years old."

"Don't you want a son, Frank?"

She watched anxiously. He was scowling at the ceiling. "I got to think about that. I'm getting old, you know."

"The hell you are."

He turned the light off. In the dark she listened to his breathing.

And then finally he said, "Hell yes."

He gathered her against him. She couldn't help it: She cried.

3

The kid bustled around the office like a termite inspector and Ezio stood out of his way by the window looking down into the traffic. He saw it when Cestone double-parked the limousine in front of the building entrance and went around the car to open the door for Frank Pastor. Frank was wearing a light-gray suit and a yellow shirt and looked boyish and foreshortened from this high angle. Ezio watched him disappear into the building.

You could tell a good deal about Frank's mood by his choice of clothes in the morning. He was wearing something light and colorful today. The meeting was going to be tricky enough; if Frank had been in a bad mood it might have gone awry.

The elevator must have been right there waiting because Frank arrived very quickly. Down in the street Cestone was still waiting for the light to change so he could pull the limousine out into the traffic. Ezio turned away from the window and Frank was in the doorway watching the kid work on a lamp.

"How's the electronic genius this morning?"

"Morning, Mr. Pastor. Doing just fine, thank you. Nothing to report, I'm happy to say. I'm just about finished up—just want to check out the door hinges before I go."

"You take your time and do your job," Frank told the kid. "We're paying for thoroughness, not speed."

Frank settled into the leather couch. Ezio said, "That rain last night sure cleaned out the air. You can see clear to Jersey."

"Beautiful day," Frank agreed.

The kid picked up his little electronic gizmos and fitted them back into his kit; he closed the case and went toward the door. "See you next week, Mr. Martin. Nice to see you, Mr. Pastor."

"So long, kid. Thanks."

The door closed behind him. Frank said, "These kids today, they're born with printed circuits and transistors in place of skin and bones."

"You look happy this morning."

"Well it's a nice day, you know how it is. Hell, I'm a free man, I got a good business, I got a great wife. I should be unhappy?"

"Sure as hell not."

Frank said, "What time the others getting here?"

"Ten-thirty. That gives us half an hour. I wanted to talk to you first."

"What about?"

"Well you know we've got a whole octopus out there trying to pin down Merle and those others." Ezio pulled the big glass ashtray toward him and leaned back in the swivel chair. "There's something curious that's come up."

"You got the jammer running, Ezio?"

"Sure. The kid checked it out and turned it back on."

"All right. Go ahead."

Ezio said, "We're blowing a great deal of money and man-hours on finding those four guys."

"You want to stop looking for them?" Frank's voice was soft and dangerous.

"No. I'm just stating a fact."

"Ezio, we need to nail those four gentlemen. For a lot of very good reasons, as you know."

"Sure. I'm just saying we've got a board of directors to answer to and some of them aren't—well they maybe don't understand some of these things. One or two of them may bring it up at the meeting. I've already heard a couple of beefs. I mean nobody's going to make a dime off this deal whether we nail those four guys or not."

"If we don't nail them we could lose a lot of dimes in the

future. People get the idea they can spit in our faces and get away with it, pretty soon we lose respect."

"You don't have to argue it with me, Frank."

"Who's been beefing?"

"A couple of the guys. Malone for one."

"Stupid Mick. Who else?"

"Lorricone."

"Mittens? *He's* beefing? All the shylock skips he's gone after and maimed?"

"Well he was making some remark about how you cut your losses after you reach a certain point. You figure you've driven him out of town, you've got him on the run, that's lesson enough."

"These four gentlemen spit in my face, Ezio."

"I know that. But I'd soft-pedal that argument with the board if I were you."

"You're not me."

"It's likely to come up in the meeting, that's all. I wanted you to be ready for it."

"I appreciate that." Frank crossed his legs. "Now you said there was something curious that came up."

"It's about Merle."

"Go ahead."

Ezio snapped the gold lighter open and fiddled with it. He felt unnerved by the abrupt coldness of Frank's voice. "Well I'm not sure about this. It's all kind of vague. What happened, we sent photographs of Merle and the other three out to a lot of contacts, particularly out on the West Coast."

"I know all that."

"Sam Ordway out in Los Angeles, you remember him?"

"Sure."

"Ordway started up a new racket out there a few years ago. It was while you were away. He's running a big executive-car operation. You know, they heist cars to order, they deliver them to South Americans and false-front movie producers and some of those fly-by-night livery and leasing outfits. The way it's set up, they mainly lift the cars from doctors, people like that, and they've got a whole chain of body and paint shops scattered around the Southwest and the Coast. They boost a car, it goes straight into the shop. It's a very smooth operation. Each item is a custom heist—they don't boost a car until they get an order for that particular kind of car—but it's pretty big business. All right, it's just a sideline to Ordway, he's got a lot of big irons in the fire, but I imagine this one clears something up in six figures every month."

"What's this got to do with Merle?"

"Just background, Frank. Ordway runs this executive-car business, he's involved in interstate car laws, right? It's FBI jurisdiction. He's got one or two FBI agents in his pocket. Not big-timers but if orders ever come down to move against his operation he'll get the word from them in time to move out. These FBI agents also pass on information to him from time to time. They sell it to him for a little extra money."

"So an FBI agent passed Ordway some information that's connected with Edward Merle. What was it?"

"Well it seems they're looking for him."

"Who's looking for who?"

"According to Ordway the FBI put out an all-points on Edward Merle, or at least on a guy who looks like him. It looks like Merle but the name is Baxter. Paul Baxter. Now the last name he was running under was Jason Greene. He was using that name up there in Arizona when George Ramiro almost ran him down."

"You're sure it's Merle? Why would the FBI put out an APB on him?"

"Your guess is as good as mine. Evidently it's not an urgent bulletin. It's just one of those ordinary daily assignment-sheet items. You know, keep an eye out for this guy and if you spot him report him to headquarters. Now maybe it isn't Merle at all, but Ordway swears it is."

Frank reached up to scratch his head and sat up irritably when he touched it; apparently he'd forgotten he was wearing the rug. "Let's take this through slowly. It's all assumptions. Assume the government gives Merle another new identity, this Paul Baxter name. Then they put out an all-points for the guy. If we assume Baxter and Merle are the same man, why do they provide him with a new name and then go looking for him? It only makes sense one way. It means Merle walked out on them."

"Refused their protection, you mean."

"It sounds that way. And if it's true it means Merle's out there in the open. Walking around loose."

"That's about the way I had it sized up but I'd like to know whether this guy really is Merle."

"You get on the horn to Ordway. You tell him to bring his FBI man back in and get that photograph away from him long enough to make a copy of it. I've got to see that picture."

"I'll get right on that."

"If they put him on the all-points sheet they must have given a reason."

"Well it's just a routine 'wanted to locate' bulletin. Agents aren't even supposed to stop and question him. They've been told this Baxter is some guy who's involved in something to do with film piracy."

"With what?"

"Film piracy. You know, guys rip off prints of movies, then they sell them to grade-B distribution chains down South or something. It's one of the petty rackets but the FBI's in it because it's interstate. The reason this FBI agent brought it to Ordway, Ordway's involved in that racket. The word on this Baxter guy is he's a contact man of some kind and they want to follow him to his sources."

"It's a cute story. Maybe it's true—maybe Baxter's just Baxter. I need that photograph, Ezio."

"We'll get it. I'll call Ordway right after the meeting."

Frank uncrossed his legs and put his elbows on his knees. "If it's Merle, it means he got disgusted with the way they were protecting him. He decided he'd have a better chance on his own. Which is stupid, of course. He hasn't got that nursemaid any more—what was his name?"

"Bradleigh."

"He hasn't got anybody to keep him out of trouble. He'll make a stupid mistake. Now our problem is to be there when he makes it."

"How?"

"On his own he'd probably do things Bradleigh would never let him do. For openers he'd probably make contact with his friends. Not anybody here in New York, that goes back too long ago, but friends he made in Los Angeles. Have you got that list?"

"Right here in the drawer." Ezio opened it and took out the Merle file.

"Find out who his closest friends were."

"All right."

"Then put people on them. Bug their phones too."

"My God, Frank, that could be an enormous operation. Cost us a fortune."

"It's eight of my years we're talking about."

"I'll do it, Frank, but it's up to you to convince the board. It's their money too."

Frank's eyes went from point to point and suddenly shifted toward him and he felt pinned against the chair.

"Frank, all I'm saying is, if it was me I don't think I could talk them into it. But you're better than I am at convincing people."

"I wish you'd put your mind on your job and find me Edward Merle."

"We found him before. We can do it again."

"I know you can, Ezio. I have every confidence in you." Frank's smile filled him with gloom.

CHAPTER ELEVEN

California: 27 August–5 September

1

WHEN THE BROWN CADILLAC CRUNCHED TO A STOP MATHIE-
son went down from the cabin to meet it. Jan went with
him; Roger and Amy waited by the cabin. The two boys were
inside manufacturing something out of Billy's Erector Set.

Diego Vasquez stepped out of the car. He smiled when
Mathieson introduced him to Jan. "A great pleasure indeed."
Vasquez bowed over her hand.

Jan was bemused. There was a chilly precision in Vasquez's
deep voice that was out of kilter with the elegance of his
attitudes. He still made Mathieson uneasy.

They went up toward the cabin. Walking behind them,
Mathieson was surprised to realize Vasquez was no taller
than Jan.

There was a round of introductions. Amy was captivated
at once. The boys came out to meet Vasquez and they were
impressed; they were inured to celebrities but Vasquez had
an odd anachronistic flamboyance. After a while Mathieson
knew what it reminded him of: radio voices from the age of
fustian—Murrow, Alex Dreier, Kaltenborn, Westbrook Van
Voorhis. It was with transparent reluctance that Roger
gathered Amy and the boys and bundled them off on the

pretext of casting a pool. The four of them went down the trail into the pines, fishing poles bobbing, lugging their picnic.

"I've enjoyed some of his films," Vasquez said. "I've never decided whether he's a competent actor but I rather doubt that matters. He cuts an impressive figure on the screen."

Mathieson said, "You know he was a rodeo champion before he came to Hollywood."

"It's more than horsemanship, I'm sure." Vasquez settled into one of the weathered rockers and glanced up at Jan. She stood with her hands in the pockets of her sheepskin coat, one shoulder tipped against the log pillar that supported the porch overhang. She watched Vasquez with tight expectant eyes. Vasquez put his whole attention on Jan. "May I assume you concur in your husband's decision?"

"Yes. Of course."

"You said that a bit casually, Mrs.—what name should I use?"

"I don't care. Suit yourself."

"You're tense. I'm sorry—I'm sure my presence only exacerbates that."

She didn't reply; she took her hands out of her pockets and folded her arms, hugging herself against the mountain chill.

Vasquez said gently, "I really ought to know how to address you."

She glanced at her husband. "Jan Mathieson."

"Thank you." Vasquez tipped the rocker back, crossed his legs and folded his hands in his lap. He looked comfortable—in command, fully assured. "You've had nasty experiences. It's natural that you should be troubled by great anxieties. We hope to allay those."

"I hope you can."

"My staff is already at work. My organization is rather unusual as you may know. You may have been misled by publicity. The news media pay attention only to climaxes. To the public I'm sure some of our operations appear reckless. I'd like to assure you that isn't the case. It may appear otherwise but we've never jeopardized innocent people. The Stedman kidnapping was a case in point. The media made it appear that the boy only escaped by great good luck. This wasn't the case. At no time was there any risk of the boy's coming under fire. Our movements were coordinated and prepared down to the inch. We had the camp under visual and electronic surveillance for sixteen hours before the moment came when we knew the boy had been left alone, temporarily, in his hut. That was when we made our move, and our first objective was the hut itself—to make sure the boy was protected. Corralling the kidnappers was only the secondary objective. Do you follow my drift?"

"Yes."

"The primary objective in your case is to insure the safety of you and your son. I won't expose you or the boy to risk, and I won't permit you to expose yourselves to it. As for your husband, he must make up his own mind as to the limits of risk; we'll conform to his decision in the matter. You've decided to counterattack those who have attacked you. This ambition is laudable only if it has a reasonable chance of success. There'd be no point in approaching it as a kamikaze mission. Does this coincide with your view?"

"I suppose so."

"You have reservations."

"It's a last resort, isn't it. This whole madness. I'd be a fool if I held out much hope."

"I understand your depression. But the forecast isn't as bleak as you may believe."

The wisp of a polite smile fled across Jan's mouth. Mathieson looked away in distress.

Vasquez said, "It's an oversimplification to state that every man has a weakness that can be exploited. What is true is that criminals like Frank Pastor are particularly vulnerable to pressure. They appear formidable but in some ways they can be reached much more easily than can honest citizens."

"Honest citizens don't retaliate by blowing up houses."

"To be sure. But we've got to push your enemies back to the corner of the chessboard and achieve, if not checkmate, at least stalemate. At the moment it's you who are in check."

"That much I understand."

"The tactics remain to be defined. The strategy, however, is quite clear—to make it so costly for Pastor to persevere in harassing you that he will withdraw his threat and leave you in peace."

Jan smiled wryly. "Even the federal government hasn't been able to do a thing about it with its thousands of agents and billions of dollars."

"Offhand I can point out three specific advantages we have over the police and the federal government. One, we don't need to secure ironclad evidence before we can move against them. Two, our actions can't be deflected or frustrated by their efforts to subvert the judicial and enforcement machinery by corrupting officials. Three, we don't need to obey the law."

"That's very glib." Jan was watching Vasquez, holding his glance too long; it became a challenge. "Suppose we put ourselves in your hands. Suppose Frank Pastor approaches you and offers to outbid us. How do we know you won't sell yourself?"

"I'm an attorney," Vasquez murmured. "You and your husband are my clients. It would be an obvious conflict of interests."

"But you consider yourself above the law. That's what you've just said."

"Unhappily there's a distinction between statutory law and moral law. I flout the one with unfortunate regularity. I am bound by the other with absolute rigidity."

"It doesn't cost you anything to say that, does it."

Vasquez turned his hands apart, palms out. "Then we're at an impasse. The only way you can determine whether you can trust a man is to trust him and see what happens."

She only brooded at him. Vasquez said at last, "I've taken you on and I won't sell you out. It would be fruitless to offer further assurances than that. Either you believe it or you don't."

"The moral law you're so concerned with—in your case it seems to include cold-blooded murder."

"Don't believe everything you read."

"That's an evasion."

"Mrs. Mathieson, I might be able to influence you by proffering slick rationalizations about the differences between murder and execution, or justifiable homicide—self-defense—

that is to say, by pointing out that the Commandment against homicide is hedged with innumerable exceptions. I've killed human beings, yes. I haven't killed many." He lowered his head. "It's fair to say only that I can't answer to your conscience—I can answer only to my own. It is clear."

In the same subdued voice and without lifting his head Vasquez said, "You've got to make a decision, you know. If you decide not to trust me there's no point going on with this."

Mathieson waited for Jan to turn and look at him. Finally she did.

He couldn't decode her expression. "I don't have a choice," she said. She turned back to Vasquez. "Neither of us does."

"Then I'm to proceed?"

"You'll have to forgive me. I don't give this much of a chance."

"Mrs. Mathieson, a sentence of death has been passed upon you by Frank Pastor's kangaroo court. You have three options. Give up and succumb. Run and hide. Or fight and hope. No human being in sound mental health would consider the first. You've already tried the second and found it wanting. Therefore, regardless how poor the chances appear, you're pretty well stuck with fight and hope."

The nervous smile, meaningless, sped across her lips again.

Vasquez seemed to take it for assent. "We'll have to arrange a program, the object of which will be to formulate our plans down to the last detail. We'll need to do a great deal of work. It will take time—time that must be unencumbered by distracting pressures of the kind Frank Pastor has been inflicting on you. This requires seclusion. I have in mind a place where we should be able to make things as comfortable for you as might reasonably be expected. There'll be no companions the boy's age but the place of which I'm thinking does have stables and horses. I understand he's a self-sufficient child."

"No child that age is self-sufficient."

"He'll have his parents with him," Vasquez said. "He'll miss school of course. The school terms are just now beginning."

"I'm aware of that." She was still cool with him. "Why can't we stay right here? There's a country school in the village—it's fourteen miles."

"We don't want to involve your friends any more than they're already involved, Mrs. Mathieson."

Vasquez let that sink in. Then he said: "I don't merely want you and the boy to be where you're safe. I want you to be where your husband knows you're safe and where I know you're safe. The only way we can avoid being distracted by concern over your safety is to have you and Ronny with us at all times. I'm afraid both of you may find it tedious but I'm sure you'll agree boredom is preferable to anxiety."

An expression tightened the skin around her mouth: It might have been an effort to choke off anger. Abruptly she went across the porch. "I suppose I'd better get packed again." Without further talk and without a glance at Mathieson she went inside the cabin.

Vasquez tipped forward in the rocker and got to his feet. He lifted an eyebrow in Mathieson's direction and stepped off the porch and walked away toward the trees. Mathieson followed him past the Cadillac to the far side of the clearing where Vasquez stopped and thrust his hands into his pockets. "I wasn't sure how soundproof those walls might be."

"Why?"

"When I undertake a commission it's not my habit to cavil over details. Don't misunderstand this, but I wish you had told me you were having marital difficulties. It may make a substantial difference."

"What makes you think——"

"I'm not an imbecile. I've got eyes."

"Things are tough on Jan right now. Tougher than they are on me."

"It's nothing that recent."

"Aren't you getting a little out of line?"

Vasquez said, "Whatever program we settle on, you can be sure it will demand your full attention. If you're going to be distracted by emotional turbulence it will undermine your efficiency. How long have you been estranged?"

"Estranged? We've never been separated."

"Don't quibble over definitions."

"We've got an understanding."

"You're still splitting hairs. I'm not prying out of seedy curiosity, you know."

He regarded Vasquez dismally over a stretching interval. The undulating rasp of a light plane somewhere above the mountains distracted him briefly; finally he said: "It goes back to the first time. When we had to pick up and leave New York. Things started going sour then."

"How old was your son?"

"Four. I suppose we both kept hoping the sores would heal. I think they still can. I want us to be the Mathiesons again, at least—we had a chance to get somewhere from that point. Things were better the last few years, much better than they'd been before. Now it's collapsed—she can't take any more of this pressure. It isn't her fault. She never asked for any of this."

"She supported you in your initial resolve to testify against Pastor."

"Yes. Maybe she didn't realize what it would cost. I know I didn't. They told me but I didn't listen. Not really—not in the gut. My own parents were dead, I was an only child—I had no one terribly close. I had to give up a number of friends. With Jan it was a lot worse. Her mother, her brother and two sisters, there was a young niece she adored. She hasn't communicated with any of them in eight years. Can you imagine what that's done to her? Her father died three years ago—we couldn't even go to the funeral. Bradleigh told us it was watched by one of Ezio Martin's goons."

"Do you blame yourself?"

"I blame Frank Pastor."

"Good. This would have no chance of success at all if you were overburdened with self-pity."

"Self-pity doesn't come into it."

Vasquez said, "Do you love your wife?"

"Of course I do."

"You said that rather quickly."

He drew a breath and closed his eyes. "You're a pill. Yes, I love her. Would I have stuck it out otherwise?"

"You might. Habit, addiction, fear of loneliness, consideration for the child. I'm sure there are men who stay with their wives even though the only feeling they have for them is hatred."

Mathieson wheeled, angry clear through; he walked away several paces. To his back Vasquez said, "In any case things are threadbare."

"You could put it that way." He snapped it out viciously; he turned to face Vasquez. "Haven't you wormed enough data out of me yet for your computer? What's the readout?"

"I have only one further question. Do you believe that solving your difficulties with Pastor will restore your marriage, or at least give you an opportunity to salvage it? Or have things gone too far for that?"

"I think we can put it back together. But you're missing an important point. Whether my wife and I love each other or detest each other, it's all the same—she's stuck with me until this is finished. What else can she do? Go out on her own? Take Ronny with her? Pastor could find them. He'd find them and he'd use them to reach me. If you were thinking of forcing things to a head and putting some kind of ultimatum to us then you'd better forget it. She stays with me until this is finished."

"I wasn't unaware of that factor." Vasquez tipped his head to one side. "But it wasn't clear whether you were."

"Then why did you bring it up?"

"You and your wife may not have a choice in the matter but I do. If she's going to be an irritant I'll put her and the boy in a safe place away from you until you've concluded your business. But if, on balance, she and the boy will render you more support and solidity than anxiety, then I'd prefer to keep you together. It's not a vital decision, perhaps, but it could prove important. And I assure you it's a decision best left to me. You're not sufficiently detached to make it sensibly. And since it must be my decision, it was necessary for me to pry."

"And what's the decision?"

"They stay with you. We go together."

"Where?"

"It's a bit of a drive. Beyond Los Angeles—not too far north of the border. We'll drive down in the morning."

2

It was in the mountains forty miles northeast of San Diego— a stand of trees along a stream, a little valley rising on all sides toward moonscape summits.

A gravel drive carried them in from the state highway. It threaded a notch in the hills and bent its way through canyons, switchbacking over a pass between peaks that were littered with gray boulders the size of great houses. On a farther slope he could see an eerie stretch of mountainside tufted with the seedlings and charcoaled stumps of an old forest fire.

The gravel road brought them up from the boxed lower end of the valley past a large pond: It was almost a lake. It didn't look stagnant and therefore there had to be some kind of earth-fault outlet that must carry its overflow under the surrounding mountains to the inland watershed beyond. Past the lake the driveway skirted along the long stand of cottonwoods and sycamores along the stream; a white three-rail fence ran along both sides of the drive. There were green paddocks and neatly maintained corrals, a huge brown barn, a variety of outbuildings. At the end there was a great lawn landscaped with stone-border flower beds and isolated evergreens trimmed into cones and balls. The driveway looped up through this rich greenery to the porte cochere of a big Victorian house—a graceful anachronism of gables and bay window and rambling wings.

"Good Lord," Jan murmured.

"Vasquez certainly has a sense of the dramatic."

Ronny said, "He owns all this?"

"It's not his," Mathieson said. "He's borrowing it. He told me that much."

Vasquez appeared on the veranda, emerging through a pair of French doors. He walked along to the porte cochere as Mathieson parked under it. He gave them the benediction of his welcoming smile.

They all got out. "What an extraordinary place," Jan said.

Vasquez said, "If it looks familiar you must be an old movie buff."

"I had a feeling I'd seen it before," Mathieson said.

"The studios used it for location work on at least a hundred pictures. All those movies about the racing gentry in Maryland and Virginia—they filmed them here. It doesn't take a terribly keen imagination to picture Joseph Cotten crossing this veranda in jodhpurs."

Vasquez came down around the car and reached inside to tap the horn: He honked it twice and the blasts startled Mathieson.

Ronny said, "Who owns all this?"

"It was the property of a man named Philip Breed—a Texas oil heir. He had several homes. At one time he produced a few motion pictures and he built this in the 1920s as his California headquarters—his company filmed a number of Tom Mix Westerns here. Breed maintained a stable of racing quarterhorses—he was one of the pioneers who built the sport up from nothing to its present level. This estate became a sort of retirement home for Breed's quarterhorses after their racing careers were ended. Some of those horses are still here. Breed died four years ago and the will is still being contested by a bewildering assortment of claimants. A trust organization maintains the property—occasionally the organization lets it out to film companies."

Mathieson said, "I'm making an effort not to think about what this is going to cost us."

"Virtually nothing, really."

"Oh?"

"The principal trustee is a former client of mine. He feels obliged to do me an occasional favor. Of course you'll pay for your food, drink, laundry and incidentals. And I intend to bill you for Homer Seidell's salary while he's here putting you in shape." Vasquez took the keys from him and opened the trunk of the car.

"Putting me in shape?"

Vasquez straightened. He turned a circle on his heels. "Where do you suppose he's hidden himself?" He looked at his watch. "By 'putting you in shape' I mean subjecting you to a training program designed to teach you competence and confidence."

Jan was listening quizzically. "What does that mean?"

"If you walk into a room with your enemy and you have absolute confidence you can beat him at any game he chooses to play, it's going to make a decided difference in the way you handle the situation."

"I see," Mathieson said.

"I'm not sure you do; but never mind, you'll find out soon enough. You could sum it up by saying we're going to war and you need to be taught some of the warrior's arts."

"That's not exactly what I had in mind when I came to you."

"You put yourself in my hands, didn't you. You're paying for my judgment." Vasquez's abrupt expression of amusement took him by surprise. "Never mind—I enjoy melodrama." Vasquez went back around the car but before he could reach the horn Mathieson saw a man appear at the corner of the house carrying a golf club.

"Ah. Homer."

The man walked forward with a sailor's gait, shoulders rolling and head rocking, legs bowed, moving on the balls of his feet. He was no taller or wider than Vasquez but he had the chest and biceps of a weight lifter. He had the pitted narrow face of a street thug.

Vasquez made introductions. Homer Seidell wasn't a knuckle-crusher but his grip was authoritative. He had an odd brief smile—as if the skin around his mouth was stretched too tight.

He lifted the suitcases out of the trunk. "We're putting you in the Ronald Colman suite. It's the best digs in the house." It was the voice of a much bigger man—husky but powerful.

Vasquez held the door for them. Ronny dashed inside fearlessly. The vast center-hall foyer was hung with oil landscapes but they might as well have been Gainsborough portraits; the space was darkly paneled and dominated by an enormous pewter chandelier and a sweeping rosewood staircase.

Homer Seidell said, with amusement, "Welcome to boot camp, Mr. Merle."

124

3

The suite had two huge rooms connected by a bathroom whose marble decor and gold-plated plumbing reminded him of the Sherry-Netherland Hotel.

Homer Seidell deposited the luggage on ottomans and Vasquez stood in the door with a proprietary air identifying the amenities and facilities: There was a Mrs. Meuth who would look after their housekeeping needs; there was a Mr. Meuth, the groundskeeper; there was Perkins who looked after the place's mechanical needs and had charge of the livestock.

"Perkins can help you pick out a steed for your adventures. It would be wise if you confined your riding to the valley. It should give you enough elbow room—there's an area of some thirty square miles to explore. Perkins prefers that the horses not be taken into the foothills. You'll understand that—it's very rocky terrain."

Ronny gulped. "Yes, sir, I understand."

Vasquez turned to Jan. "It's an ideal topography for us. This house sits on the highest spot in the valley. On horseback the boy will be able to see the house from any point, and be seen from it."

She took his meaning. Vasquez told her, "This will be your home for a while. Settle in, make yourselves comfortable. Incidentally you'll find quite a good film collection in the library—prints of several hundred excellent motion pictures. Mrs. Meuth can help you with the projectors. There's also television throughout the house, of course. Meuth does the shopping, usually twice a week, and he always returns with newspapers and magazines. The swimming pool is immediately behind the house. There's an indoor pool as well, in the north basement, but it isn't kept heated this time of year. If you prefer golf there are three holes laid out on the west lawn. Mrs. Meuth is employed to provide cooking for whatever guests are present but she doesn't take offense if you care to do your own from time to time. If you'd like to choose your own menus you may give Mr. Meuth a shopping list—his next scheduled trip is tomorrow morning."

"Are we confined to the estate?"

"You're not prisoners here, Mrs. Mathieson, but if you elect to go off on excursions I should appreciate your giving me twenty-four hours' notice so that I may bring down a few members of my staff to escort you." He glanced at Mathieson: "Naturally such services will be billed to you. But you understand the necessity."

"Yes."

"We'll take your husband off now. I'm afraid you and the young man will have to fend for yourselves most of the time."

"We'll manage. Thank you." Her face came around toward Mathieson. "Good luck." She was smiling but he couldn't fathom what might be behind the smile. Unnerved he followed Vasquez down the corridor with Homer Seidell; they went downstairs and Vasquez strode right out the front door. "May I have the keys to your car?"

He passed them over and Vasquez handed them to Homer. When Homer pulled the car away Vasquez said, "If you want the car it will be in the garage beside the main barn. The keys will be in it—we don't have thieves up here."

"Are you trying to reassure me?"

"You'll begin to feel like a prisoner of war here after a bit. It will be important that you realize that escape is dead easy. That knowledge, I think, will encourage you to stay and stick it out."

"Stick what out? You still haven't really explained the program."

"Homer facetiously described it as boot camp but it was quite apt. We're going to be rough on you. You've got to be conditioned out of some of your most comfortable habits. It will be modeled to some extent on the army's basic-training techniques, although there's one significant difference—we're not concerned with inculcating obedience; quite the contrary. What needs development is your initiative. Essentially I want to see you become comfortable with a variety of methods and techniques that will strike you at first as unfamiliar and perhaps unpleasant. We'll present you with challenges that you'll be forced to meet with a combination of trained responses and imagination. Bear in mind you're going to be fighting formidable antagonists who regard violence as an acceptable and even commonplace solution to nearly any sort of problem. I'm not forgetting your prejudices—you may not wish to initiate violence but you've got to know how to deal with it when you're faced with it."

"Sounds ominous."

"I assure you it is. But you know the seriousness of it better than I do."

"How long does all this take?"

"You're impatient."

"Of course I'm impatient, damn it."

"It shouldn't take terribly long. We can't expect to make you over. A few basics—and we do need to restore you to first-rate physical condition. Fortunately you seem to have the remains of a good constitution, according to Doctor Wylie. But that sort of training is peripheral at most. Mainly we'll be acquiring information and improvising our schemes based on that information. My organization is already casting its lines and in a very short time I expect to have dossiers on each of your enemies."

At the edge of the trees Homer Seidell came in sight. He walked up the driveway with his rolling determined gait.

Vasquez said, "Homer has instructions to be rough with you. Try to remember who your real enemies are. Homer's a very good man."

Vasquez turned away, disappearing back into the house. He left Mathieson feeling uneasy.

4

He jogged in tennis shoes and a gray sweat suit with a towel flopping around his neck. Homer Seidell paced him effortlessly and Mathieson was embarrassed by his own puffing and the streaming sweat.

They came around the corner of the fence. It was still a quarter of a mile up to the house and he didn't think he was going to make it but he was determined to try, if only because of the half-concealed contempt with which Homer had treated him all day.

Momentum and the slight downslope of the driveway were all that kept him from collapse. When he reached the porte cochere he sat on the steps of the porch panting for breath. There was a roaring in his ears.

Homer went bouncing into the house without breaking the rhythm of his stride—up the steps three at a time . . . Mathieson was still gulping for air when Homer appeared with a bottle of mineral water and two tumblers. He set them down and handed two chalky tablets to Mathieson. They looked like oversized aspirin.

"Salt," Homer explained. "Take them with the water. But wait till you've got your breath."

It was a while before he could speak. "How far . . . did we run?"

"About a mile. That's not running. Man your age doesn't start out running the first day. We'll get your legs stretched out first—legs and chest. You need to learn how to control your wind first."

"I'll try it."

"For a desk man you're in better-than-average shape. For an athlete—forget it."

"I didn't expect to have to learn to be a decathlon contender."

Homer said, "Think of yourself as Eliza Doolittle."

"Are you an actor?"

"I have been. Found it a little dull."

"How'd you get associated with Diego Vasquez?"

"He's got a small staff. Eleven of us, not counting the office help. We're all ex-cops and ex-federals. I spent six years in foreign service before the technocrats got to me. I could take working with dummies but when your superiors are imbeciles it begins to dawn on you that you're in the wrong game."

"Is 'foreign service' a euphemism for the CIA?"

"No, but it was something like that. The Defense Intelligence Agency. We didn't drag down the kind of headlines the CIA gets but then we didn't have a public relations staff."

"Tell me about Vasquez."

"He's a fine man to work for." That was all Homer had to say on the subject: It was a measure of Homer's loyalty to his employer and it also said something about Vasquez that he could command that kind of loyalty from a man who clearly did not bestow his respect easily.

Homer wore a scuba-diver's wristwatch with a complexity of dials and buttons. He turned his wrist over to consult it. "You've got four more minutes."

"Then what?"

"Ever done any boxing?"

"No."

"I won't make a prizefighter out of you but I'll teach you a bit of footwork. Half an hour ought to do it for today. Then you'll have a shower and a swim. You do swim?"

"I know the strokes."

"We'll have you doing forty laps. All right, after the swim you can relax a little while. Then lunch, then the handgun range, then rifles. Later on we'll do another jog around the fence. You won't feel like it but if we don't keep doing it your muscles will knot up. Tomorrow morning you'll feel like a cripple."

5

Vasquez flipped open the photo album on the dining table. His slender finger tapped a photograph of a sharp-faced young man in a metallic suit. "Him?"

"C. K. Gillespie."

The pages turned. "Him?"

"Sam Urban."

"What does he do? What's his connection?"

Mathieson studied the photograph. "He's the manager of a restaurant. He's the collection point for numbers slips――"

"What restaurant, Mr. Merle?"

"It's slipped my mind."

"The Cheshire Cat, Route Nine-W, Englewood Cliffs, New Jersey."

"I did remember it was New Jersey."

"Why?"

"Because it's safer for them to collect New York numbers slips in another state."

"Will you forget it again?"

"The Cheshire Cat, Englewood Cliffs. I'll remember it now." Vasquez flipped the page over. "Him?"

"George Ramiro."

"Function? Connection?"

"I'm not quite clear on the relationship. I know what he does."

"His wife is a cousin of Frank Pastor's. She's Ezio Martin's half sister. Ramiro is an immigrant, from the Azores. He eloped fifteen years ago with the girl, who was an ugly duckling destined to be the family wallflower. Pastor and Martin either had to kill him or hire him. They hired him, and Ramiro turned out to be useful and completely ruthless. You know his function?"

"Essentially he's in charge of security around Pastor and Martin—he runs the security system and staffs around their houses and offices and cars."

"If you go in after them by stealth or force, he's the one you'll be contending with."

"I may not do it that way."

"That's up to you, of course. But study the backgroundings on Ramiro. You may spot a weak point here and there."

"Have you spotted any?"

"He plays around with whores sometimes. I realize that's not much of a lever but it's all we've found."

Another page. "Her?"

"Anna Pastor. Pastor's wife."

"Good-looking woman," Vasquez remarked, and turned another page. "Him?"

"Cestone. Gregory Cestone."

There was a knock; it was Homer Seidell. "Just about time for the afternoon workout."

Vasquez pushed the photos aside. "Come in a moment."

Homer shut the door and approached the table. Vasquez inclined his head toward a chair; Homer pulled it out and sat. Vasquez said, "I'm going to have to return to the office for two days to try to catch up on the most urgent tasks on my desk. You'll have to take Mr. Merle through a number of things."

"Such as?"

"Procedures. Methods. Practices. He's going to have to learn how to recognize a hundred different kinds of locks and know how to get into them with picks. How to field-strip a wall safe or hot-wire a car. How to plant explosives on an engine block——"

Mathieson stiffened. "I'm not blowing anybody up."

"Granted. But you want to know what to look for. Suppose someone tries to do it to you?" Vasquez went back, matter-of-factly, to Homer: "He'll have to learn the rudiments of burglar alarm systems—how to spot them and how to get through them. Bugs, wiretaps, infrared camera techniques."

Mathieson said gloomily, "There's a lot to it, then."

6

"He's got me lifting weights," he complained. Gingerly he stretched his legs out across the bed and arched his head back into the pillow but there was no comfortable position.

"This was your idea," she said.

"I could use a little sympathy."

"It's the best thing that's happened to you in years, I imagine. You're going to end up with the physique of Muhammad Ali."

He scowled at her. "I've always detested cheerful types who make fun of somebody else's agony."

"Yes, dear."

He grumbled. "They can't really expect to turn me into Charles Atlas in a matter of weeks, can they?"

"Vasquez seems to think that's up to you. How long do you think it will take?"

"I have no idea; this is just phase one. I don't have too many illusions about this—even if we can bring something off, it won't be done overnight."

He rolled over on his side but that was just as painful. She said, "What?" and glanced at him in the mirror.

"Nothing. That was a grunt of anguish."

"Lift dem weights, tote dat barge. Hadn't you better start getting dressed?"

"Whose idea was it to dress for dinner around here, anyway?"

"Mine."

"I suppose you had your reasons."

"It suits the surroundings." She drew her mouth into a puckered O to apply lipstick.

He left the bed painfully and climbed into his slacks. "How are the kid's bruises?"

"Healing. He seems to be ignoring them."

"Teach him to try to ride the wildest horse in the place."

"He gets that from his old man."

"Christ I haven't even seen him in two days."

"Whose fault is that? But we ought to be thankful he's occupying himself."

"And he's not even coming down to dinner tonight?"

"He made a deal with Mrs. Meuth. There's a TV movie he's desperate to see. He promised to put the dishes in the dishwasher afterward."

Mathieson turned up his shirt collar and wrapped the necktie around it. She put the eye-shadow brush down and turned to look at him. "You've got that all askew. Come over here and use the mirror."

He had to get down on one knee behind her ottoman to see himself in the mirror. "Paying court to the queen," he observed.

"Very gallant."

He got the knot centered. Her face hovered discomfitingly near. She had gone bolt still.

"What's the matter?"

"I'm jittery," she said. "I keep feeling as if I'm on the verge of a crisis. Every little disturbance feels like a major calamity."

He reached for her hand but she was turning away; she stood up and walked swiftly to the wardrobe. He got to his feet and watched her step into the dress. "Zip me up?"

He crossed the room and pulled the zipper up and dropped

both hands on her shoulders. "How long are we going to go on being polite to each other in cool voices?"

She leaned back against him. "I wish I knew the answer to that. I'm just too neurotic to think."

He slid his hands around her waist but she pushed them away. "Let's go down to dinner. I'm famished."

7

Mathieson dragged himself to the dinner table and tried to ignore what he was sure was Homer's smirk. The chandelier threw a yellow glow along the immense dining table. Vasquez remarked, "I know. It feels rather like a set for a 1946 Warner Brothers film—something with Sydney Greenstreet." Vasquez among his oddities had a penchant for old movies and an apparent total recall concerning their stories, casts, directors and writers.

Unceremoniously Mrs. Meuth laid their plates before them and retired. Something in the kitchen began to grind and clatter. Mathieson looked at the thick red steak, the buttered zucchini, the salad, the glass of ice water. He was not hungry.

"I know," Homer said, "but eat it anyway. You need the protein."

"Been running my tail off for a week, you'd think I'd be famished."

"It doesn't work that way unless you're conditioned to it," Vasquez told him. "Unaccustomed exercise mutes a sedentary man's appetite. I'm not sure why."

Homer said, "Go ahead, eat up. It won't put weight on you—that's diet margarine, not butter."

Mrs. Meuth bustled in with a pitcher of iced tea. She slammed it on to the table and left, her feet falling like bowling pins. She was overweight but not a huge woman by any means; nevertheless everything she did seemed to require the accompaniment of loud noises.

Vasquez remarked, "These are surroundings to which one wouldn't mind becoming accustomed."

Jan said, "Is everything you touch this glamorous?"

"Hardly. Most often our work is sheer boredom. Homer can confirm that, I'm sure."

Mathieson said, "Not excepting present company. It drives Homer up the wall, being coach and trainer to an inept middle-aged idiot."

Homer squinted at him. "Do I look bored? This is the best vacation I've had in four years working for Vasquez Inc. A lot better than repossessing cars and skip-tracing."

Jan said, "Is that your bread and butter?"

"Sometimes. Actually most of our work is company spying."

"Industrial counterespionage," Vasquez said. "I do spend a good part of my time training business executives in security techniques."

Jan poured iced tea into the four glasses. When she set the pitcher down she said, "I'd like to call some friends." She looked directly at Vasquez. "Would that be all right?"

"Certainly. But I'd prefer you didn't call them from here. And it would be better if you didn't tell them exactly where we are. Mr. Meuth will be driving into town in the morning —you and I could ride with him."

"Thank you. I only want to find out if Roger and Amy are all right."

"Any reason why they shouldn't be, Mrs. Mathieson?"

She made a gesture and almost overturned the glass; she caught it in time. "I feel—stranded up here. I need some thread of contact with the world."

"Perfectly understandable." Vasquez's glance lifted from the rescued iced tea to Jan's face. "I'm sure you're thoroughly annoyed with the obsessive lengths to which my paranoia has taken us. But in the interest of your safety I've tried to cut off every conceivable lead to your whereabouts. It's unlikely that your friends would be under surveillance or that their telephones would be tapped. But possible. You understand?"

"I suppose so."

Homer jabbed his fork toward Mathieson's plate again. "Come on, you're stalling."

"They always told me it was healthy to eat slowly."

"Sure it is." Homer's smile was belligerent. "Eat."

CHAPTER TWELVE

New York: 8 September

1

EZIO BLEW CUBAN SMOKE TOWARD THE CEILING AND BEAMED expansively when Frank walked into the office. "Man you were right, Frank, son of a bitch paid off."

"You were mysterious as hell on the phone."

"You want me to spell anything out on a Goddamned telephone?"

"Of course not. But you're getting a little fancy with that million-seller hit record nonsense. What's it supposed to mean? Since when am I in the record business?"

Ezio opened the drawer and pushed the rewind switch on the tape deck. "We've got Merle's wife on tape. Is that a hit record, or isn't it?"

Frank walked around the desk and looked down at the recorder. "You don't say."

"Here." Ezio handed him the typescript from the desk. "I typed up a transcript while I was waiting for you."

Frank glanced down the first page. "Who are these people?"

"The first voice is Merle's wife. The one they call Jan. The second woman is Roger Gilfillan's wife, name of Amy——"

"Roger Gilfillan the movie star?"

"You remember, he's on that list of Merle's friends."

"Right, OK. So the 'Roger' here, that's Gilfillan."

"Just the three of them. There's some damn interesting

stuff. So anyhow I just identified the speakers with initials—J for Merle's wife, A for Gilfillan's wife, R for Gilfillan."

"The tap is on Gilfillan's phone, right?"

"We've had two shifts watching him come and go. He's shooting a TV special on one of the lots in Burbank; he goes to work every morning at seven. The phone call came in two days ago, Saturday morning; he was home."

He watched Frank page through the transcript. Frank said, "We'll listen to it in a minute. What's the bottom line here?"

"She tells them she's with her husband and kid hiding out someplace down around San Diego. She's not supposed to tell them where—she's calling from a pay phone. You get the operator coming in a couple of times there, telling her to deposit more change. From the phone rates we worked it out it's somewhere in San Diego county all right but we couldn't pin it down too close, except its north or northeast of San Diego because the charges are a dime less than they'd be all the way to the city."

"So?"

"At least we know they're in Southern California, Frank. That's a lot more than we knew before."

"Only a few million people in that part of the country, Ezio. What's this here about 'turning Fred into Tarzan'?"

"I don't know, I admit there's some of it that didn't make much sense to me. I figured you could listen to it, maybe you'd come up with something."

"Fred—that's Edward Merle?"

"The name he went under the last eight years in Los Angeles. Fred Mathieson." Something sour leaked out of the cigar onto his tongue and Ezio picked it off with his fingers. "You maybe haven't noticed the part where she talks about the kid and all the horses he gets to ride from the stables. Not that many places down there with private stables full of quarterhorses, Frank. I've already got people looking."

2

After they listened to the tape Ezio pushed the "off" button. "You want to hear it again?"

"No. Everything's on paper here. I didn't know you could type that fast."

"I just didn't want anybody else to hear this tape until you decided how you want to handle it."

"The riding-stable angle's a good one. You keep on that. And there's another thing we could try."

"Name it."

Frank said, "She said she'd call them back again next Saturday."

"Yeah, I caught that part."

"See if you can get to somebody on the cops out there. Use Ordway if you have to. See if they can set up a trace next time she phones."

"It's a pay phone, Frank. Maybe she won't use the same one twice."

"At least it would tell us what town to look in."

"Sure, I get you. I'll give it a try. It might not work—you can't do a phone trace without a bunch of people knowing about it. Some of those people would have to be straights."

Frank nodded. Ezio glanced at him again. He was getting used to seeing the toupee but there was something else different about Frank. He looked a lot healthier; he'd turned brown and smooth.

"I've got another idea," Frank said. "She's going to call them Saturday. All right. Friday you have a couple of our people crowd them a little."

"Crowd Gilfillan?"

"Nothing big. Don't rough them up. But tell them to put a clumsy tail on them."

"I don't get it."

Frank smiled. "Who's running it out there?"

"Still Deffeldorf. Fritz Deffeldorf."

"Using what, a bunch of Ordway's people?"

"A few. Some free lances."

Frank's mind was working. "Ezio, you didn't tell me, is the FBI still looking for Merle?"

"No. They canceled the bulletin."

"They didn't just let it dry up—they made a point of canceling it?"

"Yes. Why?"

"I wonder why they did that."

"At the time I figured it meant they must have found Merle. But they didn't. At least Ordway says they didn't. It was canceled on orders from Washington."

"He's all by himself out there and the FBI isn't interested anymore. That makes things easier."

"What's this idea you had? Crowding Gilfillan, I mean."

"Put three or four guys on him. Say they tail him home from the TV studio Friday night. Say they crowd him so tight he can't help but notice he's being shadowed."

"So?"

"So Saturday morning Merle's wife phones and Gilfillan tells her he's being followed around by this bunch of tough-looking guys."

"I still don't get it, Frank."

Frank got out of the chair. He folded the transcript and put it in his pocket. "Sometimes when you're up against a stone wall the best thing is to do something unexpected. Random, whatever, doesn't matter what it is, just so it stirs things up, gets things moving again. We've been stalled on this thing long enough. I want to prod Merle, that's all. Maybe this riding-stable idea works, maybe not. But we get his buddy Gilfillan all nervous and jittery, he's going to tell Merle's wife about it, and then maybe something will bust loose."

CHAPTER THIRTEEN

California: 12–13 September

1

NOW IT FELT GOOD TO RUN. HE STRETCHED HIS LONG LEGS out and left Homer behind and went up the last stretch of driveway feeling winged. When he stopped at the porte cochere his breathing was deep but without urgency and he gave Homer an arch look when he came up.

Homer dragged the back of his hand across his mouth. "Your legs are a foot longer than mine, wiseass. You want to prove something I'll take you on for a ten-mile run, we'll see who comes in first."

"No bet."

"I hate cocky bastards." But Homer's tight quick smile showed pleasure: He was proud of his handiwork.

"Tell me something. Were you in on the Stedman rescue?"

"I was there."

"Not talking about it, is that it?"

"It's not classified. I'm not crazy about the way that one worked out."

"Why?"

"I don't know if I can exactly explain it. Why are you asking?"

"I'm trying to sort a few things out. Humor me." He was still trying to get a handle on Diego Vasquez, that was what it came down to; he didn't want to put it to Homer that way.

"It left a sour taste, you know, that whole mess. They were

freaked-out junkies. The ones who snatched the Stedman kid."

"Some kind of radicals, weren't they?"

Homer shook his head, not in denial but in disgust. "Look, you turn on the TV, the radio, you look in the newspapers, all you see day after day is hijacks and terrorists. All over the world. These little bastards—the Stedman case—calling themselves revolutionaries. The truth is they're just crazies. A pack of hophead jerk-offs. Any cheap psycho with a gun can call himself a revolutionary but what the fuck does that mean?"

"What happened down there that's got you so worked up?"

"I don't know. Vasquez and I went in there alone first. The kids started blazing away. We dumped Stedman on the floor under his cot and we held the front door—it was the only way in, there weren't any windows. There were seven of those junkies with enough guns between them to fight World War Three and they decided to charge us. I suppose they expected to grab Stedman and use him for a shield. They saw we were only two guys, so they came at us. It just wasn't any contest at all. It never is when the pros go up against the amateurs. We had all seven of them dead or shot up or handcuffed inside of thirty seconds. But it's the dead ones that get to you. We killed two of them on the spot and a couple of others died in the hospital later on. It leaves a bad taste. I never thought so much of myself that I believed I had God's right to decide who lives and who dies."

"I take it the boss doesn't think the same way."

It was a while before Homer replied. "Diego Vasquez has his own way of looking at things. And his own reasons. You'd need to know something about him. His background and all."

"Such as?"

"I'd rather you asked him. Come on—time to put the gloves on."

2

When he saw Ronny trot past the gate he walked over to the barn to meet him. The boy brought the horse into the corral at an easy single-foot, knowing better than to run it;

its coat was a little damp but obviously he'd walked it most of the way home from the lake to cool it down.

Mathieson helped him strip the saddle off; he lugged it to its peg in the barn and watched Ronny rub the horse down and take out the currycomb. They talked about inconsequentials and the boy seemed to be enjoying his company but when he stripped the bridle off and drove the horse out into the paddock he turned suddenly after closing the gate and said, "How long are we going to be stuck here?"

"I thought you liked it."

"I like it fine. I like living like a king. I like having my pick of a bunch of great horses. I like everything about it. But there's *nobody around*."

"No kids your own age, you mean."

"Dad, I can't exactly have a ball with old Perkins or Mr. Meuth, can I. I mean you can only spend so much time on a horse."

"It's not as if there wasn't plenty to do, Ronny. Besides ride."

"I've read a dozen books in the library. I've looked at movies until I've started seeing everything in Technicolor. But I can't spend the whole day like that. You know what I mean, Dad?"

"I know what you mean." He heard the car before he saw it; he looked down the long driveway. "Here comes your mother."

"I wish I'd changed my mind and gone to town with them. At least it would have been a change."

"Why didn't you?"

"I didn't feel like it," Ronny said obscurely. They went up to the house and got there by the time Meuth parked it by the kitchen delivery entrance. Mrs. Meuth came out to help unload. Vasquez and Jan came up to the steps. There was stress in Jan's face.

"Anything wrong?"

"Some trouble at the Gilfillans."

"Trouble?"

"Your friends are being watched," Vasquez said. "By a group of improbably clumsy goons."

"Goons? Pastor's people?"

Vasquez's glance slid across Ronny and back to Mathieson. "I shouldn't be alarmed. It's almost textbook, really. Probably they're hoping to reach you through your friends—hoping their harassment of Roger Gilfillan will bring you out of hiding. I find it encouraging, actually—it indicates they're clutching at straws."

That wasn't all it indicated to Mathieson but he held his tongue until Jan and Ronny had gone inside the house. Vasquez returned to the car with the evident intent of putting it away. Mathieson walked around it and got into the passenger seat. "You're taking it too casually."

"I didn't want to alarm your wife unnecessarily. She's high-strung enough as it is."

"You see what it means, don't you? They've found out I'm not under federal protection. Otherwise they'd never bother trying to locate us through our friends."

"That's true. But it doesn't really put them any closer to you, does it."

"It suggests the leak in Washington was never really plugged. And that means Pastor may know we're going under the name of Baxter."

"What of it? You haven't used any names at all in this area." Vasquez shook his head. "That's not what troubles me."

"Then what does?"

As usual Vasquez provided an answer in his own roundabout way; his apparent non sequiturs always led to the point eventually but Mathieson's patience was goaded. Vasquez said, "Your friend Glenn Bradleigh and his colleagues are professionals. A great many of their regulations are the results of experience. One of their most steadfast rules in the relocation and protection of their charges is the complete break of all past associations—family and friends. Undoubtedly this is the most difficult thing their clients must adjust to. Undoubtedly the government has spent years trying to find alternatives. They have discovered none. Therefore they maintain the rule as an absolute."

He saw what Vasquez was getting at.

Vasquez said, "When you came to me you were already in touch with the Gilfillans. There was nothing I could do to undo that thread of contact; therefore I wasted no effort in the attempt. But you must recognize now that it was exceedingly unwise."

"Maybe it was. I had no one else to turn to."

"You could have turned to me. Directly, without involving your friends."

"If it hadn't been for Roger I'm not sure I ever would have made the decision to come to you."

Vasquez reached for the key and started the car. "All right. It's useless recriminating."

He drove it sedately around the loop and up past the paddock toward the barn, talking steadily.

"I suspect Pastor's men have tapped the Gilfillan phone. Pastor would have no reason to disturb Gilfillan if he didn't know you were in communication with him. Now if we can assume that Pastor knows you are in contact with Gilfillan, then you are vulnerable."

Perkins's tractor was on the far slope dragging a block of rock salt toward the water trough. Vasquez said, "For the moment Pastor may be satisfied to stir things up and wait to see whether the stirring brings you to the surface. When it doesn't he may decide to use one of the Gilfillans as hostage for the acquisition of Edward Merle. It would not require kidnapping. It would require merely a threat, delivered anonymously and easily to Roger Gilfillan, stating that if Edward Merle were not produced then an unfortunate accident might deprive young Billy Gilfillan of his eyes, or his legs, or his life. The nature of the threat isn't important; the pattern is clear enough. If Pastor made such a threat and Gilfillan passed it on to you, what would you do?"

Vasquez racked the station wagon beside the other cars in the barn. He switched it off. In the dead silence he inspected Mathieson's face.

"Don't be too dismayed. There's a countermove available to us—the only course of action I'd recommend." Vasquez opened the door. As he was getting out he said, "We'll have to persuade the Gilfillans to join us here."

He needed something to do; he insisted on doing the driving. Vasquez rode with him and on the way they rehearsed the scheme.

"We're assuming their phone is tapped," Vasquez said. "What does that suggest to you?"

"We've got to get them to another phone."

"Very good. How?"

"Just tell him to go down to the shopping center and use a pay phone. They can't tap it that fast."

"That's fine, Mr. Merle, but how do we tell him what number to call? Or do you happen to know the number of the pay phone offhand?"

"No. I could call him at a friend's house . . ."

"And involve another friend in this? Think again."

"Suppose I ask him to drive over to the studio. I could call him there."

"It's a bit clumsy—and you'd be talking through the studio's switchboard. No, I think the simplest method is to give him a phone number where he can reach us. And do it in such a way that eavesdroppers won't understand it."

"How?"

"Do you know anything of the rudiments of codes and ciphers? All it requires is a key."

Mathieson made the turn into the county road. A hot wind sawed in through the windows. Piercing reflections of sunlight shot back from mica particles in the rocks. Mirages wavered in the road surface, retreating before them.

Vasquez took out a notebook and his pencil. "There must be a fairly close friend the two of you had in common. Pick one whose phone number you remember. Someone whom you can identify to Gilfillan without mentioning a name."

"All right."

"What is the friend's phone number."

"Well say it's Charlie Dern. It's two-seven-five five-three-oh-three."

"That's fine. Now all we need do is copy down the number of the public phone in town and do a bit of subtraction.

4

In the booth he wrote down the number of the pay phone immediately above Charlie Dern's number. Then he made the computation:

$$714\text{-}895\text{-}8214$$
$$-\ 213\text{-}275\text{-}5303$$
$$\overline{501\text{-}620\text{-}2911}$$

He dialed Roger's home and got Billy on the line. "Get your dad on the phone, will you, Billy?"

"Sure, Mr. Mathieson. Just a minute."

He glanced through the glass doors. Vasquez was standing beside the car alertly watching everything at once.

"Hey, old horse, how're they hanging?"

"Roger, I want you to do something for me. It's important and it's urgent. Get a pencil and paper."

"What? Hell, hang on a sec . . . OK, shoot."

"I want you to write down a number at the top of the sheet. Ready?"

"Go ahead."

"Five-oh-one, six-two-oh, two-nine-one-one."

"Got it."

"Read it back to me, will you?"

"Five-zero-one, six-two-zero, two-nine-one-one. Area code and phone number, right?"

"In a way. Now here's what you do. Don't mention a name but we have a friend who has ulcers. You know who I mean."

"Sure. What about him."

"Write down his phone number. Including area code. Right beneath the number I just gave you. Don't repeat the number on this phone."

"You think I'm being bugged for Christ's sake?"

"I'm pretty sure you are."

145

"Jesus . . . Hold on, I'm writin' it down."

"Now add up the two numbers. Don't do it out loud."

"I get you . . . OK. Now what?"

"Get to a pay phone and call me. You've got my number there."

"Hey that's damn smart, old horse. OK, take me five, ten minutes to get down there."

"I'll be waiting."

He stepped out of the stifling booth and left its door open; he crossed the curb to the car. Vasquez said, "All right?"

"He'll call back in a few minutes."

"When he does, don't soft-pedal it."

"It's hard knowing how to break it to him."

"Tell him the complete truth."

"He'll have every right to tear me limb from limb."

"It can't be helped."

"He's probably in the middle of shooting that special. He can't just walk out on it."

"He'll have to."

"How? He's under contract."

"It doesn't matter. He'll have to do it—you'll have to convince him."

"Roger can be a stubborn guy."

"So can you, Mr. Merle. Just bear in mind that several lives may depend on it."

CHAPTER FOURTEEN

Long Island Sound: 14 September

1

OUT ON THE SOUND A FLOTILLA OF SAILBOATS MADE BUTTER-fly patterns. Anna sat lotioned and lazy in her bikini on the transom of the *Sandora,* her face thrown back to the sun. She watched Sandy on the flying bridge guiding the cruiser under Frank's watchful instruction. In the sport-fishing chair Nora was pretending she had a whale on her line.

The twin diesels made a guttural mutter in the water beneath the stern. *Sandora* curled slowly toward the forested banks of the inlet they'd chosen.

Frank shouted something and Nora bounded out of the fishing chair. Smiling, Anna watched her drop the anchor. The engines were throttled right down; she felt it when the cable brought her up; then Sandy switched everything off and there was no sound except the lapping of the water against the hull.

Frank came down the ladder. "You girls want to eat first or swim first?"

Sandy was still up top. She was shading her eyes, looking out toward the Sound. "Isn't that our outboard?"

Frank went halfway up the ladder and squinted into the dazzle. "Jesus God. Can't a man have a little privacy with his own family even on a Sunday afternoon?"

Anna stood up. "What is it?"

"The pest. Ezio."

She made a face. Frank came back down onto the deck. "You kids better have your swim first."

Nora pouted. "Is *he* going to stay for the picnic, Daddy?"

"Not if I can help it."

The motor boat came slapping into the inlet leaving a shallow white vee of a wake; Ezio throttled back and brought it smoothly alongside.

Ezio was in a mood. "Why the hell don't you ever turn on your ship-to-shore? I been trying to reach you for an hour."

"I go on this boat to get away from telephones, Ezio."

"You can't just do that, Frank. What if something important comes up?"

"Then you'll get in the outboard and come after me the way you just did. I left word where we'd be, didn't I?"

"Took me half the afternoon to find this place. Suppose it was really urgent?"

Frank showed his exasperation. "You kids go for a swim, OK?"

Nora said, "I'm hungry. You make it short."

"Damn right I will."

Anna watched the two of them go off into the water like dolphins. They went cleaving toward shore, racing each other. It wasn't much of a contest. Sandy's crawl was smooth enough for an Olympic; Nora splashed great thuds and geysers.

Ezio said, "Maybe Mrs. Pastor wants a swim too."

"What's it about, Ezio? This Merle business?"

"Yeah."

"Then she stays if she wants to."

She nodded and stayed where she was. Ezio showed his resentment in a brief pinching of his lips. Then he sat down and retied the laces of his plimsolls. "Gilfillan took off."

"Took off?"

"The whole family. Right into thin air."

2

"We had two cars and a phone tap on those people, Ezio. Now what do you mean telling me they 'took off'?"

"They had help, Frank."

148

"Whose help? This Bradleigh?"

"I don't think so."

"Suppose you tell it from the top. And try not to blow my whole Sunday afternoon, all right?"

"I know you're sore being disturbed like this, Frank, but we've got to decide how to handle this and the trail's already getting colder while we sit here talking."

"Then hurry up."

"Well yesterday morning—Saturday—Mrs. Merle called the Gilfillans again the way she said she would last week. We had a tap on it. The call came in from a pay phone in San Diego county. No telling if it was the same pay phone she used last time. We'd played it the way you figured, we let Gilfillan know he had a tail Friday afternoon, so they told Mrs. Merle."

"How'd she react?"

"I guess you'd say baffled, Frank. But it seems like she must have gone straight to where they're hiding out and told Merle about it because a couple hours later Merle calls Gilfillan."

Frank smiled. "I knew it. I knew it would bring the son of a bitch out in the open."

"Well anyhow Merle calls and he just gives Gilfillan this code of some kind, a bunch of numbers that Gilfillan can figure out a phone number from. There was no way we could get that number, the way he did it. You want me to spell it out?"

"No. Just let's have the meat."

"Our guys follow Gilfillan down to a shopping center in Culver City, right? He goes to a phone booth, he makes a call. Then Gilfillan goes back home. Now it takes a little time for things to get relayed, Frank, you know how it is. A couple of hours later I get a call from Deffeldorf out there. I tell him to put a couple extra guys on Gilfillan and watch him like a hawk, right? So now we got three cars, six guys, watching Gilfillan's place, and we got two more guys in the panel truck up the street manning the phone tap. Eight men on him. Four vehicles. Now that ought to be enough. I figured we had him sewed up."

"So what happened?"

"So about four o'clock Los Angeles time Gilfillan backs his car out of his garage. It's a Chrysler wagon. Him, his wife and his kid. Some luggage in the back, right? Our guys figure this is it, he's heading for a meet with Merle. They're on him like glue."

"This is yesterday?"

"Yeah, it's yesterday. They drive out to Riverside on the freeways. Maybe they know they're tailed, I don't know, but they don't pull anything, they just drive out to Riverside, right? No trouble following them."

"Ezio . . ."

"I'm getting there. So these Gilfillans pull in at this classy type restaurant out there. It's maybe five-thirty. They park the wagon, the three of them walk into this restaurant. Our guys park their cars the right way—one goes around behind the place, the other two bracket the Chrysler. What happens, they hardly get time to settle down and the Gilfillan people come trooping back out of the restaurant. They've been in there ten minutes tops."

"Making phone calls, probably."

"All we know is they get back in the car and they lead our guys a merry goose chase over half of Southern California. They head out to El Centro, they cut back toward Santa Ana, they go all over the damn place. They stop for gas, our guys stop for gas. Our guys check in by phone when they get a chance but what the hell can I tell them?"

"Bottom line, Ezio."

"Bottom line, yeah. They're out in one of those boondock areas—little farm towns, secondary roads, citrus farms. You know, it gets to be maybe eleven o'clock at night. They stop at some café, one of those drive-in things, they get hamburgers, they kill some time. Midnight, they're still driving around. Like they're sightseeing, you know, only it's the middle of the night. They turn down this farm road—dirt road—they go out of sight of our guys for a minute around a bend. Our guys hit the bend and there's this U-Haul truck skewed right across the road. No way to get past it. Irrigation ditches on both sides of the road and it's just one of those narrow little farm dirt-tracks, you know. One-lane wide. This truck right across the road."

"I have the picture, Ezio. Who was in the truck?"

"Nobody."

"So it was a setup. The guy in the truck waits there, they arranged it by phone. He waits, the Gilfillans come along. He puts the truck across the road behind their car, then he gets in their car and they all drive away."

"That's the size of it, Frank."

"This happened at midnight?"

"Naturally the guys screwed around for a while out there, they busted into the truck; finally they got it knocked apart enough to get things moving and they shoved it off the road. But by the time they got all that done, the Gilfillan car was long gone. There are two freeways and a dozen fairly major highways in the area. No way to trace them fast. Right now Deffeldorf's got people swarming all over the area trying to find out if anybody saw the Chrysler wagon but hell, it was one o'clock in the morning by then, most places were shut up tight and they'd just filled the tank. Not much chance we'll find anybody who spotted the car."

Frank toyed with the game-fishing rig in its socket by the swivel chair. He said mildly, "Who rented the U-Haul?"

"Papers in the glove compartment said it was hired out by a guy with a name and an address. There's no such name at that address in Los Angeles."

"But it's a Los Angeles truck?"

"Right."

"Then probably it wasn't Merle."

"What does that tell us?"

"Tells us he's got help, doesn't it."

"I don't see where that helps us much, Frank."

"It's got to be somebody professional. Your ordinary citizen isn't equipped to walk into a U-Haul agency and plunk down the driver's license and the credit cards you've got to show them to rent a truck . . ."

"Maybe the feds got Merle back under their wing."

151

"I get a feeling it's not federals. This whole elaborate business—it doesn't sound like federals to me. It sounds like some bright free-lance operation."

"That's kind of farfetched. What's he going to do with mercenaries?"

"Make war," Frank said calmly. "You send out feelers, Ezio, find out if there is any word about anybody getting hired for a job like that."

"All right. It probably won't get us anything. Those guys mainly work through mail drops. Like Deffeldorf and Arnie Tyrone."

"What about the riding stables?"

"We've checked out a lot of them. Nothing yet. There's a lot of ranches and farms down there, Frank. It could take months and we still might not find anything."

Frank turned; his face indicated his interest in the grass bank of the inlet under the trees. The girls were sliding into the water, swimming out from shore. Frank said, "I handled the son of a bitch with kid gloves because he's a movie star, I figured we couldn't afford to fuck around with a big movie star like that, get all the newspapers on it and everything. I was wrong, Ezio."

"Crying over spilt milk, Frank."

"Well it's a mistake I won't make again if I get the chance. . . ."

CHAPTER FIFTEEN

Southern California: 14–17 September

1

MATHIESON WALKED DOWN THE PADDOCK AT AN EASY PACE, arms swinging. Watching the fence and the barn and the trees: alert but trying to keep relaxed. Homer's voice boomed behind him:

"*Now!*"

He swiveled, saw the bull's-eye target on the tree, drove his hand inside his jacket and dropped to one knee while he raised the Police Special, cocked the hammer with his thumb, brought up left forearm with elbow on knee . . .

The movements were coming with synchronized automatic precision now: left hand locking up under the right wrist, target sights leveling.

Squeeze the trigger but squeeze it fast: The .38 charge exploded with an earsplitting boom. The revolver rocked in his fist and drove his shoulder back into the socket.

He forced it down, aimed instantaneously and fired the second one.

It kicked high and he brought it down ready to fire again.

"Maggie's drawers," Homer said disgustedly.

He heard hoofbeats—a fast rataplan—and when he turned

153

he saw the horseman rush the fence like a charging cavalry general; a whoop, a flap of winglike elbows and the horse came soaring over the paddock rails. Mathieson wheeled back in terror.

The horse came down from its steeplechase leap with beautiful balance and Roger Gilfillan wheeled it on the spot, came unglued from his easy seat, lighted on both boots and spun away toward the paper target—the picture of the movie gunslinger. The single-action roared, five steady unhurried blasts, and went spinning back into its holster while Roger turned toward him with his high whinnying laugh and swept off his hat, bowing over it like Buffalo Bill to the crowd.

Homer stared at him. "Sweet jumping Jesus Christ."

Roger was still laughing. He took out the big revolver and started plugging the empties out. "Would've been a mite fancier if you boys had the foresight to set up a half-dozen whiskey bottles on the fenceposts. That's the way they usually shoot that scene."

Mathieson reloaded the Police Special. "You crazy buffoon. Damn near gave me cardiac arrest."

"That's what you're here for, ain't it? Learn to grapple with the unexpected, like?"

Homer came back. He looked stunned. "You put all five of them in the black."

"Did I now. Well how about that."

Homer shook his head in awe, still staring at Roger. "Sweet jumping Jesus Christ. And I always thought they had stunt experts with rifles behind the camera doing all that stuff for the actors."

"That's me, old son. How'd you think I started in this binness? Stunt ridin' and stunt shootin'. I wasn't always an actress, you know." He turned to Mathieson. "Now you didn't do too good, did you."

"I've never been much of a hand with guns." His ears were ringing and whistling.

Homer said, "I've tried all the usual tricks. Hard to tell what he's doing wrong. I've about run out of ideas."

"Probably not bringin' the focus down," Roger said offhandedly. He took Mathieson's revolver and sighted experimentally at the target. "Good square sights on this piece. Shouldn't be no trouble. You sighted this, Homer?"

"Benchrest at a hundred yards. I ran a box of shells through it. Good tight group. Nothing wrong with the sights."

Roger cocked the hammer and the racket startled Mathieson when Roger began firing like a gunslinger. The bullets chewed splinters visibly out of the mangled center of the target.

In the sudden uneasy silence that followed the shooting Roger snapped the cylinder open and punched the hot cases out onto the little brass pile by Mathieson's feet.

"Here. Load it up and let's see if we can't clear up this little problem."

Mathieson fumbled cartridges into the cylinder and began to lift it toward the target; he heard Roger's steady talk: "Now gentle down, take it easy. You want the front sight level with the rear notch. A straight line across the top. OK? Now you want the target on top of the front sight. Good so far?"

"Fine."

"Take in some air and hold your breath where it's comfortable. Squeeze easy."

He had his eye on the target and the sights wavered a little and he relaxed the pressure until they steadied. When it went off it surprised him, as it was supposed to.

"Low and left," Homer remarked.

Roger moved around him to his left side. "Try it again, old horse."

He lifted it, cocked it, dropped his right wrist into his left hand . . .

"Oh for Christ's sake."

" 'S the matter?"

Roger was turning toward Homer. "He always shoot like that with one eye shut?"

"I don't——"

"No wonder." Roger threw up his hands. "Both eyes, you dumb dude."

"But you can only use one eye to——"

"Both eyes, old horse. Focus on that front sight. Not the target—the front sight. You can still see the target back there but it's the gun you're aiming, not the damn target. Focus on the sights and that way you know where the gun is. Homer, who taught you how to shoot?"

Homer's mouth was pinched resentfully. "Army."

"That figures."

The essence of magic is simplicity: This was magic—he emptied the revolver and each of them went home dead center; he lowered the gun slowly in disbelief. Roger shot a crafty sidewise glance in Homer's direction. "I think he's gettin' the idea. Old horse, load up and try it again."

He emptied the cartridge cases onto the pile and bounced the unfamiliar weight of the revolver in his open hand. "I don't think so."

Homer pivoted toward him. "Say again?"

The thought formed in his mind as he expressed it; it took him by surprise: "It's something I can do if I have to. That's all I need to know."

Homer's puzzlement turned into accusation. He addressed himself to Roger: "What's the matter with him?"

"Better ask him."

Mathieson put the empty revolver in Homer's hand. Before he walked away he said, "Nobody's making a killer out of me."

2

They were eight at dinner and Vasquez presided with a movie monologue filled with Byzantine digressions: He was encyclopedic, wistful, opinionated and almost sycophantic when he spoke names like Cooper and Welles.

Roger refused to be baited and Vasquez's frustration led him into outrageous overstatements. Roger stirred in his chair. "Movies are my living, not my life. I don't go to the things unless I have to."

Vasquez scowled belligerently at him. "Amazing."

Roger stood up, detesting straight chairs. "You younkers take off. We've got grown-up talking to do. Only bore the hell out of you."

Ronny and Billy glanced at each other like French underground conspirators and sped from the room. Amy said,

"Those two together go like a match and a stick of dynamite. Don't be surprised if this house gets demolished."

Jan laughed—to Mathieson it sounded brittle. Homer stood up. "You going to want me?"

Vasquez said, "An extra viewpoint never hurts."

In the big front room Roger slumped into a Queen Anne chair. Amy sat down on the floor and leaned her head back against his knee. Homer perched on a small chair by the wall as though expecting to bolt the room. Mathieson took a place beside Jan on the couch; she gave him a glance and, hesitantly after a moment, her hand. It was cold.

There was a bench seat built into the bay window and covered with velvet upholstery. Vasquez sat straight up, centered on it. Casually he had positioned himself precisely at the focus of intersecting attentions, giving himself command of the scene.

In the corner of his vision Mathieson picked up the quick amused smile that fled briefly across Homer's tight cheeks; probably he was accustomed to Vasquez's seances and expected pyrotechnics tonight. But Mathieson couldn't imagine Vasquez producing anything spectacular this time; the situation was too glum.

Vasquez began politely: "I commend your efficiency. I'm sure it wasn't easy to break away on such short notice."

"You had it all set up—Homer with that U-Haul truck. All we did was follow the script."

"Nevertheless. You must have had difficulty breaking your commitment to the producers. The program you were filming."

"Taping, not filming. Television horse shit."

"How did you manage it?"

"It's one of those documentary things. The life of the working cowhand. You know the kind of crap. All I was there for was the narration. Hell, I just called this kid up in Vegas that does nightclub impressions? You know, Cagney and all. Kid's pretty good, does me better than I do me. Then I told my manager to clear it with the producers. Amos got a tongue like old-fashioned snake oil, he'll sell it to them. That kid's real good. It'd take a voice-print graph to tell it wasn't me talking. Nobody'll ever know."

"Ingenious," Vasquez said. "The fact remains, your lives have been egregiously disrupted. It's an error for which I share blame. Among other things I'd like to try and ascertain what the appropriate redress might be."

Roger said, "You and me, we share the same bad habit—puttin' on airs. Mine's harmless—I'm a professional Texan and I talk like one. But we'd get along a little faster if you'd come down off the Oxford Dictionary and talk plain English." He glanced at Mathieson. "As far as blame goes, I'd just as soon not waste half the night arguing about who among us ought to put on sackcloth and ashes. Let's us get down to the business at hand."

Vasquez's long jaw crept forward, pugnacious in quarter profile; he jabbed a finger toward Roger. "You're about as rustic and unsophisticated as an Apollo moon rocket."

"Son, just because I talk like a country boy don't make me nobody's fool. My daddy didn't raise no stupid children."

Vasquez's finger lowered. In the corner Homer shoved his nose into his cup of coffee.

Vasquez said, "The fact remains, you came into this inadvertently, as a bystander."

"Bystander hell. They put their men on us. Tapped our phone. Next thing you know they'd start shooting at us. Don't be so damn exclusive—it's our fight too."

"If you choose to make it so."

Mathieson said, "It's not your fight. I'm sorry you're involved—it was my stupid fault—but it's not your fight, Roger."

"Old horse." Roger leaned back until he was almost supine. His eyes slid shut. After a moment without opening them he said, "Like the man says, we choose to make it ours. You want to try and keep us out of it? You want that kind of trouble with me?"

Amy said wistfully, "Roger surely does love a good fight, Fred, don't you go denying him his pleasures."

Vasquez said, "Very well. You're in."

"Thank you kindly." Roger's drawl was complacent.

Amy said, "Did any of you folks know what I used to be when I was a liberated woman before I met this here macho chauvinist pig? Happens I used to teach seventh grade in Del Rio, Texas."

With his eyes comfortably shut Roger said, "Don't mind her. She's had a couple of drinks."

"I'm making perfect sense, curmudgeon. We got two boys in this house and ain't neither one of them likely to see the inside of a classroom for a spell. Nobody wants them to grow up like ignorant slobs like you."

Roger opened one eye. "To whom would you be referrin', my deah?"

"It'll give me something useful to do. Next time anybody goes into town we pick up a few schoolbooks and we put these spoiled younkers to work."

Jan said, "That's a fine idea." To Mathieson's ear it sounded hollow: wholly without enthusiasm. He realized why. It would only isolate Jan more than ever.

Roger closed his eye. "That fresh pond down the valley— any fish in that thing?"

"A few," Homer said.

"Trout?"

"No. Carp, I think. Meuth claims there's a catfish or two."

"Reckon I'll find out for myself. While old Fred's puffin' around the track, I mean. Personally I got no use for exercise for its own sake." Suddenly he got up on his elbow and peered at Vasquez. "But I'd be obliged to sit in on your strategy sessions."

Mathieson said, "You will."

"Certainly," Vasquez agreed.

"That's all right then. I always did want a crack at a passel of real live bad guys."

3

He came out of the pool after the fortieth lap and dried himself in the sun. A sudden gnashing noise startled him: He peered over his shoulder. A door stood open and beyond it Mrs. Meuth was in the corridor swinging her electric buffer from side to side, leaving arcs of shined wax on the floor.

He took his towel around to the far side of the pool and

rested a hip against the filter-pump housing. In a rack beside it were the cleaning tools—the long-handled net, the sections of vacuum hose, all of it half concealed in shrubbery. Beyond the pool's apron the garden sloped away from the house. The pale sky seemed vast.

A cardinal took flight from the stone birdbath. Instinct startled him and intelligence informed him: Something had frightened the bird.

He wheeled just in time.

A looming figure rushed him from the sun. Mathieson caught the fragmented glitter reflecting off the knife blade.

There was no time to adjust to it. Before he realized what he was doing he had the aluminum net-pole in both hands, swinging toward the assailant . . .

Homer stopped, lowered the knife, stepped to one side out of the glare, smiling. "Pretty good."

"All right." Mathieson put the pole back in its clips. "But how often am I going to be carrying one of these around?"

"You made use of what you had at hand. That's the thing. At least you didn't stand there paralyzed. If you hadn't had the pipe you'd have tried to drop-kick me or you'd have made a run for it, right? You'd find the nearest available weapon and you'd head for it. He could be a genius with a knife but you can still beat him if you can hit him from outside the radius of his reach."

"It wouldn't help against a gun, Homer."

"You'd do the right thing."

"What's the right thing?"

"Depends, doesn't it. What you've got at hand—what cover you've got. Sometimes you can't do a damn thing. Sometimes the best thing's simple. Off the cuff. Do the unexpected. At least it may throw their aim off."

"Comforting."

"There's no magic anyplace. But at least you'll know your options—that's the best I can do for you. You're as ready as anybody could possibly be with a few weeks of intensive training. There's a point of diminishing returns. Some field experience and another eight, ten months of training you could

160

become a professional. You've got most of the instincts. But——"

"A professional what?"

"That'd be up to you, wouldn't it."

It was five o'clock and it had been a long day. He moved past the corner of the apron to one of the granite benches; he sat on it and watched butterflies jazz around the garden. Down below he saw Meuth come along with his tractor and pull out winch cable to remove a dispirited palm tree.

Homer put one foot up against the end of the bench and rested his elbow on his knee. He blinked in the sunshine. "Your buddy caught some kind of a bass down there. I didn't know there were any."

"Maybe he——"

"Mr. Merle." It was Vasquez. He had come out on to the end of the apron; now he turned away toward the corner of the house, beckoning over his shoulder. Mathieson followed him around the house and by the time he crossed the driveway Vasquez had hiked himself onto the top rail of the paddock fence to watch the two boys far down the hillside chasing each other at full gallop. The rataplan of hoofbeats came faintly to Mathieson's ears.

"I've just received more information on Pastor and his associates."

Mathieson climbed onto the top rail. "And?"

"We're still about thirty bricks short of a full load. But we're approaching the point at which I think we'll have all the useful information we can expect to obtain. After a while one begins to suck up more muck than treasure. Besides, our time here appears to be drawing short."

"Why?"

Vasquez launched himself outward and landed delicately on both feet. He looked up at Mathieson, squinting. "I can't see you against that sun. Come along." He walked away briskly down the drive. Mathieson followed irritably.

At the edge of the trees Vasquez turned and waited for him in the shadows. Vasquez looked at him—as if he were a curiosity in a zoo cage: Vasquez stood still for such a long time that his very motionlessness became menacing and Mathieson was reminded of those truly vicious dogs—the sort that do not bark.

Finally Vasquez spoke. "Glenn Bradleigh's superiors overruled him. They felt as a matter of policy that you should be found and returned to the fold. They distributed your photograph and the Paul Baxter identity to the FBI. The FBI put out a bulletin on you and we assume a copy of it fell into the hands of someone associated with Pastor. One may surmise that the existence of the bulletin suggested to Pastor that you were on the loose. Subsequently Mr. Bradleigh has been able to persuade his superiors to revoke their first decision. Accordingly the FBI bulletin has been withdrawn; but the damage has been done."

The sun hung well over westward. In his bathing trunks Mathieson felt the wind. He wrapped the damp towel about his shoulders.

Vasquez said, "For freedoms such as those you are trying to regain, men have always been ready to kill."

"We're not getting into that again, are we?"

"The net is drawing up around us, Mr. Merle. Thus far the best we've produced is the lackluster idea of trying to goad them into ill-considered actions—a program I might suggest as a last resort but certainly not as a first one. In my judgment you may find yourself locked into a situation in which you've no choice other than to kill or to back away. The only alternative to running may be to bully them into taking the first shot, and then kill them in self-defense. It's a time-honored tactic of course, but it's effective."

"I won't do it that way. I won't be dragged down to their level."

"The difference may exist only in your imagination. You're after revenge and so are they. I believe you're being unrealistic —you insist on hunting big game with an unloaded gun."

"You knew my position."

"I thought your experiences here might change your mind."

"They haven't."

"I suppose I should admire your resolution." Vasquez hooked a finger inside the turtleneck collar and pulled it away from his throat. "Do you know why we walked down into these trees?"

"No."

"To put solid objects between us and any possibility of a parabolic microphone."

"Here?"

"The habit of paranoia is a key to survival. Take nothing for granted."

Vasquez began to dismantle a pine cone piece by piece with his thumbnail.

Mathieson said, "Something's got you on edge."

"Yes."

"You said the net was drawing tight. What net?"

"Did you expect your enemies to be idle? They're systematically combing Southern California for riding stables."

"Stables?"

"One must assume your wife mentioned Ronny's horsemanship to the Gilfillans the first time she spoke with them. Pastor's men would have picked it up on their phone taps. They've begun to filter into this part of the county. They've an enormous area to cover and a great many clues to trace but they'll come, probably in the guise of fire inspectors or something of that kind."

A sinking feeling overwhelmed him. He clutched the towel around his neck. "How long do you think?"

"Two days? A week? No telling."

In the shifting light he couldn't be sure of Vasquez's expression.

"Shit."

"I'd say we have three options. One, find a new hiding place. Personally I'd vote against it if only because we'd be hard put to find a more ideal spot than the one we've got right now. Two, stand our ground, fight them, trap them if possible —take them and squeeze them, learn what we can. But that leads to bitter consequences. What to do with them afterward? Neither of those is acceptable. It leaves one other choice— risky but worth the risk, I think."

"Yes?"

"Remain here. Hide. Attic, basement, lofts. Remove all

traces of our presence. Allow them to enter the estate and search it at will. They'll see the Meuths and Mr. Perkins. They'll ask questions and get answers. They'll find no trace of our having been here. To them this will be merely one of scores of places they'll have been inspecting."

"Why not just check into a motel until they've come through here?"

"We could but we don't know when they'll come—it may be a week or more; we'd waste that time. Simpler to post Perkins on the roof of the house. He'll see them coming up the valley and we'll have ample warning to get into concealment. In the meantime we can proceed without interruption. Once they've entered the valley there's no way we can get out of it unseen—that's to our advantage of course."

"Ours?"

"Certainly. It should convince them the place is innocent."

"It's dangerous. Suppose we forgot some tiny detail? It wouldn't take much to make them suspicious."

"I'm rather professional at that sort of thing."

"So was Glenn Bradleigh."

"Bradleigh's well-meaning but he's a bureaucrat. Inevitably his mind's been stultified by manuals of procedure."

Mathieson clenched his fists around the damp ends of the towel. "It'll put a strain on our group."

"On your wife, you mean. Do you want me to tell her?"

"No. I'll do it." Feeling as if things had gone altogether out of his control he walked back up toward the house, treading gingerly in his bare feet.

CHAPTER SIXTEEN

Southern California: 18–22 September

1

HE CAME AWAKE SLUGGISHLY WITH THE MEMORY OF A frightening dream. He reached for her in the darkness and she slid down against him, throwing the sheet back. She accepted him; it was enough. His fears dwindled away in the heat of love-making. Afterward he was overcome by a debilitating melancholy but he did not sleep.

In the darkness she spoke drowsily: "I'm sorry I took it so hard last night. That wasn't fair to any of you."

"You didn't bring any of this on yourself. I brought it on you. You've got a right to——"

"I haven't got a right to go to pieces like that in front of everyone. Dear God. I'm scared to death all the time, I'm wretchedly depressed—I've turned into a useless neurotic; I feel like Blanche DuBois."

He thought, And that's something else Frank Pastor can pay for.

In the morning after breakfast he took her down past the copse of trees; he took her hand and they watched Roger chase the two boys around the paddock on horseback, twirling a rope. They were keeping close to the barn.

A flight of geese went overhead in formation. Sunlight

dappled the creek that fed down into the pond a mile away. The water flashed white where it birled over the stones. The smell of early autumn was strong—pine resin on dry dawn-chilled air.

Mathieson ran a hand over his brush-cut hair. The bristle still took him by surprise; it was the first short haircut he'd had since he'd been in the army.

He spoke gently. "What do you think? Can we make it?"

"Sometimes I think we can." She withdrew her hand and put her back to him, watching the boys on horseback. "Sometimes I don't even want to."

"If I can settle this thing—get Pastor off our backs——"

"What's the sense talking about it? We don't know what's going to happen. You don't even know if you can do anything yet—you haven't got any idea how to approach it."

"I'm beginning to see how it can be done."

"Are you?" She didn't sound reassured. She looked around at him, wary as a fawn. "I'm afraid. Let's go back to the house?"

2

Vasquez opened the photo album on the dining table. Roger Gilfillan pulled his chair closer; Mathieson stood behind Vasquez's shoulder.

"This one?"

"Sandra Pastor. The older daughter. Fourteen."

"Chubby kid," Roger observed. "Too much of that there spaghetti."

Vasquez turned the picture over and slid the next out of the folder. "Him?"

"Hard to say." Mathieson leaned forward. "It's a lousy picture. It could be a rear-quarter profile of Ezio Martin."

"It is. You're getting quite good. Either of you recognize these two men?"

Roger shook his head; Mathieson said, "No. Should we?"

"This one's name is Fritz Deffeldorf. The mug shots date back four years, the other two were taken by my people in the past few weeks. Now the other one. I'm afraid the pictures aren't as good—he's camera-shy. He's Arnold Tyrone."

"Tyrone?"

"It's an Anglicization of something or other."

Roger asked, "Where do these two hairpins fit in?"

"We believe they're the men who bombed the house."

Mathieson leaned over the photographs and burned them into his memory. "Tell me about it."

"What we have is mainly circumstantial. It wouldn't hold up in court."

"Come on, come on." He shifted the mug shot to get another angle on it.

"We managed to check the passenger lists on flights into Los Angeles International. They both arrived in Los Angeles the morning of the bombing—not together, they were on separate planes."

"Using their real names?"

"Yes. It's not unusual. Deffeldorf came in on a nonstop from Newark airport. Tyrone came in from Oklahoma City airport. That's the airport that serves Norman, Oklahoma."

"Then Tyrone may be the man who shot Walter Benson."

"It seems a reasonable assumption. Tyrone flew back to Newark about ten days later. From Albuquerque."

Mathieson looked up. "After they lost Glenn Bradleigh in Gallup."

"That isn't a supportable conclusion yet. But it's an allowable surmise."

"Go on."

"Fritz Deffeldorf is a specialist for hire. His specialty is demolitions."

"You've done a lot of digging."

"I've had weeks to do it, Mr. Merle. But I must point out to you that your friend Bradleigh may have more information than I have about these two men. I haven't approached him—I assume you don't want my connection with you known. Now then. Arnold Tyrone. He owns and manages a sporting goods store in Trenton, New Jersey. Through his business front he procures weapons and hardware for those who need them. He's said to be one of the best marksmen in the country. He may be, as I said, the one who shot Walter

Benson in Oklahoma. By the same chain of reasoning I suspect he's *not* the man who fired at you from the ridge above your house—the man with the motorcycle. That one missed."

"Then who was that sniper? Deffeldorf?"

"I doubt it. Deffeldorf's expertise is in explosives, not rifles. You told me that Bradleigh was followed to Arizona by men in separate cars. That sort of operation usually entails at least three cars with two men in each car. Six men, then. Even if we assume two of them were Deffeldorf and Tyrone, there remain four men unaccounted for. There's also reason to believe that at least three men were involved in the attack on your house. I'd guess that Tyrone drove the car, Deffeldorf threw the bomb from it, and a third man with a motorcycle was stationed on top of the ridge to cover the house in case anyone came out of it after the bomb was thrown. We're still trying to identify him, as well as others who must have joined the team to shadow Mr. Bradleigh. We're also trying to identify the four men who are combing San Diego County for riding stables. We've had descriptions of them—sufficient to indicate that none of them is Deffeldorf or Tyrone or, for that matter, anyone familiar to our operatives. But that's not surprising. It's a menial sort of assignment and I'm sure the four men are local hoodlums, perhaps from San Diego itself."

"Then where are Deffeldorf and Tyrone now?"

"At home managing their separate businesses."

Roger said, "You mean they just cut out and head back home right in the middle of the job?"

"Their part of the job is probably concluded. Such men are free lances."

Vasquez tapped a fingertip on Arnold Tyrone's grainy face. "When Pastor and Ezio Martin decided to employ assassins to seek out you and Walter Benson and the others, they shopped around to find out who'd be available for the work. They'd never use one of their own for this kind of assignment. It's *de rigueur* to hire outside talent, and to hire it through an anonymous chain of intermediaries. Then if the talent is apprehended and decides to confess, nothing can be traced back to the source."

"Make your point."

"Contain your impatience. You have an annoying tendency to try to reduce everything to straight-line simplicities. There are things in life that aren't subject to that kind of reduction. An organization like Pastor's is not going to dry up and blow away if its taproot is severed. Remove Frank Pastor and the organization will go on quite happily without him. By personalizing your vendetta you render it meaningless."

"Are you suggesting I should go after the entire organization?"

"I suggest, Mr. Merle, that you decide once and for all which it is that you want—the removal of the threat against you and your family, or revenge against your enemies."

"You're making an artificial distinction."

"Not at all. If you're after revenge then by all means fill your hands with pistols and go roaring off in pursuit of Mr. Deffeldorf and Mr. Tyrone. I'm quite certain they're the men who assaulted your home and hired the sniper who shot at you. But if you're after the removal of the threat then you must forget Deffeldorf and Tyrone. Individually they constitute no threat to you. If Frank Pastor were removed from the scene you can be sure the hired hands would forget you instantly—they do only those jobs for which they can reasonably expect recompense, and there would be no profit in their continuing to harass you."

Mathieson pushed the photographs away. He walked to the window and stared through it. Meuth's tractor pulled a mower across the skyline, making a distant racket. Roger cleared his throat.

Vasquez hammered home his point. "You've no need to deal with outsiders who have no personal stake in your living or dying. Forget Deffeldorf and Tyrone. Forget the sniper, whoever he may have been. Focus your attentions on those who have compelling reasons to threaten you."

"Frank Pastor."

"Not merely Pastor. Think about the kind of importance these people attach to revenge. It is a familial obligation—a duty of the blood. If Frank Pastor is harmed, his family is obliged to retaliate. Anna Pastor, his wife. George Ramiro, who must maintain his reputation as the family's enforcer. C. K. Gillespie, who has designs on the family's fortunes and is, I'm told, merely waiting for the eldest Pastor daughter to reach the age of consent so that he may marry her. Ezio Martin who is a second cousin of Pastor's, his closest friend and heir apparent. Alicia Ramiro, Martin's stepsister, the wife of George Ramiro and again a cousin of Pastor's. Sandra and Nora Pastor, the daughters."

He turned away from the window and found Vasquez watching him with a peculiar narrowed eagerness. Mathieson said, "Teen-age girls?"

"They're your enemies. Make no mistake. Leave those two innocent little girls free to act and the time will come when they'll seek revenge on you. It's born in them—they have no choice. Therefore *you* have no choice."

"My God. This is absurd."

"Do you want to reconsider?"

"Why are you always after me to change my mind?"

"Answer my question, please."

"No. I can't reconsider. I've got to get them off my back."

Vasquez watched, unblinking.

Mathieson said, "You're testing me, aren't you."

"Testing your resolve, yes."

"Why?"

"Because you must realize the depth of your commitment. Once you start, there will be no turning back. Go after one of them and you must go after them all. You can't leave the job half done." Vasquez gathered up the photographs, squared them neatly and slid them into the envelope. "Suppose your campaign achieves the intended results—the neutralization, somehow, of the threat posed by Frank Pastor. I can't conceive of your accomplishing that without incurring the rage of his family." Vasquez paused significantly. "Suppose in achieving your first goal—Pastor—you find you've offended your own moral sensibilities. Suppose you find yourself filled with self-loathing. Suppose self-disgust tempts you to take to your heels. You must realize now—before we really begin —that such a train of events would leave you and your wife and son and your friends in a far worse predicament than the one they're in now."

"How could it?"

"Your death has been a matter of sport to Frank Pastor. It's inconsequential. He's gone through the motions, he's honored the traditions to which he's obligated, but he hasn't yet devoted extraordinary energies to pursuing you. The attacks on you may have been engineered by a subordinate—perhaps Ezio Martin—and they were incidentals in Frank Pastor's life. Your demise is something he desires. But it's hardly a vital issue to him. Now if you should carry your attack directly to Pastor and do injury to him, then he and his family would drop absolutely everything in the rush to avenge themselves on you. Where a relatively insignificant proportion of their energies heretofore has been devoted to your harassment, now you would find that the entire force of their violent resources would be brought to bear in an intense concentration against you and your family."

The tractor sputtered to a stop. In the abrupt silence he could hear the breath whistling through Roger's nostrils.

Vasquez said, "I doubt you'd stand one chance in a million. You and your wife and son would not merely be tracked, found and taken. You'd very likely be subjected to punishments of agonizing painfulness before you were eventually slaughtered. As for Mr. Gilfillan and his family, one can't be sure whether their hunger for vengeance would stretch that far but it's possible."

Mathieson pulled out a chair and sat down slowly at the table. He laid both arms out flat along the tabletop and looked at the backs of his hands. Beside him Roger reached out; he felt the solid grip of Roger's fingers on his shoulder.

Vasquez was behind him and Mathieson did not look around. Eventually it forced Vasquez to walk around the table and stand on the far side looking at him. Mathieson raised his head.

In a kinder voice Vasquez said, "I have a responsibility to force you to think these things right through before you decide on a course of action. You resent it, of course—it would be unnatural if you didn't. I've thrown a few of your assumptions off the track. I've managed to depress you. I've made what already appeared difficult become all but impossible to conceive."

Roger's hand fell away; his chair scraped and Mathieson heard him stand up. "Tell you what you've done to me, you've made me start wondering whether you're getting a case of cold feet."

"I intend going all the way with this," Vasquez said. "Make no mistake about that."

"How do we know that? So far all I've seen is some athletics and some smoke screens."

Mathieson looked up at Roger in surprise: the anger in Roger's voice was unmistakable.

"I signed on to *do* something—not just set around and look at pictures and listen to your long-winded flapdoodle and wait on our butts for these four fire inspectors to come find us hidin' in the hayloft. So far all's I've seen you do is spend a lot of Fred's money on man-hours for your own operatives compiling these here beautiful plastic-bound Xerox dossiers, and now you're trying to tell us we can ignore Deffeldorf and Tyrone, just throw all that money and time away. Hell, the way you go at it we could all set around here waitin' for inspiration until we got long white whiskers on us."

Vasquez scowled. "We can't fight from ignorance. We'd get nowhere. Surely you can understand that. We need facts before we can move. We've got the facts now. We're sorting through them. In time we'll find facts we can use. It takes time—I'm sorry, I won't be held accountable for that, or for your impatience."

"You make it sound right reasonable. But somebody else might take a look at all this and call it foot-draggin'."

"In other words you don't trust me."

"Why should I? Why should Fred, for that matter? Just because you say out loud that you aim to go all the way with this, we supposed to believe you? Vasquez, I been listening to producers and directors talk real sweet to me all my life, and the only thing I really learned out of all that was that ninety-nine times out of a hundred those old boys are just yakking to practice their lying."

Vasquez looked at Mathieson. "Do you share your friend's distrust of me?"

"I'd like to know what your intentions are. I'd like to know your reasons—why you took this on in the first place, especially if you thought it was such a poor gamble."

"My reasons are personal."

"Something between you and Frank Pastor?"

"No. I've never had dealings with the man."

"Then what is it?" Mathieson sat up straight. "I realize it's an impertinent question."

"Impertinent? It's personal. But then the only things that matter are." Vasquez thrust his hands into his pockets. His face drew back defensively, chin tucked toward the plaid collar of his open shirt. "Call them my private demons. Matters of vanity and eccentric conviction. I'd prefer to leave it at that."

"Ain't enough," Roger said.

Mathieson said, "I agree with Roger. I'm sorry to pry but we've got a right to be satisfied on this. I don't want to be crude—but it's my money you're spending."

"And my time you're wasting," Roger said. "All of us, our time."

"An extraordinary amount of my own time as well," Vasquez said. "Do you know how many other cases I've had to turn away or set on the back burner?"

Mathieson's fist hit the table: "Why? You've got to tell us why."

Vasquez blinked. His shoulders rolled around and settled; his chin poked forward until he looked querulous. "Are you religious, Mr. Merle?"

It took him aback. "What? No—not particularly."

"You?"

Roger shook his head.

Vasquez said, "People who believe in God can leave the ultimate sortings-out to Him. Rewards and punishments.

Heaven and Hell. When one has no faith in that, one must pay some attention to justice here and now. Otherwise it's all meaningless chaos."

Roger snapped at him: "We didn't ask for a course in philosophy."

"You're going to get one. You asked a question. I'm answering it." Vasquez's eyes swiveled bleakly toward Mathieson. "My reasons have to do with the fact that I lost my faith in God a long time ago. Do you understand at all? I'm a Chicano, Mr. Merle, I have experience of injustice."

Roger said, "You don't talk like no ignorant *barrio* slum."

"Nevertheless I was born in one. I was born on the south side of Tucson, Arizona. An adobe slum."

"So now we get into ethnic stuff?"

Vasquez shook his head. "I believe with Edmund Burke that the only thing necessary for the triumph of evil is for good men to do nothing. You see I may have lost faith but I still carry the burden of absolutism—I was raised in the Church. I believe in absolute distinctions between good and evil. It would have been easier if I'd been able to adapt myself to the current fashions in flexible morality. But I can't—I won't be corrupted, it would make my existence so complicated it would be impossible."

Mathieson stared at him. Was it possible Vasquez's reluctance had been caused solely by a fear of ridicule?

Vasquez said, "One meets decent people but most of them are decent largely because their lives have contained little hardship, little pain and little temptation. Mr. Merle is all but unique—he has faced those challenges and has not been ground down by them. He's made his choices from principle rather than expediency. I can't tell you how much I admire that."

Roger watched, skepticism undiminished. Vasquez pulled out a chair and arranged himself in it. His voice dropped; it took on the dense foggy bass tones of a church organ. "My son was drafted into the army in 1969. He submitted to the draft but petitioned to be treated as a conscientious objector. We had long arguments. He insisted he would not kill. He

174

said that was his credo. He's a Catholic and as you know that's a congregation not noted for its pacifism, but I had no doubt of his sincerity. I put a hypothesis to him. If someone were to point a gun at his mother with the unmistakable intention of killing her, what would he do?"

Mathieson said, "What did he say?"

"The question at this juncture is what do *you* say?"

"I don't know what I might do. I'd try not to kill him. I'd stop him, or maybe get shot trying. But no, I wouldn't deliberately kill him."

"Those might have been my son's exact words."

Roger said, "What happened to him?"

"He was classified I-A-o. Assigned as a noncombatant, a medical attendant. Near Hue, in 1970, he disappeared. He's still listed as missing."

Mathieson said, "I'm very sorry."

"Your sorrow isn't of much use."

It angered him. "I'm not a surrogate for your son. Don't work out your penances on me."

"Don't be idiotic. Or at least don't proclaim your idiocy. I'm not confusing you with my son. I'm trying to explain why I've had occasion to think these issues out."

Mathieson felt exhausted. "Do you want to argue metaphysics all day?"

Vasquez disregarded him. "A man does the sort of thing you're doing only after a great deal of considered analysis. To face such dangers requires a unique devotion to moral principle."

"If you say so. Seems to me I'd face more danger if I did anything else."

"Don't be disingenuous. It's not worthy of you. As we both know, you could always run."

Roger came toward the table. "To where?"

"Anywhere."

"Reckon that's the same as nowhere."

"We've tried it," Mathieson said.

Vasquez glanced from one to the other. "In any case you asked what my motives were. Are you satisfied?"

Roger gripped the edge of the table and leaned on his arms. For a long time he studied Vasquez. "I believe it. Don't ask me why."

"Very few men would believe it," Vasquez said. "It's a cynical age."

Mathieson was about to speak when he heard the door. Mrs. Meuth appeared. "Mr. Vasquez——"

"What is it?"

"Perkins says those men are coming up the road, sir."

Mathieson was out of his chair before she completed the sentence.

CHAPTER SEVENTEEN

Southern California: 22 September

1

THEY DISPERSED ON THE RUN. MATHIESON FOUND THE BOYS in the stable unsaddling. Perkins and Meuth came striding into the runway and Mathieson surprised himself by how calmly he spoke: "Leave that. Let's get up to the house."

Perkins said, "We'll take the horses, boys." Meuth reached for the trailing reins.

Ronny balked. "But they'll——"

Meuth had a tart New England nasality. "They see two sweaty horses, they'll want to know who was riding them. It'll have to be me and Perkins. You boys git, now."

Perkins's thatch of white hair seemed to glow in the dim stable. He looked at Mathieson: "You've got maybe four minutes."

"Come on—come on." He took the boys across the drive-way at full steam, leading the way with his long legs.

They caromed inside. Ronny was anxious: Mathieson saw him reach for Billy's arm. "Wait a minute. What I was trying to say—the stirrups. What if they notice your stirrups?"

"Dudes," Billy said with an echo of his father's prairie twang. "Never notice it in a million years. Come on."

Mathieson stopped halfway to the stairs. "Ronny may have

a point. Get on upstairs—I'll be right there." He swiveled and ran back outside: went off the porch in a single flying leap, skidded on the gravel under the porte cochere and sprinted full-tilt across the lawn. He spared a glance to his right. There was nothing in sight—the trees masked the lower valley beyond the farther bend in the driveway.

Meuth and Perkins were leading the two geldings out into the paddock. Mathieson stopped in the stable door; if he went outside he'd be visible from below. "Meuth!"

He saw the man's cap-bill turn.

"Lengthen those stirrups!"

Meuth shook his head; he looked away toward the end of the paddock fence. "No time. Run for it, man!"

Mathieson made his dash. If the car came around the bend before he got inside the house . . .

But it didn't. He took the main stairs three at a time and pounded down the upstairs corridor.

Homer was waiting by the open door to the utility closet. "Where the hell you been? Never mind—here, I'll give you a boost."

He pulled himself up through the trapdoor onto the rafters. They'd rehearsed it twice several days ago: He knew enough to move with care, balancing his weight on the beams—there was nothing between them but the light wire framing of the plaster ceilings covered by six inches of foam insulation and if you put a foot down on that it might go straight through.

He laid himself painfully belly-flat across the rafters and reached down the trapdoor. Beneath him Homer was stacking soapboxes back on the shelves they'd used for ladder-holds. Homer tipped the ironing board back into place and then there were no footholds. He made his jump from a crouch; Mathieson caught his arm and manhandled him up far enough. Homer's fingers gripped the box of rafters around the traphole and Mathieson slid back to give him room to chin himself up through the opening.

Homer rolled away from the hole and Mathieson slid the painted sheet of three-quarter plywood down into it, closing the door. He turned, barking a knee on a two-by-eight, picking up the faint guide of illumination falling through the angled louver-slats of the attic vent up near the peak of the wall at the far end of the crawl space. It was enough to steer by; he followed Homer awkwardly along the rafters on hands and knees, using the beams like railway tracks until they reached the central crawl-planking. It was two feet wide and ran the length of the attic—a service platform for access to the air-conditioning ductwork.

Even under the roofbeam the space was only three feet high and they had to scull the plank on hands and knees. A breeze hit him in the face, drawn through by the throbbing exhaust fan down the length of the house behind him.

Two heads blocked some of the light from the shutter-slits of the vent—Vasquez and Roger, peering down through the openings. The long attic was architecturally a nave; at the end to either side garbled dormers made symmetrical wings. Back in those narrow triangular spaces the side-vents threw enough light for him to make out the rumpled shapes of human figures and the crowded stacks of luggage, piled like bricks, neatly fitted into the corners. Everything they possessed was up here.

His eyes were dilating in the dimness and when he moved forward he distinguished Amy Gilfillan's silhouette; the dark figure before her was Jan. He looked the other way and found Ronny and Billy crowded up against the side-vent of the left wing, trying to see down through the slats. That one overlooked the swimming pool and the back slope of garden.

Behind him Homer brushed his ankle, climbing across the beams into the wing by the two boys. Mathieson put one foot on a rafter and reached out for Jan's shoulder. Her hand found his and squeezed it. He moved ahead down the planking; Vasquez and Roger made room for him.

The vent was about a foot square. Its wooden louvers were tilted down against the rain. The fan sucked a powerful wind through the screening. He moved close to it and the changing focus of his eyes blurred the mesh of the wire screen. The view was restricted by the four-inch depth of the louvers: He could see a piece of the driveway, grass on either side of it, one end of the stable and a patch of paddock beyond it.

The car squatted in the gravel drive and by squinting and

moving his head from side to side against the screen he was able to piece out the lettering in the gold decal on the front door of the pale blue car: *County of San Diego—Utilities Board.*

Vasquez moved his lips close to Mathieson's ear. "Electrical inspectors. It's an excellent ploy—gives them the excuse to pry into nooks and crannies." The sibilants of his whisper hissed in the wind.

Roger said, "They over in the paddock talkin' to Meuth and Perkins right now. Over to the right a bit—you can't see them right now."

Mathieson said, "Well at least we didn't go to all this trouble on a false alarm. While I was banging my knees on those rafters I was thinking how sore I'd be if it turned out to be Meuth's sister-in-law or some Sunday driver who lost his way."

"He'd have to be real good and lost," Roger remarked. "Today's Monday."

"Is it?" He'd lost track. Nothing stirred in the quadrangle of his view. His knees began to ache; he gingerly shifted position on the sharp-edged beams. "They're taking a long time out there."

"Establishing their credentials," Vasquez guessed.

"Maybe. But there could be a problem. Meuth and Perkins still have the horses with them?"

"Yes."

Roger said, "Meuth's probably stalling them, give us more time to get settled down."

"I hope that's it. We didn't have time to lengthen Billy's stirrups."

He felt Roger stiffen beside him. Billy was a head shorter than Ronny; the stirrups on his saddle had been hiked up several notches to accommodate his short legs. An alert observer would notice it.

Roger said, "Perkins knows?"

"Yes."

"Then I reckon it's all right. They get curious, he'll just allow he shortened the stirrups to ride knee-high race form. He was Breed's trainer, you know. Sometimes they ride quar-

180

terhorses short-stirrup, get 'em used to pancake saddles."

But his heart kept pounding. He didn't know Perkins at all: Did the man have brains enough?

Then they moved into sight. He nudged Roger. The three of them pressed their faces to the screen.

Meuth trudged across the driveway, moving with an elderly foot-dragging slowness that wasn't typical of him. Stalling them, Mathieson judged. Meuth was talking rapid fire, waving his arms about—probably extolling the glories of the estate, putting on an act and evidently doing a good job of it.

The two electrical inspectors wore casual outfits—open sport shirts, khakis, sneakers. One of them was a big man with a veined bald skull; the back of his head was flat. His companion had crew-cut gray hair and a beer belly. They didn't look sinister. They looked like weary civil servants.

On the lawn the three men paused, Meuth still talking expansively. The bald man nodded to acknowledge something Meuth said. The gray-haired man peered around, turning on his heels, taking in everything. His face lifted and his eyes seemed to focus directly on the grilled vent. Mathieson had the impulse to jerk back away from the opening. Vasquez's hand gripped his arm: "Steady. He can't see us. But don't move—he might see the shadows shift." The whispered words were carried away behind them by the thrumming fan.

The bald man had a well-used metal tool kit box. He led the other two out of sight toward the porte cochere.

Vasquez pulled back away from the vent. "Pick a comfortable spot and settle down. They'll be here a while. Don't move around—they might hear creaking."

He saw Perkins lead the two saddled horses into the stable. Faintly he heard the bang of the house's front door. Probably Meuth—slamming it to warn them in the attic.

Vasquez was climbing into the side wing with Homer and the two boys. Mathieson made his way over the rafters, palm and knee, brushing past the stacked suitcases and into the little false cave behind them where Jan and Amy were hunched under the low dormer roof. The space was tight, most of it taken up by the luggage. Jan was watching him but in the dimness her expression had the false serenity of withdrawal.

He guessed she had simply thrown all the gears into neutral. He fitted himself down onto a beam beside her and captured her cool hand; he rubbed it gently between his palms but she only gave him a distracted wisp of a smile.

Roger eased in opposite him and Amy flashed her teeth, squeezing to the side to make room. Mathieson saw the mischievous grin pass between them—a game of hide-and-seek: Amy, who lived a life of splendid carelessness, was enjoying this. Her pixie face was faintly aglow with wide-eyed excitement.

Then they waited.

Disquieted by uneasy imaginings he ran his mind back over the preparations they had made, trying to discern whether they'd overlooked anything. They'd picked this hiding place because it was big enough to accommodate eight people and their possessions; they'd studied it by flashlight from the top of the trapdoor and they'd placed the luggage back far enough from the nave so that it wouldn't be seen by anyone who didn't actually crawl most of the length of the attic. There'd been a bigger, more comfortable and more obvious pair of dormer wings at the opposite end of the house but that was right by the big attic fan and they'd ruled it out when Vasquez pointed out that the noise of the fan would prevent them from hearing anyone's approach. Homer, Vasquez and Roger were armed with revolvers and if they were discovered the plan was to try and get the drop on the hoodlums; after that they'd have no choice but to keep the prisoners incommunicado for an indefinite period. But if that happened it would be a costly risk: When the two electrical inspectors disappeared their colleagues would trace their movements.

Somewhere in the house there was a faint thud—probably another door slamming.

Mathieson's shoulder was jammed up against an overhead rafter and he had to keep his head bent below the sloping roof; his muscles began to ache. Across the way he could only just make out the huddled shadows of Ronny, Billy, Vasquez and Homer. The three vents threw just enough light to distinguish outlines but not colors. He remembered the rehearsals up here last week—Vasquez urging him to keep a gun in his pocket, growing angry over Mathieson's repeated refusals. *If it comes to shooting it'll make no difference whether you're armed or not—you're still part of it.*

He kept looking at the luminous dial of his watch. Beside him Jan shifted her position slightly. He tensed; but there was no sound. The beam on which he sat was pinching a groove into his rump. He wanted, of all things, a cigarette—he hadn't smoked in years.

Thirty-five minutes had passed. It was almost noon. Despite the exhaust fan's powerful circulation the corner was close with musty heat; he was sweating heavily.

The faintest of clicks—his eyes flashed toward Roger and he saw a pale flash ripple along the blued gun barrel as it lifted. The cords stood out in Roger's neck.

Mathieson turned his face a bit and then he caught it on the flats of his eardrums: the scrape of wood on wood.

There was light—dim irregular reflections that moved the shadows under the center roofbeam. In alarm he watched the shadows dance, faint as ghosts. He knew what it was: Someone had come up through the trapdoor and was playing a flashlight around; what he was seeing was secondary and tertiary reflections of the light beam.

Beads of sweat stood out on Roger's forehead. His knuckles went pale on the grip of the revolver. Its muzzle stirred, pushing toward the central runway where, if the searchers advanced this far, they would appear.

Across the way Mathieson could see subtle movements—Homer and Vasquez preparing themselves; he caught, once, a glint of light on steel.

Cramp put a stitch in Mathieson's neck. He opened his mouth and drew a shallow breath. Jan sat absolutely still except for her eyelids: She was blinking very fast, staring sightlessly and fixedly at an indeterminate shadow amid the suitcases. A pale movement—it drew his eye: Amy, lifting her hand to chew on a fingernail.

The vague dappling of lights grew dimmer. He guessed they were prowling toward the far end—toward the attraction of noise and movement: the exhaust fan.

Then a voice. It startled him by its very faintness; the fan, drawing air, sent the sound away and made it seem to reach him from a great distance downwind:

"It's just a fan."

An ordinary voice—no menace in it—but the skin of his back crawled.

His nerves were so keyed up that the tiniest movement in the corner of his vision drew his alarmed attention. It was Roger: his thumb curling over the hammer of the revolver.

A creaking of planks. The lights came lancing down the attic—the flashlights pointing this way now. Two of them: the beams crisscrossed, bobbing around the rafters, throwing the shadows into sharp relief. Against the sudden light Jan's profile in silhouette was preternaturally still like something carved out of stone. Then he heard something catch in her throat: She dipped her face, stifling it. With great care he slid his arm around her shoulders. She was rigid.

"This insulation's making me all itchy. Come on, there's nothing up here."

The lights receded. He heard the scrape of the trapdoor. Darkness returned.

He let the breath out of him; he sagged back against the roof.

Jan stirred. His grip clenched her shoulder. "No." He mouthed the whisper against her ear. "Wait till they've gone—wait till we hear the car."

"God—God . . ."

"Take it easy. It's all over."

2

His back ached and his arms were getting weak; he took a break and set the ax beside the stacked logs. In the night the cool breeze brushed his cheeks. Lamplight from the windows of the house made little pools on the lawn above him. He filled his lungs and dragged another limb to the sawhorses: Meuth had pruned the maples during the week and dragged the limbs around behind the barn with his tractor and they'd been waiting for the ax. Mathieson had volunteered for it because he

184

needed to be alone and because he needed to work hard with his hands and body, exhaust himself to the extreme so that there wouldn't be any strength left for feeling and thinking.

In the end his muscles rebelled and he had to quit. He put the ax away and left the barn, walking stiffly in slow weariness, guiding on the porch lights.

He stopped under the porte cochere, reluctant to go inside. The scene still reverberated in his skull. They had fought many times but never quite like this. *God, the things I said*. At its climax she had burst into screaming tears. They were real tears —it was real emotion—but her histrionics had been so theatrical he'd found himself unmoved; and that had frightened him more than the rest. He'd rushed outside.

On the porch steps he sat down with his elbows on his knees, face in his hands.

An insubstantial cloud drifted across the moon; he forced himself to his feet and stumbled inside and up the stairs.

He looked in on Ronny. The boy lay asleep on the bed, covers thrown back, positioned as if he'd tripped while running in sand. Mathieson pulled the door silently shut and went on along the hall.

She was at the dressing table prospecting for pins in her hair. She had a headache again: He could see the pain across her eyes. She looked up, locking glances with him in the mirror, and he saw her breathe in through her nose, slowly and expressively, pinching her lips together. Her hair, still fresh from washing, shimmered in the lamplight; the portable dryer was in the open suitcase; now she was taking her hair down. She twisted half around to look at him directly and his glance traveled the long column of her back—even in anger she still had the capacity to arouse him deeply.

She swung her legs around and crossed them and leaned forward as though she had a severe pain in her stomach: She held that attitude, watching him, anxiety behind the surface anger in her eyes. Her arms hugged her upraised knee.

"I'm sorry," he said.

"Are you?"

"I'll make it up to you."

"How?"

"I don't know yet."

"I'm going to pieces, Fred."

"You can't. Not yet."

"Easy to say. Easy for you to say."

"When I put Ronny to bed he said something to me. He said, 'I want to be a rodeo rider if I grow up.' "

She only looked at him blankly.

" '*If* I grow up.' "

Comprehension changed her face.

"That's why you've got to hang on."

She turned away from him and her hands plucked blindly at things on the dressing table. She picked up the hair brush and put it down, prodded a lipstick without lifting it, found a pin left in her hair but didn't take it out—merely touching things as if there were communication in the act.

He said, "You've got to try."

"I feel like Humpty Dumpty—a lot of little pieces nobody will ever put back together."

"I know."

"I'm learning to hate you."

"I'm learning to hate myself."

She took the pin out and put it down very gently in the little box. Then with growing ferocity she began to brush out her hair.

He stripped off his sweat-sodden clothes and went into the shower. When he came out of the bathroom the lights were turned off in the bedroom; before he switched off the bathroom light he saw her in the bed, lying on her side, facing away from him, crowded as far over as she could get without falling off.

He turned it off and felt his way to the bed and got in. He was careful not to touch her.

Too charged to sleep, he just lay there. Something Homer had taught him kept coming back: *A man comes at you hand-to-hand, there's one way to put him out and it works every time if he doesn't know to look for it. Doesn't take much of a blow. Hit him with the heel of your palm—bring it up, short and hard, right up into his nose. Drive the nasal cartilage right up into the head. You hit a man hard enough that way, just once, it'll drive the splinters right up into his brain and kill him instantly.*

The thought had sickened him at the time and he'd changed the subject immediately. But now in fevered visions he saw himself slamming his palm up with vicious rage into face after face—Gillespie, George Ramiro, Deffeldorf, Tyrone, Ezio Martin, Frank Pastor . . .

And then all at once he had it, the structure of the plan. It brought him bolt upright in bed.

He got up and left the room, striding down the hall barefoot, belting his robe. At Vasquez's door he banged impatiently and when he heard a grunt he pushed inside.

Vasquez lay across the bed, reaching for the lamp. When it came on he flinched from the light and sat up squinting. He was wearing satin pajamas—bright green. "What the devil?"

"I've got to talk to you."

"Evidently." Vasquez reached for the clock and turned it toward him. "At half past two it had better be utterly fascinating."

"I've figured it out."

"Have you?" Vasquez threw the sheet back and slid his feet into a pair of moccasins. "I can't really see you. You'll have to wait a moment." He padded to the bathroom.

Mathieson was too keyed up to sit; he walked to the door and back. Vasquez hadn't shut the bathroom door and when Mathieson passed the foot of the bed he saw Vasquez bending over the sink, running water, prying his eyelids open one at a time.

Contact lenses, he thought. I'll be damned.

From a hook Vasquez took down a green-lapeled dressing gown; he folded it around his trim shape and crossed to the straight chair at the writing desk. He sat down before he spoke. "Proceed."

"We've been making a mistake in our whole approach to this thing. I just figured it out."

187

"Indeed."

"We've been trying to contrive some cockeyed scheme to nail them all together—simultaneously."

"It's hardly cockeyed. We can't attack one or two at a time and leave the rest free to retaliate."

"Sure we can. That's been our mistake. You ever go bowling?"

"Not for a good many years."

"Neither have I. But that was the image. We've been trying to bowl a strike—figure out how to hit all ten pins with one ball. But if you bowl a strike into the pocket—you know the term?"

"Yes."

"Then think about what really happens. The ball doesn't actually hit all ten pins. At most it hits three of them. Those three pins take care of the rest. *They* knock the other pins down."

"That's attractive," Vasquez said, "but I've never put much trust in analogies. We're not dealing with bowling pins. Suppose you bowl a spare instead of a strike? You've got one pin left standing. But this one would be a bowling pin that can shoot you to death."

"All right, it's a sloppy metaphor. But it got me to thinking. There's no reason why we have to go after them all at the same time. If we can peel them off one at a time——"

"We've gone over all that. While we're peeling them off one at a time, what do you suppose the others are doing?"

"They'd have to know who to come after and where to find us. If we start taking them out individually, and if we do it in such a way that nobody else knows what's really happening . . ."

"Starting where? At the bottom? We've discussed that before. We can't hope to disrupt their operations by stinging individual enterprises. You might annoy them a bit by hitting a few front operations but that sort of campaign would be like trying to kill an elephant with sandpaper. In any case it would be stupid to disperse our attacks—we haven't the manpower. Save up your punch and when you use it, use all of it in intense concentration. Mr. Merle, none of this is new. Some-

188

times an idea coined at two in the morning seems brilliant but loses its luster in the light of day. We've already demonstrated that you can't injure Frank Pastor by hitting his subsidiaries. There are too many of them and in any case those operations are protected by the police . . ."

"You're getting off the track."

"Am I? You're talking about taking them out individually. I suggested that at the outset. But the only effective method of achieving that is to kill them. I still suggest your preclusion of murder is an artificial stricture—because the methods you'll be forced to use are bound to be as reprehensible as murder or more so."

"I can think of very few things as reprehensible as murder."

"You're wrong. Whatever method you choose, it must lead to the same end—the willful destruction of your enemies. Nothing less than that will suffice. You may leave them alive and breathing but you must destroy something vital—if only their freedom to make choices. Ultimately you'll be forced to assume absolute power over their decisions and their lives. You must see that much. I'm not as certain that you also see the inevitable consequence. Such power will corrode your soul."

"It can be done without killing," Mathieson said.

"Very well. How?"

He pulled the chair closer to Vasquez and sat down. "We start with C. K. Gillespie."

PART THREE

THE HUNTER

CHAPTER EIGHTEEN

California–Illinois: 29 September

1

HE SAID HIS GOODBYES TO AMY AND BILLY AND THE MEUTHS; he carried the suitcase down to the car and put it in the back seat and walked off beyond earshot with Jan and Ronny.

Because of the boy they were both holding back a great deal. Ronny shook his hand gravely. Mathieson fought back the impulse to embrace him: Ronny would hate it in front of the others.

"I want you to take damn good care of your mother. Don't sass her."

He took Jan in his arms. "It's going to work, you know. Things are going to be all right."

"Sure." She kissed him. He was startled by the ferocity with which she clenched him against her as if she could draw strength from him.

Ronny said, "You still look lousy in that moustache. It makes you look like Zachary Scott."

"What have you got against Zachary Scott?"

"He's dead," Ronny said and turned away.

"I'm not dead, Ronny. Listen to me."

The boy turned reluctantly.

"Are you listening?"

"Sure I am."

"Put a little trust in your old man. I'm going to pin these bastards like butterflies. They'll never touch us again. I want you to stop feeling sorry for yourself. If you don't, you'll feel like a damn fool afterward—all that sour worry for nothing. Understand me?"

"I just don't want you to get hurt. You don't even have a gun."

"Guns don't answer any questions, Ron."

"Who's asking questions? They just want to kill us."

"They won't get the chance. Believe that."

"All right."

"I mean it now."

But the boy wasn't convinced and he couldn't think of any way to reassure him.

Jan said, "You'll miss your plane." It was the next thing to a whisper.

He kissed her again, trying to mean it. Then he walked away from them to the car.

Vasquez got in behind the wheel.

Homer held the passenger door. Mathieson shook his hand. "I'll see you in Washington."

"And me in little old New York," Roger said. "Ride easy, old horse."

"You know this is going to work," Mathieson said.

"Damn right I do." Roger smiled a little; of them all Roger was the one who had no reservations.

"Take care now, old horse."

Vasquez drove him down past the paddock fence. Behind them Jan and Ronny stood in the driveway waving.

They rolled very fast down the gravel track. The dust lifted high and their passage exploded birds out of the trees. Vasquez said, "I'll have four men down here by tonight to keep watch. Don't alarm yourself over their safety. No one will get through to them. If there's an attempt my men have orders to use their weapons."

"If there's no other choice."

"There won't be if Pastor's men come here again. They'll come only if they know they've got the right place. But I still believe they're safest here. Pastor has already searched it—he'll have no reason to come back."

"I hope you're right."

Vasquez slowed for the turning into the county road. "You're one of the most closely guarded people I've ever met. Have you always been remote or is it something that's happened since these attacks began?"

"You're a great one to talk."

"I haven't got a marriage to save."

Mathieson closed his eyes. Vasquez's smugness made him want to snarl. "You've got a wife."

"In name," Vasquez said. "We don't share premises. You're evading the point."

"I don't need two-penny psychoanalysis from you."

"You're frightened. It's understandable. But aren't you confusing the source of your fears? It's not your friends or your wife you need to fear."

2

When the flight was called he left Vasquez and went along to the boarding gate, being careful to stay in the center of the crowd, neither first nor last.

The plane was not crowded; to his relief the seat next to his was empty. Stewardesses went down the aisle looking at passengers' seat belts and offering magazines and headphones. At takeoff he felt a belly-churning sensation when the wheels thudded up into their sockets while the plane still seemed only inches off the ground. Then they were climbing steeply and he relaxed his grip on the arms of the seat.

He spent the three hours neither sleeping nor reading; he stared at the clouds and worked out pieces of the scheme in his mind. But anxious thoughts about Jan kept distracting him.

At O'Hare he took the first taxi in the rank. He was empty-handed; the bag was checked through and he had four hours between planes.

The taxi dropped him at the John Hancock tower. It was a chill bleak day, the heavy overcast scudding quickly overhead, pedestrians chasing their hats in the Chicago winds.

He went into the tower and cruised through the basement arcade of shops, making an aimless circuit, emerging from the side entrance and crossing briskly to the hotel garage opposite; he hired a nondescript small car there and drove it down Lake Shore Drive to the Loop.

He was not particularly well acquainted with Chicago but he knew the main landmarks and found his way without difficulty to his destination. He had arrived early for the meeting in order to see who went into the hotel. He recognized no one until he saw Bradleigh step out of a taxi and walk inside, hatless and ruddy, the tails of his open topcoat flapping in the gray wind.

He gave Bradleigh a five-minute lead, saw nothing that alarmed him, got out of the car, locked it and crossed the street just as rain began to slant onto the pavement. By the time he reached the hotel it was pouring.

Bradleigh was in the bar at a side table, cigarette smoke trailing from his mouth and nostrils. Mathieson went straight to him but Bradleigh's glance passed over him twice without recognition until he was within three paces; then Bradleigh beamed, humor in the gentle eyes: "I didn't recognize you."

"That's good." He pulled the chair out and sat down.

"It's not just the hair and the moustache. You move differently. Have you lost weight?"

"Redistributed it."

"You look ten years younger."

"I'm in a little bit of a hurry, Glenn. Can we let that suffice for the amenities?"

"Do you want a drink?"

"No. I'd like to know what you've found out—how things are going, if anywhere."

"That's a little brusque, isn't it?"

"I haven't got much time."

"I'm beginning to wonder who's doing a favor for whom by coming here."

"Glenn, you still owe me a debt. I'm not letting you off the hook." For the first time in months he was making a contact that might be noticed—he was exposing himself and it made him nervous.

Bradleigh smiled reassuringly. "Don't worry. I took all the standard measures and then some. We're not being watched."

"Not unless someone found out about this appointment."

"No one did. Count on it." The ritual lighting of a fresh filter tip; then Bradleigh said, "We've picked up a few tidbits on C. K. Gillespie. We'll be ready to nail him before long. When we do we expect him to sing."

"How long before you pounce?"

"A week, ten days. It depends on developments. If he doesn't let a few more things slip where our bugs can pick them up, we'll use what we've got and grab him anyway. We've got leads on at least four men who probably were involved in the Los Angeles business and the Oklahoma shooting——"

"Including Deffeldorf and Tyrone?"

Bradleigh's jaw dropped. "Where did you get those names?"

"A Ouija board."

"Have you been playing at amateur sleuth?"

"No."

"Then I don't get——"

"Just out of curiosity, who are the other two you're investigating? Aside from Tyrone and Deffeldorf?"

"A motorcycle freak named Ortiz and a friend of his by the name of Tony Senno."

"Angelinos?"

"From the area, yes. Burbank."

"Have you got hard evidence?"

"We're building a pretty good case."

"I hope you make it stick."

"We will. We're taking our time, we want to make sure it's airtight before we make the grab. The biggest break was Ortiz's rifle. We found it where he ditched it in a street trash can. He'd broken it down into components but we got enough to prove it's the rifle that fired at you—and the serial numbers that trace it back to Ortiz."

"Fingerprints?"

"No. Nobody's that stupid. It's mainly circumstantial at the moment but we're convinced they're the right men. We'll take all four of them simultaneously. Then we'll work on them individually. Whichever one cracks, that's the one we'll use to pin the other three to the wall. OK, that's the good news. The bad news, of course, is that there's no chance any of them will ever be able to lead us back to Frank Pastor in a way that would stand up in court."

"We knew that before."

Bradleigh shook his head. "I get my nocturnal emissions from dreaming that someday I'll find enough rope around Pastor's neck to hang him with."

"Have you got anything at all on Pastor or Ezio Martin or George Ramiro?"

"I don't—— Where'd you get Ramiro's name?"

"It's a talkative Ouija board."

"I don't know if I'm obliged to give you every scrap that I've got."

"It's damn well the least you can give me, Glenn."

Bradleigh showed his discomfiture. "Well as you know we've been bugging Gillespie every way from Sunday. Mostly he talks with Ezio Martin and mostly they do their talking in Martin's office in Manhattan. It's fully equipped—for example with an electronic jammer. All we get is static."

"But you do have those bits and pieces."

"Yes. For one thing, we're not the only ones who've been bugging Gillespie."

"No?"

"There are three sets of microphones in his office and his apartment. One set, each, is ours."

"And the other two?"

"We think Gillespie installed one set himself. The Nixon syndrome—the compulsion to record his own crimes for posterity. In case he ever has to go back and find out what actually happened. These people deal in lies all the time. Sometimes they need to check back, find out what lies they told somebody so that they can remember to stick to the story the next time they meet the same person."

"I see. And the third set?"

"We think it's Ezio Martin. We think maybe Ezio's getting a little jealous. Maybe he bugged Gillespie to try and get something on him so he can discredit Gillespie with Pastor. Martin would love to drive a wedge between them."

"That makes sense."

198

"Anyway we know the bugs aren't another government agency."

"Any evidence stronger than guesswork?"

"Yes. Fairly strong evidence. But I'd rather not divulge it."

"Just out of curiosity, if Gillespie happened across the two sets of microphones in his office—the ones he didn't plant himself—could he tell the difference between yours and Martin's? Would he know one bug was official and one wasn't?"

"He might, if he knew what to look for."

"Namely?"

"Why are you pumping me about it?"

"If I'm ever bugged," Mathieson lied, "I'd like to know how to tell whether it's official or private."

"There's no way to tell for sure. Gillespie's an easy obvious case. The next one might not be."

"Tell me anyway."

"Hell, it's simple enough. Ezio's equipment is wireless. He's got the best stuff money can buy—voice-activated miniature transmitters. Somewhere in the neighborhood there'll be a small receiving set and a cassette recorder attached to it. The recorder doesn't start running until somebody starts talking. It's not the most reliable system but it's the most practical, especially for an organization that doesn't have unlimited man-hours to spend on monitoring. But we prefer the old-fashioned wire, ourselves. A wire isn't subject to interference by radio-jamming equipment. The reception isn't affected by static in the air or neon lights in the vicinity. Anyhow that's the difference and it's easy enough to spot. The official microphones have wires attached to them. The other stuff—the mikes we think are Ezio Martin's—they don't have any wires on them."

"What about the bugs you said he planted on himself?"

"They're wired right into his own tape recorders in the desk drawers. They're activated by switches hidden under the desks."

"What about the phones?"

"We tapped the incoming lines. The other outfit puts bugs in the receivers. As a matter of fact that's where most of Ezio's mikes are—in the phones. It's as good a place to hide them as any." Bradleigh smiled vaguely. "I wish we'd been able to get wires into Ezio Martin's offices in New York. All we've been able to use has been bugs sewn into the buttons of Gillespie's clothes and they've been wiped out by jammers whenever he goes inside. If we could get wires into Ezio's office we'd probably get enough on them to put them all away for consecutive five-hundred-year prison terms."

"Tell me what else you've found out."

"This may come as a shock to you, old buddy, but a lot of things don't have the remotest thing to do with you."

"Anything that has to do with Frank Pastor has to do with me. The more I know about him, the better I can keep out of his way."

"You're clutching at straws."

"Let me be the judge of that."

"I'm sorry. It just isn't included in the price of your ticket."

"My ticket came pretty high, Glenn. For instance when you people put my face and the Paul Baxter name out on a national FBI bulletin. Did you think that wouldn't get back to Pastor?"

"It wasn't my doing. I put a stop to it as fast as I humanly could. Who's been feeding you all this information about Deffeldorf and Tyrone and Ramiro and the FBI bulletin? Did you hire a private security outfit?"

"No," he lied. He had to put Bradleigh at ease and it had to be plausible. "Pastor found out I was off your hook and he decided I might get in touch with my old friends. He staked some of them out. We made the mistake of phoning one of them. His phone was tapped. Pastor's hoodlums started putting pressure on my friend, so my friend did some inquiring— he wanted to find out who was harassing him. He's a man with contacts in Los Angeles—big executives who have access to police officials. He found out about Deffeldorf and the FBI bulletin and all that. He told me about it—from a pay phone, of course."

"What friend was this?"

"He's out of it now. They've been leaving him alone. I don't want him interrogated by your people—I don't want him dragged back into it."

Bradleigh tapped his cigarette on the tabletop and lighted it. "What name are you going under?"

"Try another one."

Bradleigh smiled, evidently without wanting to. "Anything you need?"

"Information."

"About what?"

"Anything you've got."

Bradleigh said, "There's nothing you'd find useful. We're talking about the results of a secret investigation that's still in progress. It's got to stay secret until we blow the whistle."

"It's been nice talking to you, Glenn. Thanks for coming on such short notice. I'll be in touch."

CHAPTER NINETEEN

Washington, D.C.: 2–4 October

1

HE SPENT TWO HOURS WITH HOMER SITTING IN THE PARKED Cadillac at a meter opposite the nine-story office building. Homer had the various photographs arranged on the seat between them—Gillespie, his junior partner, the two secretaries, the clerk and the receptionist.

At 4:30 the clerk appeared with a briefcase and walked to the corner to wait for a bus. Homer said, "Probably an errand to do on his way home. At this hour he won't be coming back."

"Let's hope."

In the next forty minutes people emerged from the building in knots and they scanned faces carefully. Mathieson checked off the receptionist and, at two minutes past five, the two secretaries. At 5:10 Homer stiffened. "There he is."

Mathieson watched C. K. Gillespie walk away toward the parking garage at the end of the block. The heels of Gillespie's polished Italian shoes threw back brisk hard echoes. Mathieson studied him keenly: You could tell a great deal about a man by his walk. Gillespie strutted: a tense man, alert, arrogant.

Mathieson said, "It's suite seven-one-six."

"What kind of locks?"

"Just one, the original equipment. Eaton Yale and Towne. Standard unit. He wouldn't keep anything incriminating in the office. But there could be a burglar alarm."

"According to our preliminary work-up there's only one alarm circuit in the building—jewelry outfit on the third floor." Homer checked his notes. "Twenty-four-hour doorman service. After six you have to sign in when you enter the building. That's why we've got to go in sometime in the next half hour."

"I'd feel more comfortable after dark."

"That's just instinct. Actually we're less conspicuous now, while there are still a lot of people in the building."

A red Thunderbird with Gillespie at the wheel rolled out of the parking garage and Mathieson watched it dwindle into the Connecticut Avenue traffic.

"That leaves one unaccounted for," Mathieson said.

They waited until 5:40. He was restless. "Where's the junior partner?"

"Maybe he's working late. Maybe he wasn't in the office today at all."

"If he's working late we've had it."

"Then we come back tomorrow afternoon, that's all." Homer looked at his watch. "We'd better go in."

"I'm not crazy about it."

"The office door has a frosted glass pane. If there's a light on inside we'll back off and try again tomorrow."

Mathieson lifted the attaché case from the back seat. They walked into the lobby, two gray-suited businessmen arriving for an after-hours appointment. The doorman was engulfed in the stream of people pouring from the elevators and flooding across to the doors; he hardly glanced at the two arrivals. When one elevator emptied itself Mathieson and Homer stepped in.

They had the cage to themselves on the way to the seventh floor. Mathieson opened the case and pawed through the half-dozen rings of keys. "Yale, but which one?"

"Probably that one." Homer singled out a master key.

Mathieson took it off the ring and put the rest of the Yale ring in his pocket. A single key was less conspicuous than a bulky ring of them. If the first key didn't work he'd have to bring out the ring.

Gillespie's door was the last on the left at the end of a forty-foot corridor. They passed two secretaries and an executive going home for the night; the executive nodded politely as they passed him.

Homer slowed the pace. Mathieson glanced over his shoulder. The secretaries and the executive were waiting for the elevator.

Sotto voce Mathieson said, "We can't just stand here."

There was no light behind the frosted glass. Mathieson tried the knob; it was locked. His palm slipped on the brass—he wiped the sweat off against the front of his suit jacket and jabbed the key into the lock.

Homer laughed loudly. "You should've seen old Charlie's face when the decision came down."

The key wouldn't turn.

Behind them the elevator doors opened. The three people disappeared into the cage.

He twisted the key but it wouldn't turn. He stepped back and reached into his pocket.

"Wait a minute," Homer said. "Let me have a try." He jiggled the master key and after a moment Mathieson heard the tumblers click. He made a face and looked over his shoulder. The corridor was empty.

They slipped inside. Homer pushed the door shut behind him. From this point forward they would not talk: The microphones were alive.

Homer moved swiftly across the reception foyer. Mathieson glanced at the switchboard to see if any lines were lighted. There was no sign of life in the place but in his mind he rehearsed a nervous explanation designed to bluff an exit if anyone appeared.

Homer was halfway down the length of the partitioned hall by the time Mathieson followed him through. Quickly they checked out the four rooms. Two side offices, a law library and filing room combined, and the big corner office—Gillespie's lair. There was no one.

The safe was in the law library; that was where he caught

up with Homer. It was a floor model, a Mosler, probably three-quarters of a ton in weight—it stood four feet high; there were two combination dials. Homer glanced at the safe, then at Mathieson and shook his head. Nobody but a top professional box man could hope to get into it without using a torch—and that would undoubtedly destroy the contents.

With gloves on their fingers they went quickly through the file drawers—looking mainly for files on Pastor, Martin, and the various names Mathieson had used. The only result was a thin folder on Ezio Martin; it contained nothing useful—a handful of Xeroxes of bills, receipts and canceled checks and copies of two real estate contracts.

He hadn't expected anything but it might have turned up a tidbit; he wasn't disappointed by the failure. They went into the corner office and Mathieson crossed toward the windows to draw the blinds but Homer shook his head violently at him and Mathieson, belatedly comprehending, withdrew without touching the cords. The drawing of blinds could be noticed from outside the building: It would have been a blunder. *I'm still a novice.* The realization alarmed him.

They took screwdrivers from the attaché case and began to prowl in search of microphones.

He was still sweating: forehead, palms, crotch. The plan had seemed simple when he'd formulated it but he was seeing holes in it now—all the things that might go wrong. Suppose Gillespie forgot something and returned to the office to get it? The search was taking far too long . . .

The wireless bug was easy; it was in the handset of one of the two phones on the desk. That was Ezio Martin's mike and after he had pointed it out to Homer he put the phone back together with the bug intact; he'd need to have that one function properly.

Homer found Bradleigh's mike when he began unscrewing the faceplates of the electric wall plug receptacles. The wires disappeared back into the baseboard, going through holes that had already been cut for the building's electric power lines. There was enough slack. Homer drew a short loop of wire out of the receptacle and went to work with the wire cutters and splicing materials from the attaché case.

Mathieson watched him. Homer's fingers were deft inside the thin cloth gloves. He spliced the new wire onto the cut ends of the microphone wiring; he ran it down out of sight behind the metal baseboard heat shield and threaded it around the room in that fashion to the molding by the office door. He mounted the miniature toggle at the edge of the baseboard just inside the door. You wouldn't notice it unless you knew what to look for; it was a thin plastic contact switch and blended neatly with the baseboard and might have been an insignificant piece of the heating apparatus. He made sure it was in the "On" position and screwed it down firmly. Then he stuffed the original wiring back into the base receptacle and screwed the faceplate into place. The bug was now functioning as it had functioned before; but a nudge of a man's heel against the newly installed switch by the door would disconnect it and another nudge would switch it on again.

They resumed the search. There was another wireless bug in the junior partner's office and a second wired mike in the receptionist's foyer; they left these intact. At 7:10 they began to go through Gillespie's desk drawers and at 7:30 they gave it up and left the office. Homer locked the door and they put the Yale keys back in the attaché case and walked toward the elevator. "We'll have to sign out, of course. Dream up a plausible name. We were visiting the Johnson Greeting Card Company."

They waited for the elevator to come. Mathieson said, "Thanks. That was a beautiful job."

"You going to tell me how it's supposed to work?"

"Afterward."

"Why not now?"

Mathieson said, "Maybe I'm just paranoid. A secret's only a secret as long as one person knows it. But you can see how it's going to work—you wired it yourself."

"All I can see is, you expect something to be said in that office, and you want it heard by Ezio Martin but not by federal agents. I don't get much out of that."

"Are you sure? Think about it."

They went down and signed out; they walked to the car and got in. Homer put the key in the ignition but didn't turn it; he was scowling. Finally he shook his head. "No. I don't get to first base."

"Good. If you can't figure it out then Bradleigh won't figure it out either. He'll know his bug's been tampered with, but he won't know why."

"Sometimes you're a pain in the ass, you know that?"

"I hope I am," Mathieson said.

2

He made the phone call at 10:30 in the morning from a pay phone in the lobby of the Hay Adams. "Is Mr. Gillespie in?"

"Who's calling please?"

"This is Walter Benson. From Oklahoma."

"I'll see if he's in . . ."

He waited, nervously impatient. He'd rehearsed it endlessly.

"Hello?"

"Mr. Gillespie?"

"Yes. Who's this?"

"I gave your secretary the name Walter Benson."

"I know you did. Who are you?"

"Actually my name is Robert Zeck but it won't mean anything to you—I'm sure you haven't heard of me." He made his voice a fruity tenor, lilting and supercilious. "I happen to have come across some items I believe would interest you."

"Yes?"

"Let me mention three names to you. Edward Merle. John Fusco. Philip Draper."

"Never heard of them. What's this all——"

"Naturally you haven't heard of them. I really rather dislike telephones, I'm sure you understand—perhaps I could drop by your office for a little chat?"

"Where are you?"

"Not far from your office. I can be there in half an hour."

"I'll be here."

He went into the coffee shop and dawdled over a cup of tea and a newspaper: partly to calm his nerves and partly because it wouldn't hurt Gillespie to stew a while. Then he went into the men's room and inspected his disguise in the mirror. It was nothing radical. The padding under his newly bought suit added the appearance of twenty pounds to his weight. The cotton wads between upper gums and cheeks broadened his face. The bleach—a rinse that could be washed out immediately—made his hair and moustache a dirty tawny blond. The glasses with black plastic frames lent pedantic seriousness and further obscured the rectangular structure of his face. Finally there were the rings—six gaudy big rings on the fingers of both hands. The sort of thing that would be remembered at the expense of other detail. The suit was an ill-cut gray pinstripe, the tie was something with dreary red-and-black diagonal stripes. The overall appearance was that of a weary civil servant.

At five minutes to eleven he left the hotel and walked to the taxi rank.

3

When he left the elevator on the seventh floor he pressed his elbow in against the hard weight of the .38 under his jacket. If the scheme worked he wouldn't need it, but Gillespie was unpredictable and it might take a show of arms.

The receptionist took him back through the partition and he trailed along as though he hadn't seen the place before. She showed him into the corner office and disengaged herself while Gillespie rose to his feet.

Gillespie was taller than he'd thought.

"Mr. Zeck." The voice and eyes were guarded.

An attack of nerves stopped him just inside the door. He cleared his throat and pushed his voice into the higher register. "Nice office. Very nice, yes." He bobbed his eyes around the room, feigned a minor loss of equilibrium and pressed the side of his shoe firmly against the switch that disconnected Bradleigh's microphone.

He pushed the door shut and stepped forward, contriving a nervous smile.

"What's this all about?"

"Let's be circumspect." He stared whimsically through his

glasses at a point a yard above Gillespie's head. "You're really quite well fixed here, aren't you."

Gillespie sidestepped to sit down and the movement brought his feet in view under the desk: He was wearing platform shoes. That explained it. Yesterday on the street Mathieson had seen him only at a distance. A short man who wanted to be tall.

Mathieson flashed a courteous unconvincing smile. He felt no pity at all: He'd thought he might but Gillespie's sharp arrogant face made such an emotion impossible. He felt a sort of pleasure. "Robert Zeck is not my name, of course."

"I'm busy, Mr. Zeck."

"I won't take long. May I sit down?"

Gillespie jerked his head toward a chair. Mathieson lowered himself and crossed his legs and flashed an unconvincing smile. "As you know, the bureaucracy works in mysterious ways its blunders to perform. Somehow even the most secret of secrets has a way of being filed away in quintuplicate. I came across your name recently on a printout from a government computer."

"My name?"

"In connection with certain reports turned in by the Witness Security Program office."

If Gillespie was surprised he didn't show it. "Do you work for the government?"

"It doesn't matter who I work for. At the moment I'm working for myself—that's all you need to know. I may be working for you, for that matter."

"For me?"

"I'm doing you a service, Mr. Gillespie. The printout had to do with confidential informants—CIs as we call them."

"I don't see what that's got to do with me."

"Normally the identities of CIs aren't put in writing. The identity of the informant usually is a private matter between him and his contact. Now and then in an excess of bureaucratic zeal the government agent makes the mistake of reporting not only the information but its source."

"I'm losing patience fast, Mr. Zeck."

"I doubt that. I've got you over a barrel."

Gillespie's laugh was a cruel snort.

Mathieson kept his voice pitched high. "A few months ago you extorted information from a secretary in the Witness Security office. She gave you the current names and addresses of four men—Merle, Benson, Fusco and Draper. You passed that information on to your clients, Frank Pastor and Ezio Martin."

"You're out of your mind."

"The Witness Security office discovered the leak. The secretary was taken into custody and persuaded to talk. Naturally she gave them your name."

"She lied, then."

"Why? Because you'd never told her your real name? It happens she took the precaution of noting down the license number of that red Thunderbird of yours. Then she identified your photograph. You know we'd get this done a lot faster if you'd stop interrupting me with pointless denials."

"Say what you came to say."

"The next step is an assumption, I admit. I can't prove it but I assume you must have realized how risky your situation was. As soon as you got the information from the secretary and passed it on to your clients, you became a member of a conspiracy. An accessory to attempted murder."

"That's a crock. I never——"

"Well you may have had some other reason, I admit that. If so, I don't know what it was. In any case I do know what happened. You had to protect yourself in case anything went wrong. Something did go wrong, of course—the secretary was arrested and she incriminated you. But you'd already prepared for that. You'd already made a clandestine contact with government agents."

"I *what?*"

"It's all on the computer printout, Mr. Gillespie. You made a deal with the government—you talked. Information in return for your own immunity. That explains why you haven't been arrested, of course."

"You're out of your mind." Gillespie's voice climbed.

"You said that before." Mathieson smiled imperturbably. Inside he felt a chilled satisfaction: It was working. Gillespie had taken the hook. "The state of my sanity is beside the point."

"You're not going to——"

"I'm going to talk and you're going to listen. You gave information to the government. Tipped off by you, the government was able to hide three of the four intended victims before Frank Pastor's killers could reach them. How else could the government have acted so fast, if you hadn't given them advance warning? They didn't even arrest the secretary until several days later. The information couldn't have come from her. It came from you."

"The hell it did. There was an attack on Benson and they put two and two together, that's all. Nobody tipped them to anything."

"I see where you'd have to take that position. But it won't hold up."

"I've never contacted anybody in that office. I never gave information about anything to anybody. I don't know where you got——"

"Your information was too late to protect Benson but it gave them time to hide the other three men. Now the field agents file weekly reports on these cases. One of those reports drew my attention. I happened to retrieve it in a batch of printouts that had to do with a computer audit. I saw the report and the significance of it was obvious. It states that you came forward privately to a government agent and told him the whole story. You're pinned like a butterfly, you know."

"You're stark raving bananas."

"Look at it this way. If that report should ever be shown to Frank Pastor or Ezio Martin, what do you suppose would happen to you?"

"Wait a minute. There's no such report and you know it."

"Not now there isn't. I agree. I erased your name from the memory bank of the computer. I substituted the phrase 'confidential informant' wherever your name appeared in the printout of that report. Do you understand now?"

"I understand that you're a——"

"I've still got two tapes of the original printout. One copy is in my possession. I don't have it here with me but I can lay my hands on it. The second copy is in a sealed envelope in the custody of a disinterested party. He has instructions to mail the tape to Frank Pastor if anything should happen to me."

"What kind of slimy game is this? What are you——"

"To put it simply, blackmail."

"You bastard."

"I've got evidence that can destroy you, Gillespie. If I put it in Pastor's hands you're a dead man. I'm willing to sell you the evidence. It's a simple straightforward proposition."

"It's a fucking lie. I never informed on——"

"The computer says you did. Computers don't lie. Now shall we discuss terms?"

"I'm not discussing anything."

"That's shortsighted."

"The whole thing's a fucking lie."

"Why should the agency lie about it?"

Gillespie squinted shrewdly at him. "You're one of them."

"One of what?"

"Corcoran and Bradleigh. One of that outfit."

"The Witness Security Program? No, I'm afraid not. Not my department at all."

"Sure you are. They sent you up here with this load of shit. It was supposed to scare me into spilling my guts."

"If you doubt the tape exists I'll be happy to make a copy of it and send it to you."

"If there's a tape it's a phony. It doesn't prove a thing."

"Let's go over this again. First, if you didn't inform, then how did the government know Merle and Fusco and Draper were in danger? Second, since the secretary implicated you months ago, why weren't you arrested? Your freedom alone is persuasive evidence that the tape isn't a fake."

"It's a fucking frame. I don't know whose idea this was, but by God——"

"The tapes will cost you one hundred thousand dollars. In cash. Small unmarked untraceable currency. Random serial numbers. When the money's in my hands I'll deliver both copies of the tape to you. Otherwise I send one copy to Frank Pastor and one copy to Ezio Martin."

Mathieson stood up. He moved quickly to the door.

Gillespie slowly rose from his chair. He stared at Mathieson with no expression at all on his sharp features. Mathieson turned brightly, pressing his foot against the switch, activating Bradleigh's microphone. "I'll be in touch in a day or two. Think it over and let me know how you want to proceed. It's up to you. I have every confidence you'll do the right thing."

Gillespie didn't say a word. Mathieson opened the door, went through it and pulled it shut behind him.

By the time he reached the elevator he was shaking badly and the sweat burst from his pores, but he had a savage sense of triumph.

CHAPTER TWENTY

Washington, D.C.: 4 October

1

GILLESPIE STEWED FOR HALF AN HOUR. THE RECEPTIONIST announced the arrival of a client; Gillespie said, "I've got to make a call. You'll have to ask him to wait." Then he picked up the private line. He put the coded card into the phone and let it dial for him.

"Bellamy Security, may I help you?"

"C. K. Gillespie. Let me talk to Ernie."

"I'll see if he's in, Mr. Gillespie."

"You do that. It's important, honey."

"Yes, sir. Hold on a minute please."

In a moment she was back: "I have Mr. Guffin for you now."

Ernie's voice was coarse; you kept wishing he'd clear his throat. "Get off the line, Mary Lou." Gillespie heard the click. "What can I do for you, counselor?"

"There was a man in my office about thirty-five minutes ago. Gave his name as Robert Zeck. Some kind of government computer technician—says he does audits on computerized files."

"What do you want about him?"

"Robert Zeck's a phony name. I want to find out who he is."

"Anything to go on?"

"Blond hair. Blond moustache, no beard. Maybe five feet eleven but he's stooped, he might be six one if he stood up straight. A hundred and ninety, two hundred pounds. Wears glasses with black frames and big rings on most of his fingers."

"What was he wearing?"

"Gray suit, pinstripe. Not expensive. Off the peg. Desk type —junior-grade bureaucrat. He may be a fag, the way he talks."

"Computer auditor. They're a fairly rare breed, counselor. Shouldn't take too long."

"I've got his voice on tape if you want it."

"First we'll try the physical description. If we have to trot around with a cassette asking people do they recognize this voice, it could take forever."

"Anyway I'd have to edit the tape before you used it."

"Yeah. What's your beef with him?"

"Just find him, all right?"

"Do my best, counselor."

"Do it fast. Spend all the money you have to."

"OK. You want daily reports?"

"Daily reports shit, Ernie, I want him turned up this afternoon."

"Sure you do. I'll call you when I get something. It may be today, it may be next week. You know how these things go."

"Push it, Ernie."

He cradled the phone and ran fingers back through his hair. "Shit."

Then he reached for the intercom. "Send him in now."

The rest of the morning was hell. His temper kept rising; he couldn't concentrate on the work. At lunchtime he stayed in the office in case Ernie should call back. By two o'clock he was pacing the office. He went to the interphone: "That four o'clock appointment. Call him and cancel it if you can—make it Monday."

"You're going out?"

"No." He switched it off.

He rewound the tape and played it back. It didn't tell him anything new. He took the spool off and put a fresh one on the machine; he put the tape in his pocket. *This thing could be dynamite.*

At three he couldn't stand it. He rang Bellamy's. "Where the hell's Ernie Guffin?"

"Why he's in his office, Mr. Gillespie. I'll connect you right away."

"Counselor?"

"Ernie, where the hell are you? I give you a dead-simple job and I don't hear a——"

"He's not an auditor, counselor. We got that in two hours flat. He might be a computer technician, service type, programmer, anything. We've had to widen the thing and it's likely to take a while. I'm sorry but that's the way it is. All I can tell you, I'll call you the minute we turn up anything."

When he hung up he scowled at the telephone. Not an auditor. Who the hell was the guy, then?

He waited until six but there was no call. He got the red car out of the garage and headed home but he realized he hadn't had lunch—his stomach was growling; he stopped in a Chinese place and ate a quick meal without tasting it.

When he drove up the avenue toward his apartment house he saw them sitting in a green hardtop right across the street from the entrance. He recognized the driver right away—the man had brought messages from Ezio Martin a few times.

They hadn't seen him; he was sure of it. He turned off a block early and went back through side streets toward the center of the city. He was shaking.

He pulled over and parked. It was a slum street off Fourteenth Street Northwest. He ignored the black kids playing on the sidewalk. He had to think. He slid down in the seat and leaned back against the headrest and closed his eyes but that wasn't any good. He started it up again and drove aimlessly.

They were waiting for him. What for? An innocent message? Perhaps. Two of them in the car. It didn't take two men to deliver a message.

Dynamite blows up in my office and nine hours later two guys are waiting for me.

The office. The answer had to be there.

He found a meter on the street; it was after seven and he didn't have to put a dime into it; he signed in at the security man's ledger and went up to the seventh floor knowing what he would find and hoping he wouldn't find it.

In his office he tore things apart methodically. He wasn't expert but he had a feeling he'd know it when he saw it. He opened the drawers and felt their bottoms. He got down flat on his back and inspected the undersides of the furniture. He unscrewed light bulbs. Then he took the desk radio apart. He inspected his own tape recorder to make sure no extra wires led away from it. Then it occurred to him to check the telephones. He started unscrewing mouthpieces and earpieces. Nothing there; he unscrewed the bottoms and opened the phones up.

He found it taped to the plastic inside the second phone. It looked a little like the kind of flat disk battery he used in his electric wristwatch but it had tiny grille holes and he knew what that meant.

He sagged back into the swivel chair. That was it, then. Ezio. It had to be Ezio. The two men in the green hardtop—he could figure out their instructions without much difficulty.

Ezio, he thought again. The computer auditor—Robert Zeck—Ezio had sent him. A plant, to give Ezio something on tape he could take to Frank. Ezio had always hated him. And Frank would buy it. And there was no way on earth he could talk Frank out of it.

He got up slowly and walked out of the office.

CHAPTER TWENTY-ONE

New York City: 5 October

1

MATHIESON LOOKED DOWN THROUGH THE WINDOW AT THE Forty-fourth Street traffic. It was thick with empty taxis coming east from Times Square after having dropped their fares in time for the 7:30 curtains. The panes were coated with an oily grime of soot.

Behind him Diego Vasquez said, "You've left him a few choices."

"Not many."

"He may even try to pay you the blackmail money."

Roger said, "That'd be fine and dandy by me."

Mathieson said, "I hope he does."

"I doubt he'll have time," Vasquez said. "Ezio Martin was taping the whole conversation. The minute he listens to the tape, you may as well have killed Gillespie."

Mathieson turned away from the window. "Is that what you think?"

"Certainly. You're making artificial distinctions."

"I think you're wrong. Gillespie's quick enough—he'll make a run for it. He's an opportunist. He'll see he's got only one way out."

"Only one?"

"I think so. He'll go to Glenn Bradleigh."

Vasquez smiled slowly. "If you're right that's a nice irony."

"He'll have to turn the bag upside down and shake it, otherwise it wouldn't be worth Bradleigh's while to give him immunity and protection."

Roger said, "By the time Gillespie stops talking there'll be enough raw meat on the floor to feed a dozen grand juries."

Vasquez took a ball-point pen from his pocket and played with it, clicking it. "Maybe—maybe. It may cause some trouble for Pastor and company. But it won't solve our problem. It doesn't cancel the threat. Oh, don't think I'm not impressed."

Vasquez sat with his legs crossed, his shoes polished, his tie neatly knotted; he looked as old-fashioned as the hotel room. It had been designed by Stanford White. "It may put Pastor off balance—then again it may only influence them to tighten security."

"That's what I want them to do. I want them to know what it feels like to know they're under attack. Not knowing where or when it's going to hit them next."

Vasquez clicked the pen. "Waste of time. They're already paranoid, by definition."

"I want them to know I'm coming."

Roger had a slow chilled smile that had thrown fear into a hundred movie villains. He drawled softly, "Now you're talkin', old horse."

A leather briefcase leaned against the base of Vasquez's chair where he'd dropped it. Vasquez opened it. "You asked for the file on George Ramiro—I assume he's your next target."

"Yes. Because he's dangerous. We don't want him behind us when we move on Pastor and Martin. What have we got on him?"

"Not a great deal. You can't expect to flush him as easily as you did Gillespie."

"No. Gillespie made it easy."

"Ramiro's not a bright man. In fact his brainlessness may make it harder to attack him. You can't be subtle with him."

"Will you stop clicking that pen?"

"Sorry." Vasquez put the pen away and opened the file folder in his lap. He set the photographs aside and scanned the typewritten pages. "Has a license—it must have cost him at least seven thousand dollars—to carry a Colt Python revolver, caliber three fifty-seven Magnum."

"A Magnum? I'll bear that in mind," Mathieson said dryly.

Vasquez flipped a page. "Seems to patronize one call girl with some regularity . . ."

"Name and address?"

"They're here but it wouldn't be a worthwhile angle of approach."

"Why not?" Roger said drowsily. "Catch him with his pants down."

"Your jokes are bad." Vasquez returned to Mathieson. "Catch him and do what? You're determined not to kill him."

Roger said, "We could have him worked over by experts. Break a few arms and legs."

"No. If he's beaten up he'll only call in six friends to get even for him. No. He's got to be taken right out of the game. The way Gillespie was."

"Tall order. Very tall," Vasquez observed.

"He can be framed," Mathieson said. "Anybody can." He looked at his watch. "I've got to go. I'll be back in an hour."

2

When he returned to the hotel from his errand he found Homer in the room with Vasquez and Roger. Mathieson hung his coat in the hall closet and rubbed his hands together.

Roger said, "Right. Us Californians get thin-blooded. I'm still not thawed."

Vasquez didn't rise from his chair. "Homer's been talking to Nick D'Alesio."

"The reporter?"

"The same," Homer said. "Very interesting guy. He knows the New York mobs as well as anybody alive outside the mobs themselves."

Mathieson opened one of the ginger ales on the room-service

tray. He scooped a handful of ice cubes into a glass. "What did you find out?"

"First you ought to know what I had to give him in trade. Detectives and reporters—we're all in the same business, you know. Information."

"So?"

"I gave him a nice scoop. Told him how the Benson shooting in Oklahoma and the bomb attack on your house in California were connected."

Mathieson looked at him sharply. "How much did you tell him?"

"I didn't tell him anything that Pastor doesn't already know. Relax. I didn't say anything about Gillespie. The only time your name was mentioned was in connection with the explosion in Sherman Oaks and the sniper on the motorcycle. It's a bit of news that hasn't been reported anywhere else. He'll have to attribute it to an informed source or something like that. I told him he couldn't use my name."

Vasquez said, "But don't be surprised if you see the name Edward Merle in the newspapers tomorrow. They'll probably go back into the morgue files to dig up a summary of your testimony against Pastor."

Mathieson said wryly, "I always like to see my name in the papers. OK, what did you get in return?"

"A lot of detail about Pastor and Martin. I'll type up my notes in the morning."

"What about George Ramiro?"

"A little. Not very much. He's not a complicated sort. Too stupid to be devious."

Roger said, "He got many friends?"

"Not many. Mostly he cares about showing off his new Cadillac and smoking Cuban cigars and driving his big power boat around Long Island Sound. A typical suburban citizen."

"He and his wife live on the same premises with the Pastors?"

"Yes. Three sets of premises. In Manhattan they're in the Park Avenue building, same floor. Next door apartment. In Brooklyn it's a semidetached, one of those big old Victorian houses that go for a quarter of a million nowadays. The Ramiros have the top floor. Summers they all go out on Long Island. The Ramiros live in the gatehouse."

"Well we're not concerned with what they do in the summertime."

Vasquez said, "Perhaps what we need to know is who his enemies are."

"He's rubbed a lot of people the wrong way. It might be a long list."

"I'm talking about serious enemies," Mathieson said.

"D'Alesio didn't mention anything specific. Ramiro's not too well liked—but mortal enemies? No, I pass."

"We may have to do some excavating," Vasquez said.

Mathieson shook his head. "Take too much time."

Vasquez said, "We've got to find an opening, haven't we. If it takes time then it takes time."

"If we can't find one we'll make one."

"How?"

Mathieson poured more ginger ale. "He's a man who's obviously done a few things that must make him nervous in the middle of the night."

Roger said, "You'd spend half of forever rooting them out."

"We don't need to. All we need is the assumption that something exists that might cause trouble for him if word of it leaked out to other hoodlums. Something that might even turn Frank Pastor against him."

Homer said, "He seems to be reasonably loyal. Anyway he's married into the family. He wouldn't pull anything that would make Pastor come down hard on him."

"Somewhere along the line he's probably slipped a little off the top for himself," Mathieson said. "That's all it needs —just the wedge of something that could make him feel guilty. Or nervous. Anyhow we'll want an update on Ramiro's movements. Find his patterns—then we'll move."

Mathieson swabbed his dry throat with ginger ale; he was trying not to think about Jan, the way she'd sounded on the phone when he'd called her. He tried to force her out of his mind. "Roger, how'd you get into the hotel without being recognized?"

"Fake beard and motorcycle shades."

Homer said, "His own mother wouldn't know him. He looks like a forty-year-old hippie."

"As long as he doesn't talk," Vasquez said. "The voice is a dead giveaway."

Mathieson said, "Anything you can do about that? Fake an English accent or anything?"

"I reckon not. It's the only way I know how to talk."

"I thought you were an actor."

"Old horse, *I* never said I was." But then Roger screwed up his outdoor eyes in concentration. "But oi suppews oi moight be able to troy. It's me dewty, innit?"

"That's the worst Cary Grant imitation I ever heard," Homer said.

Mathieson said, "But it didn't sound like Roger Gilfillan, did it. Can you sustain that accent?"

"If oi must, old chep, but I should think it could become bloody tiahsome." Roger lapsed into prairie twang. "What you fixin' to have me do?"

"We're going to need some movie equipment. Sixteen millimeter, I'd think."

"Silent or sound?"

"Sound. Preferably sound-on-film. We won't want to have to monkey around with a separate tape-recording system."

"What's it for?"

"We'll get to that," Mathieson said. "What we need is a sound camera, a microphone, color film—the new fast kind that can be used indoors under ordinary artificial light. We'll need a projector and a screen. Now we'll want the most compact equipment that's available. Oh, and a tripod camera mount."

"What kind of lenses?"

"A normal zoom should do it. We don't need telephoto."

"How fast you want it?"

"No hurry. We've got other things to take care of first."

"Old horse, that ain't much of a chore. Anybody could do it."

"I've watched you on the set, Roger. The other actors play poker and swap lies. You hang around the cameramen and the sound engineers every chance you get. You're probably more of an expert than they are by now. This equipment has got to work well and it's got to be manned by a professional. You're in charge of it."

Vasquez said, "What's the next step?"

"Glenn Bradleigh," Mathieson said.

CHAPTER TWENTY-TWO

New York City: 7 October

1

ANNA WAS LATE GETTING BACK TO THE PARK AVENUE apartment. In her euphoria she nearly forgot to pay the taxi driver. The doorman's surly face changed when he opened the door for her: She decided it must be the infectiousness of her radiance. It was the first time she'd ever seen a real smile on his face.

She stopped on the curb and looked up. It was one of those rare evenings: the sky autumn-clear, the Park Avenue glass towers sharply etched against the blue. Dry and cool and beautiful.

After a solitary elevator ride she arrived at the apartment and rang the bell; her key wouldn't work—the police bar would be in place. She glanced up at the lens of the closed-circuit camera.

It wasn't Frank who opened the door; it was Sandy, her hair in curlers, belted into a terrycloth robe. "Hi."

"Hi yourself. How's school?"

"You always ask me that." Sandy closed the door and slammed the police bar across it and went toward the hallway that went back to the girls' rooms. "And I always say the same thing. It was all right. It was school. What can you say about school?"

"Dad home?"

"In there." Sandy pointed toward the study. The door was closed.

"Alone?"

"Ezio's here." She made a face. "I'm watching the *Star Trek* rerun and I've got to get back under the dryer, OK?"

"Get it combed out in time for dinner."

"Sure, sure." Sandy disappeared on the run.

She knocked. When she heard Frank's voice she went in.

Ezio gave her a glance and a nod; he didn't rise from his chair. Frank was at the desk. She went around it and kissed him.

Frank said, "You're in a good mood."

"I'm glad you noticed. You two look like the building just fell down around your ankles."

"It did. Gillespie hasn't turned up."

She went toward the recliner chair, peeling off her gloves. "He's scared. He's hiding somewhere."

"Scared for sure," Ezio said. "He didn't even go home for his toothbrush that night."

The jammer's light glowed red. The plastic cover was on the pool table and Ezio's topcoat was thrown across it. She put her gloves neatly in her lap. Narrow bands of sunlight fell through the Venetian blinds of the south window.

Frank told her, "Ernie Guffin still hasn't got a make on——"

"Ernie who?"

"The detective in Washington," Ezio explained. "He still hasn't got a make on Robert Zeck. Nobody meets the description. We told you all this before, Anna."

"There's been a lot going on," she said.

Ezio turned toward Frank. "You listen to the tape again?"

"Three times."

"So what do you think?"

"Anna thinks Zeck's a federal."

Ezio blinked. "And what do you think?"

"It's as good a guess as any. If Zeck didn't get that stuff off a computer like he said he did, then where'd he get it? He had to get it officially. And that makes him a fed."

"Beats shit out of me," Ezio said.

"Mind your language." Frank said it gently. Anna covered a smile with her hand; Frank winked at her.

Frank said, "C.K. probably found the microphones, he found out the office was bugged. He figures you had him bugged, Ezio, he knows I must have heard the tape. That's why he disappeared. He's afraid maybe I'll believe this Zeck stuff."

"You mean you don't believe it?"

"I don't know. I'll tell you this much. If C.K.'s straight with us and if he uses his head, what he'll do, he'll think it over and then he'll come to me. He's putting himself in my hands because he knows I'm a fair guy and I'll give him a hearing and all that baloney. He comes in, he shows a white flag, he tells me Zeck was lying. Then he says, 'Look, Frank, here's how we prove who's telling the truth. This guy Zeck, he'll come back to my office or he'll telephone and tell me how to deliver that hundred kay, the payoff money.' That's when we set a trap and we grab Zeck when he comes for the money. We find out the truth from Zeck and that lets C.K. off the hook. That's what C.K. will do if he's using his head."

Ezio said, "That's supposing Charlie's been on the level with us."

Anna said, "Even if he has, I wouldn't count on him doing that. He knows how we work. He's not going to take the chance of walking in here. He's never had much courage."

Ezio said, "That's for sure. Plenty of brains and oily as hell but no guts at all, you ask me."

Frank said, "Anna's got something there. If he's too scared to come to us there's only one other place he could go."

She said, "That's what worries me."

"You mean the feds," Ezio said. "Spill his guts."

"It could put us in a very tough place. He knows a lot."

"He's a lawyer," Ezio pointed out. "He can't spill confidential information."

"Can't he? Who's going to stop him?"

"Even if he does, they can't use anything in court. Privileged communications."

Anna said, "He could tell them what rocks to start looking under. That could be trouble enough."

"I think," Frank said, "I think we pay attention to what Anna says here, Ezio. I think maybe you ought to sort things out and see what tracks we can start covering. Anything that C.K. had a piece of, anything he could tie us to. You may have to burn some papers and things. It may force us to cancel some deals."

"We've sweated these things out before," Ezio said. "I guess we can do it again this time. But I'd rather cancel Charlie Gillespie, myself."

"If you can find him. But you haven't been finding people too well lately."

"We're working hard on that, Frank, you know we are."

"Then show me some results."

"We're looking for needles in haystacks."

Frank brooded at the desk top. "I know you are."

2

They watched a half hour of the Carson show and then Frank reached for the remote switch on the bedside table and turned it off. "Too many goddamn commercials."

She stretched and smiled drowsily. Frank rubbed the skin on top of his head; then he placed both hands over it and leaned back against the pillows. "I've got trouble you know."

"We'll get through it. We always have."

"Big trouble. Word gets around that you're losing your grip, that's the biggest trouble you can have. Too many things slipping through my fingers, Anna. First Merle and those others. Now this C. K. Gillespie mess."

His head swiveled under his hands. He looked down at her.

"We're alive, Frank. We've got a lot of good things."

"That could end real sudden. Word gets around, old Frank Pastor spent too much time in the slammer, he got softened up, he's lost his edge. They start moving in on you like hyenas. You start that kind of a fight, you don't win it."

"Then do something spectacular to take their minds off it. To convince them you're still the top."

"Like what?"

She said, "I was in the doctor's office, in the waiting room.

I was reading the Sunday *Times*. You know in the main news section they have that follow-up column about——"

"What were you doing in a doctor's office?"

"Finding out about the tests."

"So you've been home six hours and you haven't told me yet?"

"The mood you've been in——"

"Anna, quit sneaking around behind me. What did the son of a bitch tell you?"

"He told me I'm pregnant."

"Jesus fucking H. Christ."

3

He romped up out of the bed and stood with his arms akimbo and his face thrust out toward her and a mock-ferocious scowl. "She comes home, she spends the whole night grinning the place up like she swallowed the canary, she doesn't say a fucking word to the old man about it. Jesus fucking H. Christ. You're going to have a kid?"

"We're going to have a kid."

"I'll be a son of a bitch." He stared at her. He didn't even blink.

He held the pose so long that her eyes widened with fear. "Frank, you're not sore at me. We talked about it months ago and you agreed I could go off the pill. You said you wanted a son. Don't be angry with——"

"Crazy little woman. You crazy woman." He put one knee on the bed and pulled her up and engulfed her, laughing in his throat.

"Damn you, Frank." Her voice was muffled against his chest.

He searched her face. "He didn't say anything about complications or anything?"

"Not a word."

"Well a man my age——"

"Men twice your age become fathers."

"A kid—did he say it's a boy?"

"It's too early."

"I thought they had ways."

"We'll have to wait a little while longer. The baby's not due till May."

"Son of a bitch." He bounded off the bed, looking for his slippers. "Celebrate," he said; then he stopped. "Can you drink? I mean——"

"I want a great big Scotch on the rocks."

"You got it." He went.

They didn't switch on lights in the living room; a soft glow came in from the buildings across the avenue. She watched Frank settle down with his feet on the coffee table. He reached for his drink. "To your very good health, little Anna—the both of you."

She lifted her glass. "Frank Junior."

"Yeah." He was delighted. "Frank Junior."

"And confusion to our enemies." She drank ceremoniously. She coughed on the Scotch and put the glass down. "I was telling you about the follow-up column in the *Times*. There was a squib about some of those radicals the FBI arrested a few years ago, the ones who broke into some FBI office and stole their files and put them on a bonfire?"

"I read about that in the slammer."

"C.K. blackmailed that secretary to get the files on Merle and the other three men. You wanted those four because they were the witnesses against you."

She saw it when he made the connection. His eyes changed. "Well now—well now."

"Eleven, twelve hundred names and addresses in those files," she said. "We make a joke out of the whole Justice Department. We make chaos all over the country. We show them who's running what. Nobody ever again will work up the nerve to testify."

Frank took his feet off the table. "And for a little bonus, yeah, we collect the new files on those four gentlemen." He got to his feet and spread his arms wide. "Anna, I love you."

CHAPTER TWENTY-THREE

New York City: 10–16 October

1

HE CALLED BRADLEIGH FROM A PHONE BOOTH IN GRAND
Central Station. "How's it going, Glenn?"

Bradleigh was cool. "Where are you?"

"What difference does that make?"

"You're supposed to be acting like a good boy. Staying out
of trouble."

"I'm not in any trouble. I'm calling because I'm curious,
that's all. Any developments?"

"Curious. Are you. Well our friend Gillespie walked in."

"Walked in?"

"Just like that. Came in here with a fairly wild story . . ."
Bradleigh went on talking.

A girl outside the phone booth was staring at him. He
realized he was grinning like an imbecile. He turned away.
"I wonder what got into him."

"Do you?"

"You're a bit chilly for a man who's just scored a triumph."

"I'll tell you something, Fred. One of our bugs had been
tampered with. In Gillespie's office."

"Oh?"

"We lost the transmission on his conversation with that
computer blackmailer I mentioned."

"You're not making much sense, Glenn. You'll have to go a little slower."

"How much do you know about electronics?"

"About enough to change a light bulb when I have to. Why?"

"Whoever set Gillespie up knew about the microphones in his office."

"So?"

"You knew about them."

"I suppose I did. You did mention it to me. Has Gillespie dropped some goodies?"

"Enough to keep the FBI busy for about ten years, I imagine. We're still extracting it, still collating. It'll be a while before we're sure what we've got but it's a rich vein. It's all unsupported for now, of course. But it's the biggest break we've had since Joe Valachi turned inside out."

"Congratulations. Maybe it'll give you enough to nail Frank Pastor again."

"Sure—in five years or so after his lawyers exhaust all their delaying tactics and Pastor runs out of public officials to buy."

"You sound jaded."

"Well it's a little outside my bag you know. I just protect them. Interrogation is the FBI's job. I'd like to see Pastor put away but right now I'm not too happy about the idea of having to nursemaid C. K. Gillespie. He's not my favorite sort of client."

"Look on it as penance."

"Why the phone call?"

"Maybe I've been doing a little investigating on my own, Glenn."

"You damn fool. You bloody idiot. If you——"

"Pipe down. You're looking a gift horse in the mouth."

"What gift horse?"

"Who do you think gave Gillespie to you?"

"So it *was* you."

"I'm the computer programmer."

"You bastard."

"I'm taking them apart, Glenn . . ."

"Oh you stupid bastard. You've gone bananas."

". . . by the seams." He couldn't help the tight little smile. "And I may have some good news pretty soon for Benson and Fusco and Draper."

"What kind of news?"

"I'd rather give it to them personally."

"Nothing doing. No addresses, no phone numbers."

"I'm not asking for addresses or phone numbers. You're in touch with them, aren't you?"

"Maybe."

"You can get a phone number to each of them. That's all I'm asking."

"Shit."

"It'll be a pay phone. No bugs. No traces."

"How can I trust you now?"

"Am I going to sell them out, Glenn? Use your head. I only want to talk to them. They call me from anywhere they like—in pay phones five hundred miles from wherever they live. I'll send you a check to pay their expenses if you want. Just have them call me."

"You've got to give me more than this to go on."

"I can't. Not now. Later."

Bradleigh said, "What the hell do you think you can accomplish? You can get yourself killed, that's all."

"I could do that just by standing still and waiting for them to find me. Come on, Glenn, come on."

"What about Jan and Ronny? What about——"

"They're safe. They're fine."

He heard the exhalation of Bradleigh's breath. "Maybe I'll see what I can do. I'll ask them if they want to talk to you."

"Tell them it could save their bacon. Tell them it could mean they'll be able to come out of hiding."

"In a pig's eye."

"Who gave you Gillespie?"

"That was a fluke but don't rub it in."

"It wasn't a fluke, Glenn."

After a pause Bradleigh said, "I don't know you at all, do I?"

"I'm not a bad fellow."

"You're a fucking lunatic."

Mathieson said cheerfully, "I'll see you."

2

Ramiro was a big heavy dark cigar-chewing jowly sour-faced man at the wheel of an overshined twelve-thousand-dollar automobile. It slid in at the curb and Mathieson watched Ramiro get out, turning the fur collar of his coat up against the drizzle.

The passenger emerged from the far side of Ramiro's car— a short truncheon of a man with vanishing gray wisps of hair and a rigid coin-slot mouth.

"Vince Damico," Homer muttered by way of identification. "Manages the restaurant-linen supply business."

From the front seat of the rented Plymouth they watched Ramiro and Damico go into the restaurant.

"They eat here every Wednesday?"

"And then they go upstairs and play poker."

"It's a gambling joint?"

"No, just a friendly poker game. Lou Tonelli runs the restaurant. He hosts the game every week."

"Funny neighborhood for it. We're only a few blocks from City Hall and the courthouses."

"Well it's still the Italian neighborhood, you know."

Traffic squeezed through the narrow street and pedestrians hurried by, topcoated under umbrellas. Mathieson said, "We're likely to be here for hours."

"That's what stakeouts amount to. The thrill and adventure of detective work."

The rain frosted the windshield but he didn't switch on the wipers; it would have been a giveaway. He could see the restaurant well enough. *ANGELO'S—Fine Italian Food.* It looked expensive.

He had never been an easy victim to boredom but it was a bleak night, autumnally cold; he thrust his hands into the pockets of his topcoat and reminded himself to buy a pair of gloves.

"Vasquez wanted to be in on this, didn't he?"

"Did he say so?"

"It was a feeling I got," Mathieson said.

"He'd have liked it. But no way. Too much chance Ramiro might recognize him."

"Does Ramiro know him?"

"A lot of people recognize him. Not as recognizable as Roger Gilfillan, maybe, but a lot of people do spot him."

"I'm surprised he exposes himself to all the publicity. I'd think it would be a handicap in such a confidential business."

"Times like this, maybe. But it's celebrity that sells popcorn. Vasquez is the best-known private detective in the world. That's what brings the clients in. It's what brought you in." Homer ruminated over his slice of cold pizza. "It's you I'm worried about. Ramiro's never met you but he must have seen your photograph."

"I'm nine years older than those photographs. Don't you think the disguise works?"

"It's the same disguise you used with Gillespie, without the glasses. I don't know—I guess it'll fool him. He'll have no reason to think of connecting us with Edward Merle. I guess it's not much of a risk. But I don't like taking any risks at all when I don't have to."

"Homer, there was no way I could wait somewhere else. I've got to be in on this—I want to see his face."

"I can understand that. But you let me do the talking, understand? You must be the silent menace. Concentrate on looking like a killer."

"What does a killer look like?"

"Silence is the main thing. Don't say a single word. It'll shake him up more than anything else would. Keep your hand on the gun in your pocket."

"Don't worry about that. I haven't forgotten he carries a Magnum."

"Well we'll have to take care of that before we do anything else, won't we."

3

Finally they came out of the restaurant—Ramiro and Damico. It was half past one in the morning; the rain had stopped and

235

a cold mist flowed through the empty street. A third man came out into the street and there was some conversation among the three; then the third man embraced Damico, turned and pumped Ramiro's arm in a politician's handshake, left hand on Ramiro's elbow.

"Lou Tonelli," Homer said. "He's the ward boss down here, among other things."

Tonelli went back into the restaurant. Ramiro and Damico climbed into the Cadillac Fleetwood and after a moment its tailpipe spouted white steam.

For three blocks Homer followed without lights; then the Cadillac turned uptown on the Bowery and Homer switched on the headlights when he fed the Plymouth into the traffic. Mathieson observed how he interposed several cars between himself and the Cadillac without getting caught behind traffic lights; it looked easy but it wasn't.

Ramiro went west on Thirteenth Street, dropped Damico on University Place and went uptown again. "All right," Homer said. "He's not going home—that's what we needed to know. We've got him. He's heading for the call girl. Forty-sixth between First and Second. Now all we've got to do is get there first." He swung off Madison Avenue and they barreled across Twenty-sixth street, jouncing in the chuckholes, running an amber light and then the tag end of a red one; Homer went squealing into Third Avenue precariously and chased the staggered traffic lights northward.

There was no traffic; they made it to Forty-fifth on the single light and Homer wheeled left into the side street opposite the United Nations Building; he parked swiftly in front of a loading bay. *No Parking.* "So we get a ticket. They won't tow it away this time of night. Come on, let's move."

Mathieson got out and turned toward the corner. Homer was retrieving something from the car—it looked like a plastic bottle of detergent fluid; and he had the styrofoam coffee cup. They went quickly around the corner. Homer was pouring liquid into the cup. He tossed the detergent bottle into the mesh waste can on the corner and they strode north to Forty-sixth Street.

Mathieson said, "What's in the cup?"

"Window cleaner. Ammonia. Less drastic than acid but it does the job." They went around the corner. "Good. He's not here yet. It's that second awning—the girl's got an apartment on the seventeenth floor."

"We go in?"

"No, there's a doorman. We wait for him outside."

They posted themselves on the curb just short of the awning where they were not within the doorman's angle of view. "Which way will he come from?"

"No telling. Depends where he finds a parking space." Homer held the styrofoam cup casually. Two friends saying good-night after an evening on the town, sobering up with a cup of takeout coffee. "Keep your hand in your pocket and your mouth shut. Use the gun if you have to—*he* won't hesitate."

He curled his hand around the .38 in his pocket. "We're not here to do any shooting, Homer."

"Sometimes something goes wrong. Just stay loose and be ready to—heads up, here he is."

The big Fleetwood growled along the street seeking a place to park. There wasn't any; the car disappeared around the corner, moving slowly.

"He'll find a space somewhere. Take it easy—don't get jumpy now, for God's sake."

Mathieson looked both ways. There was no one on the street. Above them numerous windows were still alight. Up at the farther intersection a woman with a heavy shopping bag walked across on Second Avenue. Eddies of mist curled like steam on the wet black surface of the street. The canvas awning dripped.

A taxi cruised past, empty, dome-signal alight; it paused hopefully but Homer shook his head and the taxi drove on. Then a pedestrian appeared at the corner of First Avenue and turned into the street, coming toward them—wide shoulders, heavy bulk, coat flapping: George Ramiro.

Homer said, "We're having a conversation, OK? I just told you a joke. You're a little drunk."

Mathieson uttered a sharp bark of laughter. It sounded unconvincing to him but he said, "Hey that's a pretty good one," his voice sounding too loud and too forced. He turned without hurry, facing Homer, his shoulder to the approaching pedestrian. He could see Ramiro out of the corner of his eye—walking steadily, unafraid, unalarmed; but his right hand stayed in his coat pocket and with it, Mathieson knew, there had to be the .357 Magnum.

As Ramiro approached, Homer gestured with the coffee cup. "So I says to him, 'Billy, the day she takes her pants down for you is the day whales start flying.' "

Ramiro was three paces away and Homer turned abruptly. "George? Hey, that you, George?"

It brought Ramiro's head around and that was when Homer flung the contents of the styrofoam cup in his face.

4

When the ammonia hit his eyes Ramiro brought both hands to his face and cried out, lurching back against the brick wall. Homer was on top of him instantly, dropping the cup, pinning Ramiro to the wall. Mathieson darted in; fumbled in Ramiro's coat pocket; found the Magnum and relieved him of it. It took no more than three seconds. He slipped the Magnum into his own pocket and Homer was pressing a handkerchief into Ramiro's hand. "Here, wipe yourself off."

Ramiro whimpered and clawed at his face. Blinded and in excruciating pain he was completely without fight. Homer batted Ramiro's arms away and wiped his eyes with the handkerchief. "Come on, it's only a little window cleaner."

"What the hell——"

"Grab an arm," Homer said.

Supporting Ramiro like a drunk between them they walked him toward the corner. He was in enough pain to disable him. They walked him around the corner and the Cadillac was just up the block.

They propped him against the back door of the car. "Keys," Homer said. Mathieson went into Ramiro's pockets again.

Ramiro was getting his breath. "I can't see . . ."

"Take it easy, George, you'll be all right in a minute."

Mathieson unlocked the car door and reached inside to pull up the knob of the back door. They got it open and shoved Ramiro into the back seat. Mathieson got into the front seat and took out the Magnum and held it against the headrest, casually aimed at Ramiro's belly.

Homer pushed Ramiro across the seat and got in beside him. The doors chunked shut.

The UN street lamps were bright; they threw reflected illumination against Ramiro's features. He clutched the handkerchief and scrubbed at his eyes. "Jesus I'm blind—I can't see. You fuckin' bastards."

Homer said, "I'm going to put some drops in your eyes; it won't hurt you. Hold your head back now."

"Fuckin' bastards." But he was still in terrible pain and he didn't fight it when Homer shoved his head back and squeezed fluid from the little plastic bottle into the inside corners of his eyes.

"Now blink. Wash them out."

Ramiro straightened slowly, blinking like a fish. He squinted, watery-eyed, trying to hold them open, lids fluttering like moths' wings.

"Settle down, George, just take it easy. We'll wait while you get your wind."

"Jesus. Jesus God that hurts. Oh God you son of a bitches."

"Just let them wash themselves out now, that's a good boy."

The inside of the car smelled of the stale sweat of habitual garlic eaters. Ramiro's breath was like the panting of an overheated dog. Mathieson shifted his grip on the heavy Magnum. If it were fired inside the car it would deafen them all. He had no intention of firing it but it made an impressive prop—especially to Ramiro who doubtless had seen the results it could effect.

Ramiro threw his head back along the rear-window platform. He took in a deep breath that swelled his chest and stomach; he let it out and shook his head violently as if to clear it. He wiped at his eyes again and began to peer narrowly through his trembling inflamed lids. "Yeah. OK, OK. I still can't see too good."

"It'll come back."

"What the hell you guys want?"

Homer said, "It could have been acid, George. It was supposed to be acid."

"Supposed to be." Ramiro still wasn't tracking too well.

"Put your hands in your lap and keep them there. It won't do your eyes any good to keep rubbing them."

"Aagh." Ramiro clawed at his face again.

Homer batted his arms down. "Now keep them in your lap. Do as you're told, George. You might live a little longer."

Ramiro blinked at the Magnum. Mathieson curled his thumb over its hammer and drew it back slowly. The series of sharp clicks seemed very loud.

"Jesus. Take it easy with that thing."

"You paying attention now, George?"

"What the fuck do you want?"

Mathieson showed him a slow cold smile. The gun in his hand was trained motionlessly on Ramiro.

Homer said, "You listening now?"

"I'm listening. Who the fuck are you guys? Do I know you?"

"No. We're imported. You don't know us."

"Imported by who? For what?"

"To waste you, George."

"To what?"

"A job of work. A hit, you know how it goes."

"Me?"

"You're George Ramiro, ain't you?"

"You must have the wrong George Ramiro, man."

"No, I guess not. It's supposed to be an acid job, George."

"What the fuck for?"

"Don't ask me."

"Who's paying you guys?"

"Even if we knew that, we'd hardly tell you. Would we."

"Well what the fuck do you want?"

"A few kays. Money, man. You know."

Ramiro's face was screwed up; he kept trying to look at them but his eyes kept squinting shut.

"See if you can follow this, George. You listening to me?"

"Yeah, yeah."

"The man gives us a down payment on you. You follow?"

"Yeah——"

"We finish the job, we're supposed to get another five kay. Between us. Twenty-five hundred apiece. Capish?"

"I hear you."

"There's talk you're a pretty rich guy, George."

"I ain't poor."

"No, I wouldn't think so. What'd this car set you back? And that boat out on the Island—fifty-two-foot power cruiser, right? Now a guy like you, comes from some foreign country someplace, he probably don't trust banks a whole lot. Probably keeps a good stash someplace. In cash. I'm right, George?"

"What do you want from me?"

"Well, here's the thing. George, you're worth five kay to us dead. Now we figure maybe you want to tell us how much you're worth to us alive."

"Huh?"

"Maybe you scratch up enough cash, George, we let you live. You understand what I'm saying?"

Ramiro peered at him through the slits of his swollen eyes. In his lap his square fingers were at war. He had been in pain; now he was afraid. Mathieson could smell the rank sweat of it.

Homer said, "We're offering you a rare opportunity, George. All we're asking in return is a little grease. We're asking for your help, see?"

"You got a strange way of asking." Ramiro glanced at the Magnum.

Homer reached out suddenly, grabbed the middle finger of Ramiro's hand and bent it back hard. Ramiro shouted and reared back in pain, clutching his hand protectively.

Mathieson moved the revolver slightly—just enough movement to draw Ramiro's eye. When Ramiro looked balefully at him, Mathieson smiled.

Homer picked at his scalp and studied his fingernail. "You see how it is, George."

"How much you want?"

"Twenty-five kay."

"Twenty-five thousand dollars?"

"Apiece, George. Each. Per person. Capish? Adds up to fifty kay if you got a slow head for figures. Fifty kay, George. You think your life's worth that much?"

"Where the fuck you think I'm going to lay my hands on fifty thousand cash this time of night?"

"You got a stash, ain't you?"

"Well I——"

"You take us to the stash, George. Easy."

"And I hand it over to you and then you turn me loose? Yeah, sure."

"George, we might be lying about that. We might knock over your stash and then waste you anyway. That's what you're thinking, isn't it." Homer turned his cold smile toward Mathieson. "You see, Al, you see how he's thinking."

Mathieson neither smiled nor spoke. He dropped the muzzle of the Magnum half an inch and centered it on Ramiro's heart.

Ramiro swallowed spasmically. Homer said, "The thing you can know for sure is we'll waste you right here if you don't turn the stash. You die here for certain or you take a chance we're straight. What do you want, George?"

"Look, how do I know——"

"George, I'll spell it out crystal clear. Now you pay attention. Al and me, we're supposed to come into town tomorrow night and waste you with acid and a knife. That's what the contract says. Tomorrow night. So we got into New York a day, two days earlier than we're supposed to. We noodged around a little, we find out George Ramiro's a big important rich guy. We can use a side profit on this deal. You see how it goes? What we do, we go with you to your stash tonight. We take our fifty kay. Anything over fifty kay you got in that stash, that's yours to keep. You take it with you. We all three of us go straight from your stash to the John F. Kennedy Airport. You following this, George?"

"I hear you talking."

"We don't care where you go. Just so it's a long way out of this country. Europe, Africa, Hong Kong. That's up to you. You pick your spot, you buy the ticket. You got a passport?"

"Yeah."

"With your stash?"

"Where else?"

"OK, OK. We walk you to the airplane and we watch you take off. Then tomorrow night Al and me, we pretend like we've just arrived, you know, in New York to take care of this contract on you, and we ask around and we find out, Jesus Christ, the guy left town. So we snoop around a little, we play private eye, we find out you bought a ticket to Europe. We report back to our contact. I mean the man didn't pay us to go all the way to Europe or Africa or Hong Kong, did he."

"What man? Who's the man?"

"Somebody very high up. That's all we know. Now maybe the man tells us the contract is off, or maybe the man hires somebody else to chase you around Europe, or maybe the man pays us extra bread to go find you and waste you. I can't say what'll happen, George. It'll be up to you to keep your head down because God knows who might come looking for you. We ain't writing guarantees on you—this ain't the Prudential Life Insurance Company. We're just giving you a head start."

"I see that."

"For fifty kay."

"I ain't got no fifty kay in my stash."

"What've you got in it?"

Ramiro rubbed his eyes and finally said with infinite disgust, "Short of forty. About thirty-eight five."

"Thirty-eight five. Al, what do you say?"

Mathieson lifted one shoulder—a shrug of contempt.

"I think maybe Al wants to waste you, George."

"Then go ahead and shoot. I knew it wasn't my night. Took a bath in poker. You want to turn my pockets out? I got maybe fifty dollars left."

"Thirty-eight five, that's a funny number. How come, George?"

"I figured I'd build it up to forty and leave it at that. I had to borrow fifteen centuries from it last week for something."

"Al, what do you say we settle for thirty-five kay. We

leave the man thirty-five hundred for his airplane ticket and expenses. What do you say?"

Mathieson repeated the shrug. The adrenaline was pumping through him, making him shake; he kept the Magnum braced against the headrest so Ramiro wouldn't see the tremor.

"That's the deal, George. You want it?"

"For thirty-five thousand dollars I ought to at least get a name. One name. Who put out this contract?"

"It's not for you to make terms, George. It's for you to accept them."

"Yeah I know. But you guys seem to be in a mood to do favors tonight. I just figured, you know."

"The contract came down through channels, George. That's all we know."

"Yeah, all right, but what channels?"

"The same channels that put paper on those guys in Oklahoma and California. The same guy on the phone who called Deffeldorf and Tyrone. More than that I can't tell you because more than that I don't know. You figure that's worth your thirty-five kay?"

Ramiro kept blinking. His eyes were filled with tears. It didn't mean anything; they'd been that way ever since they'd got into the car; but Mathieson thought he could see the ponderous slow brain working behind the ravaged face. Ramiro said bitterly, "Oh Jesus H. Christ. What the fuck. What the fuck did I do?"

"You stepped on somebody's sore corn, I guess."

Mathieson wiggled the Magnum. It was his entire contribution to the discussion but it drew Ramiro's attention.

"I got a wife, what about my wife?"

"You got your life, George. You worry about that first."

"But I——"

"Maybe two, three months go by and the heat cools. Maybe then you call your wife on the transoceanic cable and you arrange for her to come join you somewhere. How's that sound?"

Ramiro bit his lower lip. "Can I just call her, tell her she shouldn't worry?"

244

That was when Mathieson knew they had him hooked.

Homer said, "Think, George, use your head. No phone calls. You can understand that, can't you?"

Mathieson wiggled the Magnum again. Homer said, "Now where's the stash?"

"I guess I ain't got much to lose."

"I guess you don't."

"Shit."

"Yeah, well those are the breaks sometimes, George. You could've been dead, you know. You still can be if you try anything humorous." He glanced at Mathieson and winked. "And with your own piece at that. Nice piece of iron. What do you use for target practice, George? Six-inch armor plate?"

There was no resistance left in Ramiro. "Look, suppose the man finds out you crossed him. The man that put out the contract on me."

"He won't find out, will he, George." Homer tapped Ramiro's sore finger. It jerked away and Homer smiled. "Where's the stash?"

Ramiro pursed his mouth and blew air through his lips. "Shit. It's right here."

"Here?"

"Where I go, this car goes. I want my stash where I can get it in a hurry, right? It stays in the car."

"Here? In the *car* for Christ's sake? You never heard of a Cadillac Fleetwood getting ripped off, George? You're *that* stupid?"

"Look, why do you care if I'm stupid or not? Shit, the organizations know whose car this is, they know the license plates. The amateurs, shit, anybody busts into this car without the right key, he gets a faceful of cyanide gas."

Homer grinned at Mathieson. "It's a good thing we used the man's own key, ain't it, Al."

"Ain't nobody going to fuck with George Ramiro's car," Ramiro said, but it was only a faint dying echo of bluster. "Anyway the stash, nobody ever finds the stash. I welded it myself. Nobody'd ever spot it."

"Where is it?"

Ramiro's raw eyes swiveled painfully toward the Magnum. "Shit. I open it and you kill me."

"It's your choice, George."

Ramiro didn't speak. Homer said, "Now we know it's in the car we could spend the next two years taking this car apart screw by screw. We know it's in the car but we ain't wasted you yet, have we? That ought to mean something."

Totally deflated Ramiro jerked his head reluctantly toward the dashboard. "Under the radio. The whole thing. You look close, you'll see two keyholes. Takes two Schlage keys to get into it."

"Let's see them."

"My shirt pocket."

Homer fished in it. Mathieson watched him extract two small brass keys and bounce them in his palm.

"Take it easy when you open it up. Everything falls out on the floor it'll take you all night to get it picked up and sorted out. You slide it out easy, it comes right out like a drawer."

Homer passed Mathieson the keys and took the Magnum from him. "Open it up, Al."

Mathieson turned around in the seat and found the keyholes low in the metal of the dashboard, deep in shadow. He turned both locks and looked for a handle. In the back seat Ramiro said, "You leave the key in the lock. You pull with the key until it comes open enough to grab the edge."

He reinserted one of the keys and pulled and it slid easily toward him—an entire section of the underside of the dash.

The drawer was irregularly shaped, crowded with canvas money packets. There was an empty money belt, a passport in a wallet, a leather zipper case filled with shaving gear and toiletries and an old-fashioned pineapple hand grenade.

He made sure the pin was secured to the grenade handle. It wasn't a booby trap. *If it had been we'd all be sky-high.*

He looked behind him. Ramiro sat rigid with his eyes squeezed shut and his fists locked on his knees, white-knuckled. If he was going to die it would come now—that was what Ramiro had to be thinking.

Homer said, "Let's go to the airport, Al."

5

Through the observation panes he watched the 747 taxi away from the ramp. Homer's narrow mouth was stretched back to the point of splitting. "Bon voyage, George."

They walked down the stairs. Homer said, "You were beautiful. You had *me* scared. That wild thing in your eyes."

"That was terror." Mathieson laughed with him.

Vasquez met them on the way out of the building. "On his way?"

"He'll keep running for a year before he stops to think," Homer said.

"Ingenious again, Mr. Merle."

Homer said, "Especially the part where we convinced him it was Pastor and Martin who put out the contract on him. That guarantees he'll never get in touch with them."

Mathieson said, "Maybe. Sooner or later he'll stop and figure out he may have been conned. But by that time we'll be done with this."

In the parking lot they transferred Ramiro's $35,000 and the rest of his goods into a suitcase. Mathieson pushed the homemade drawer shut and locked it with both keys. He locked the Cadillac and they walked across the lot to Vasquez's car. Mathieson put the suitcase in the back seat. "At any rate this will cover our expenses."

Vasquez got behind the wheel and they drove out of the lot. "In due course his car will be discovered. Evidently abandoned. A cursory investigation will disclose that Ramiro bought a ticket to Lisbon and flew there today. The police doubtless will report this information back to Frank Pastor. Pastor will assume that Ramiro absconded, the result of some transgression. Suspicion is all those people need—proof of malfeasance isn't required. Ramiro is acting suspiciously, therefore Ramiro must be dealt with. A genuine contract will be put out. You realized that from the outset, I presume?"

"It won't happen."

"Why won't it?"

"Because it will be a long time before that car is noticed.

People leave their cars at airports for weeks on end—even on those twenty-four-hour lots. By the time Ramiro is traced to Portugal he'll have a month's jump on them at least. They may go after him but it'll be a cold trail unless Ramiro does something idiotic."

"Like sending for his wife, perhaps?"

"He knows he's on the run. He knows he's got to hide. It's more chance than they gave me." Mathieson felt a sour bile of anger in his throat. "He'll spend the rest of his life on the run. All right, it was my doing. Do you think I was wrong?"

"I think you may have inspired his murder, in the long run. I think you've stepped over that invisible line you're so scrupulous about."

"No. That's like blaming Hiroshima for positioning itself under the Bomb. All I've done is conned one man into running for his life. If another man ends up killing him, it's not on my conscience—it's their own doing."

"I thoroughly agree. But it marks a shift in your position."

"I don't see any shift."

"Put it this way. What has George Ramiro ever done to you?"

"He has existed," Mathieson said, "and that's enough."

CHAPTER TWENTY-FOUR

Washington, D.C.: 21 October

1

THE FALL COLORS IN ROCK CREEK PARK WERE STUNNING. Mathieson watched them shimmer in the wind.

The wind muffled the sound of Homer's approach; Mathieson didn't know he was there until he felt weight behind him. He turned in alarm.

Homer grinned at him. "Old Indian Joe."

"Scared half the life out of me."

"Just practicing," Homer said. "He's coming." He pointed off through the trees, down the path.

"Alone?"

"Yes."

"All right."

Homer said, "He's probably wired for sound."

"If he is it'll be a recorder, not a transmitter. He's going against company policy by meeting me."

"He says he is. Maybe it's true."

"I know him, Homer."

"I just don't trust these guys." Homer turned back into the woods. "I'll be watching." He patted the revolver under his tweed jacket.

Mathieson crossed the path and sat down on the bench.

Above him Bradleigh appeared. He came down the slope with his hands in the pockets of his topcoat. He stood above Mathieson for a moment and then turned around and sat down at the far end of the bench. "I never recognize you anymore. Somebody's been giving you makeup treatments."

"I'm rehearsing for the remake of *Man of a Thousand Faces*," Mathieson said. "You look a little peaked, Glenn."

"I've been losing too much sleep."

"Not on my account, I hope."

"Yes, on your account. Now what's all the mystery?"

"Are you carrying a wire?"

"Just a recorder."

"Mind if I see it?"

"Suppose I do?" Bradleigh kept his hands in his pockets.

"I don't want to be taped, Glenn. This is private."

"It doesn't look like anybody's ever taped you. Christ and I thought I knew you, once upon a time." But he went inside his lapels and pulled out a flat little recorder and held it up in plain sight while he switched it off. He put it down on the bench between them.

"I hope that's the only one you're carrying."

"No, I've got eighteen others distributed about my person. You want to tell me why I'm here?"

"George Ramiro's gone, did you know that?"

"Gone?"

"Left the country last week."

"Where?"

"It doesn't matter. He's on the run. He'll never be back."

Bradleigh studied him as if he were something on the marquee placard of a freak show. "Your doing, I take it? First Gillespie, now Ramiro."

"That's right."

"You've got a reason for telling me this."

Mathieson glanced idly up through the woods. He couldn't see Homer anywhere but he knew Homer was there.

He said, "The point should be obvious enough. I've taken two of them out of the game and put one of them in the government's hands eager to give up every scrap of information he's got."

250

"You're saying you've proved you're capable of doing things we've failed to do."

"That's right, Glenn. And in return I want a favor."

"We'll see."

"I expect you to say, 'Name it.'"

"Come off it," Bradleigh said. "I don't sign blank checks like that."

A group of riders went by, cantering. Mathieson said, "Did you talk to Benson and the other two?"

"I talked to them."

"And?"

"They want to know more about what you want to talk to them about."

"All they need to do is call me and find out."

"For them to go to a phone is a big risk."

"Talk them into it."

"That the favor you're asking?"

"Part of it. You can tell them to call me, Glenn. Don't ask. Tell them." He took the slip of paper out of his pocket and wedged it under a corner of the tape recorder to keep the wind from picking it up. "That's three phone numbers. They're all pay phones in New York. Beside each phone number I've written a date and a time. One for Benson, one for Fusco and one for Draper."

Bradleigh pulled the paper out and read it and put it in his pocket. "I'll see."

"You'll tell them to make those calls, Glenn."

"They don't have to take orders from me, you know that."

"You can be persuasive."

"I'll try. The way you're going about this, I'm not sure I even owe you that much. You're not even giving me a scrap to go on."

Mathieson said, "What I'm doing is counterattacking. That ought to be obvious enough."

"You can't get them all."

"I don't have to. All I have to do is neutralize Frank Pastor. If I force him into a position where he's got to leave me alone, then he's got to pass the word down to his troops and his friends to keep their hands off me."

"I don't see how you hope to accomplish that by picking off small fry like Gillespie and Ramiro."

"That's just to put him off balance, make him nervous. I need him nervous."

"You're out of your mind. You know that, of course."

"I'm not under your protection anymore. If I'm wiped out it won't be on your conscience."

"I wish I saw it that way." Bradleigh sighed with exasperation.

"I'm doing a favor for Benson and Fusco and Draper. I want to let them in on this. It won't put them in any more danger than they're already in. Pastor hasn't found me—he won't find them either. And if it works it gets all four of us off the hook. And our families."

Bradleigh said, "What if I refuse to cooperate with you?"

"I can pull a few things."

"Feeling your oats, aren't you. But Pastor's a lot tougher to crack than penny-ante types like Gillespie and Ramiro."

"I know that, Glenn. I had to start somewhere. Call it practice."

"What is it you want, then?"

"One or two of them may want to come to New York after I've talked to them. Maybe all three of them."

"Benson, Fus——"

"Right. I want them protected."

"You mean you want me to keep them away from New York?"

"Just the contrary. I want them in New York if they're willing to come. I want their help."

"Of all the incredible balls——"

"I'm not going to force them to do anything. But if they want to come, I want them protected every step of the way. Even if it means you have to send Caruso and Cuernavan and ten other people out there to escort them. Even if it means you have to charter a private executive jet."

Bradleigh exploded. "It's out of the question, of course. We can't give support to any cockeyed private schemes. I told you you were out of your mind. This proves it. To even ask for——"

252

"Well, it's more than just a casual request, Glenn."

Bradleigh sighed again. "It figured there'd be teeth in it."

"I'd rather keep it on the level of favors between friends."

"Would you."

"I don't want to put a gun to your head."

Bradleigh said, "I guess you don't have to spell it out. All it would take would be a word from you in the FBI director's ear. That after I blew you twice to Pastor you went out on your own and handed us C. K. Gillespie on a platter. I'd be out on my ass. I'd probably deserve it, too."

"Then don't force me to threaten you with it. Come on, Glenn, I don't want to be the instrument of your disgrace and you don't want it either. I'm not going to the FBI or anybody else."

"If that's a promise then your threat just sprang a leak."

"It's not a threat. It's a favor. I'm asking one in return."

"Jesus, you're a devious son of a bitch."

"The only thing I'm putting pressure on is your conscience."

"You bastard."

"Then you'll arrange it all."

Bradleigh didn't reply. But his quick angry nod was as good as a promise.

Mathieson stood up. "Tell them to call me."

"Sure, sure." Bradleigh didn't look at him. He reached out for the cassette recorder and shoved it inside his coat. Then he rammed his hands into his pockets. "I always hate the fall. Makes me know winter's coming on."

"Can spring be far behind?"

"Jesus. Get out of here with your fucking platitudes." He still didn't look up. After a moment Mathieson stepped forward, made a fist, nudged his shoulder with it and then walked away up the hill. Homer picked him up beyond Bradleigh's view and they walked on through the park to the car.

CHAPTER TWENTY-FIVE

New York City: 23 October

1

IT WAS A HIGH-PRICED PRIVATE SCHOOL THAT OCCUPIED three interconnected brownstones on Eighty-ninth Street between Fifth and Madison avenues. The neighborhood suggested old wealth. Trim blonde matrons in Diors and Givenchys went heel-clipping along under their umbrellas. In better weather you'd see nurses wheeling infants in perambulators to and from Central Park. The only black face was that of the occasional supermarket delivery boy on his box-fronted tricycle.

Mathieson and Roger Gilfillan sat in the car. They were parked at a hydrant in front of a narrow stone house with discreet small bronze plaques on its wrought-iron gate advertising the presence of two MDs who were probably psychoanalysts. That conclusion had been reached after the first half day on the stakeout when it became apparent that only two patients arrived in each hour.

None of them took any notice of the Plymouth with its two occupants parked at the same fire hydrant day after day.

Every few hours a police car would cruise past but they were never asked to move on. Had the car been unoccupied it probably would have been towed away.

Each morning the gray Mercedes arrived and discharged

its two passengers. They would join the throng trooping into the school. Each afternoon promptly at half past three the Mercedes drew up and the two passengers came from the school and got in. Now it was 2:45 P.M. and raining.

The older girl was Sandra—fourteen, a bit on the plump side, ample of bosom: athletic and attractive but she would be matronly in ten years' time. She had a round face, almost cherubic, surrounded by a frizzy explosion of dark hair. Her sister Nora, twelve years old, was slender, pubescent, tall for her age. She wore her dark hair long and straight and it framed a piquant triangular face with extraordinarily large eyes.

There were always two men in the Mercedes that delivered and collected them.

The driver was a chauffeur who went by the name of Lloyd Belmont.

The bodyguard was Gregory Cestone, a large hard man whose face reminded Mathieson of a lunar landscape. It was a disquietingly immobile face that had been badly burned.

Belmont and Cestone in the Mercedes were due to appear in forty-five minutes. Roger shot his cuff over his watch. "Reckon I'll go over to Madison and use the little boy's room while there's time. You want to go first?"

"No, I'm all right. Pick up a pack of Life Savers or something, will you? I feel peckish."

Roger walked away in the rain and disappeared around the corner.

It was stuffy in the car and Mathieson rolled the window down. A fine spray of rain drifted against his face. It came across the park off the Hudson estuary and carried the tang of sea salt.

If we can only bring this off. He had set Monday as the target date because if Gregory Cestone didn't lead them to a connection by Friday evening it would still leave them the weekend to find another source. Right now Vasquez and Homer would be shadowing Cestone; they would drop the baton here at half past three; Mathieson and Roger would pick it up.

But the Mercedes was early.

In the side mirror he saw it come into the street from Madison. It drew up slightly behind him, stopping in front of the school; its horn tooted three times. In the intersection Mathieson saw Vasquez's brown Cadillac slide slowly by—it couldn't turn into the street because it would have had to squeeze past the double-parked Mercedes and that would have given Cestone and Belmont a close look at Vasquez.

Mathieson reached out as if to adjust the side mirror. It was the signal to Vasquez that he was picking up the relay. There was nothing else he could do. From that distance Vasquez would have no way of seeing there weren't two men in the Plymouth but it couldn't be helped.

He saw no sign of Roger on the sidewalk.

The two girls came down the steps. Cestone held the rear door open for them. Sandra carried an umbrella; she folded it as they got into the car. Cestone got back into the car and Belmont moved the Mercedes away.

It came past at a crawl and when it was dead abreast Cestone abruptly looked point-blank into Mathieson's face.

Mathieson felt the stab of panic. He bluffed: looked at his watch, looked in the rearview mirror, made a face as if awaiting a date who hadn't shown up on time. He was sure it wasn't convincing.

The Mercedes rolled on. Inside it Cestone twisted his face close to the rain-mottled window, staring back at Mathieson.

It dwindled toward the far corner. Mathieson turned the key and started the engine. He began to back up. Then he saw Roger running forward along the curb. Roger dived into the car grinning.

Up ahead the Mercedes was at the end of the block waiting for the signal to change.

Mathieson could no longer see Cestone's rigid face. Was he looking back past the girls through the rear window? The rain made it impossible to tell. Had he seen Roger get into the car or had he turned to face front by then?

"Maybe we blew it," Mathieson said.

"Hell, old horse, take the chance. Reckon we got nothing to lose."

When the signal changed the Mercedes made the left into

Fifth Avenue and Mathieson let it go out of sight before he pulled away from the hydrant; the tires squealed and he turned left through the light just as it changed.

At the far end of the block the staggered signal went green and the cars began to surge away but he was only half a block behind the Mercedes.

"This could backfire."

Roger said, "Supposin' we just see what happens."

"If there's any talking I'll do it. You hide behind your beard and keep your mouth shut."

"Yes sir, General sir."

"Don't make a joke out of it, Roger."

"Just hankering for a gun in my pocket about now."

"Just as well you haven't got one—you won't be tempted to wave it around." There was no point carrying guns around New York; if you were caught with one in your pocket it could cost you ten years.

The cars knotted up, crowding past the snag of buses in front of the Metropolitan Museum; afterward it was an easy run in light traffic down into the lower Sixties and Mathieson let the Mercedes stretch its lead to three blocks. A bus arrogantly shouldered in front of him; for a moment he lost sight of the quarry. He crowded a small car aside and went out past the bus in time to see the Mercedes swing east on Fifty-sixth.

"Taking the girls home early? Why?"

He squirted between taxis and looked for openings but the light went red at Fifty-seventh and he had to wait it out.

"Goddamn it." Homer wouldn't have got caught that way.

But he kept going when the traffic began to move; he pried through the pedestrians at the turn and had a glimpse of the Mercedes two blocks away, snarled in crosstown traffic, its right-hand light flashing for a turn into Park Avenue.

"Sure enough," Roger said, "taking them home."

By the time Mathieson inched through the intersection the Mercedes had pulled up, the doorman had it open and Cestone was out on the curb. A group of adolescent girls converged on the canopied doorway and Cestone produced a small gift-wrapped box from his pocket and handed it to Nora Pastor:

The girl beamed up at Cestone and went running inside with her sister and the five or six friends. Mathieson thought back, printed the dossier on the screen of his mind: *Nora Pastor, b. 23 Oct. 1963, NYC (Women's Hosp), dtr. Frank & Carola Pastor.*

It was her birthday—that explained it.

The traffic carried them abreast the Mercedes. In the rain they couldn't see much; Cestone was getting back into the car. The flow pushed Mathieson on by.

Behind them the Mercedes pulled out into the avenue. "What now?" If he pulled over immediately and let it go by they'd certainly notice.

Obligingly the Mercedes went over to the far lane and its signal-flasher started up a block and a half short of the next available left turn at Fifty-second; Mathieson had time to get there first and swing into the pass between the islands. The light was with them and they got across into the side street while the Mercedes was still bottled in Park Avenue.

He went down half the length of the block and pulled up ahead of a heavy double-parked truck; he backed up until he was nearly against its front bumper. Then he waited, half hidden there. He switched off the wipers.

The Mercedes was the first car through and it went by at a good clip. Roger said, "Go." Four cars followed it and Mathieson pulled out behind them. The Mercedes left him behind at the Lexington Avenue light but he made it up at Third. He kept the four cars between them. One of them turned south at Second Avenue; the others trailed the Mercedes east as far as First Avenue where everything turned left. Within a few blocks of here they had waylaid George Ramiro a few nights ago. Now he followed the Mercedes uptown and it coasted unhurriedly with the traffic and he had no difficulty keeping his position half concealed in the stop-and-go East Side tangle.

Roger said, "Take it easy now. Don't spook 'em."

At Ninety-sixth Street it went out into the FDR Drive and they trailed it north in a coagulation of traffic toward the Triboro Bridge. Roger said, "Maybe you ought to tell me one more time where this is supposed to get us."

"If we get the stuff from Cestone's connection then Pastor will know it's the real thing—not a bluff."

"You can buy the real thing on any street corner around here. I hear tell it comes in brand-name packages these days."

The Mercedes led them across the Triboro and down the Grand Central Parkway. Heading for what? An airport?

But it went right past La Guardia and left the parkway at Northern Boulevard. He had a harder time keeping up now because he didn't know this section. Fortunately the Mercedes was in no hurry.

Roger said mildly, "Those two boys ain't hardly wet behind the ears no more, old horse."

"I know." He took Roger's meaning: By now Belmont and Cestone probably knew they were being followed.

"Wild-goose chase maybe," Roger said. "They could be just funnin' with us."

"They'll want to find out who we are and what we're up to. Otherwise they'd have ditched us before this."

"Meanin'?"

"Meaning they won't just stop and blaze away at us. They'll want to ask questions."

"Figure we got answers that'll satisfy them?"

"Well I hope so, Roger, because if we don't we could be in a little trouble."

"That's real comforting."

The quarry led them into a dreary endless commerce of used-car lots and franchise service shops, fast-food diners and cut-rate haberdasheries. Bayside, Queens.

A left turn at—what? He searched for the street sign: They'd need to know their way back.

Bell Boulevard. The sign was half hidden. He followed along, two blocks behind the squat gray limousine. They were twenty miles from midtown Manhattan; the area looked like the broken-down hub of an upstate industrial town. A corner of his mind was bemused by the realization that this was still New York City—a part that didn't exist outside the minds of the people who inhabited it.

It was nearly four o'clock. The rain was intractable. The wipers batted noisily, keeping tempo to the chug of his pulse.

Roger said, "If push comes to shove, you distract 'em and I'll rush 'em."

"Other way around, Roger. It's my party."

Fat women browsed under the awnings of open-front vegetable shops, waving flies off the fruit, squeezing things experimentally.

"You hear me?"

"All right, old horse, I hear you."

Just ahead of them a bright yellow car pulled out of a parking space. He almost collided with it. His tires skidded on the oil-wet paving. The car, something from a drag strip, made an ear-shattering roar and slithered wildly away, spewing a wake that sheeted across Mathieson's windshield and blinded him. Roger grunted: "Weasel."

When the wipers cleared it away he had a glimpse of the Mercedes turning right.

The yellow racer veered away, leaving a scalloped set of tracks in the wet. Mathieson slowed when he approached the intersection where the Mercedes had turned. A warehouse on the near corner; an abandoned five-and-ten on the other, its windows exed with the white paint of condemnation. He made the turn.

Right ahead of him the street bent out of sight around a forty-five-degree turn.

He accelerated a little. This might be what they had been waiting for.

There was no curb: The street skirted close by a heavy brick corner of the looming warehouse. He had to twist the wheel hard through the abruptly narrowing gap.

The paving was chuckholed and muddy. In front of him the street petered out: a morass and a cul-de-sac against a high mesh fence. Rain coursed down past the fence—he had a vague gray-green impression of earth falling away: an old embankment, a railroad cut or canal or highway.

There was no sign of the Mercedes.

Roger had time to say, "Hoo boy. They've done this before, old horse—they had this set up."

Because there must have been a *Dead End* sign at the corner back there and they must have had it removed.

Behind him in the mirror as he stopped the car he saw the gray bulk of the Mercedes ooze out of an opening in the brick wall and position itself crosswise in the neck of the alley. Like a stopper, bottling them in.

"Boxed like sheep," Roger said contemptuously. "Shee-yit."

Cestone and Belmont came walking forward in the rain.

He looked at Roger. Roger lifted his eyebrows. "Might as well, old horse."

They got out of the car to meet it.

2

Bleakly he watched the gun in Belmont's hand. Cestone looked them up and down, nothing in his face moving except his eyes. Cestone had his hatless head lowered against the rain and his hands in his coat pockets.

The two men stopped three paces away. Roger edged away from Mathieson. He saw Belmont's lip twitch—in amusement? Belmont kept wiping water off his forehead with his free hand.

Cestone never touched his face. Possibly the nerves were gone.

"What you people want with us?" Cestone's voice was petulant and high-pitched. Behind him the Mercedes blocked the entire width of the only exit. Its wipers flapped steadily.

"I want to talk to you," Mathieson said.

"Me? I don't know you, man. Who are you? What you want then?" Cestone's speech had curious rhythms: It was almost Jamaican.

"A little business."

"You had to shadow us all afternoon? Why don't you just come to me and say, Gregory, I want to talk a little business? Why don't you just do that?"

"I'm doing it now," Mathieson pointed out.

"What kind of business, man?"

"We want to make a connection."

Cestone uttered a sound that might have been a laugh. It chilled Mathieson because the face displayed nothing at all.

"What kind of stupid cops are you?"

"No cops." Mathieson held both hands out from his sides, palms out. Out of the corner of his eye he saw Roger take his hands out of his pockets, empty.

"No cops. Look, we figured we'd follow you to your man and make our own connection with him afterward. That's all. We're from out of town, see? Your name's the only name we know."

"That's a load of shit, man."

"It's the truth."

"You don't look like no junkies."

"It's for somebody else."

"Sure it is."

Belmont showed his teeth. "Who?" It was the first word he'd spoken.

"What's the difference?" Mathieson said. "You wouldn't know her. We're both from out West."

Cestone said, "I don't buy this, man."

"Please listen to me. Either we're cops or we're not. If we're cops you don't want to shoot us—you'd get heat all over you. If we're not cops then we're telling the truth. What have you got to lose? Either way you're going to have to let us out of here."

"Man, I don't *have* to let you do nothing. I can leave you here all shot to pieces. Nobody ever knows it was Cestone."

"If we're cops then the rest of the cops know who we're shadowing. But then if we're cops we wouldn't travel alone, would we. We'd be wired—there'd be a radio truck out there on Bell Boulevard listening to this conversation and they've heard your voices and your name."

"I didn't see no radio truck," Belmont said.

Cestone glanced at him. "I think we rough them up a little, teach them about tailing people."

Mathieson said, "Take it easy. We haven't done anything to you. We only want to talk."

"You annoy me, man."

"I wasn't trying to——"

Belmont scowled. "Wait a minute, Gregory."

"What, man?"

262

"Wait a minute—wait a minute. I know him."

"Who?"

"He's changed his face a little. I ain't seen him in years. But the voice—yeah, it's him. Merle. Eddie Merle, the lawyer. Gregory, there's a contract out on him."

3

Right now had to be their move because Cestone was still absorbing the slow process of the chauffeur's recognition and both men were in the grip of surprise.

Mathieson flashed a glance at Roger and saw the muscles tense under Roger's coat.

Do the unexpected. At least it may throw their aim off. Homer's voice echoed in his recollection.

Roger was diving away—back toward the car—and Belmont's gun instinctively turned that way and it gave Mathieson room to move.

Two long sudden strides put him right between them.

His left hand had been outraised. He snapped it down against Belmont's revolver. Deflected the weapon. Made a grab for Belmont's wrist—and missed.

Still turning: wheeling, staying in motion, mingling, circling. Alarm had propelled Cestone backward and he had his automatic out very fast but he couldn't fire because Mathieson kept moving and spinning, his grip fastened on Belmont's sleeve—Cestone couldn't shoot without risking Belmont; and then Roger was all over Cestone, a bear hug from behind, locking Cestone's arms down.

Wrist lock, Mr. Merle, and don't ever be dainty—these people don't hand out second chances. Use both hands. Use them hard.

Still wheeling, he clapped his right hand over Belmont's fist, revolver and all. Left hand on the elbow. Stop, whip the knee up, smash Belmont's arm down against it. Fulcrum-pivot. Like cracking a stick of kindling across an upraised knee.

The bones were tough; Belmont's forearm did not snap, but he heard the grunt and saw the pain in Belmont's eyes and felt the revolver hit his own knee when it fell from Belmont's numbed hand.

Don't turn loose too fast. A little hurt's no guarantee you've taken the fight out of the man. Or the man out of the fight.

Rain in his eyes—hard to see. He flung Belmont in front of him, whirling close behind the man, hanging on to the injured arm with his right fist, twisting it up behind the man's back. Belmont cried out at last. Mathieson hooked his left arm around the neck, around the windpipe, pulling the head back against his chest. Using Belmont as a shield against Cestone's gun because things were uncertain in the downpour, he couldn't tell who had the upper hand there.

Belmont tried to struggle. Mathieson twisted the bruised arm. Belmont screamed—a raucous terrible noise.

Cestone was big; Roger was on his back but Cestone broke loose and Mathieson saw him lift the automatic—Cestone was going to shoot, right across the top of Belmont's shoulder.

Mathieson put his knee in Belmont's back and shoved him against Cestone.

Collision. Cestone's feet slid on the mud; he went over on his back. Belmont fell on top of him. Roger was getting to his feet, sliding in the muck, scrambling. Mathieson walked right in. Cestone's arms had gone out behind him to break his fall; he was pushing Belmont off him, looking for a gun; Mathieson found the automatic and kicked out, full force, right foot. From the feel of it he couldn't tell whether he'd kicked the gun or the hand but it was all the same: The automatic slithered away.

But he'd lost his own footing on the slick. He fell on his side and bruised his hip against his pocketful of coins.

It was right against his nose—the revolver that Belmont had dropped.

He got one knee under him and thrust the revolver out at arm's length. "All *right*."

Roger was standing up—casual, a grin behind the beard, eyes flashing: enjoying this.

Cestone was half erect. He straightened slowly, feet spaced wide. The immobility of his face was horrifying.

Belmont crawled around in the mud in a circle, moaning,

moving like a half-crushed beetle. Roger kicked him in the rump. Mathieson said, "On your feet, you're not hurt."

Belmont kept whimpering and crawling. Mathieson said mildly, "I kicked the automatic away. You won't find it."

Belmont let out a sigh of disgust and got to his feet.

Cestone had come up from hands and knees. His fists had been in mud and Mathieson should have thought of that. He detected it too late. Cestone flung the mud in his face.

He threw up his left hand. Not in time: The muck of gravel and soaked earth stung his face, blinding him.

He fell back, unbalanced, slipping; down hard on his rump. Kept his grip on the revolver; desperately raked mud out of his eyes. In one instant's flash he felt bitter irony: the ammonia in George Ramiro's eyes—it was a kind of justice.

He heard a whack of fist on flesh. Eyes on fire he stepped back and to one side. If one of them grabbed for the gun now . . .

The slurp of shoes in mud; another scuffle, another fist fell. He swung the gun savagely back and forth in front of him and kept clawing at his eyes with his left hand. He squeezed his cheeks up, squinted tight and tried to peer through the caked lids.

A shadow wavered in the blurred translucence of his vision: diminishing, fading—he began to hear the running footfalls.

One of them was running away.

He cleared his eyes enough to see Cestone leap over the front corner of the Mercedes and run past the brick corner.

Belmont swung a wild blow at Roger; it whistled past Roger and Mathieson saw him move in to strike but Roger's foot slipped an inch and it threw him off just enough. Belmont wheeled away and ran.

Roger stood in a fury. "Shoot the son of a bitch."

But Mathieson let him go.

Roger spread his feet apart for support and propped his arms akimbo. "Shee-yit."

Mathieson turned angrily and threw the revolver with a pitcher's might, soaring it above the mesh fence, down into the embankment cut.

Roger started laughing. "Look at us. Couple of tar babies."

Too enraged to speak, Mathieson walked to the Mercedes. The engine was still running. He backed it into the doorway and took the keys with him when he got out; he threw the keys far out into the mud pond. He walked right past Roger and got into their own car. Backing and switching, he reversed the car carefully, wheels spinning in the mud. When he drew up beside Roger he leaned across and pushed the door open. "Get in, damn it."

Roger got in, coated with mud. "You got to admit it's funny. Two big heroes making asshole fools out of theirselves."

"Goddamnit."

"Hey, old horse, gentle down. Look here, we hurt them more'n they hurt us. Mexican standoff at worst but I think maybe we won the fight on points."

"Points. Aagh. We lost Cestone, we lost his connection. We blew it, Roger."

"Ain't nothing can't be got at from some other angle, old horse. It's not as if we blew the whole enchilada or anything."

"I guess I'm just feeling like a stupid fool. If we pull anything that clumsy again we may get our heads handed to us."

Trembling badly he put it in gear and eased through the passage to the boulevard.

4

"You're both lucky to be alive." Vasquez was angry. "What was it, sheer bravado? Now they know who you are, they know you're in New York. You've brought us a great deal of trouble."

"I don't think so."

"Don't be a stubborn fool. Of course you have. They know they're under attack now. They didn't know it before. It makes all the difference. They'll batten everything down."

Homer sat on the bed with a sour smile on his small mouth. He watched Mathieson and Roger scrape the mud from their coats. After a moment Homer stood up. "Better give me your car keys."

"What for?"

"Got to assume Cestone got a make on the license plate.

I'll turn the car in and go to some other rental outfit and get another one."

"And that's one more thing," Vasquez said. "On the rental voucher we used the address of this hotel. We'll have to move. Now—tonight."

"All right, we'll move."

Roger gave up trying to repair his coat. He stood up. "I'm headin' for the showers. Clean clothes. *Then* I'll pack and join you gents. First things first."

"We'll call you when we're ready," Vasquez said.

Roger left. Mathieson threw his coat aside. "You're over-reacting, Diego. I'm surprised. Sooner or later Pastor had to find out who was after him. If it hadn't happened this way I'd have told him myself."

"You should have waited. Our job's become much harder now. We may not reach him at all."

"We'll reach him. What's really on your mind?"

Vasquez had the bureau drawer open. He was slapping stacks of folded clothing into the suitcase. Abruptly he stopped, turned and faced Mathieson. The anger was still flashing in his eyes.

Mathieson prompted him: "Well?"

"You employed the services of my firm. You gave us an assignment, albeit unique, that I have done my best to carry out, and now you seem to wish to persist in getting in the way of it."

"Don't be silly. I only——"

"You very nearly blew it. You may in fact have blown it. And yet you insist on keeping me in the dark about the most vital part of your scheme."

"And you resent that. Is that what this is about?"

"It raises the question who's in command here."

"I am. We settled that a long time ago."

"Not quite," Vasquez said. "You're my client, not my commander. When you employ the services of a firm such as mine, it's understood that tactical decisions and methodology are my perquisites. I'm the professional here."

"Do you want to withdraw?"

"I want to know what's in your mind, as a first step. I

want to know why you wanted to trace Gregory Cestone to his heroin connection. I want to know what importance a shabby drug peddler can have in your scheme. I don't intend to proceed without that knowledge."

Mathieson opened the second drawer and transferred the underwear into the suitcase. He went into the bathroom, gathered his toiletries, dumped the armload into the suitcase, bagged his dirty shoes in plastic and put them on top. It was an untidy job and he had to sit on the suitcase to close it. He brought out the second bag and opened it—it was half filled with packets of Ramiro's money, the hand grenade from Ramiro's car, the kit of tools and the makeup kit that he'd used. He stripped off his suit and crumpled it into the suitcase and shut it. He went back to the closet and got into his remaining suit and his clean shoes.

Finally he set both bags by the door and turned to face Vasquez. The detective stood between the bureau and the window, one shoulder propped against the wall, tapping a pencil against his teeth like a professor waiting impatiently for a student to respond with the right answer to a complicated classroom question.

Mathieson said, "Has it occurred to you that I may have kept you in the dark for your own protection?"

"Against what?"

"Against the possibility of your being charged with complicity in a serious legal offense."

"I've already conspired with you in the commission of several criminal acts."

"Those aren't likely to be reported—and even if they were they're relatively trivial. You'd never go to trial for any part you've played up to now. Maybe the worst you could face would be a charge of conspiracy to commit extortion, but there'd never be enough hard evidence to put you in serious trouble."

"And now you're contemplating something more dangerous."

"If it goes wrong," Mathieson said, "I could be had up for a capital felony charge. I don't want you dragged into that."

"What capital felony? Murder?"

"No. We've already discussed that."

"Kidnapping?"

He hesitated. "Yes. If it goes wrong."

Vasquez shook his head—an expression of disbelief. "You amaze me. You draw the line at a simple killing, yet you don't turn a hair at the prospect of kidnapping, which can be the vilest of human sins."

"I will not kill. It's that simple."

"You're absurd, Mr. Merle. Absurd."

"That's your opinion. Are you willing to proceed, knowing we may get involved in that kind of risk?"

"Certainly. If I know the nature of the scheme and if in my judgment it has an appropriate chance to succeed. Unlike you, Mr. Merle, I don't draw artificial lines. I've never quite understood people who did. I've known dope dealers who drew the line at rape. I've known killers who drew the line at dealing drugs. I've never understood any of them. Once one crosses the line of morality any further distinctions are arbitrary and capricious."

"You're a fundamentalist."

"A meaningless label. I distinguish between good and evil. I think I do so far more realistically than you do."

"A moralist who's cheerfully willing to indulge in extortion, fraud, illegal entry, kidnapping and God knows what other offenses."

"Offenses against what, Mr. Merle? Against evil men. I justify my existence by jousting with evil. But I've never defrauded an innocent man or extorted anything from an honest citizen."

"Robin Hood, are you?"

"I'm Diego Vasquez, Mr. Merle. Perhaps I make my own legend but I certainly don't model myself on others'."

"You're extraordinary, you know that?"

"Are you going to tell me what your scheme is so that I may evaluate it?"

"I suppose I'll have to, won't I. All right. You may as well sit down."

CHAPTER TWENTY-SIX

New York City: 24 October

1

THE BUILDING WAS EMPTYING OUT. WHEN THE LAST STRAG-
glers had disappeared Ezio locked the door of the office and
returned through the anteroom to his desk. He picked up the
phone and punched ten digits.

"Ordway Enterprises."

"Ezio Martin. Mr. Ordway in?"

"Yes, sir."

"Ezio. That you?"

"Me. Turn on your scrambler," Ezio said.

"Just a minute . . ."

Ezio opened the drawer and switched on his scrambler.
"OK, you hear me?"

"Good enough." Ordway's voice was distorted now.

"That order I placed yesterday morning. You got anything
yet?"

"Working on it, Ezio. It takes a little time, it's a complicated order."

"I'm waiting for Mr. Pastor in my office now, that's why I
called. Thought I'd give him the latest."

"We ought to have a crew for you in maybe forty-eight
hours."

"Clean?"

"Squeaky clean. That's what you asked for."

"Mr. Pastor's going to appreciate that."

Ordway said, "I don't suppose you want to tell me anything at all, do you?"

"Out of bounds right now. You'll make a nice profit on it, though. Mind telling me who you're sending us?"

"Well we haven't got them yet, Ezio. But two of the men we're trying to get, they're a couple of soldiers. I mean real army soldiers, they were out in Vietnam. Officers, Green Berets. No police records at all. Squeaky clean."

"But their fingerprints would be on file."

"Hell, anybody's fingerprints are on file, Ezio. So they wear gloves, whatever it is. These guys are into demolitions, communications, you name it."

"We're not expecting to invade a Vietcong village," Ezio said. "I'm not sure it's a bright idea. The operation we've got in mind, it needs to be real quiet. This doesn't want demolitions types, it wants second-story types."

"These are good men, Ezio. They ran some shit into the country for us from Nam. They did it efficient and quiet. These are not loud guys."

"I told you I wanted three men."

"The third guy, I was thinking maybe Tony Senno up in Burbank."

"No. Definitely out."

"Why?"

"Because we've used him before. I told you, nobody we've ever used before. Senno drove the car for Deffeldorf, right?"

"Then I'll cancel him, get you somebody else. No sweat, Ezio."

"You don't mention our names to whoever it is, you understand that. They're not going to know who they're working for. You'll call me back when they're ready to take off."

"Today's Friday. I'll probably send them out Sunday on a plane. Where do I reach you?"

"It'll have to be here, the office, because I've got the scrambler here. I'll come in around noon, that's nine in the morning your time, you call me here then."

"Fine. So long, Ezio."

Ten minutes later Frank arrived. He tossed his coat and hat on the couch and shot his cuffs. "So?"

Ezio told him about his conversation with Ordway.

"Fine, fine. What about the schedule?"

"Everybody arrives in New York by Sunday night."

"Assembly point?"

"Midnight Sunday, one of the piers in Brooklyn. It'll be empty—no ships in, no cargoes waiting. We slipped the watchman a few bucks, he won't see anything."

"That's fine, Ezio."

"Who briefs them?"

"You do. Buy some longshoreman's clothes, wear a stocking over your face, don't talk unless you have to. Rent a typewriter and have the instructions typed up, pass it around, make sure they understand. If they ask questions you answer them with a pencil, you write the answer down in block letters so they can't figure the handwriting, you let them read it and then you burn it."

"Down payments?"

"Two thousand a man. The other eight thousand each when they bring us the files."

"You worked out a plan for the drop or do you want me to take care of that?"

"Use a truck. They drive it to a given point, you pick it up there. You personally. Nobody else is in on this, Ezio."

"Right."

"Keep it that way."

"I pay them off when I pick up the truck, then."

"Yes. Treat them square, this is a hard job for them."

"Got you," Ezio said.

2

She put down five tiles and scored it. Frank rotated the board and scowled.

She said, "What now? Another seven-letter word?"

"No. How do you spell 'harass'?"

"One are, two esses."

"No good." He lapsed into silent contemplation.

She said, "How long will it take them to do it, Frank?"

"How long will it take who to do what?"

"The files."

"No telling." He rearranged tiles on his rack. "First they'll have to scout the place, every inch. Find out what the security setup is. How many people work there weekends and nights. Bringing in one guy from Minneapolis who used to install alarm systems—he's supposed to figure out a way across whatever they've got but it may take equipment and time. You can't pull off anything this big overnight. And they've got to get away clean—it means working out complicated maneuvers, trucks inside trucks, diversions, all that kind of crap. It's a Goddamn military operation."

"But it can be done. I'm sure it can."

"Anything can be done," he said. "Once they pull it off there's going to be all hell breaks loose. You know what we're going to do? We're going to put the stuff in the mail."

"In the mail?"

He was smiling. "Sure. Bust it up in little packages, wrap it up in plain brown paper, mail them out from all kinds of little branch post offices to guys all over the country who got testified against. Then we sit back and watch it all hit the fan. The government hasn't got enough agents to cover all of them at once. Eleven hundred witnesses? Eight, nine hundred of them be dead by the time the federals start catching up. And the first four are going to be Merle, Benson, Draper and Fusco."

"If they still have a file on Merle."

"There's that. But it doesn't bother me anymore. We miss Merle, OK, we miss one man. But we make our point, that's the important thing."

"Then you still think Gregory was mistaken."

"Sure, the both of them. Couldn't have been Merle. What's Merle want with a junkie connection? It doesn't make any sense. It was just some cop trying to run a bluff. Couple of clumsy cops running a poor tail, they got caught, they had to dream up some story."

"But Belmont said he recognized him."

"He backed off, you know. It's been nearly ten years. Ezio took him over the photographs again and Belmont admitted he wasn't sure, it was just a resemblance. I mean I'd love to think we had Merle right in our own backyard but things just don't work out that easy. Forget it. We'll find Merle—we'll find him in San Diego County, I'll bet you on that."

"I never bet with you, Frank, I always lose."

"The hell you do." He grinned at her. "But that's the right thing to say."

CHAPTER TWENTY-SEVEN

New York City: 24–31 October

1

MATHIESON RETURNED TO THE HOTEL IN A SEVERE DEPRESSION. When he walked into the suite he found Vasquez and Homer going through real estate ads in the *Times*. Roger was fiddling with the Arriflex camera, checking its lens settings against the recommendations on the film pack. Roger looked up; it was clear that one glance at Mathieson's face told him the answer to the question in his mind; he didn't speak but Homer voiced it: "How're they doing?"

"Fine—fine."

Vasquez was cold. "She's still upset. Very well—she'd have needed to be superhuman."

"Don't we all."

"Don't take on like that, old horse."

"Amy's all right. A little itchy. The boys are raising some hell."

"Expected that," Roger said. "You et?"

He had to think. "No."

"Then go down and get yourself around some grub. Might improve your disposition some."

Without arguing he went downstairs, debating the dining rooms, settled on the coffee shop. Afterward he had a drink in one of the bars, a double, and felt slightly mellowed when he returned to the suite. Roger inspected him critically. "My turn to call tomorrow. I hope it don't have the same effect on me."

"Hell, Roger, you've got the best marriage in the world."

"Always tend to agree when people tell me that. Strange thing is, it's true."

Vasquez folded the newspaper and put it away. "Mr. Merle, you didn't honestly expect your marriage to survive this. It would be imbecilic to blame its failure solely on these experiences."

"I don't need undercutting—not from my wife and certainly not from you."

"You do, however, need a clear mind. You've half-persuaded yourself that if you were to give up your quixotic quest, even at this late date, you'd have a chance of recovering your marriage. You've convinced yourself somehow that it's an either-or situation—that you can have Pastor or you can have your wife, but you can't have both. It's idiotic. If you accede to these irrational pressures you'll surely lose both of them."

Roger said, "I hate to say this but I agree with the man."

Acidly Mathieson turned to Homer. "What about you? Nobody seems to have asked your opinion."

"Haven't got one, Mr. Merle. I don't mess in other people's private lives. Done enough messing in my own. I've got a back trail littered with ex-wives—three of them."

Roger said, "I never knew that."

Neither did Mathieson but it wasn't enough of a surprise to distract him. He said savagely, "Nobody said anything about giving anything up. Have I even hinted I ever thought about quitting?"

"That's beside the point," Vasquez said. "You've created a talisman—the superstitious belief that if you succeed against Pastor it will cost you your marriage. I'm bringing it out in the open now because I believe it's the kind of superstition that may become a trip wire. Whatever happens to your marriage, it will not be the result of anything that occurs here. The two matters are completely unrelated. You must admit it—without reservation. Otherwise we're in peril."

"You may be right. I may have been putting it to myself

like that. I don't know. I haven't been able to think clearly about it."

"Then do so now." Vasquez left his chair and stood looking down at Homer. "I've been thinking that perhaps you should leave us, Homer."

"What?"

"Return to Los Angeles. There are tasks waiting at the home office. Things have piled up during my inexcusable absence."

"You've never thrown me off a case in the middle."

"There are things that will transpire here, things you don't need to participate in. Please don't be whimsically gallant. I need you more at the home office than here."

Mathieson's rage shifted toward the available target: "Is that the thanks he gets? At least Homer deserves to be in at the finish."

"Please stay out of this, Mr. Merle. Homer knows nothing of your plans. If we exposed the scheme to him he would find it anathema. It would go against every principle in him. But he would insist on backing us to the hilt out of his loyalty to me. I don't wish to confront him with that dilemma."

Homer was on his feet. "Talk to me, not about me."

"I've done so. You have your instructions."

"It must be something that stinks pretty awful. I've gone a long way down a lot of roads with you. Where did you change? I didn't spot it. Where'd you all of a sudden park your values, Diego?"

"I never had a shot at evil so large before."

"And all of a sudden it's the end that justifies the means?"

"The means are, to say the least, appropriate."

Abruptly Homer turned to Mathieson. "We've had fun so far. Does it have to go sour now?"

"I was never playing for fun, Homer."

"That's too bad. You play the game better than anybody I know outside of Diego." He turned back to Vasquez. "I'm not going."

"Don't presume to——"

"Diego, I'm not going. You want to fire me, then fire me. I imagine Mr. Merle will put me on the payroll."

Mathieson said, "If that's what you want."

Vasquez turned away. "It's a bloody mutiny."

"No," Homer said. "Just a touch of insubordination. You've never hired lackeys—what do you expect?"

"I'm rather touched, Homer."

"Is that sarcasm?"

"No. It's the simple truth."

"Then I stay."

"I'd prefer you didn't."

"Your exception is noted."

"Very well." Capitulating, Vasquez sat down again. But distaste was ground into his features. He scrutinized Mathieson. "It's reprehensible. Despicable."

"Think of an alternative."

"Easily. Kill them."

"No. I won't do that."

"You're a terrible man, Mr. Merle."

"Then clear out."

"You couldn't possibly handle it alone. It will be supremely difficult for four of us."

"Then why did you try to send Homer away?"

"For exactly the reasons I gave. I don't lie about such things."

"If you're so reluctant you may only be a burden to me."

"I'll carry my share of the weight—and the guilt." Vasquez lifted his coat off the back of the chair. "There's little sense wasting time. Let's find a dealer."

"How? I blew it with Cestone—he never led us to the connection."

"Cestone's connection is not the only source in New York. I made several calls while you were on the line to California."

"And you found a connection just by making a few phone calls?"

"I've been in my profession a great many years . . ."

Roger said, "I take it you got names."

"Names and likely places where we can look for the bearers of those names. You have your revolver?"

"Yes."

"Very well. Follow my lead and don't speak unless you must."

"I'm becoming an expert at looking sinister." Mathieson didn't smile at all. "Do you know how to use the stuff?"

Vasquez hesitated. Something happened in him—an emotion had been provoked. He turned away. "Oddly enough yes, I do."

"I wish we'd found Cestone's connection."

"Why?"

"It would have been neater. Using Pastor's own heroin."

"Heroin is all the same. The vein can't tell whose it was."

"Just the same, I'm going to tell Pastor that it was his own dope."

2

The trivial things always ruin a schedule and in this case it was the tedious matter of the hideout. In the end they had to settle on something farther from the city than they'd anticipated—a broker's summer home on Culver Lake near the Water Gap in northwest New Jersey; it was nearly a two-hour run from the city and that made for a dangerously long period in transit but it couldn't be helped because they'd already used up four days in the search and it was the first suitable property they'd found. It was isolated; there were no close neighbors. Vasquez took it on a month's rental at an exorbitant price; they posed as businessmen looking for a quiet place to hold a series of high-echelon management conferences. The house was furnished, it was sturdy, and the owner thoughtfully had prepared it against break-ins by installing heavy bars over the ground-floor windows. They also would serve to keep a prisoner in.

Vasquez made only one change in the house. In a hardware store he bought a heavy dead-bolt lock and installed it on the corridor door of the downstairs guest bedroom. It could not be opened from either side of the door without a key. Two keys were provided with the lock. Mathieson kept them both.

It was Wednesday night when the four of them left to return to Manhattan but there was still one chore to do en route. In a sleeping Leonia street they unscrewed the license plates of a parked car and drove several blocks and stopped again to remove their rent-a-car's New York plates; they put the stolen Jersey plates on the car, stowed the New York plates in the trunk and drove on across the George Washington Bridge. It would be a little while before the owner of the Leonia car would notice the absence of his license plates; by the time he reported them stolen—if he reported it at all—the plates would be in a trash can somewhere.

Vasquez had never worked in New York before and Mathieson was baffled by the number of people there who seemed to owe favors to someone who, in turn, owed Vasquez a favor. They had an absurdly easy time making the heroin buy; Vasquez judged the price exorbitant but paid it without balking— it was, after all, George Ramiro's money.

Now it was a pharmacist on West Seventy-second Street who provided, at a price but without prescription, a phial of sodium pentothal and a large bottle of chloral hydrate capsules and two cartons each of which contained forty-eight disposable syringes.

By midnight they were back at the hotel. Mathieson unlocked the door to his room. Vasquez walked on toward his own room, then stopped and looked back at him. "You're convinced this is the only way."

"Can you think of another?"

"One, but we've already been through that."

"Nothing else?"

"Nothing else comes to mind. Variations on the same sort of scheme—all of them equally reprehensible."

"There aren't any clean ways of dealing with vermin."

Vasquez said, "Get some sleep. We'll check out of here in the morning."

3

Friday was the day scheduled for the calls—Halloween.

The first was due at two in the afternoon; the phone was in a booth in the Plaza Hotel; he was in the booth at eight minutes to two, pretending to be talking into the phone. Then

280

the woman in the fur stole found another booth and Mathieson put the receiver back on the hook and waited for it to ring.

Two o'clock came and went. At five minutes past the hour he decided Benson wasn't going to call. Bradleigh had made a mistake somewhere—put on too little pressure or perhaps too much. But he'd give it another ten minutes.

It rang at 2:12.

"You're still there. Sorry. We had busy circuits. This really Edward Merle? Talk to me, let me hear your voice."

"It's me, Walter. It's been a long time but I don't think my voice has changed much."

"Been a lot of blood passed under the bridge, hasn't there." Benson's voice hadn't changed either: precise, thin, prissy. He'd been a bookkeeper in a numbers operation in Brooklyn but he hadn't been born there; his voice still had the Midwest in it. Of course he'd been living in Oklahoma for eight years.

Benson went right on—he'd always been filled with chatter. "How's that lovely wife of yours? How've you all been doing?"

"We're just fine, Walter. Look, I don't think we should spend more time on this line than we have to."

"It's secure at both ends. You're in a phone booth, aren't you?"

"Yes."

"So am I. But then I'm paying for the call so I suppose we'd better keep it short. I'm not exactly rolling in money these days."

"Walter, did Glenn Bradleigh give you any idea what this is about?"

"Very vague. Very vague. Enough to make it sound interesting. He said you were trying to pull something that might force the boys to leave us alone. He didn't say any more than that but he said it often enough that I got curious. That's why I'm here."

"I think we've rigged up a foolproof trap," Mathieson said. "It'll take your help to spring it."

"Well now wait a minute, just what does that include?"

"About one day of your time. That's all. I'll want you to fly to a place—not New York, it'll be Pennsylvania. Fly there, I'll meet you. We'll need you for about three hours. Then we'll take you back to the airport. I have no interest in knowing where you're coming from or where you go from there."

"Very mysterious. I don't like mysteries much."

"I can't tell you exactly what it involves until you agree to come in with us."

"Who's 'us'?"

"I have some associates working with me. No names, Walter."

"They know my name, don't they?"

"Walter Benson is the only name they know. I have no idea what name you're using now and neither do they. This has nothing to do with Bradleigh's office. It's a private matter between the four of us and the people who've been trying to find us. There won't be any publicity."

"Well Bradleigh did say this was something you'd cooked up yourself. He said he wasn't taking any responsibility, just relaying a message."

"That was the truth."

"This three hours you want out of my life. What's the risk?"

"No more risk than you'd stand by traveling anywhere."

"The way things are, that's pretty risky by itself."

"Bradleigh has agreed to provide a private plane. He'll fly you in and out. There won't be any airline reservations on the record."

"It sounds pretty cute but I'm leery. You can understand that. Can't you tell me anything at all about what I'll be expected to do?"

"Mainly wait around while we focus a movie camera," Mathieson said. "I need you on a few feet of film that we're going to show to the other side. Now if you've made any changes in your appearance, I'd like you to be ready to change back to your old self as much as you can—we'll want them to recognize you as the old Walter Benson. I don't know what you look like now so I can't suggest what it may require. Hair dye, a wig, a shave, whatever."

"I'm ten years older and twenty pounds heavier. I can't exactly strip that away overnight."

"Just so you feel they'll recognize you."

"What do we do in this home movie? Thumb our noses at the camera?"

"Something like that."

"If I didn't know you I'd think this was some kind of very bad practical joke."

"Believe me it isn't."

"No, you aren't the type. But you haven't convinced me it's in my interests to go along with it."

"It's got a damn good chance of getting them off our backs permanently, Walter. And if it doesn't work you haven't lost anything. I'm paying all expenses."

He could hear Benson breathing into the phone through his mouth. The man was very nervous. "When would this be?"

"Next Sunday. Nine days from now. Nine November. You come in the morning, you go out the same afternoon. I don't know how far away you are but you should be able to do the whole trip the same day, or break it up if you prefer. That's between you and Bradleigh—he's handling the travel arrangements. All I'm concerned with is that you show up at the Scranton–Wilkes-Barre airport at twelve noon on Sunday the ninth."

"Wait a minute, I'm writing it down. Scranton–Wilkes-Barre, nine November Sunday, twelve noon. You'll be there in person?"

"That's right. You'll recognize me."

"What about Draper and John Fusco, you talked to them?"

"Not yet. They're due to call this afternoon."

"Be like old home week," Benson said without audible enthusiasm. "Look, level with me, you really think this has a chance?"

"A damn good chance. When you get there I'll tell you."

"How soon will we know whether it's worked or not?"

"Six weeks maybe." Mathieson gripped the handle of the booth's door. He closed his eyes. "How about it—you think you'll make it, Walter?"

"I've been running my ass off, I got shot in the back, I'm still hiding like some hermit out here. Why the hell not. I'll be there."

When he hung up and left the booth Mathieson was smiling. The other two would be easier: He'd be able to tell them Benson had already agreed to it. That would carry weight with them.

4

Fusco was no trouble: Fusco had always been a fighter. It was Draper who gave him a few bad minutes but finally he brought Draper around with the promise of security.

He had arranged to take the three calls in lobby booths in the three luxury hotels clustered around Fifth Avenue and Central Park South—the Plaza, the Pierre and the Sherry-Netherland—and afterward he walked to the St. Regis to make his fourth call; there was no reason to walk the extra blocks— there were ample public telephones—but it suited his sense of compositional balance. He realized that Vasquez was right: He was making talismans out of everything, the way a child was careful never to step on a crack in the sidewalk.

The call from the St. Regis was to Bradleigh's office. Bradleigh wasn't there. He was expected Monday.

Mathieson tried Bradleigh's home phone. He got an answering machine. Mathieson identified himself, said he would call back Saturday evening at six.

CHAPTER TWENTY-EIGHT

New Jersey–New York: 1–6 November

1

HE DROVE TO THE LAKE HOUSE AND LET HIMSELF IN. VASQUEZ and Homer were in New York for the day doing surveillance on Pastor and his family. Mathieson found Roger in the house fiddling with lamps, taking experimental footage with the Arriflex. The living room had a cathedral ceiling and high glass doors across the length of one wall: They gave a view of most of the lake.

Roger was bundled in sweater and jacket. "My feet are colder'n a witch's tittie."

"Try a bucket of hot water."

"You talk like my grandma. You get Bradleigh all right?"

"It's all set. Any trouble with the camera?"

"No. Go set in that chair, let me take a bead on you and run a few frames, we'll see how the lighting works out."

Mathieson sat down with the *Times* and let Roger photograph him from various angles, moving the tripod clumsily around the room and zooming the lens in and out. Mathieson said, "You've got both black-and-white and color, right?"

"Right. High-speed color, the new stuff. Otherwise we'd need klieg lights all over the place."

"These two kinds of film, they're compatible? I mean they can be spliced together?"

"Sure. Same sprockets, same sound-on-film tracks. We use the same splicer on everything. It'd go easier with a Movieola but it would've cost a fortune and I couldn't find one to rent. We'll make out with what we've got."

"You've got a week to practice. Get it right."

"Old horse, time I get through with this even old Jack Ford would be proud of me."

"Or rolling over in his grave." Mathieson put the newspaper down. "It's time we wrote the script for the first piece of film."

"You write the script, old horse, I'll direct it."

"We'll both write it. It's got to be right."

"Go ahead. I'll take a peek over your shoulder now and then."

"We've got four days," Mathieson said. "Thursday, as they say in the vernacular, the snatch goes down."

"Why Thursday in particular?"

"Because it's her birthday."

2

She let her mind drift; under the dryer she neither read nor spoke. Alexandre returned after forty-five minutes and lifted the cone off her head and removed the curlers and began to brush her hair out. "Glorious," he intoned with professional cheer. "Madam is a vision."

She inspected herself critically in the mirrors. "It's nice, Alexandre. A really fine job."

"Thank you. I'm thrilled that madam is pleased."

He helped her into her full-length suede coat. She gave him a smile that seemed to brighten his day; he went to the door and held it for her.

It was another of those crystal fall days and she blinked when the brightness hit her eyes; she found the sunglasses in her handbag and put them on.

The limousine was not at the curb; there were no parking spaces. She looked at her watch: 11:40. She'd told Belmont to pick her up at a quarter to twelve. She looked down the length of Madison and didn't see it anywhere; probably he was waiting double-parked in a side street—Belmont was always punctual, it was what he was paid for. She window-shopped antiques and paintings for a few minutes, not really looking at them. She was still thinking about the child. Frank Junior. She still heard Frank's laughter last night: *Let's hope the kid has your looks and your brains.* She caught her own smile in the window's reflection—and behind it she saw the long Mercedes draw up.

She crossed the curb toward it; Belmont was just getting out, starting to come around the car to open the door for her; people straggled by along the sidewalk, topcoated against the chill; two men were coming toward her, deep in animated conversation, and she hurried briskly across their path toward the car. She stepped off the curb between two parked cars and suddenly the two men crowded against her.

"Anna—Anna Pastor, isn't it?"

The voice was vaguely familiar and she turned with a polite hesitant half-smile. Belmont came around the back of the limousine and she glanced at him. Then she froze. It wasn't Belmont.

The man who had spoken was reaching amiably for her arm. Something glinted in his hand. She drew back instinctively but his companion moved in closer and when she took a backward step she felt hard fists grip her by both arms from behind: the man who wasn't Belmont.

She opened her mouth but the taller man, the bearded one, said in a low voice, "Honey, I wouldn't do that was I you. You could get hurt real bad."

In a terrified confusion she glanced down. The man who had spoken first—the one with the moustache and glasses —had a firm grip on her right arm and now for the first time she saw the syringe clearly.

There was no time to react, no time for anything. The needle plunged into the soft web of skin between her thumb and forefinger. All three men held her tightly: She couldn't move. The bearded man loomed, screening her from the curb. A bus went by with a swishing roar, filling the air with a noxious stink. The man behind her had something against her mouth—a handkerchief, she thought dispassionately. *To keep me from screaming.* It all went so fast . . .

They were pushing her into the car. She kept waiting for a shout of discovery from the people crowding past on the sidewalk.

She found herself in the back seat between the two tall men. The man in the chauffeur's uniform got in behind the wheel. The doors shut, sealing her off from the world.

She cleared her throat. "What was in that needle?"

The man with the moustache said, "Sodium pentothal. It won't hurt you. You'll go to sleep for a while."

The voice: Finally she recognized it. She turned and stared in horror at the man with the moustache.

"Merle."

"Just take it easy, Mrs. Pastor. Nobody's going to hurt you."

The bearded man said, "Move it on out, driver."

"I don't see the boss's car."

"Probably hung up in traffic. Get going—he'll catch us up."

The limousine eased out into the knotted traffic. Anna tried to reach the door. Merle gripped her arm—surprisingly gentle; he forced her back in the seat between them. "Easy now."

Her head swam. "My God this stuff works fast." By the time she spoke the last of the six words her tongue was thick. She tried to rouse herself, to stay awake. In five seconds she gave up the struggle and plunged into darkness.

3

She awoke with a sensation of having been asleep for a very long time. But they were still in the car, still moving. She seemed unable to open her eyes. She could hear and understand but her body was still asleep. She listened to their voices.

"Transfer point coming up."

"She should come around in a minute. That stuff wears off fast."

"Gave me a turn, old horse. Right out there in front of God and everybody. But nobody raised an eyebrow."

"It's all a matter of plausibility. People see it happen in broad daylight on a crowded avenue, they can't believe it's a real abduction. Everything moving so fast, it looked as if she'd had a fainting spell, that's all. She was too surprised to put up a fight—we counted on that."

"Likely fight like a bobcat when she comes to. You get that needle ready, old horse."

"It's all set when we need it."

The car rolled to a stop. Her eyelids fluttered. She felt the car sway—someone getting out. Voices outside—the chauffeur and an unfamiliar voice:

"Anybody behind us?"

"No. But someone may have noted the license number. Have you made sure of fingerprints?"

"We're all wearing these plastic gloves. Haven't touched the car anywhere bare-handed."

"Fine. Leave it here then. Let's go."

They were pulling her out, sliding her across the seat. She tried to resist it but the muscles were sluggish. She opened her eyes: They wouldn't focus. The sunglasses had slipped down on her nose; the daylight was painful.

They hustled her across a few yards of pavement. She had a vague impression of shopping center and parking lot. They lifted her into the back seat of another car. She licked her dry lips.

"She's awake."

"It'll be a few minutes before she starts tracking properly."

Doors slamming; once again she was between Merle and the bearded man. Hazily she saw the other two men in the front seat. The car began to move.

Merle said, "Can you understand me, Mrs. Pastor?"

"Yes." A croak: She cleared her throat and tried again. "Yes."

"If you've had time to think about it you can understand that I've got no interest in hurting you. Quite the opposite. You're only of use to me alive. So please don't fear for your safety."

"Where's Belmont?" She slurred the words and felt angry with herself: so little control.

"Waiting in his limousine to pick you up at Saks Fifth Avenue at twelve-thirty. That was the message we gave him."

"But the car——"

"That wasn't your limousine, Mrs. Pastor. We hired it from a livery leasing outfit."

"I don't know what you expect to prove by this," she said. "You'll all be killed, you know that. If it takes the rest of Frank's life and every penny he's got."

The bearded man patted her knee. "Ma'am, don't fret yourself none, just relax and enjoy the ride."

The man in the front seat said, "Give her the shot, Mr. Merle. She's not to know where we're going."

She tried to fight it but it was no use: She went under again.

4

It was a small bedroom, cheerfully decorated with print wallpaper. The double bed had a good hard mattress. The first thing she noticed was the bars on the windows. Through the glass she could see trees, almost bare of leaves now except for a few tall pines.

She turned her head on the pillow. A man sat on a chair near the door. The door was closed; there was a large brass lock on it that appeared new.

The man's face was deep in shadow until he reached up to switch on the lamp on the table beside him. Edward Merle.

"You're in a house in the country. I suppose you can see that for yourself. You've been asleep for about two hours."

"Two hours?"

"It was a different drug this time. Chloral hydrate. You'll probably want to sleep several more hours to get it out of your system. The only thing that's keeping you awake now is anxiety."

"You know everything, do you?"

Merle didn't reply.

"Where do you think this is going to get you?"

"I intend to get free of your husband and his pack of animals, Mrs. Pastor. You're the instrument of that freedom."

"You're out of your mind."

"Maybe. Would you like coffee? Anything to eat?"

"No."

"Don't be stubborn. You're probably thirsty—drugs do

that, of course. There's a plastic pitcher of ice water on the bedside table there, if you didn't notice it. If you want anything at any time, just knock on the door. One of us will be outside at all times."

"How considerate."

"We're not going to harm you. I want you to understand that. We may want to sedate you now and then, merely to benefit our own freedom of movement at certain times. Don't be alarmed when you see hypodermic needles. It's more humane than tying you up and putting a gag in your mouth."

"How long do you intend to keep me here?"

"As long as it takes to convince Frank Pastor."

"Convince him of what?"

"That he's vulnerable." Merle stood up. "You'd better try to sleep it off now."

He left the room; she heard the lock slam home. She tried to think but drowsiness overcame her.

CHAPTER TWENTY-NINE

New York City: 6–7 November

1

FRANK WAS A PASSIONATE MAN BUT EZIO HAD NEVER SEEN him in such a towering rage.

The guests had come and waited and gone; the party had been limp and awkward without its guest of honor. Now the children had been sent to their rooms, Ezio's wife and Ramiro's were in the kitchen putting loads into the dishwasher, Belmont and Gregory Cestone were in the front room awaiting orders and Ezio sat locked in the study watching Frank pace back and forth like something in a zoo cage, darting savage glances toward the telephone as if willing it to ring.

"Let's go over it one more time."

"Frank, we've been over it a hundred times."

"Get Belmont in here."

"What for? We know everything he knows."

"Maybe he forgot something."

"We pumped him half a dozen times. There's nothing wrong with his memory."

"Get him in here."

Ezio got up and went to the door. He crooked a finger at Belmont. Cestone sat near the door looking at the monitor screen. There were two men in the hallway, standing there. No one else; the elevator doors were shut. Ezio said, "Gregory, see if those two guys want some coffee or anything."

Cestone went out through the foyer. Ezio returned to the study and closed the door. Frank was talking to Belmont: "I want to go over it again. Maybe you'll remember something else."

"I'm sure willing to try, Mr. Pastor."

"I know you are. All right. You dropped her at the beauty parlor at ten-fifteen, right?"

"Yes, sir."

"She told you to come back and pick her up in an hour and a half."

"Right."

"You got back when?"

"About eleven-thirty. I parked at Fifty-third right at the corner. At a hydrant. I figured at a quarter to twelve I'd pull out around the corner and pick her up."

"You were just sitting there parked at the hydrant, reading the *Daily News,* right?"

"Yes, sir."

"And this guy walked over and tapped on the car window."

"Yeah."

"Did you actually see him come out of the beauty parlor?"

"No. He came from that direction."

"Describe the guy again."

"Small guy. Kind of wiry, you know, but he looked like he had muscles. Built like an acrobat, sort of."

"Clean shaven?"

"Yeah. Dark hair, kind of narrow face, little tiny mouth. I never saw him before."

"What about the clothes? You said he was wearing a dark suit."

"Black. No topcoat or anything. Just the black suit. I think he had a colored shirt on, yellow or pink or something. He was wearing a tie—I couldn't say what color."

"What about his voice?"

"I didn't notice anything unusual about it. He didn't have an accent or anything. He talked clear, like a radio announcer, you know, the guys that get all the accent rubbed out of their voices in broadcasting school."

"Tell me again what he said."

"He said he was just coming outside, a lady in there asked him to pass a message to me, she said she wanted to pick up something at Saks and she felt like a walk, and would I pick her up at Saks at twelve-thirty."

"Before you said he asked if it was Mrs. Pastor's car."

"That's right, he asked me that first. And he said the reason she asked him to deliver the message she was under the hair dryer and couldn't come out."

"Can you remember any of his exact words?"

"I don't think so, I'm no good at that kind of thing. I'm sorry, Mr. Pastor. I'm doing my best."

Ezio said, "We know you are. Nobody's blaming you."

Frank was scratching the top of his head through the toupee. "Why don't we hear from them?"

"Trying to make us nervous," Ezio said. "Sometimes they do that. They snatch the wife and let the husband spend the night alone, missing her. Then they make the call in the morning. Don't be surprised if we don't hear until morning."

He saw the rage in Frank and he added quickly, "Listen, it's an occupational hazard. Guys in our business, they know we won't go to the cops. But you think about all the snatches you heard about people in our business. They usually handle the victim with a lot of care and they don't hold you up for an arm and a leg. That Galleone kid, what was his name, they took him three-four years ago, somebody out in Kansas City. They called Galleone, they told him to drop twenty kay in small bills. He made the drop, they delivered the kid safe and sound. They don't mess up the merchandise and they don't ask for too much money because they know that would bring the whole organization down on them. . . . That's all this is, Frank. Tomorrow night, Saturday morning, I bet you she's home right here in perfect health. You want to try and take it easy."

"I don't think you're reading it right, Ezio."

"It's not professionals, Frank. Professionals don't kidnap people in the first place because the odds are wrong. In the second place nobody in the business is going to mess with Frank Pastor's wife. So it's a bunch of amateurs, maybe long-hair kids or something, they want some quick money."

"This guy that decoyed Belmont away from the beauty shop wasn't any longhair kid."

"So maybe they're a bunch of middle-class middle-age businessmen that fell on hard times. Somebody he's in trouble. I don't know who they are but I'll bet you they're not professionals. It's not some rival guy trying to put any kind of pressure on you. That leaves amateurs. Amateurs get scared, they don't want trouble, they take the ransom and give her back safe."

"Amateurs get scared, they start killing. You know that as well as I do. Don't try to soft-soap me with reassuring lies, Ezio. I don't need that crap."

"I still say they're not going to hurt Anna. Nobody's that stupid."

"I hope to God you're right."

2

It wasn't a phone call. It was a small package, marked *Personal*, delivered by hand messenger at eleven-fifteen Friday morning.

Ezio signed for the package. Behind him in the foyer Frank said, "That's probably it."

"Sure."

Frank said to the messenger, "What's the name of your outfit?"

"MRDS. Midtown Rapid Delivery Service.

"Where'd you pick the package up?"

"Forty-second Street Library. The main reading room." The messenger was an old man without teeth; his jaw chopped up and down like a marionette's when he talked.

Frank went into his pocket and took out his roll. He peeled off a twenty. "Describe the man who gave it to you."

The old man gaped at the money. "Well I don't know as I noticed him all that much. Young man, he was. Not a kid,

you know, but young. A little younger than you, anyway."
He laughed, high-pitched and nervous.

"For twenty bucks you can do a little better than that, old
man." Frank held the bill up a yard from the messenger's nose.

"Well he was kind of dark, I remember that. Not Negro,
a white man but he had dark hair, dark clothes."

Ezio said, "Black suit?"

"Maybe. I guess it was. Young man, dark hair, that's it.
Not very big. No bigger than me."

"What kind of voice did he have? How did he sound?"

"Ordinary. Nothing special. He wasn't no foreigner or anything."

Ezio said, "Sounds like the same guy."

Frank pushed the twenty-dollar bill into the old man's
hand and Cestone ushered him out.

They opened the parcel on the pool table. There were
two enclosures: a cassette of recording tape and a small gold
ring. Frank held the ring up and squinted at the tiny inscrip-
tion engraved inside it. "Anna's wedding ring all right."

"Got a recorder to play this tape on?"

"The kids have them. I'll be right back."

While Frank was gone Ezio examined the cassette. On
Side One it had the words *Frank Pastor* printed in block
letters in pencil. There was nothing written on Side Two. It
was an ordinary half-hour cassette; you could buy the brand
in any electronics shop.

Frank came into the study carrying a small recorder. They
plugged the cassette in and Ezio punched the "start" button.
The tape ran silently for a bit; then there was a click and
a hollow noise as if the microphone had banged against
something when it was picked up.

Ezio clenched his fists and prepared to listen.

3

"This is for Frank Pastor's ears only. And I suppose Ezio
Martin's if it's unavoidable."

Ezio looked up. He couldn't read Frank's face.

"I'm sure you recognize my voice, although it's been a long time since you've heard it."

"I recognize it, Merle."

". . . We've invited Mrs. Pastor to spend a vacation with us. She's a little run-down, I think she needs a holiday."

"Vicious bastard," Frank said. He swung roughly away but not before Ezio saw the moisture in his eyes.

"We have a few requests to make of you. They're simple and you shouldn't have any trouble following them. You may have thought that your wife had been kidnapped, but that's not true. She's taking a vacation, that's all. Nobody is asking for ransom money or anything of the kind."

Ezio said, "That's in case we brought a few friendly cops in."

Frank said irritably, "Shut up," and because they'd missed a few words he pushed the "stop" button and rewound the tape slightly. Then he started the machine again.

". . . vacation, that's all. Nobody is asking for ransom money or anything of the kind. Your wife is in perfectly good health, she's just a little tired. The rest should do her good. The only thing that could endanger her health, and the health of the baby, would be an attack on her or the place where she's resting. I'm sure you understand what that means.

"We don't know yet how long Anna will choose to stay here. That's up to her, of course. It depends on how well she responds to therapeutic treatment.

"She doesn't want you to worry, but I think you should. We'll be in touch at fairly regular intervals. Expect to hear from us again in a week or so. In the meantime, as I said before, we have a few simple requests and recommendations.

"First, it would be unwise for you to issue an alarm. Mrs. Pastor doesn't need excitement right now. It could be injurious to her. Please don't make any efforts to find her, or to find us. We'd hear about them and we'd act accordingly.

"Second, we'd like you to equip yourself with a motion-picture projector. It should be a sixteen millimeter sound-on-film projector, the standard kind that uses magnetic sound-reproduction and has a single row of sprockets rather than a double row. You'll need this equipment in the next week or two because Mrs. Pastor will be sending you some movie film.

"Third, Mrs. Pastor feels that you should stop hunting for me and for Mr. Benson, Mr. Fusco and Mr. Draper. She said that unless you call off the search immediately, you may not see her again. Ever. She's quite serious about this.

"Fourth, all communications from Mrs. Pastor and from me and my associates will be in the form of messenger-delivered tapes and films. Therefore there is no need for you to install expensive taps and tracing equipment on your telephones. We won't be using telephones.

"Possibly this experience will be good for you. It may teach you what it's like to be frantically concerned for the life and well-being of your wife and your child."

4

Ezio expected him to explode but Frank only ran the tape back to the beginning and listened to it again. Then he made his way to the leather chair and sank into it.

Ezio said, "The guy's gone psycho."

"Looks like it."

"What do you want to do, Frank?"

"Think."

"You want me to go?"

"No."

Ezio rewound the tape and stood awkwardly with his hands in his pockets waiting for Frank to speak.

After a while Frank said, "Well we can call off those people in San Diego County, at least."

"It's for sure he's not down there," Ezio agreed. "What about the other three?"

"He's trying to make us think the four of them are in this together. I'm having a little trouble swallowing that. I think he just wants to make himself look more formidable than he is."

"Formidable enough. He's got Anna."

"He won't keep her forever. And he won't kill her because

if he did that he'd know nothing would stop us pulling him apart a hair at a time." Frank examined his fingernails bleakly. "The movie projector thing, that's what worries me. What kind of home movies does this nut want to show us?"

"I don't know, Frank."

"He's got her someplace around here. Maybe right here in the city. He didn't have time to take her very far, and he's got at least one guy with him who decoyed Belmont yesterday and delivered this tape to the messenger this morning. They're right around here someplace."

"Fifteen million people right around here, Frank."

"You don't have to give me population figures."

Ezio said, "What about the Virginia operation? Those guys are already down there casing it. Do we call the whole thing off on account of this business with Anna?"

"Hell no. We don't call anything off except San Diego."

"He's acting like he's got connections, Frank. Like he's got ears in places where they can hear things. Maybe we ought to call off the memos on Fusco and Draper and Benson."

"All right. For the time being. Call them off."

"You want to set anything up to start looking for Anna?"

"No. I don't want to take the chance of him getting wind of anything like that."

"He's gone nutty, Frank. How can we trust him to keep her alive?"

"He may be nutty but he was never stupid. He knows if he kills her he kills himself."

"Maybe he's aiming for that. Maybe he doesn't mind going down if he can hurt you doing it."

"He'd have killed her already if it was that way."

"Maybe he has."

"I don't think so. If he had, why string us along with tapes and movie projectors?"

"To buy himself time to get away."

"There wouldn't be any point in it, Ezio. He's not that crazy. If he was just out to kill Anna to get revenge on me, he'd have killed her and left the body around where we'd find it." Frank got out of the chair and crossed to the table. He put his finger on the tape recorder. "But I still can't figure out what he's up to. He must think he's going to accomplish something but I can't see what it is."

"Me neither. But what are you going to do right now?"

"Nothing," Frank said. "Sit it out. Wait for the next one. What the hell else can we do? He's got us over a barrel right now. It won't last forever but that's the way it is right now." Frank pushed the button again.

CHAPTER THIRTY

Pennsylvania–New Jersey: 7–9 November

1

FRIDAY MORNING MATHIESON DROVE WEST WITH HOMER, OUT Interstate 80 across the Delaware River into the Poconos. They checked out the airport at Scranton–Wilkes-Barre and then drove deeper into the hills through Hazleton, looking for back roads, exploring them for half the day until they found what they sought.

It no longer had a name. At one time it had been a small community; there were a dozen derelict houses, none of them much more than a shack, and along the curving ungraded road stood three large structures that had been barns and possibly a local general store. It was the remains of a coal pocket; the coal had been worked out and the miners had moved on, most of them toward Appalachia; it had been abandoned at least fifty years. The depressed hills of northern Pennsylvania were littered with burnt-out diggings and deserted hamlets. Lying outside the attractive tourist belt of the Poconos and far beyond commuters' radius of New York and Philadelphia, they attracted no interest and stood untended to rot.

The shacks had low stone foundations and plank-board walls; no clapboards, no shingles. Only one of them still had a roof—a patchwork of corrugated rusty metal and frayed tar paper. Homer explored it with his revolver out: There was a possibility of snakes.

The floor was rammed earth covered by the splintered remains of a few rotted floorboards. The window openings had been boarded up long ago; light seeped through the cracks and fell through the open doorways of the two rooms.

"It'll do," Mathieson said. He marked its position on the road map and they got back in the car to drive back.

They timed the drive to the airport. Just under an hour.

He examined the map and found a route from the ghost town straight across forest and farm land to the banks of the Delaware south of Easton. That would be their return route.

They took another reconnoiter around the airport. The general-aviation hangar was set well back from the commercial terminal and there was a separate entrance from the highway.

"We'll meet them right at the plane. Drive the car out on the runway."

"Sure," Homer said. "Nobody gets a look at faces that way."

"The security measures may be a little extreme," Mathieson said, "but I'll feel safer."

"So will I."

"That about wraps it up then. Let's go home."

2

Roger opened the door; evidently he'd been alerted by the crunch of their tires on the gravel; Mathieson glimpsed the revolver before Roger put it away under his pullover.

"Everything check out over there?"

"Everything checks out." Roger locked the door behind them. Mathieson hung his coat on a peg by the door and went directly down the hall to the bedroom. He turned both locks and glanced behind him—Roger was watching from the end of the hall; his glance slid away and he moved out of sight toward the kitchen.

Troubled by Roger's expression, Mathieson pushed the door open and stepped into the bedroom.

She was sitting in the chair watching him. She hadn't been reading or watching television or smoking or fidgeting; she'd simply been sitting there. The hate in her eyes was almost corporeal.

He shut the door behind him and shot the lock home. "Good evening, Mrs. Pastor."

3

When Mathieson came into the kitchen Vasquez glanced up at him and then went back to examining the interior of the coffeepot as if he were a shaman consulting a pot of mystic entrails. Finally he set the pot back on the hot red ring of the electric stove. "I take it the reconnaissance was a success."

"It looks good, better than we hoped. We can go over the maps later."

Homer said, "How's the lady?"

"She wants to kill somebody. Preferably me."

"There's a big surprise," Roger said.

Vasquez put the lid on the pot. "I went into the village and made several telephone calls. There doesn't seem to have been the slightest rustle on any grapevine, except that apparently Pastor has obeyed instructions to the extent that his hunters have been recalled from the San Diego area."

Roger said, "Takes the heat off our kids and womenfolk."

"It's what we hoped for," Mathieson said, "for openers."

The water began to bubble. Vasquez spooned coffee into it. "In any event it seems quite certain the police haven't been alerted. It's something of a relief to have one's anticipations confirmed."

Roger said, "Hadn't we ought to get some chow down the lady?"

Mathieson sat down at the kitchen table. "She claims she's not hungry. We'll make dinner a little later."

"Reckon she's too groggy to eat. You keep her shot full of that sleeping stuff, it's likely to do a lot of harm to that kid she's carrying. But I guess you know that."

"She's been sedated only when I wasn't here. And I don't expect to make any more excursions."

"You know we could have looked after her fine, old horse, without the mickey finns."

"Nobody goes in that room except me," Mathieson said. "I keep the keys. That was the understanding from the beginning."

He pressed the point. "I want it clear with all of you. I'm the only one she has contact with. It's for your sakes—things could still go sour."

"Sour?" Vasquez took down cups and saucers. "It's already gone far past that." He glanced up at the clock. "We really should get some nourishment and liquids into her, walk her around, let her exercise for an hour before you give her the next fix."

4

The Lear Jet touched down. When the door opened and the steps came down Mathieson already had the station wagon in motion. He drew up at the foot of the steps and got out.

Caruso and Cuernavan stood in the plane's open doorway surveying the airfield.

Mathieson smiled. "It's secure. Nobody knew you were coming. How are you fellows? Nice to see you."

"Didn't recognize you at first," Caruso said. He came down the steps and shook hands. "You all alone?"

"I'm the only one whose face you're going to see."

Caruso looked up over his shoulder. Cuernavan nodded; he stayed put at the top of the stairs. Caruso ducked to look under the belly of the plane, examining everything in sight. He walked around the station wagon, opened a door and inspected the interior. When he backed out and closed the door he turned to Mathieson. "You see how it is. I'll need to talk to your wife and son now."

"That's part of the arrangement. There's a pay phone in the hangar. I'll drive you over."

Caruso said to Cuernavan, "Hang on, we'll be back in a minute." Mathieson waited while he got into the car; then he drove across the macadam and put it in park. The phone was in a booth outside the building. "Wait in the car until I've dialed the number."

"OK. Glenn Bradleigh told us to play along."

He put his pocketful of coins on the shelf beneath the phone, dialed the number direct and obeyed the operator's instructions by inserting nearly half a pound of quarters. Mrs. Meuth answered the phone: "Yes, sir, they're here waiting for your call. I'll put them right on."

Jan sounded cheerful. "Well here you are, right on time again." It had a false echo.

"Caruso's here with me."

"Tell me how you are, at least."

He smiled for Caruso's benefit. "I'm fine. We're on the homestretch and everything's working beautifully."

"You sound strung up."

"Nervous. Can't be helped," he said. "It's a tricky day today—a lot of intricate business. Ronny there?"

"I'll put him on."

"Hey, Dad . . ."

"How're you making it, Ron?"

"Oh we're OK, everything's OK. You going to be finished pretty soon now?"

"A week ought to do it. Then we're going to rebuild the house on Beverly Glen and things will be just like they always were."

"I got bucked off yesterday. You'd think I'd know better by now. I got a real black eye, you wouldn't *believe* the shiner."

"Everybody gets bucked off now and then, I guess. You and Billy still hitting the books?"

"Well she makes up these exams, you know, like the College Boards or something. It's a lot tougher than we figured it'd be."

"You'll make it."

"Yeah, I guess."

"How's your mom?"

"Kind of bored. You know."

"I know. It's hard on her. But it'll be over very soon. Put your mother on again, will you?"

"Dad——"

"Yes?"

"Nothing. I kind of miss you, that's all."

"I miss you too, Ron."

"Here, hang on a minute."

Jan came on the line; Mathieson said, "I'm going to put Caruso on. He wants to make sure you're both all right. Answer any questions he asks but don't tell him where you are."

"Yes, I understand."

"It's right down to the wire. We're almost there with this thing. One week—that's the timetable."

"I hope so, Fred. I hope so. Good luck."

There was a click; a woman said, "Your three minutes are up, sir."

He plugged money into the phone and beckoned to Caruso. Jan said, "When will you call again?"

"Make it Wednesday at six. I may have more to report by then. Here's Caruso."

He handed the receiver over. Caruso gave him an apologetic glance and Mathieson walked back around the station wagon and got in. Through the window he watched Caruso but the man's face told him very little. Caruso was patient and thorough, asking brief questions, listening carefully to the answers: probably listening more to the tone than to the content. It was obvious when Ronny took over the phone; Caruso began to smile broadly and became more animated talking to the boy. Mathieson saw him scoop up some of the coins he'd left on the shelf and put them in the phone. The conversation went on at length; evidently Caruso was talking with Jan again; finally he cradled the phone and got into the car.

Mathieson said, "All right?"

"Yes. Nobody's holding a gun on them. You understand why we had to do this. We had to make sure."

"Pastor hasn't got a lever on me, you know. It's the other way around." Mathieson drove back out toward the plane.

306

"What kind of lever?"

"Take my word for it, you don't want to know that."

"If it works I'm in favor, whatever it is."

He drew up at the foot of the stairs and Caruso got out and made a hand signal to Cuernavan. "OK, bring them out."

5

They had changed as one expected men to change after an interval of more than eight years. Benson's shoulders had rounded, he'd lost a lot of hair on top, he'd developed a paunch and he squinted through his glasses. Draper had always been cadaverous and he'd put on no weight, but the years had engraved deep brackets around his mouth and had crosshatched his skin as if he'd been using a rabbit-wire screen for a pillow. John Fusco was still the same squat hard fireplug of a man but his kinky hair had gone gray and he had scars on his face that hadn't been there before.

They'd never had anything in common except their testimony against Frank Pastor. Benson had been a bookkeeper in one of Pastor's operations and had seen Pastor on the premises two or three times when illegal money had changed hands. Draper had been a gopher in Ezio Martin's office; he was the one who had gone to the bank that day and withdrawn the cash and delivered it to Pastor—the cash that Pastor had put into a white envelope and handed to the judge in the courthouse men's room. John Fusco had been an enforcer, George Ramiro's aide-de-camp; he'd been nailed in a truck hijacking and had testified against Pastor in return for immunity from prosecution on the hijacking charge. None of their evidence had been crucial to the case but it had contributed: Defense attorneys had tried to discredit the three men but the weight of their testimony, coupled with Mathieson's, had been enough to convince the jury.

Mathieson had no idea what Fusco or Draper had been doing since he'd last seen them in the courtroom. He knew that Benson had been managing a store in Oklahoma. They were four strangers thrown together by a common enemy.

Driving down narrow roads through the Pennsylvania

mountains he briefed them to the extent that the situation required:

"We're putting pressure on him. Part of the pressure consists of informing him that the odds against him are high. The more people we can show him on our side, the more impressive we look and the more convincing our operation becomes. We want him to think there are so many people in this thing that he couldn't possibly reach all of us before some of us strike back. I can't fill in too many details today.

"When we've had the films developed and edited we'll prepare copies of all the important materials and have a complete set delivered to each one of you through Glenn Bradleigh's office. I'd suggest you each make independent arrangements with someone you trust—maybe a lawyer—to put the tapes and films in safekeeping with a letter of instructions to be opened in the event anything happens to you. That part will be up to you, of course. That's how I'm handling it myself and it's always the most sensible method of protecting yourself against retaliation from people like Pastor. Now you'd better not ask me what it's in retaliation for. You'll be finding that out for yourselves.

"What we're going to do today is gather our group in front of a movie camera. There'll be the four of us and three other men who've been working with me. Two of the men you're going to meet will be wearing stocking masks at all times. You'll never find out who they are. That's to give us insurance against Pastor trying to put pressure on any of you to identify all the members of the group. Pastor himself will never find out who those two men are. Therefore he'll never know where the attack comes from, if he tries anything against the rest of us.

"That sums up the highlights. I'll try to answer questions if you've got them."

6

When he drove the station wagon into the ghost town he saw the glint of the lens in the window of the shack at the top of the slope. He had a glimpse of Anna Pastor's dark hair framed in the window as well. Roger was up there, working the zoom lens, holding Anna Pastor in the foreground of the picture while in the background he focused on the station wagon as its four occupants emerged. Vasquez and Homer, unrecognizable in stocking masks, emerged from one of the tumbledown structures and joined Mathieson by the car.

"Two of my associates. There's no need for names. These are Mr. Benson, Mr. Draper and Mr. Fusco." He turned and lifted an arm in signal to Roger; then he walked up the hill and entered the cabin, leaving the five men on the road below.

Roger picked up the camera on its tripod. "Now I go down and take group shots and two-shots while they mingle, right?"

"Right. I'll be down in a minute."

Roger carried the Arriflex out. Mathieson turned his attention to Anna Pastor.

Her arms were tied behind her and her legs were roped to the chair. Mathieson walked past her and pulled the improvised shutter across the window; he didn't want her to be seen or recognized by the visitors.

"We're ten miles from the nearest house," he said. "I'm not going to put a gag in your mouth because nobody would hear you if you screamed. Nobody except my own people. We're having a little convention, as you may have gathered."

"To celebrate your funeral, I imagine."

"There's only one door and we'll be watching it from outside. I can give you another shot or leave you tied to the chair. Which do you prefer?"

"I've had enough drugs pumped into me to last ten years. If you're giving me a choice I'll stay like this."

"It'll be an hour or two. Then we head home."

"Home," she said. Even in the dimness her eyes burned.

"Take it easy, Mrs. Pastor. If those three men knew you were here you might not get out of this shack alive. After what your husband's done to them they'd probably be happy to take you apart bone by bone. You'd be well advised to keep absolutely quiet up here until they've gone."

She didn't speak to him again. After a moment he left the

shack and walked down the hill. Roger was moving around with the camera, telling people where to stand and what to do. It was apparent that the newcomers were baffled: He was disguising his voice and they had not quite recognized him behind the beard but his presence, as always, was commanding.

As Mathieson approached he saw the camera swing toward him. He looked straight into the lens and felt atavistic rage; he hoped it showed.

Homer was distributing coffee in plastic containers. His face under the stocking mask looked weirdly distorted. Mathieson took a cup of coffee and sipped it; he looked up and found the tripod-mounted camera panning past him and he contrived a grim smile for it before it went past.

Roger locked the camera in position, left it running and stepped around in front of it, showing only his back to the camera but adding his bodily presence to the group's number. Then he backed out of range and returned to the camera and picked it up to carry it down the hill and take a group shot from another angle.

Benson said, "You mean this is all you want from us? Just some film of us standing around drinking coffee?"

"It'll do the job," Mathieson said.

John Fusco snorted. "You're a little crazy if you think Frank Pastor's going to get scared out of his shoes just by seeing some movies of the four of us together. He was never scared of us before. Why should he start now?"

"Because we never organized ourselves against him before. We were always solitary targets. I want to convince him we're unified against him."

He went across to the porch of one of the half-decomposed buildings and picked up the stack of placards. While he carried them back to the group he saw Roger setting up the camera above the road. It wasn't cranking.

He put the placards down. "I doubt any of you has much experience with cue cards but we've got a few lines for each of you to read. You'll be on camera while you talk but I want to rehearse these performances before we put them on film.

310

It'll have the best effect if it doesn't look like you're reading the lines. Try to be as natural as you can. If you can't get your mouth around the wording, put it in your own words. All right, let's start with Walter."

CHAPTER THIRTY-ONE

New Jersey: 10–14 November

1

HE SAT HUDDLED BY THE BOATHOUSE ON THE PIER. THE COLD wind shot sprays of foam off the lake into his face; he sat with his arms wrapped around his knees and did not move when he heard the car enter the driveway.

He heard the front door slam. Homer bringing in the groceries. Mathieson didn't stir.

The sun filtered weakly through a brittle haze. Pointed reflections ran along the surface of the water. All around the lake the trees were stark and bare. On the far shore a boy rode his bicycle along the road. There was no other sign of life.

It was a while before he was disturbed. He heard the glass doors slide open and someone's footsteps on the path.

"Time to feed Mrs. Pastor, I believe." Vasquez.

He didn't move.

Vasquez's hand fell on his shoulder. "Come on, get up. You'll catch pneumonia."

He shook the hand off.

"Don't be silly, Mr. Merle."

When he still didn't look up Vasquez sat down beside him. "Having second thoughts, are you?"

"Everybody's entitled to a mood now and then."

"You're a thousand miles past the point where you could have turned back, if that's what you're contemplating. Think of your own wife—what will happen to her if you don't carry it through. Your own child as well."

"I had no idea she'd be pregnant, Diego." His speech sounded rusty in his own ears: slow, painful, searching for words. "An innocent unborn child. It's harder to sink lower than that."

"I'm sure Genghis Khan was innocent in the womb."

"Don't patronize me with ad-lib aphorisms."

"Come on, Mr. Merle, it's time to take her supper to her before it gets cold. Or give me the key and I'll be waiter tonight."

"No. I'm the only one who goes in there."

"As you wish."

He got to his feet; suddenly he was very cold. He began to shiver.

2

He rubbed his eyes and watched the mixture cook up on the stove. When it was heated he drew it up carefully into the syringe. He switched off the heat.

He felt the others' eyes on him when he carried the syringe through the hallway, holding it up ahead of him like a uniformed doctor. With his free hand he turned the keys in the locks; then he went into the room, careful not to brush anything with the needle.

She rolled over on the bed and stared at him. Her eyes were utterly blank.

3

On his way into the living room he paused by the thermostat. It was on its highest setting. He rubbed his hands together and buttoned his sweater all the way up.

Vasquez looked up from his crossword puzzle. "Another day or two and you should be able to begin withholding the drug until she begins to need it. It shouldn't take very long before she's convinced beyond all doubt that she cannot survive without having the injection at regular intervals. You'll have to impress the mythology on her."

Roger said, "What mythology?"

"Drug addiction is in large part psychological, you know."

Roger looked at Homer across the checkerboard. "What's he talking about now?"

Vasquez said, "Those stories you've heard about addicts dying from cold-turkey withdrawal are largely hokum. Of all the deaths attributed to heroin, virtually none has been caused by withdrawal. It's a painful process to be sure but rarely a deadly one. It isn't the physical need for the drug that controls the victim—it's the mind. The mind becomes convinced that survival is impossible without the drug. If she weren't aware it was heroin that was being injected into her veins, she'd realize only that she felt sick in the absence of injections. She'd feel terrible but she wouldn't know why. Given enough time, her sickness would pass. She'd return to normal health and never entertain the desire for another shot of heroin— because she'd never know it was what she'd been receiving in the first place. Do any of you understand what I'm saying?"

Mathieson said, "I always understood it was a physical addiction."

"To a great extent it is. But the mind needs to be aware of it. The human mind is the great betrayer."

Homer cleared his throat. "Can't we talk about something else?"

"No. We must be clear on this. We cannot flinch from it. This thing must be done in such a way that her knowledge of absolute need becomes the overriding factor in her life. We must continually reinforce her conviction that she has become a hopelessly addicted slave to whom the withholding of her regular injection would be unthinkably agonizing."

Mathieson sat down. Vasquez stared at him. "By letting her go a bit too long between shots you will let her feel the touch of withdrawal anguish. Merely a taste of it. You cannot make the final move until you've accomplished that."

Mathieson rubbed his face with both palms.

Vasquez's voice softened. "Actually I'd worry more if you

weren't having such a strong reaction to these events. If you took them in stride I'd have to put you in the same category of subhuman existence to which verminous cretins like Frank Pastor belong."

Mathieson let his hands fall onto the arms of the chair and leaned his head back against the cushion. "Roger, we'll want to film some close-ups tomorrow of the scabs on her arms. The needle tracks."

CHAPTER THIRTY-TWO

New York City: 16 November

1

THIS TIME THE MESSENGER WAS A RETARDED YOUTH WITH a club foot; there was no information in him. Ezio signed for the package and Cestone escorted the limping messenger to the elevators.

It contained a single reel of 16mm film. Ezio set up the projector on the pool table and unrolled the screen against the book shelves. Frank shut the door and turned off the lights. Enough illumination came through the closed Venetian blinds to thread the projector. Ezio set up the speaker box and plugged in the wires.

Frank said brutally, "Enjoy the show, folks."

It began with a close-up of Anna. Apparently she was sitting in a chair; the frame showed only her shoulders and head. She looked contemptuously toward the camera and then away.

It was in color with good resolution: very professional. But Anna's movement, her turn away from the camera, was sluggish and her eyes looked dull. She looked doped, Ezio thought. He glanced at Frank to see whether the same thought had occurred to him but Frank stared unblinkingly at the screen and the quiet anger in his face registered no change; he had been in a deadly calm for ten days now—running things with chilly precision but an utter absence of visible feeling. It was a state in which Ezio had never seen him before.

The image of Anna remained on the screen for several seconds in complete silence; there was only the grind of the projector and the hum of the speaker. Ezio was about to check the sound system when abruptly Edward Merle's voice boomed, filling the room.

"She is, as you see, quite alive."

There was a sudden cut: a daylight close-up of Merle, looking into the camera. Ezio felt Frank stiffen. He reached for the volume knob and turned it down a bit.

"She'll stay alive if you do certain things. First, you're to cancel immediately the contract on my life and my family. I want you to spread the word where *everybody* hears it. I want it to be heard where it will be reported back to me. In addition, you will similarly cancel the contracts on these three men: Walter Benson."

Another cut: Benson was there, looking into the camera, showing his teeth—in defiance.

". . . John Fusco."

Fusco, his hair gone gray, his eyes hidden in shadow, his jaw squared in determination.

". . . Paul Draper."

Draper's fine hair moved slowly in the breeze like seaweed. He stared blankly at them from the screen.

Ezio heard Frank murmur, "So they're in this together."

There was another tight shot of Anna; another setting—it looked like a bedroom; Ezio saw a barred window at the edge of the frame. She was sitting on the edge of the bed. The camera moved and the image jerked: The camera was being hand-held and perhaps this was a different photographer's work; the resolution was less clear. Anna got up and walked slowly to the window and the camera followed her, panning across the room. It was as if she had been told to stand up and walk to the window; she obeyed listlessly. At the window she was in silhouette. The camera zoomed forward slowly until her torso's outline filled the frame. Just before it went to black there was an abrupt cut to a close-up of an arm.

"You'll notice the punctures in the flesh above the vein.

These are the tracks of mainline needles." The voice was harsh and cold.

The camera drew back, tipping upward; Anna's face came into the picture. So it wasn't a fake; that was really her own arm.

"At the moment her maintenance dose has been increased steadily to five nickel bags per day."

Ezio gripped his head in both hands. *Jesus.*

Abruptly Walter Benson was on the screen. He talked straight into the camera. Ezio had no trouble recognizing the reedy voice. "I've got a bullet in my back from your contract. It won't happen again, and we're going to tell you why."

Cut: Now it was Draper, speaking with slow gravity. "There are more of us than you can ever handle. We want you to know that."

And then Fusco. "We've had it, Pastor. One more move against any of us . . ."

Cut to Merle: ". . . and we all come down on you like a ton of bricks. That's a promise."

Now there was a repeat of the opening shot; Anna, head and shoulders, first looking into the camera and then, as if in woozy disgust, looking away. The camera moved up slightly and began to zoom forward through the window beyond her; it kept her head steadily in the frame in the lower corner but she went gradually out of focus as the image went out through the window and picked up a scene of abandoned shacks, barren gray earth, rock-studded hills beyond. At the foot of the slope the camera discovered a knot of men milling slowly about. The lens zoomed forward to high telephoto resolution. Ezio counted five men in the picture: He recognized three of them; the other two were not in focus.

There was a cut that disoriented him momentarily; the camera seemed to be prying its way through a group of people, pushing foreground figures away to the sides, finding more people beyond. Draper looked at the camera and made an obscene gesture. Fusco made a fist. Benson, with an ironic twist to his mouth, lifted a plastic cup toward the camera as if in toast, and then drank. Merle was coming down the slope from a cabin above them; the camera focused on him until he moved into the group. In the background two other figures moved in and out of the view—Ezio realized they were wearing stockings over their heads. Both of them wore pullover sweaters, dark slacks, dark shoes and leather gloves. Six so far, he thought. Then the camera steadied and a seventh man appeared at one side of the frame. He did not face it; Ezio had an impression of bulk, a full reddish beard, long unkempt hair. The man milled among the others, keeping his back to the camera, and soon went out of sight to one side.

The camera cut to another view of the group, taken from a point slightly above them; Merle's voice startled Ezio from the speaker. "These are a few of our group. There are others. You'll notice that you can't recognize three of the people you've seen in these pictures. Remember that. These three are close friends of ours. They've joined us to fight you. You don't know who they are, and therefore you can't reach them before they reach you."

Close-up of Merle; behind him nothing but a blank off-white plaster wall. Talking directly into the camera.

"We've grown into a sizable force. You're not dealing with helpless individuals anymore. We took your wife to prove a point. You're vulnerable. You're just as vulnerable as we are. Your wife and your unborn child are at our mercy. We've made a hopeless heroin addict out of her in a matter of weeks, with carefully controlled increasing doses. We can do a lot worse than that if you force it."

Anna's face appeared. She was sitting in the front seat of a car. It was a close-up; not enough of the car was visible to determine its make or design. The picture had been taken from outside the car, looking in through the open window. She wasn't looking at the camera. She reached up and ran her hand through her hair, dragging it back from her face. Ezio noticed abstractedly that her hair needed washing.

Merle's voice droned on: "You'll hear from us in a little while. You'll receive instructions. Obey them."

Another shot of Anna: a reverse of an earlier shot, Ezio saw. From Anna's face the camera moved down to her arm;

it zoomed in tight on the scabs and open sores. Then the screen went bright with a reprise of the downhill shot of Benson and the others; the camera drew back—it was the same shot as the opening frame, in reverse—through the window to a close-up of Anna in the chair; she was looking away and then she turned to face the camera and the screen went motionless, freezing frame on her as she stared into the lens. Now Ezio saw the fear and appeal in her eyes.

The screen went white; the film flapped through to its end.

2

Ezio didn't speak. He rewound the film to its beginning and threaded the projector and left it set up that way in case Frank wanted to look at it again.

Frank showed no inclination to review it. He sat in the leather chair with his fingers steepled below his chin.

Ezio opened the blinds. The light made him squint. He stood by the window waiting for Frank to speak. Outside it was snowing.

But it was the telephone that broke the silence.

Merle, he thought. He crossed the room, glancing at Frank; Frank didn't even look up. Ezio picked up the receiver. "Yes?"

"It's Belmont, Mr. Martin. I need to talk to you."

"Where are you?"

"Down at your office. Something's come up."

"To do with Mrs. Pastor?"

"No. Something else. That other matter, down around Washington."

"Can it wait?"

"It could but I don't think it ought to. It's pretty bad news."

"I'll get to a pay phone and call you back. Wait there." He hung up.

Frank lifted his face slowly.

"I've got to go out for a few minutes."

Frank nodded.

3

When he returned with snow on his coat Frank was still in the chair; he appeared not to have moved at all. But he looked up alertly. "Well?"

"Bad news from Washington. Very bad. They had to abort the raid on those files."

"Why?"

"Because there aren't any files any more."

Frank gave him a sour look. He didn't flare up; he only sighed. "Par."

"What?"

"Par for the course," Frank said. "Everything else goes rotten, I should've known this would fall apart too. What happened to the files?"

"They put them in code and fed the code into a computer bank. Only three or four people alive have the code. Corcoran, Bradleigh, one or two others high up in the department. Nobody can retrieve the information without the key code. So there's no way we can get at them any more."

Frank nodded. "They probably put that in motion as soon as they found out we'd been getting files from the Janowicz woman."

"They must have. It'd take them quite a while to program the whole thing into computers, let alone code it."

"You'll have to pay those men off and send them home."

"I know," Ezio said. "I wish I had some good news for you for a change."

Frank's mouth twisted into a half-smile. "What's left, Ezio? Just what the fucking hell is left?"

4

When the phone rang again Ezio picked it up expecting nothing.

Without preamble the voice said, "Put Frank Pastor on."

Ezio held the receiver out toward Frank. "Him."

Frank took it. "Yeah, I know who it is. Talk." Then he looked up at Ezio and mouthed the word *paper* and snapped his fingers. Ezio handed him the notebook and pencil from the desk. Frank wrote something down. "All right. Ten minutes," he said and hung up the phone. He tore the paper off the pad and rammed it into his pocket, getting to his feet. "Wants to call me back at a pay phone."

"Smart. He figures this one's tapped."

"Let's go. Might as well find out how much it's going to cost me."

CHAPTER THIRTY-THREE

New York–New Jersey: 16 November

1

MATHIESON CHECKED HIS WATCH.

Time. He put the dime in and dialed.

Pastor was there on the first ring. "All right. Talk to me, you bastard."

"Instructions. Are you listening?"

"You're dead, Merle."

"No. If I die Anna dies. Get that through your head."

"I'm listening."

"I want you to meet me. Alone. No wires, no bugs and no guns."

"When?"

"One hour."

"Where?"

"The southbound service area on the Palisades Parkway in Englewood Cliffs."

"I can't go to New Jersey."

"You'll have to."

"And go back inside for five years on violation of parole?"

"That's your problem. You'll have to go up the parkway from the George Washington Bridge and make a U-turn at the Palisade Avenue exit and come back along the southbound lane to the service area. One hour from now—one o'clock. Alone. No outriders, no passengers, no microphones, no tape recorders and no guns. Play it my way or you'll never see Anna again and your child will never be born."

2

He drove back across the bridge into Fort Lee and parked in the motel lot. Vasquez evidently had been watching from the window—he came outside immediately. Mathieson said, "Picked your spot?"

"Phone booth right across the street."

Mathieson looked that way. It was on the apron of an Exxon station. "Too close. He may spot you."

"It doesn't matter. His wife has seen my face a hundred times. My only real protection is your protection." Vasquez drew a slip of paper from his pocket. "This is the number of that telephone across the street. Just in case. And here's something else." He pulled a bulky paper bag out of his coat pocket. "Keep it wrapped up until you're safely hidden inside the car."

"What is it?"

"George Ramiro's three fifty-seven Magnum."

"I don't want it."

"I know you don't; but will you humor me?"

He tossed the bag into the car. "All right. But I think Pastor will play it straight."

"You can't predict what these creatures may do. It's best to take every precaution. It's fifteen minutes to one, Mr. Merle. You'd better be on your way."

3

It was an oppressive gray day. The bare trees were limp, heavy with wet snow. Wind stirred at the upper branches and white pillows fell with plopping crunches. He stepped across the curb and went through the trees—a little copse of them that masked the town streets from the parkway.

324

He walked through the trees until he had a good view of the service area—the station a bit to his right, the gasoline-pump islands dead ahead, cars entering the area from his left. By his watch it was 12:53.

Waiting laid a frost on his nerves; it mingled with the dreary chill in the damp air. The snow had quit falling but there was the threat of more. Cars on the service area apron had ground the stuff into filthy slush. He waited just within the trees, motionless in the shadows.

It was a white Continental streaked with filth from its drive. It pulled past the pumps and parked against the corner of the repair station. Frank Pastor, his nose tucked inside the upturned collar of his coat, stepped out of the car and stood there trying to spot Mathieson. The small round face was just the same—neat, almost distinguished, hardly a hoodlum's countenance. Perhaps it was the air of unruffled self-confidence that had made him a leader; or perhaps leadership had created the air. In either case he was inevitably a man arrogant with power and that was a quality which could be used against him.

A sudden attack of nerves: He imagined someone was coming after him, running through the trees in deadly silence —he looked all around, terror-stricken. There was no one.

He stepped out into the bitter wind, holding the heavy .357 Magnum in his coat pocket.

Then Pastor turned and the expression in his eyes electrified the skin of Mathieson's spine. Pastor's cold animal stare triggered all Mathieson's warning systems but he kept walking.

"You cocksucking motherfucker." Pastor spat the words out as if they were insects that had flown into his mouth. But he removed his hands from his pockets, empty and ungloved. A vein rose and throbbed above his eyebrow, embossed by rage. "It's your game. What's the next move?"

"You come with me."

Without waiting for a reply he turned on his heel and strode away, following his own tracks back through the woods. He could hear Pastor behind him, treading heavily in the wet.

"Get in." He took the wheel of the Pinto and when Pastor

got in beside him he threw it in reverse and backed into another parked car and left a little red glass in the road when he pulled away from the curb.

Pastor did not ask questions; he did not speak at all. He stared straight ahead, his mouth pressed tight as if to contain the threat of an outburst.

Mathieson parked the car in the slot in front of the motel room door. He unlocked it and went in ahead of Pastor. His enemy entered the room boldly behind him, wearing an expression of contempt as if to indicate that he didn't care whether it was a trap.

"Strip down to your shirt-sleeves."

"What for?"

"I want to find out if you're bugged."

"I'm not."

"Want me to take your word for that?"

Pastor got out of his coat and threw it on the bed. He tossed his jacket on top of it and stepped back. He was unarmed. Inside his shirt he seemed surprisingly thin; he looked as brittle as a dead sapling.

Mathieson went through the coat and jacket carefully with especially close attention to the buttons. There were no microphones that he could find. He found nothing other than Pastor's wallet; it contained nothing that interested him.

"Empty out your pockets. Let me have your belt."

He proceeded methodically with everything including the shoes and shirt buttons and even the zipper of the trousers. When he was satisfied he tossed the shirt and slacks back to Pastor. "You can put them back on."

Pastor got dressed without saying a word. Then he posted himself in the middle of the room, hands at his sides. "How many copies of that movie are there?"

"Quite a few. Benson has one. Fusco, Draper, each of the other three men you saw in the various shots." Mathieson went to the window and looked out along the motel lot. Across the street he vaguely made out the shadow of a man inside the phone booth on the Exxon apron—Vasquez.

"You may have worked out some clever kind of trap for me," Mathieson said. "If so, I think you should know that we've got your wife near here and if I don't telephone at specific intervals to let them know I'm all right, she'll be taken away to a place where you'll never get her back."

"There's no trap. What's your price?"

Mathieson studied him for a long time. There was no satisfaction in it but he detected the bitterness of defeat in his enemy. Finally Mathieson said, by way of a test, "You're too calm to suit me."

Pastor made a quarter turn on the carpet to face him squarely. His voice was utterly without tone. "I made up my mind I'd play your game. Whatever it takes to get Anna back. You want to kill me, then you'll kill me. No gimmicks, no cross, no tricks. I came here to find out the price. You've got me over the barrel, all right, I've played the game before. Quit shitting me—quit wasting time. What's the price?"

"Freedom."

"You already got that."

"Only as long as I've got your wife. The real price is our freedom after you get her back."

"You've got the floor."

"We hooked her on heroin, Pastor. Your heroin, from one of your own pushers. We hooked her bad. She's a falling-down freaked-out hopeless helpless junkie. She needs smack so bad she'd cut herself open and put her insides on exhibit if it would buy her a fix."

In his coat pocket he gripped the Magnum but Pastor didn't move off his stance. He blinked several times and looked at the floor.

Mathieson said, "You've seen some of the members of my group. On the film. There are others you've never seen. Do you get the point of all this?"

"Suppose you spell it out."

"We can reach you, Pastor. You're not impregnable. If they can assassinate presidents then people like you can be reached just as easily. Now I know about your laws of revenge. I know you can put up with the idea of an enemy who wants to kill you. What you can't put up with is the knowledge that if anything ever happens to me or Paul Draper or John Fusco or Walter Benson, then the target for all the survivors will be not merely you personally but your wife and your two daughters and your child who's about to be born. That's my edge, Pastor, and that's why we took your wife and made a junkie out of her. We did it to prove we could do it. To prove we can do it again if you force us to. All it takes is one bullet, aimed at any of us, and the rest of us will tear your family apart limb from limb. That's the pact we've made among us. That's what you've got to know."

For a moment Pastor closed his eyes. Then they snapped open. "Suppose you get run over by a bus that has nothing to do with me?"

"That's your hard luck." Mathieson watched him warily—tried to see what was going on behind the eyes.

"Merle, everybody's got to die."

"I'm not offering you a way out. I'm offering you time. You can have your family as long as the four of us and our families stay alive. That's all I'm promising. With some luck it might be twenty or thirty years. It's more than you ever offered us."

Pastor's face gleamed unhealthily. He rubbed his thumb across the pads of his fingers. "When do I get her back?"

"When you see my point."

"Hell, I see your point, Merle."

Pastor's face gave away nothing—not anger, not even contempt. It was too easy. Mathieson felt the need to provoke a reaction: He needed to know he'd struck bedrock. He said, "You might like to know I was the one who put Gillespie and George Ramiro out of the way."

"Did you."

"Don't you care?"

"You'll never know what I care about. What is it, Merle, you want to see me grovel? That what you want, the satisfaction? Look, you played the game and you won it. I haven't got any surprises up my sleeve, I'm not a magician. I don't like the way this turned out but all right, Anna's hooked on smack, there's worse things, I'll just get her unhooked. All right, the game's over, you won it, now you want to stand around here and gloat over it, is that what you want?"

"I want to know I'm free of you. Now and forever.

Wherever I go, whatever I choose to do. That's what I want."

"Merle, I'd kill you in half a second. I'll hate you to my last breath and my grandchildren will grow up hating you and yours. And someday they'll come for their revenge. But then you knew that before. You said it yourself—all you're trying to buy is some time. All right, you've bought the time. I'll see you around, maybe, in twenty or thirty years. In the meantime you got what you want—you're free of me."

Mathieson stared at him. Slowly he took it out of his pocket: the .357 Magnum. "I should have killed you after all."

"You want to do it, do it now, get it over with."

"George Ramiro's gun. I could leave it here next to your corpse and they'd pin it on Ramiro."

"You won't use it."

"What makes you think I won't?"

"Because you had too much fun setting this up," Pastor said. "Because I'm going to spend the next twenty years eating my guts out hating you and that's why you set this whole fucking stinking thing up and you don't figure to throw it all over for one lousy quick shot at me."

Mathieson put the gun back in his pocket. Dismally he turned to the door. "Wait here. In a few minutes you'll get a phone call telling you where to pick her up."

"Sure," Pastor said. "Good-bye, Merle."

Mathieson walked out.

4

He got into the car and drove out of the motel. He drove two blocks and stopped in a shopping center and used the sidewalk phone. He dipped into his pocket for the number Vasquez had given him.

"Me."

Vasquez said, "Roger and Homer are just getting into their car. They're backing out now."

"Pastor still inside the other room?"

"Yes. Here comes the car. I'll go now. Give us three minutes or so. You're in the shopping center?"

"Yes."

"Don't call him until you see us drive into sight."

He broke the connection and waited patiently.

When the car rolled into the parking area he looked at it long enough to make sure all three men were in it. Then he dialed the number of the motel and said, "Mr. Johnson, please, Room Ten."

Pastor answered the phone. "Yeah."

"It's Merle."

"Go ahead."

"One thing first. I lied about the heroin."

"Come again?"

"We didn't hook her on anything. The tracks on her arms are from a harmless glucose solution. She's in perfectly good health. No addiction."

"What the fuck are you trying to prove, Merle?"

"That we can do it to you if we have to. Any time at all. Remember it, Pastor. Write it high in letters of fire and never forget it."

"Where is she?"

"Upstairs above you. Room Twenty-two. The door's unlocked. You'll find her inside, tied to a chair."

He hung up and left the booth.

CHAPTER THIRTY-FOUR

Southern California: 17 November

1

THEY GATHERED AROUND THE LONG TABLE AT SEVEN: VAS-
quez remarked that there was an irresistible human proclivity
to solemnize transitional events with rites of food and drink.
He expounded on the biological reasons for such traditions.
His thesis followed its nose inevitably into movieography.
Roger sighed when Vasquez resolutely began to catalog film
scenes that supported his point.

Mrs. Meuth tramped noisily in and out. Billy Gilfillan and
Ronny fell to giggling. Vasquez had picked something heroic
to play on the stereo; the volume was low but it sounded like
a movie sound-track score—something by Steiner or Tiom-
kin. The steaks were blood rare and Mathieson found himself
eating with unexpected gusto. He looked up once and caught
Homer leering at him in amusement.

Amy kept glancing slyly toward Roger beside her; his face
was a study in attempted gravity but now and then a corner
of his mouth would twitch—she was teasing him under the
table with ribald glee while she kept her innocent attention
on Vasquez and his monologue.

It wasn't pomposity. Vasquez was setting them at ease. It
was an evening for which they had prepared through the hard

uncertain months; now it had come and Vasquez, sensitive to their awkwardness, was guiding them through it with gentle distraction. Mathieson found it a remarkable performance.

Jan sat beside him pecking at her food. When he caught her eye she would smile tentatively. She'd had very little to say in the hours since they'd met at the airport. He had not known what to expect and therefore he had been prepared for anything. She had put warmth into the first greeting; the rest of the day had passed gingerly as if they were agreed unspokenly to suspend everything and rediscover each other like acquaintances meeting for the first time after a long separation.

He had shaved off the moustache and tried to wash the dye from his hair; it was the best he could do until it grew out but he wanted as much as possible to resume his identity—Fred Mathieson's identity: Edward Merle had achieved the justification that had completed his being; now it was up to Fred Mathieson to complete his own.

But the estrangement was still with them. A day's celebratory truce meant nothing. In Jan's hesitant smiles he saw possibility but not conclusion. It depends, he thought, it depends. Listening to the drone of Vasquez's voice he reached for the wine, caught Homer's eye and contrived a smile.

After dinner they drifted into the big front room. The two boys stuck close, aching for reports of adventure; Homer entertained them with an edited account that made heroes of Roger and Mathieson. Roger chose his customary place on the Queen Anne chair with Amy on the carpet beside him. Jan was listening to Homer's recital; she glanced quizzically at Mathieson; he managed to laugh, deprecating Homer's version. She lifted her face to him and he tasted her kiss; her eyes were open. He couldn't determine what was in them—whether it was simply relief or something more.

Vasquez touched his arm. It startled him: Vasquez ordinarily avoided physical contact.

"May I have him for a minute?"

Jan smiled. "Of course."

"A word, if you don't mind." And Vasquez went toward the French doors.

Outside the house he followed Vasquez across the driveway. Vasquez kept walking until he reached the paddock fence. He hooked his elbows on it and craned his head back to peer at the sky. It was cool but not cold; a few clouds scudded across the stars and there was a three-quarter moon on the rise, its shadow-pittings startlingly visible. "Quite a beautiful evening. That's fitting, I think."

"Yes." Mathieson was mystified.

"Something I've been meaning to ask you."

"Go ahead. Ask."

"I fail to understand why you chose not to inform any of us that the doses you were administering to Mrs. Pastor were not the real drug."

"If I could convince you three then I could convince Pastor. It had to be absolutely believable. There couldn't be any doubt in his mind that I was capable of it."

"But you weren't capable of it. He knows that now."

"No. I'd have done it if I'd had to. I didn't have to. Pastor understands that."

Vasquez said, "Then that explains it."

"Explains what?"

"The thing that's troubling you. *You'd have done it if you'd had to*—that's what you just told me. You've discovered what you're capable of. It alarms you."

"Maybe."

"Mr. Mathieson. Fred, if I may. You were a good man when you began this. You've made yourself into something of a sinner—you've committed offenses against your own moral code. Extortion, fraud, blackmail, kidnapping, dire threats. But insofar as I can see you've done irreparable damage to no one. Those who've been damaged—like Gillespie and Ramiro—have done the harm to themselves. All you did was trigger their fears."

"Is this the Confessional?"

"At this moment from the look of you and from the sound of your voice I should say you're not merely a preternaturally weary man; you're a man experiencing a profound emptiness —a sense of guilt and anticlimax. You feel you may have de-

333

stroyed yourself along with your enemy—you may have brought yourself down nearly to his level in your search for retribution and freedom from the enslavement of fear."

Mathieson rested his forearm along the top of the fence. "You enjoy exposition too much," he murmured. "Have you ever had an unexpressed thought?"

"You need reassurance. You feel everything is a shambles. You've won what ought to be a victory and yet you're uncertain. You're concerned about your marriage. All the things you've put out of your mind during the past months. Your future weighs on you. You can't picture yourself going back to an office and dickering over meaningless details in dispassionate contracts. You can't picture yourself living a quiet life of contentment in a suburban house with two cars and swimming pool and boredom heavy on your hands."

"This mind-reading act—what are you using? Palmistry or a crystal ball?"

"Neither. Let's try cards. Let's put them face up on the table. I believe you're missing a vital discovery."

"Am I."

"You feel you've a burnt-out life—that anything henceforth must be anticlimax."

"Go on."

"You've given up your soul for freedom, in a sense. To regain your soul—your *raison d'être*—it's my feeling you have no choice but to put your freedom back on the line."

"What?"

"Nothing less will satisfy your need to justify your continued existence."

Mathieson watched him with passionate desperation. "Tell me . . ."

"You've tasted the hunt," Vasquez said. "Haven't you?"

He stood up straighter. "I'm beginning to see."

"You've savored the chase." Vasquez's voice dropped with a resolute intensity. "You'll be satisfied with nothing else, ever again. You've trapped yourself—an exquisite trap. You may hate it. But you've demonstrated the most incredible talent for the chase that it's ever been my experience to observe. You're a master. You're the best hunter I've ever met. And you do not kill. You're unique."

Mathieson inhaled until his chest was filled. He threw his head back and emptied it out. The oxygen made him giddy. He watched a cloud put a brief haze around the moon. "What's your offer, Diego?"

"There are other Frank Pastors. For you and for me."

"Yes."

"Full partnership," Vasquez said.

He was looking up toward the house. He saw the French doors open, saw Jan's inquiring silhouette.

Vasquez said, "Salvation for both of us—that's what it could be."

Mathieson pushed himself away from the fence and began to walk up toward the house. In the doorway Jan's silhouette turned—she'd spotted him. He walked toward her.

Behind him Vasquez spoke quietly. "What will it be, then?"

"I don't know."